Stealing the Preacher

Books by Karen Witemeyer

A Tailor-Made Bride

Head in the Clouds

To Win Her Heart

Short-Straw Bride

Stealing the Preacher

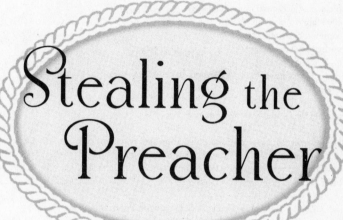

Stealing the Preacher

KAREN WITEMEYER

BETHANYHOUSE

a division of Baker Publishing Group
Minneapolis, Minnesota

Published by Bethany House Publishers
11400 Hampshire Avenue South
Bloomington, Minnesota 55438
www.bethanyhouse.com

Bethany House Publishers is a division of
Baker Publishing Group, Grand Rapids, Michigan

Printed in the United States of America

Library of Congress Cataloging-in-Publication Data
Witemeyer, Karen.
    Stealing the preacher / Karen Witemeyer.
        pages cm
    Summary: "Forced off a train in 1885 Texas and delivered to an outlaw's
daughter for her birthday, is it possible this stolen preacher ended up right
where he belongs?"—Provided by publisher.
    ISBN 978-0-7642-0966-6 (pbk.)
    1. Preachers—Fiction. 2. Kidnapping—Fiction. 3. Texas—
History—1846–1950—Fiction. I. Title.
PS3623.I864S73 2013
813'.6—dc23   2013002695

Scripture quotations are from the King James Version of the Bible.

Cover design by Dan Thornberg, Design Source Creative Services

Author represented by WordServe Literary Group

13   14   15   16   17   18   19   7   6   5   4   3   2   1

To all the ministers who proclaim God's truth
with boldness and care for his flock with loving-kindness.
Thank you for answering his call,
even when the path he directs you to
is not the one you expected.

A man's heart deviseth his way:
but the Lord directeth his steps.

PROVERBS 16:9

1

Crockett Archer stretched his legs into the aisle as the train pulled away from the Caldwell station. Only a brief stop in Somerville remained before his arrival in Brenham—the place where his life's work would begin. A wide grin spread across his face as he contemplated his future.

Was this how Abraham felt as he'd journeyed to Canaan? Anticipation thrumming through his veins. Certainty of purpose pumping with every heartbeat. That rare sense of satisfaction that came only when one responded to the direct call of the Lord.

"Mama, that man is laughing at your hat." A young boy peered over the seat in front of Crockett, pointing an accusing finger at him.

His mother huffed and reached up to pat the back of her hat—as if it might have had its feelings hurt. "Some people have no manners," she muttered, shooting a scathing glance over her shoulder as she grasped her son's arm and tried to get him to turn around.

"I meant no disrespect to your hat, ma'am." Crockett leaned

forward to offer an apology, but in truth, as he focused on the millinery atrocity in question, the desire to laugh threatened to choke him. Blue feathers poked out at all angles, as if a family of jays had used it as a perch while molting. Forcing down his amusement, he schooled his features into a serious mien. "My thoughts were elsewhere entirely, I assure you."

"Then why was you smilin' so big?" Suspicion laced the boy's tone.

And no wonder. If the sample before him was any indication of the woman's usual taste in headwear, the poor lad probably battled for his mother's millinery honor constantly.

"I was simply thinking of all the exciting things that await me at the end of this trip, and it made me happy." Crockett winked at the kid. "Are you looking forward to the end of your trip?"

The boy shrugged. "Not really. We're goin' to see my great-aunt Ida." He gave Crockett a beleaguered look. "She smells funny."

"Andrew Michael Bailey! How could you say such a thing? And to a stranger, no less." Andrew's mother yanked him around, and Crockett beat a hasty retreat, leaning back in his seat while the woman lectured her son in strident whispers.

At least she seemed to have forgotten about the hat incident. Crockett decided to count that as a blessing. If dear old Aunt Ida lived in Brenham, it would be best if her niece was more concerned with her son's slip of the tongue than the new preacher's opinions on her hat.

The new preacher. His heart swelled in his chest.

After three years of apprenticing with the minister in Palestine, Texas, near the ranch where he'd grown up, and guest-speaking at any church in the area that would let him into the pulpit, he finally was being offered the opportunity to preach full time.

Oh, there was another fellow competing for the position, but Crockett knew in his gut that his time had come.

The Lord had been leading him to this day since the summer he'd turned fifteen and his older brother, Travis, suggested he take over the spiritual instruction of the family. At first it had simply been a chore like any other, but it soon developed into a ministry. With their parents deceased and their lives isolated and uncertain, the four Archer brothers had needed a faith that ran deeper than the occasional blessing over supper. They'd needed a faith that penetrated every aspect of their lives. Crockett assumed the responsibility of nurturing his family's souls, but as he and his brothers reached manhood, an ever-increasing pressure to reach beyond his household drove him to stretch his boundaries.

Apparently, he'd be stretching them all the way to Brenham.

Crockett rested his elbow on the satchel that sat on the seat beside him and mentally ran through the key points of the sermon he'd written and rehearsed for tomorrow's service. His concentration shifted inward, and the scenery chugging past his window blurred. He silently mouthed a verse from 1 Peter, but before he could complete the quotation, the passenger car gave a violent lurch.

His hand caught the seat back in front of him at the last second, narrowly preventing a spill into the aisle when his weight was thrown forward. The locomotive's wheels screeched against the rails. Passengers flew about the car. Women gasped. Children whimpered. The train slowed slightly as the screeching continued.

"What's happening, Mama?" Andrew wailed as his mother curled her body protectively around her son.

"There's probably something on the tracks." Crockett raised his voice above the chaos. "Once the train stops, the crew will clear it away and we'll resume our trip. No need to be afraid, little man."

Yet even as he spoke the words, a tingle of unease crept between Crockett's shoulder blades. A woman a few rows up let out a shrill scream and pointed at something beyond her window. The man at her side pushed forward for a better look, then shouted the one word guaranteed to strike fear in any traveler's heart.

"Bandits!"

Crockett instinctively reached for his hip only to come up empty. He'd left his guns at the ranch. For more than a decade he'd worked the Archer spread with a rifle within constant reach or a pistol strapped to his thigh. Usually both. Now he was stuck facing a band of train robbers with nothing more than his wits because his mentor assured him that circuit riders were the only preachers who traveled armed.

He should have listened to Travis when his brother advised him to pack a weapon in his bag. Maybe then he wouldn't be sitting here defenseless. But he'd been too intent on making a good impression.

Not one to sit idle, however, Crockett lurched to his feet and fought the forward momentum of the slowing train. Lunging across the aisle, he locked his hands onto a pair of seat backs and hunched over a salesman's sample case to peer out the sooty window.

He counted four men. Guns drawn. Faces covered. Their horses quickly closing the gap between them and the train.

"God help us," Crockett prayed under his breath.

As the train slowed to a near stop, the outlaws drew abreast of the passenger car. One rider fell back, disappearing from Crockett's line of sight. The other three surged ahead.

A thump echoed from the rear of the car. The first man was aboard.

Crockett reclaimed his seat.

Just as the rear door crashed open, two other bandits burst into the coach from the front.

"Ever'body put your hands where I can see 'em!" The lead man pulled a second pistol from his left holster. With a weapon in each hand, he took aim at both sides of the railcar, eyeing the male passengers who seemed most likely to interfere.

As he did so, the train came to a full stop, jerking the passengers a final time. The leader's stance never wavered. He stood as steady as an old sea dog on a ship's deck.

Panicked murmurs slithered through the coach, gradually rising in pitch until one lady shot to her feet.

"I have to get out. Let me out!"

The leader's left gun immediately shifted aim to her chest. "Better control your woman, mister." His steely eyes narrowed above the black bandana he wore over his mouth and nose. "I ain't planning to shoot nobody, but plans can change real fast."

The woman's companion snatched her from behind and hauled her back down into the seat. She whined but turned her face into the shelter of the man's arm and made no further comment.

Satisfied, the outlaw turned his attention to the crowd at large. "There's no reason to get all worked up, folks. As soon as we get what we came for, we'll be on our way."

He took a step down the aisle. Then another. The bandit who'd entered with him hung back by the coal stove at the front of the car.

Crockett stole a glance at the man in the rear. He blocked the exit, his gun hand steady. Crockett shifted his attention back to the leader.

Something was off about these outlaws. From accounts he'd read and stories he'd heard, robberies usually featured hotheaded, cocky kids eager to prove they were fast with their guns. This group seemed too steady. Too self-controlled. Too . . . *old*.

Crockett examined them more closely. The one by the stove turned to glance out the window, and Crockett spotted graying hair at his collar beneath his hat. The middle one had leathery skin—what little was visible above the bandana. Deep creases around his eyes testified to a life lived outdoors, squinting against the sun. And though his glare was intent, the slightly crooked posture of the man at the back reminded Crockett of his sixty-year-old mentor when the man's joints were paining him after too much work in the garden.

Crockett was still chewing on his observations when a man in a business suit held out a fancy gold watch, the chain dangling from his fist.

"Here. Take it and leave."

The leader scowled down at the watch as if it offended him. "Put your valuables away," he groused. "That's not what we came for."

Why would they take over the passenger car if they didn't intend to rob the passengers? Were they simply keeping the crowd in check while the fourth man rummaged through the baggage car?

Crockett leaned forward, just enough to see out the opposite window. The fourth man had gathered the horses on the west side of the tracks and was pointing a rifle in the direction of the engine.

"Then what *did* you come for?" the man with the watch demanded. "Tell us so we can hand it over and be done with you and your gang."

The creases around the outlaw's eyes deepened as he scanned the coach for what he sought. When his gaze touched on

Crockett, it hovered a moment before moving on. Crockett's mouth went dry.

The man's brows formed a V of displeasure as he concluded his search. A growl rumbled in his throat seconds before his intention exploded across the coach.

"I came for the preacher!"

2

C rockett stiffened.

He came for the . . . what? Surely his mind was playing tricks on him. The man couldn't have said what he thought he'd heard.

The outlaw glared at the passengers and waved his guns from side to side. "Which one of you is the parson? Don't think you can trick me by not wearin' one of them white collars. I know he's on this train, and I ain't leaving 'til I find him."

Crockett's hand nearly lifted to the string tie at his neck, but he halted the movement before giving himself away. He'd never worn a clerical collar. Brother Ralston insisted that a man's character, not his clothing, should identify his calling. Following in his mentor's footsteps might have saved his life.

"You!" the outlaw barked at the salesman across the aisle. "You look like a preacher with your fancy duds and soft hands."

"N-n-no, sir." The man who had raised his hands in surrender the minute the bandits boarded the train now turned his palms inward, worry creasing his brow as he inspected his smooth palms. "I'm j-j-just a drummer. See?" Slowly he opened his traveling case. "Patent medicines."

"Bah!" The outlaw turned away in disgust and swung around to face Crockett.

Pale, steel-blue eyes took his measure. Accustomed to staring down unwanted strangers after years of protecting his ranch from interlopers, Crockett held the man's gaze, although the task had been much easier when he'd been the one holding the gun. The outlaw's eyes narrowed to slits, then turned their attention to Crockett's suit. One brow lifted to the brim of the man's dark hat as he took in the formal attire, but after a glance at Crockett's work-roughened hands, the bandit grunted and strode past.

Never had Crockett been more thankful for calluses and scars.

As the outlaw continued his progress through the car, Crockett made his own assessment of the passengers. Which one was the preacher the bandits were looking for? The man at the front who had offered his watch? The one two rows up dressed like a farmer but whose head was bowed like a man in prayer?

The coincidence of the robbers invading this particular train in search of a preacher didn't sit easily on Crockett's shoulders. Yet he was sure they couldn't be searching for him. He'd never been in this area before. Shoot. Until a couple years ago, he'd never been *anywhere*. No one knew he was on this train except his family, Brother Ralston, and the elders at Brenham.

"I'm losin' patience, folks." The leader growled his warning as he stomped back up the aisle. "If the preacher man don't fess up, I'm liable to get a might upset. And my trigger finger tends to get twitchy when I'm upset."

"Mama, is that man gonna shoot us?" Andrew's tiny voice cut through Crockett's heart.

"Hush, Andy," his mother hissed as she tucked him more firmly under her arm.

Crockett set his jaw. *This isn't right.* Tormenting women and children. Something had to be done. "How do you know that the man you seek is even on this train?" Crockett slowly pushed to his feet, careful to keep his hands raised.

Steel Eyes met his challenge without flinching. "Read him the handbill." He barked the order over his shoulder with a jerk of his chin.

The man by the stove reached into his jacket and pulled out a folded sheet of paper. Holding it by one edge, he shook it open. "'Meet the . . .'" He paused, cleared his throat once, and then stretched the handbill farther away from his face and squinted. "'Meet the preachers. Welcome our two cand-i-dates at Brenham Station on Saturday afternoon. They will arrive on the noon train from Houston and the two fifteen from Milano. Cookies and lemonade will be served.'"

A heaviness pressed against Crockett's chest as the bandit's stilted words drove into him like nails into a coffin.

How . . . ? How could he be the preacher they sought? Denial raged through him, but he smothered it and straightened his shoulders. The *why* didn't matter. What mattered was getting these bandits off the train.

"I'm your man."

"You ain't no parson." The leader waved his gun at him. "Sit down."

Crockett stood his ground. "Check my bag. You'll find my Bible, and inside the front cover is a folded page of sermon notes."

Steel Eyes cocked the pistol in his right hand and pointed the barrel an inch from Crockett's chest. "Step aside, son."

Crockett obeyed, moving into the aisle.

Keeping his stare locked on Crockett, the outlaw holstered his left gun and reached for the satchel. Crockett gave serious thought to knocking the pistol out of his hand the minute he glanced down to open the bag, but the man never gave him the chance. Once he had a grip on the satchel, he tossed it to his partner at the rear of the coach, all without taking his eyes from Crockett's face.

"It's here, boss," the third bandit called in confirmation. "The Bible. The notes. He's even got some journals underneath—all with religious-type names."

"Well, folks," Steel Eyes announced. "It looks like we found what we came for." He latched onto Crockett's arm with an iron grip. "Now, Mr. Preacher Man, let's get you off this train so these good people can enjoy the rest of their trip."

Crockett submitted to the forced escort, the pistol barrel jammed into his back keeping him in check. The outlaws might have the upper hand now, but he'd bide his time. Once away from the women and children, Crockett wouldn't have to worry about an innocent getting caught in the crossfire. He'd make his move when the time was right.

He had an appointment to keep and a job to win. No gang of long-in-the-tooth train robbers was going to derail his plans.

An hour of hard riding later, the leader finally called a halt near a stream bed. Crockett had managed to stay in the saddle during the grueling ride despite the fact that his hands were tied behind his back. His shoulders burned from the awkward position, and his thighs ached from working so hard to keep him atop his mount. The pain had kept him alert, however, and his mind sharp.

The man who had stayed with the horses during the abduction was the first to dismount. "We still got it, eh, Silas?" He eyed the gang's leader. "Don't get that kind of excitement herding cattle, do ya?" He tugged his bandana down to his neck and took a long drink from his canteen, apparently unconcerned that Crockett could see his face.

"I'm too old for that kind of excitement." The man to Crockett's right released a mighty groan as he stood in the stirrups. "You didn't have to jump the train, Carl. I swear I ain't gonna be able to walk right for a month after slammin' my hip into that railcar." He rubbed the offending spot and made a great show of hobbling as he led his horse over to the stream.

"Quit your whining, Frank." Silas kept a firm grip on the reins to Crockett's horse as he swung down out of the saddle. He'd had them in hand the entire way, not trusting his captive to follow meekly.

Smart fellow.

Crockett had already concluded that they needed him for a particular purpose, and whatever that purpose was, it would probably keep them from lodging a bullet in his back should he make a run for it. But it was unlikely he could keep his seat at a full-out gallop with his hands bound behind him, even if Silas relinquished the reins. So, instead, he'd spent his time plotting what he would do when they stopped.

Now that they had, it was time for action. All he needed was for Steel Eyes to come a little closer.

Silas moved, but only as far as the head of Crockett's horse. He paused to stroke the animal's muzzle. Crockett bit back his disappointment.

"Jasper, bring the preacher man your canteen. He looks a little parched."

The third bandit did as ordered, but as he approached, Crockett caught a glimpse of the censorious look he turned on his leader. "This is crazy, boss." His low voice barely carried, but with little noise around them, Crockett was just able to hear his quiet words. "You promised Miss Martha to give up your thievin' ways. I've never known you to go back on your word. Especially to your wife. We've been livin' honest for too long to risk it all on some fool stunt like this."

"I haven't broken my word," Silas growled, his face reddening as he clearly fought to control his fury. "Martha was the best thing that ever happened to me, and I'd not dishonor her memory by soiling a vow I made to her. I didn't steal a single trinket today, and you know it."

"You stole the parson." Jasper tilted his head in Crockett's direction, though neither of them looked his way. Good thing—since they might have noticed him slipping his boots out of the stirrups or loosening his bonds as he stretched them on the cantle.

"I didn't steal him," Silas insisted. "I just borrowed him. We'll let him go when Joe's through with him."

Jasper sighed and shook his head, his long gray mustache doing nothing to hide his frown. "I know you love that kid of yours, Si. We all do. But this ain't right."

"I'll decide what's right for my family." Silas snatched the canteen away from Jasper and stalked over to Crockett's left side.

Carl and Frank were watering their horses several yards away. Jasper had his back turned. There wouldn't be a better opportunity.

Crockett flung up his knee, planted his left boot against the man's chest, and shoved with all his might. The canteen clattered to the ground. Silas stumbled back, his bellow sounding an alarm. Crockett leapt from the horse's back and managed to wrench his right arm free of his bindings. He smashed his fist into Silas's jaw before the man could regain his balance. The outlaw tumbled backward, the horse's reins still tangled in his fingers.

The horse whinnied at the rough treatment and thrashed about, trying to gain his freedom. Crockett used the diversion to make a run for the trees. A building of some kind lay to the north. A building meant people. People meant help. He just prayed he'd been right about the bandits not wanting to lodge a bullet in him.

A shot rang out, followed by angry shouts demanding he stop. But no lead slammed into him, so Crockett kept running.

He ducked beneath post oak branches and zigzagged from one tree to another, taking advantage of any cover the terrain afforded.

The building was getting closer. A barn, maybe? He just had to keep his legs under him.

Hooves pounded into the earth behind him. Crockett's heart rate tripled. They were running him down. And he was running out of trees.

Open grassland lay between him and a fenced pasture. Keeping to the trees would only allow him to delay capture, not elude it. His only chance was to scale that fence and hope that Silas and his gang wouldn't risk discovery by pursuing him onto private property.

Lungs on fire, Crockett burst out of the woods and sprinted for the fence. The hoofbeats behind him escalated.

A soft whirring caught his ear a second before a lariat dropped over his head and shoulders. Crockett made a desperate grab for the rope, but before he could get his thumbs hooked, the noose tightened around his chest and yanked him backward. In a flash he was flat on his back, staring at the sky.

He'd just been lassoed like a new calf at branding time. Lying still, head throbbing from where it had collided with the earth, Crockett prayed there'd be no hot iron involved when Silas presented him to his son. Then again, whoever this Joe person was, he was bound to be as off his rocker as everyone else involved in this farce. Who knew what the kid would do? After all, he was the one who'd talked his outlaw father into stealing a preacher in the first place.

3

Silas Robbins didn't know what to make of the man at the end of Jasper's rope. All the sermonizers he'd ever come across were soft, bookish men partial to the sound of their own voices. Silas rubbed his bruised jaw with one hand as he shifted in his saddle and glared at the preacher struggling to gain his feet.

This parson was anything but soft.

"I thought you fellers believed in turnin' the other cheek." Silas's saddle creaked as he leaned forward. The preacher man's fine black suit was covered in dust, his hat lay upended a few feet away, and his arms were pinned to his side by a snare that wouldn't give an inch. Yet the man met his stare without a hint of fear.

"King David was a mighty warrior," the parson answered, "and the Bible calls him a man after God's own heart. If he can slay his enemies and stand before the Lord with a clean conscience, I think I can defend myself and do the same."

Silas straightened, a grudging respect poking him like a mosquito prick. In other circumstances, he could imagine himself liking this fellow. But a preacher? He'd run barefoot across a bed of cactus before he'd give his hand in friendship to one of them holy hypocrites.

"Whatever lets you sleep at night, Parson. Heaven knows the only man better than a lawyer at twisting truth to serve his own purpose is a preacher." Silas crossed his wrists over his saddle horn and waited for the man's reaction.

Would he sputter denials? Call down curses? Staunchly defend his profession?

Nope.

All the fellow did was arch an eyebrow and make a quiet observation. "Seems odd that you would go to so much trouble to collect a clergyman when you hold the occupation in such low esteem."

Odd? It was downright unnatural. But what a man chose to do for his kin was none of this sermonizer's concern.

"To the house, boys." Silas gave the signal to head out. He trotted his gray gelding to where the preacher's hat lay on the ground. Without slowing, he pulled his rifle from the scabbard, leaned deeply to the right, and plucked the thing off the ground by jabbing the gun's muzzle into the head hole. Guiding his horse with his knees, he unhooked the black felt slouch hat from his rifle barrel and slapped it onto the parson's head.

Gotta have the man looking respectable for Jo.

It gave him a sense of satisfaction to have the upper hand again. The preacher might be a couple decades younger and fleeter of foot, but Silas Robbins still had a few tricks up his sleeve. King David, here, wouldn't be getting the drop on him again.

"You want me to put him up on his horse, boss?" Jasper wrapped the end of the rope around the saddle horn and prepared to dismount, but Silas stopped him with a shake of his head.

"He seemed so all-fired anxious to run across our pasture, I figure we might as well grant him his wish."

The parson's attention snapped to meet Silas's before shifting to the barn and back again. The disbelief lining his face was priceless. The poor fellow thought he'd been running for freedom when all along he'd been heading directly into the den of the thieves he'd meant to escape. If there hadn't been the little problem of him ruining Jo's surprise, Silas might have let him go just to see his expression when they rode into the yard and met him at the barn door. Might've made catching the parson's fist with his jaw worthwhile.

Silas set a leisurely pace as they circled the pasture's perimeter. The man leashed to Jasper's horse masked his fatigue well, but he had to be tuckered out after that mad dash through the trees.

Besides, everyone knew preachers were only good for one thing—talking. It stood to reason that if Jo wanted a preacher, she'd want to talk to the fellow. What kind of gift would the hypocrite make if he was so out of breath when he met her that he couldn't get a word out? If Silas was going to all the trouble of surprising her with this gift, it'd be foolish to break it before she could use it.

But would she like it?

Last-minute doubts nibbled the corners of his confidence. Martha had always been the one who'd selected Jo's birthday gifts in the past. Last year, their grief had been too raw over Martha's passing to celebrate anything. But this year Jo was turning twenty-one. She deserved something large, something meaningful, something she never dreamed she'd actually receive.

Ah, Martha. As they gained the road that led to his ranch, Silas turned his eyes heavenward. *I miss you something fierce, love. You should be the one arranging things for our Jo. Not me.*

Jasper was right. Martha never would have approved of his methods, but somehow he thought she'd approve of the gift. She always was partial to preachin' and church-goin'. And Jo followed in her mama's footsteps.

When he'd asked her last week what she wanted for her birthday and she'd told him she wanted a preacher, Silas had seen the truth of her words in her eyes—eyes so like her mother's. She'd laughed afterward and tried to play like she'd just been foolin', but he'd known better. His Jo was hurtin', and for some reason she thought a preacher man would make it better. Silas had no patience for religion, but if Jo wanted a preacher, by George, he'd get her a preacher.

It was only as they pulled up in the yard and the door to the ranch house cracked open that it occurred to Silas that he maybe should have tried to fashion a bow out of some of the rope around the parson's middle to make him look more like a present and less like a prisoner.

Joanna Robbins stepped from the house, her gaze, as always, drawn to her father. The dappled gray he rode stood out among the brown quarter horses, just as he stood out from his men. Mama used to say he was a man born to lead, and Joanna had to agree. He exuded authority, but it was his unwavering dedication to those closest to him that won their loyalty. His men would follow wherever he led. As would she. Yet in the one thing that mattered above all else, she needed him to follow *her*, and that he would not do.

But he was her daddy, and she loved him. So when a smile crinkled his eyes as he swung down from his horse, and his arms stretched wide in invitation, Joanna banished her worries and ran to him.

His strong arms surrounded her with the love and acceptance he'd shown her all her life. She reveled in it as she circled his waist and squeezed her own love back into him, nestling her head against his chest.

"Three days is a long time, Daddy. I missed you."

"I missed you, too, darlin'." His grip loosened, and he leaned back. "But I brought you something real special."

"For my birthday?" Giddy anticipation bubbled up inside her, as if she were a girl turning twelve, not twenty-one. But the men were looking on, so Joanna harnessed her excitement.

Saddle leather groaned, drawing Joanna's attention to Jasper Mullins, her father's foreman. He swung a leg over his mount's back and unwound a rope from the saddle horn. He dragged his hat from his head, exposing a circular crease in his white-gray hair, then leaned forward and bussed her cheek. The tickle of his droopy mustache made her smile, but the rope he placed in her hand brought a furrow to her brow.

"Happy birthday, Miss Jo."

"Thank you, Jasper."

Frank Pickens and Carl Hurst called out similar well-wishes before making themselves scarce by following Jasper to the barn. It was only when they'd all led their horses away that she got a clear view of what stood tethered to the end of her rope.

"You brought me a . . . rustler?"

The tall man was dressed better than any rustler she'd ever seen—not that she'd ever really seen any. But she imagined they'd wear something more practical for their thieving. Denim trousers, perhaps. And a cotton work shirt. Not a fancy suit and tie. Although the coat *was* rather rumpled, and the trousers were coated with a thick layer of dust.

"He's not a rustler, Jo." Her father's deep voice penetrated her thoughts.

She questioned him with her eyes.

He struggled to meet her gaze and failed. Blowing out a heavy breath, he plucked the hat from his head and beat it against his thigh. "Dad-burn it, girl. You said you wanted a preacher, so that's what I brung ya."

A preacher?

Joanna's knees nearly buckled. She dropped the rope as if it had become a snake and pressed her empty hand to her belly. A preacher. How fervently she had prayed for a man of God to cross her path, one who would aid her in fulfilling her calling. This should be a time of great rejoicing and thanksgiving. Instead she felt ill.

"You stole him?" She bit back a moan. "Daddy, how could you?"

"I didn't steal him," he shouted at her back as she rushed to the preacher's side and began loosening the knot. "I just encouraged him to pay you a visit for your birthday. That's all."

Joanna didn't respond. Nor did she meet the parson's eye. She just focused on the knot above his waist.

"I was real careful not to hurt him none—which is more than I can say for him. That preacher man nearly broke my jaw!"

That brought her head up. "You did?" she whispered.

The man shrugged. "Seemed prudent at the time. I was trying to escape a band of ruthless kidnappers."

Lord have mercy, but the man was handsome. His eyes were the exact shade of the Caledonian brown pigment in her paint set, though infused with a light that would be nearly impossible to duplicate on canvas. His jaw was strong and slightly squared. His nose perfectly proportioned to the rest of his face.

The artist in her had begun cataloging the position of his ears and the line of his throat when he wiggled against his bindings and reminded her of more pressing matters.

"I'm so sorry," she said, fumbling once again with the knot. Finally it loosened enough for her to expand the loop and free his hands. He immediately flung the lasso over his head and rolled his shoulders.

She instinctively stepped back, not sure what he would do. The sound of a gun being cocked directly behind her made it clear her father was taking no chances, either.

The parson seemed unruffled by the show of force, however. He simply continued rubbing his arms and wiggling his fingers in an effort to repair his circulation.

Curious. Most men of her acquaintance had difficulty standing up to her father when he was in a stern mood, even without a gun pointed in their direction. But this preacher, if he truly was a man of the cloth—she was beginning to have her doubts—acted as if standing in a yard at gunpoint was an everyday occurrence.

"Who are you?" She hadn't realized she'd spoken the thought aloud until he turned to her.

He swept his hat from his head, revealing russet hair neatly trimmed. "Crockett Archer, miss." He dipped his chin politely.

She stepped closer. "I'm Joanna Robbins."

"Well, Miss Robbins. As much as I've enjoyed this little side trip, and as delighted as I am to have the honor of wishing you felicitations on your birthday, I really must take my leave. I'm afraid I have a prior engagement that is of the utmost importance. A congregation awaits my arrival in Brenham."

His gaze held no malice, and his smile seemed genuine enough, but she sensed a layer of iron beneath his words.

"You ain't going nowhere, preacher man." Her father moved to her side, his gun less than a foot from Mr. Archer's chest. "Not until my Jo gets what she wants from you."

Joanna's eyes slid closed in mortification. What *his Jo* wanted right now was for the earth to open up and swallow her whole.

4

It appears I am at your disposal, Miss Robbins." Crockett made little effort to hide his irritation, and only felt the tiniest twinge of guilt when his abductor's daughter winced.

What in heaven's name did the girl want with a preacher, anyhow? Did she have some potential husband tied up inside the house waiting to be hitched? Poor wretch had probably been kidnapped, too. Gagged and chained to the stove, no doubt.

Not that this woman would need chains to capture a man's attention under normal circumstances. Her milky skin, soft eyes, and that mad riot of reddish-gold corkscrew curls that gave her a pixie-like appearance would see to that task. But with a train robber for a father and his gang having free rein on her ranch, circumstances were anything but normal.

Part of him wished she was indeed the *Joe* he'd imagined. At least then he could fight his way free. Her being a woman complicated matters. And this ridiculous situation was complicated enough already.

Joanna Robbins raised her head, her gaze meeting his for only an instant before skittering away to somewhere near his

28

chin. "If Mr. Archer agrees to accompany me on a short stroll, I'd be happy to loan him a mount so he can ride into Deanville later this evening. From there he can arrange transportation to Caldwell and be on about his business."

The gun pointed at Crockett's chest lowered a few inches as Silas turned to study his daughter. "That's all you're wanting, Jo? A stroll?"

Crockett found it hard to believe, as well. Yet her voice rang with a quiet earnestness he couldn't discount.

Slowly she raised her chin. Her blue-gray eyes pleaded with him. "It's not all I want, but it's all I'm asking."

How was a man supposed to fight against that? Crockett sighed inwardly. To deny her request would be well within his rights. Yet even considering the notion left him feeling small and petty. No. He'd been called to a higher road, a narrower road.

Besides, if taking a stroll with the gal satisfied her father and thereby gained him his freedom, it'd be worth the concession. He needed to get to a town as soon as possible and wire the elders in Brenham. They would have heard what had happened by now and were surely concerned. And while he wanted to allay their fears, what he really wanted was to allay his own by rescheduling his audition. The elders had communicated their wish to have a decision made and a permanent minister installed as soon as possible. Today's delay, no matter how outrageous the circumstances, would not do him any favors.

"I'd be pleased to escort you wherever you wish to go." Crockett sketched a brief bow, then fit his hat to his head and offered her his arm.

Joanna's lashes dipped over her eyes and pink stained her cheeks, but she only hesitated a moment before sliding her fingers into the crook of his arm. A tiny smile wavered upon her lips. "Thank you."

She swiveled to face her father next. "We'll just walk down to the churchyard and back, Daddy. We won't be long."

"You won't be alone, either," Silas groused. "I plan to keep my eye on you." He spoke to his daughter, but Crockett had no doubt where the implied threat was aimed.

"No." The solidity of the single word brought Crockett's head around to the woman he'd thought docile. "I need privacy for my conversation with the parson. The churchyard is visible from the dormer windows in the attic. You can watch us from there if you feel you must. You can even use your spyglass. But we walk alone."

Silas took hold of Joanna's free arm and tugged her away from Crockett. "I don't like it, Jo. He's a stranger."

"You're the one who brought him here, Daddy."

Crockett hid a grin. Joanna might not wield a Colt .45 like her father did, but her marksmanship was flawless nonetheless. The old man looked as if he'd swallowed a prickly pear.

"He's a preacher," she reminded her father as she gently yet firmly extricated herself from his hold. "I'll be fine."

Joanna moved to Crockett's side and reclaimed his arm. "Shall we?" Her smile was all for show. He could tell by the tremble of her fingers against his coat sleeve and the way her gaze flitted between his eyes and his left ear.

He deliberately waited to respond until her eyes flickered back to his. Then he winked, feeling more himself than he had in hours.

Her brows arched and her eyes widened. Then the edge of her mouth twitched with the beginnings of a genuine grin.

The stress he'd carried since being forced off the train fell from Crockett's shoulders, and he found himself answering her grin with one of his own. "Lead the way, Miss Robbins."

"You got yer knife?" Silas barked out from behind them.

Joanna sighed but twisted her neck to answer. "Yes, sir."

Crockett glanced over his shoulder, as well, and was immediately gutted by a glare that promised dire consequences should any harm befall the lady at his side.

"She knows how to use a blade, Parson." Silas retrieved his own knife from the sheath attached to his gun belt and ran his thumb along the sharpened edge. "Taught her myself. You might wanna keep that in mind during your stroll."

"A comforting notion, indeed," Crockett quipped, "seeing as how I'm without a weapon. I'll be sure to let her take charge of our defense should we come across any bandits."

Silas glowered at his barb, but Crockett ignored it. Joanna Robbins could probably handle a variety of weapons with a skill that would put most men to shame, but Crockett's gut told him she wasn't the type to use them unless forced.

And the more he watched Silas interact with his daughter, the more certain Crockett became that the man was more bluster than bite. In fact, he reminded him a lot of his brother Travis. Oh, if push came to shove, he would strike and strike hard. Until then, however, he'd just growl out the meanest warnings he could think of.

"I'll be watching, preacher man." With a flick of his wrist, Silas flung his knife. The tip of the blade stabbed the earth a mere inch from Crockett's boot.

Crockett's pulse ricocheted in his neck, but he resisted the urge to jump back. Raising his gaze from the hilt of the knife to Silas's face, Crockett watched victory flare in his adversary's eyes. Perhaps the old dog had teeth after all.

"And Joanna," Silas said with a point of his finger, "if you're not back in an hour, I'm comin' to fetch you, private matter or not. Understand me?"

"Yes, Daddy."

Apparently the pixie had challenged the dragon enough for one day.

Feeling as if she were trapped in an hourglass with sand threatening to bury her if she didn't get all her words out in time, Joanna blurted out her desires the moment they reached the road and were safely out of her father's hearing.

"I prayed for a preacher to come."

Mr. Archer's stride stuttered a bit, but he recovered quickly. "Why do you need one?"

She tugged her hand from his arm and focused on the ground in front of her as they walked. Touching him was a distraction she could ill afford at that moment. And though his voice sounded kind and politely curious, she suddenly felt very young and foolish. Why was it that thoughts and plans always made more sense when confined to one's mind than when they exited one's mouth?

"To save my father's soul."

The crunch of the parson's footfalls ceased. Joanna plodded on, however, sure he would snap out of his stupor momentarily. Besides, it was easier to keep moving than to look at whatever shocked expression surely lined his face.

"He's a good-hearted man." She rushed to add, "Truly," before he could dispute the point. "My father might not open himself up to many, but when he does, he gives his all. You should have seen the way he loved my mother. She softened him, he said. Made him laugh. Made him a better man. I tend to think he was always a good man; he just needed someone to believe in him. Losing her nearly broke him."

They passed beneath the shadow of a large oak, and Joanna fought down the sadness that stirred at the thought of her mother. "He made a point to stay strong for me. For his men. For our ranch. He's not one to let down the people who depend on him."

"Yet he holds up trains." Brother Archer's long legs caught him up to her quickly.

She snuck a peek at him. His furrowed brow spoke more of a man wrestling to make sense of a contradiction than of one handing down tacit disapproval. Thanking the Lord for small miracles, she continued her explanation.

"He's been an honest rancher for sixteen years." Joanna kicked at a pebble in the road in front of her, her hackles rising in her father's defense. "In his younger days he might have robbed a few stagecoaches and a handful of trains, but he's reformed."

"Begging your pardon, miss," the parson interrupted her. The laughter she heard in his voice rankled. "But the man I met today held a carload of rail passengers at gunpoint and abducted one of them. He doesn't seem all that reformed to me."

Joanna spun to face him, words coiling inside her like a nest of baby rattlers. "Can't you see that he only did what he did out of love?" Her hand slashed the air. "I don't condone his methods, but his motives were pure. He had no idea what I wanted with a preacher. If he did, he likely never would have fetched you. All he knew was that I missed my mama. Since she and I always attended services together, he must've hoped that having a preacher at hand would ease my grief a little. That's what drove him. Not some twisted need to terrorize people."

Mr. Archer said nothing. He simply stared at her as if she were an oddity in a curiosity shop. Maybe that's what she was. Heaven knew that's how she felt most days. Odd Joanna Robbins. The girl who'd rather hide away in her father's loft with her paints than attend a barn dance. The one who never knew what to say or how to fit in. Whose skin was too pale, freckles too plentiful, and eyes too colorless to ever catch a beau. Hair that resembled copper wire fresh from the spool, its coils springing every which way no matter how many pins she scraped against her scalp.

Some of the starch went out of her. What did she expect? That this stranger whom her father had held at gunpoint and dragged all over creation would be moved by her impassioned plea? The man was only walking with her as a means to an end. He wanted his freedom, and she was the price he was being forced to pay. Man of God he might be, but he was still a man—one who had every right to resent her and her family.

Joanna turned from him and set off through the trees. Thankfully, he followed. She could hear his boots crunching the dry grass and dead twigs behind her. The usual route between her house and the church took about twenty minutes, and while she lived closer to the building than any of her neighbors, today the distance stretched too far. Cutting across the open field would save them about five minutes. With her father no doubt counting down each tick of the clock until he could storm out to fetch her, five minutes might prove crucial.

Soon the back of the old church came into view. A door at the rear led to the previous parson's personal quarters, which he'd built onto the building so as not to be a burden to the area families who felt obligated to take him into their already overcrowded homes.

Hackberry trees lined the sides of the weathered clapboard structure, their small, dark purple fruit littering the ground. Joanna tromped past them and rounded the corner to the steepled front entrance.

Whether Mr. Crockett Archer was a direct answer to her prayers or just some unfortunate fellow her father happened to kidnap, he was here, and she wasn't about to pass up the opportunity she'd been given.

She waited until her companion emerged from around the corner, then gestured to the decaying building. "Do you see this church, Mr. Archer?"

The long-legged stranger propped a boot on one of the front

steps and pressed his forearm into his thigh. He made a great show of examining the old structure, tilting his head back to take in the very tip of the spire. "Yes, ma'am. I do."

Joanna inhaled a fortifying breath, braced her hand against the balustrade, and set her chin. "I want to bring it back to life."

5

Bring it back to life?" Crockett echoed, pretty sure his strolling partner was talking about more than slapping on a new coat of paint but wanting to hear the details from her. He'd stopped making assumptions when it came to the Robbins clan.

"Yes." Joanna stared him down as if expecting him to laugh, but Crockett felt no such compulsion. What he felt was a burgeoning curiosity.

Unless he'd missed his guess, Miss Joanna Robbins possessed the soul of a missionary. How that had come to be when she'd been raised by an outlaw and his gang, Crockett couldn't fathom. Yet he sensed her passion. Respected it. He'd not belittle her dream.

Crockett straightened his stance and angled his head toward her. "I'm listening."

The defiance in her eyes softened, as did her posture. She loosened her grip on the balustrade and used it as a pivot to swing herself toward the chapel steps. After climbing three, she smoothed her navy blue skirt beneath her and took a seat on one of the slightly warped boards that had once been a proper stair.

Joanna nibbled the edge of her bottom lip and turned her attention to the sky, as if searching for a place to start. While he waited for her to find the words she sought, Crockett claimed the bottom step, braced his back against the rails, and stretched his legs across the width of the stairs.

"My mother was a godly woman who believed her life's foremost duty lay in leading the members of her family to Christ." His companion's quiet voice drew Crockett's head around. Joanna's gaze no longer peered into the heavens but rested firmly upon her lap, where her palms lay open like a book that held a story only her eyes could see.

"When she died last year, that responsibility fell to me." A quiver vibrated her breath as she paused to inhale. "I'm afraid I'm not up to the task."

An urge to debate that point shot through Crockett, startling him with its vehemence. Why he should feel the need to defend her against her own self-criticism, he couldn't imagine. He'd just met the girl, knew next to nothing about her. However, the burden she carried was palpable, to the point of nearly being visible upon her slender shoulders. Her capabilities or lack thereof were not the issue at the moment. Her weary spirit was begging for someone to lighten her load—if only for a few minutes. God had placed him here to be that someone. Crockett held his tongue and waited for Joanna to continue. He'd take on as much as he could for as long as he could, and when he left, if God was merciful, he'd take it with him.

"She begged me not to give up on Daddy. To keep sowing seeds and praying that the Lord would lead them to fertile ground so they could take root." Joanna gave a tiny sniff and jerked her chin skyward again, blinking against the afternoon sunlight. Or an unwanted tear. "I've tried. Lord knows how I've tried. But I don't have Mama's patience. And without her to lean on, the discouragement grows too heavy."

Finally her eyes met his. "I need help, Mr. Archer. I need a preacher to bring this old church back to life. One who can inspire a community to revive its dormant faith and reach past the barricades erected around a stubborn ex-outlaw's heart to save the bruised soul within."

Pieces of the sermon he'd prepared for the church in Brenham rose unbidden in Crockett's mind. His fiery call to evangelism. His encouragement to seek out lost souls from among those close to home. To testify with actions as well as words. How no soul is beyond the reach of grace. Crockett raised a hand and rubbed away the prickle at the base of his neck.

"I understand you have another commitment, so I will not ask you to take on this mission," Joanna said. "But surely you know other ministers—men who might be interested in such a position. All I ask is that you pass on word of our need. And if you see fit, make a recommendation."

"A recommendation?" Crockett sputtered before he could stop himself.

Joanna stiffened, her shoulders squaring off as she thrust out her chin. "And why not? Our pasture may be small, but our sheep are just as worthy of a shepherd as any other. Or are you the type to condemn an entire community for the mistake of one man?"

"Mistake? It's not like what happened to me was an accident, Miss Robbins. Your father plotted his actions in advance, and as far as I can tell, feels not one speck of remorse."

"Because his motives were pure!"

Crockett held his hands up in conciliation. "Fine. I'll concede that his actions were driven by his desire to please his daughter, but that doesn't make them acceptable. How can I honestly recommend a position here to a colleague? The only men I've met out here are train robbers and kidnappers."

"'They that are whole have no need of the physician, but they that are sick,'" Joanna recited.

The words of Christ pierced Crockett's heart and deflated his defenses. "'I came not to call the righteous, but sinners to repentance.'" The remainder of the quote fell from his lips and lashed his conscience like a whip. "Forgive me, Miss Robbins. You're right, of course. I *can* recommend. With caution, certainly, but with sincerity, too."

And if the Lord was leading him in the direction Crockett believed, there just might be a young minister who would be grateful for an alternative position once the elders in Brenham made their decision. He'd be sure to mention the possibility to him.

"Thank you, Brother Archer. I'll be praying that God will lead the right man to us. *Without* my father's help this time."

Her smile asserted itself once again, and Crockett found himself returning it.

He laughed a deep chuckle that unknotted his belly and expelled the last of his resentment. Joanna's soft chimes added to the music, and for the first time, Crockett was actually glad to be exactly where he was.

"So, how did this old place come to be abandoned?" he asked, his gaze lifting to trace the outline of the neglected building.

"A few years back, the folks over at Deanville offered our preacher a church in town. They already had a cotton gin and grist mill and plans for a school. New families were moving in. It was a good opportunity for him, and I don't blame him for taking it."

"But it left you without a minister."

She nodded, looking back at her hands. "Some of the folks who live farther north make the trip into town on Sundays for services. Most in the area, though, find the journey too long. It's a good ten miles into Deanville from our place, and many live farther away." Joanna grasped the rail nearest her hip and stroked it as if it were the arm of a dear friend. "This old building sits right in the center of the largest cluster of farms and ranches. No one in the area has to travel more than five miles to reach its doors. We still gather here for socials on occasion, but we haven't come together for worship in over two years. I miss it."

The longing in her voice struck a familiar chord. Hadn't he hungered for the same thing? For a community of believers to worship with outside his immediate family? His brothers had been his church for longer than he could remember, and while he loved them and found their encouragement and support invaluable, something within him had cried out for a broader community. For different opinions and perspectives. For friendship. For mentorship. For prayer. When Amos Ralston took Crockett under his wing and introduced him to the congregation in Palestine, he'd felt as if he'd been invited to a feast. What an emptiness it would leave to have that taken away.

Crockett leaned forward and touched Joanna's hand. "I will help you find a new preacher. I promise."

She stared at him a long moment, then nodded. "I believe you."

Joanna quickly ducked her chin and tugged her hand from his. She pushed to her feet, and minding his manners, Crockett stood, as well. His attention lagged behind, however, remembering the passion in her eyes, the determination etching her brow.

In the last three years, he'd met many women. Young. Old. Pretty. Plain. Devout. Flirtatious. After living only among men for years, he found he enjoyed the company of women. Their gracious manners. Their gentle ways. Their lovely figures. But never had he felt anything deeper than a surface admiration. Perhaps because he'd been so focused on his training. Yet after only a handful of minutes, Joanna Robbins had touched something deep inside him, as only a kindred spirit could do.

She'd experienced the Lord's call on her life as surely as he had. And while he'd been called to minister to many, she'd been called for one. Who was he to say her calling was any less significant than his own? In fact, her dedication to the one in her care humbled him, gave him a perspective he'd been lacking. In other circumstances, he could easily imagine the two of them becoming friends. Maybe after he settled in Brenham, he could write to her, encourage her.

One thing was for certain. He'd keep his promise. An Archer never went back on his word. Joanna Robbins would get her preacher. It just wouldn't be him.

"So I guess this means I owe you the use of a horse." She smiled up at him as she dusted her hands together. "You held up your end of the bargain, after all."

Crockett tipped his hat. "As much as I've enjoyed our walk, I really do need to be on my way. I'm sure the congregation in Brenham is concerned for my safety."

She led him to a path that meandered back toward the road. "Is that where you preach?"

"I've spoken there on two occasions," Crockett answered. "Tomorrow was to be my third. I'm hoping to be selected for a permanent position there."

"And my father's ill-timed interruption has put that position in jeopardy, hasn't it." She halted, her expression pained. "I'm truly sorry."

Crockett drew even with her and gestured for her to continue on. "Don't fret, Miss Robbins. My future is in God's hands. All will be well."

"I wish I had your faith," she said, not yet moving.

"I wish I had your horse." He shot her a wink to let her know he was teasing. Mostly.

Joanna grinned, then dutifully resumed her march toward home. Crockett stayed close to her side, enjoying her company now that the tension hovering over them had lifted.

She was telling him something about the creek that ran behind the old church when his senses suddenly sharpened.

Someone was watching them.

Crockett swiveled his head, searching the empty road behind him and then scanning the trees like he used to do at the ranch when standing guard. A movement caught his eye. Furtive. Menacing. Near the blackjack oak they'd just passed to the left of the road. His muscles grew taut, and for the second time that day, he reached for a holster that wasn't there.

A figure jumped from behind the tree. The glimpse of a rifle barrel was all Crockett needed. He grabbed Joanna, ignoring her startled cry as well as her resistance. He pressed her to his chest and curved his larger body around hers, shielding her from the attack.

"Get your hands off my woman, mister, or I'm gonna put a new crease in them fancy duds of yours."

6

Joanna wiggled against the parson's protective hold. She recognized that bothersome voice. And as soon as she found her freedom, she was gonna strangle the scrawny throat it came from.

She shoved against Brother Archer's chest, a rather firm and well-muscled chest that never would have given way to her puny efforts, she was sure, had she not muttered some disparaging comment about the man's intelligence that finally seemed to clue him in to their lack of true danger.

Once free, Joanna darted around the preacher, dodged the rapidly lowering rifle, and smacked Jackson Spivey upside the head.

"Owww, Jo," the twelve-year-old whined as he jerked away. "What'd ya go and do that for? He's the one that grabbed ya."

"He never laid a hand on me until you jumped out at us like some crazed coyote. What were you thinking, waving a gun around like that? You could've hurt somebody!" Joanna's chest heaved as she dug her fingernails into her palm in a bid for control. "You got no business spying on me, Jackson, or making ridiculous claims on me."

The sandy-haired boy set his mouth in a mutinous line and stretched himself to his full height, which put the top of his head at least an inch above hers. How was she supposed to give him a good dressing down when she had to look up to do it?

"It ain't ridiculous, Jo." His rebellious eyes dared her to contradict him. "Soon as I get old enough to offer for you all proper like, I'm gonna. I done told ya that. And I won't hold with no fancy-pants rooster moving in on my territory in the meantime."

Jackson's eyes narrowed and shifted to Joanna's right, where Brother Archer had come to stand.

Could mortification kill a person? Because at that moment, she was feeling precariously close to expiring.

"You do much hunting, Jackson?" The parson's deep voice rumbled beside her, but it was his question that took her off guard. So nonchalant and . . . well . . . man-to-manish.

Jackson glowered at him. "Now and then."

"Winchester's a good gun. That the '73 Carbine?" The parson stepped forward, his attention on the rifle.

"Yep."

"I prefer the sporting rifle, myself. Longer barrel, more cartridges. But the carbine is lighter weight. Better for when a man's on foot. You clean it after every hunt?"

"Yes, sir."

Joanna's jaw nearly came unhinged. With a few simple questions, Brother Archer had drained all the posturing right out of the boy. Jackson was even holding the rifle up to the preacher for his inspection.

"That's good." The parson smiled and clasped the boy's shoulder in praise. Something that almost looked like pride flashed across Jackson's face. "Make sure you keep it oiled even when you're not hunting. A man's weapon can save his life. You can't get lazy with its upkeep."

"No, sir. I always clean it real good. Pa's, too, when he's . . . ah . . . sick." Jackson's gaze dropped to the ground and stayed there while he kicked at a dirt clod.

Joanna ached for Jackson's embarrassment. He might be a pest and the cause of more headaches than she cared to count, but he only acted that way because he was starved for attention. His pa was a no-account drunk who spent more time at the saloon in Deanville than at home. Jackson had basically been rearing himself for the five years since his ma up and ran off. Which was why Joanna usually didn't put up much of a fuss when he came around and pestered her. But today he'd gone too far.

Brother Archer didn't seem offended, though. Instead he smiled at the boy as if Jackson hadn't just aimed the very weapon they were discussing at his back and threatened bodily harm. As far as she could tell, the parson had no intention of taking the boy to task for his actions. Yet the next man Jackson took aim at might not be so forgiving. *Someone* had to set the boy straight, and apparently that duty fell to her.

"Your pa get sick often?" Brother Archer asked before Joanna could regain her footing in the conversation.

Jackson shrugged, still staring at the dirt. "Often enough."

"Ever had to use your gun to ward off trouble when he was feelin' poorly?"

He ventured a glance up, his eyes wary. "Some."

"Two-legged trouble?" The parson's passive face revealed nothing of his thoughts. His voice remained calm, giving no sign that he felt any of the alarm rising within her own breast. She knew Jackson had it hard, but she never imagined him fighting off trouble harsh enough to require weaponry.

"Once or twice." The boy's matter-of-fact tone left Joanna certain that he'd understated the frequency.

"Why didn't you tell me, Jackson?" Joanna reached out a hand to him, but he shied away, shooting her a glare that made it clear he'd not welcome her pity. "You should have asked for help. My father could have—"

"I handle my own problems."

"With what? A gun?"

He bristled at her, but she didn't care. The kid was twelve years old, for pity's sake. He shouldn't be wielding anything more deadly than a slingshot.

Brother Archer's hand came to rest at the small of her back. The touch was so brief she barely registered the warmth of his fingers before it disappeared, but the surprise of it scattered her thoughts.

"Sometimes it takes a gun."

Shock stole Joanna's breath. How could he stand there and say such a thing? He was a man of God. A man of peace. "He's just a boy!" She flung the accusation at him, but it bounced off his stoic shoulders without an ounce of impact.

"Some boys grow into men slowly," Brother Archer said, his attention trained on Jackson, as if his answer were more for him than Joanna. "Others have manhood thrust upon them whether they're ready for it or not.

"I was eleven when my father died, leaving my brother, Travis, and me to run the ranch, care for our two younger brothers, and defend our home from those who thought they could take it from us. We grew up fast because we had to. Used our guns for the same reason. But all those years, the fear that I might one day have to kill a man haunted me. Nothing scars a man's soul like taking a life, whether justified or not."

A shiver crept down Joanna's back. What kind of parson was this? Weren't preachers supposed to be gentle, compassionate creatures, preferring words to weapons? Crockett Archer sounded more like her outlaw father than a preacher. Perhaps it was a good thing he had other ministerial commitments keeping him from starting up her church.

"Did ya ever hafta do it?" Jackson's low tone rumbled with trepidation. "Kill a man?"

Joanna held her breath, waiting for the answer.

"No, thank the Lord." Brother Archer lifted his face heavenward and closed his eyes for a moment before turning back to Jackson. "Every time you point a gun at someone, though, you run that risk." He paused to glance meaningfully at the carbine in the boy's hand. "A wise man draws his weapon only in the direst of circumstances."

Jackson swallowed hard, his Adam's apple bobbing in his throat. But he nodded—nodded with the maturity of a young man, not a boy. And suddenly Joanna didn't care if Crockett Archer was like other preachers. He had a gift for reaching people. A gift that could make him more valuable to her than the most rousing speaker or genteel scholar.

"Name's Crockett, by the way," the parson said, his face breaking into a smile that banished the solemnity hovering over the trio. "Crockett Archer." He offered his hand, and Jackson shifted the hold on his rifle in order to shake it.

"Crockett? As in Davy Crockett?"

"Yep." The twinkle Joanna had noted earlier returned to the parson's eyes. "My ma named all us boys after men who fought at the Alamo."

Jackson scrunched up his nose. "Why didn't she just call ya Davy?"

Brother Archer laughed, and the rich sound spread through Joanna's chest like molasses on hot oatmeal. "Crockett's not so bad. My younger brother got saddled with Bowie."

"Yer pullin' my leg."

"Nope. That's his name. Although Pa eventually took pity on

him and dubbed him Jim. We only use Bowie now when we're wantin' to needle him."

He spoke of his brothers with such affection, Joanna found herself wanting to delve deeper into the Archer clan's history. Until she remembered he was leaving.

"Jackson," she said, feeling a bit like an interloper when two sets of male eyes fastened on her as if they'd just been reminded of her presence. "Mr. Archer needs to get back to the ranch. He has to ride into Deanville before nightfall."

"What's the rush? Ain't he gonna stay for your birthday supper?"

For a boy who'd tried to run the man off a few minutes ago, he sure seemed eager for him to stay.

"He has a previous engagement."

Jackson's brow furrowed. "If it's so important, why'd he come here in the first place?"

"Ha!" The preacher grinned and elbowed Jackson in the ribs. "Her father kid—"

"—*interrupted* his travel plans and persuaded Mr. Archer to come for a short visit in honor of my birthday tomorrow." Joanna shot Crockett a glance that begged him to keep the details to himself. "Unfortunately, because of a pressing appointment, he won't be staying for this evening's supper. But I fully expect to see you there, Jackson. Six o'clock, sharp. You hear?"

"You still gonna have cake?"

"Made a chocolate one this morning."

His grin nearly engulfed his face. "I'll be there."

Joanna hid her pleasure as the boy set off across the field. She'd guessed right. She'd questioned him the other day under the guise of having him help her decide what dessert to use to celebrate her birthday but hoping to discern *his* favorite. Her mama had always made apple pie, knowing Joanna preferred the fruity pastry over cake. But making a pie without Mama didn't seem right, so she'd opted to celebrate with something new. Watching Jackson devour her cake would be a gift in itself.

"Why'd you cut me off back there?" The parson's question brought Joanna back to the present. "I had a great yarn ready to go."

She much preferred his current good humor to the barely leashed indignation he'd displayed when her father had first presented him to her, but she couldn't let him endanger her family, even with a seemingly harmless tale.

"Jackson doesn't know about my father's past. No one outside the ranch does."

"But . . ." His voice trailed off.

Joanna bit back the retort that sprang to her lips. There was no reason for Brother Archer to act so surprised. It wasn't as if reformed outlaws went around telling tales of their exploits at parties to entertain the neighbors.

"I already told you that he's been making an honest living as a rancher for the last sixteen years. Folks around here know him as the owner of the Lazy R. That's all they need to know. That's who he is." She crossed her arms over her middle, determined to drive her point home, when all at once it occurred to her there was another risk she'd managed to overlook.

Crockett Archer.

He knew the truth about her father, had experienced it first-hand. When he got to Deanville, the town marshal was sure to hound him with questions.

Her arms went limp and unfolded of their own accord. "Will you turn him in?" She stepped closer to him, wanting to grab the lapels of his coat but fisting her hands in her skirt instead. "Please. He meant no harm. You were inconvenienced"—a vision of him trussed up like a calf at roundup time flashed through her mind, stirring her conscience—"and mistreated to a certain extent, I suppose, but surely not to the point where you wouldn't be able to extend forgiveness to a man who was simply trying to give his daughter a gift."

The parson's brown eyes hardened, but when his palm closed around her shoulder, the gentleness of his touch instilled hope.

"I won't lie to cover up anything, Miss Robbins," he said, "but neither will I seek retribution. You have my word."

"And if the marshal presses you for details?"

"I'll do my best to be vague, but I will not dishonor my calling with lying. Sin carries consequences. And while a man might escape earthly repercussions, his soul cannot escape the eternal ones. Not without a Savior."

"I know," Joanna murmured, her heart squeezing painfully in her chest. "That's why my father needs more time. Please give him that."

Brother Archer tightened his grip on her shoulder for an instant, then stepped away. "I'll do what I can."

But would it be enough?

7

Crockett couldn't seem to extricate Joanna Robbins from his mind during his ride to Deanville. Every time he started to mentally compose a telegram message for the Brenham elders or review his sermon points, memories of a certain redhead intruded.

The woman was a series of contradictions. His first impression had marked her as a shy, timid creature, yet she defended her father with fiery passion. And when given the chance to solicit help for her mission, she finagled time alone to plead with a stranger. Her wild hair and elfin features were more girlish than womanly when it came to feminine charms; but when her eyes sparked with humor or enthusiasm, her face lit up in a way that made his breath catch. And though she fussed at Jackson Spivey as if he were the bane of her existence, she went out of her way to include him in her birthday supper.

Yep. Joanna Robbins was the kind of woman a man could take his whole life trying to figure out. Not that he was in the market for that kind of puzzle. He had enough to worry about with solidifying his position in Brenham.

Perhaps he could check in on her after he was settled, though. They'd forged an odd sort of friendship, after all, during their brief encounter. Then again, that might prove awkward for whomever she found to fill the pulpit of that old church of hers. Better to focus on the here and now and let tomorrow take care of itself.

Deanville was a tiny place compared to Palestine and Brenham, but it boasted all the necessities of an up-and-coming town—general store, schoolhouse, cotton gin, grist mill, saloon, and two churches. He wondered which of the two was shepherded by the preacher who'd left Joanna's church.

Crockett dropped his horse off at the livery and paid for its board, instructing the stable hand that the animal would be collected by someone from the Lazy R in a day or two. Then, after untying his travel bag, which Joanna's father had returned to him with a belligerent glare, he solicited directions to the telegraph office.

Crossing to the opposite side of the road, Crockett side-stepped a farmer hefting a pair of feed sacks into a wagon bed and tipped his hat to a middle-aged woman carrying a market basket who'd halted to stare at him outside a shop window that read *Dean's Store*.

"Ma'am." He offered one of his most charming smiles. The woman nodded in return, yet he felt her disapproving stare follow him down the street. He was several steps past the store when the rattle of the door and the soft jangle of a bell announced the end of her perusal and the resumption of her shopping.

He probably looked a sight in his rumpled suit coat and dirt-stained trousers. The Lord only knew what the woman must've thought of him. A hot bath and change of clothes would work wonders, but they would have to wait. He had to contact the Brenham church.

The telegraph office stood a few yards north of the general

store, a tiny shack of a building with wires strung from wooden poles stationed behind it. Crockett entered and strode to the counter. A short man wearing black sleeve protectors sat hunched over a desk, scribbling furiously as the machine beside him clicked out a pattern of long and short signals. When the clicks ceased, the operator tapped back a brief response, then pushed to his feet.

"What can I do for you, mister?" The fellow's mustache twitched as he talked.

Crockett grinned. "I need to send a wire to Brenham."

The operator shoved a tablet across the counter to him and reached above his ear to extricate a pencil. "Nickel a word."

"Thanks." Crockett wrote out his message, then struck through as many words as possible. He handed the paper back to the operator and tossed a fifty-cent piece onto the counter.

ABDUCTED FROM TRAIN.
RELEASED.
IN DEANVILLE.
WILL ARRIVE LATE TOMORROW.

As the operator scanned the message, his eyebrows arched high onto his forehead. "I done heard about that holdup this morning. The wire's been buzzin' with it for hours. You telling me *you're* the fellow those bandits took from the train?"

Crockett hardened his gaze. If he answered one question it would only open the floodgate for myriad more. "Just send the telegram, please. To Mr. Lukas Hoffmann."

"How'd you escape?" The little man leaned his elbows on the counter and stared up at him, nearly salivating in anticipation of a tale Crockett had no intention of telling. Telegram contents were supposed to remain confidential, but something told him this particular operator relished juicy tidbits too much to keep them to himself.

Crockett braced his palms atop the counter near the operator's elbows and bent his head close enough to growl his response in the man's ear. "Send the telegram."

The man jerked backward. "No need to get your dander up, mister. I's just curious." He carried the paper back to his desk. "Wanna wait for a reply?"

"I'll stop back in after I clean up a bit. That is, if you can direct me to a place where a fella can buy a bath."

"Harold's Barber Shop, across the street. And the boardinghouse is around the corner if you need a place to hang your hat for the night."

"Thanks." Crockett nodded to the operator and turned for the door, his gut telling him that news of his arrival would be all over town before his bathwater cooled.

Maybe he was wrong. Maybe the little operator with the big mustache really did keep things to himself. Maybe he just wanted to assuage his own curiosity. But as Crockett approached the barber shop, a reflection flashed in the window of a man with dark sleeve protectors scurrying down the street. Crockett sighed. Maybe he better make his bath a quick one.

Fifteen minutes later, dressed in his spare trousers and a clean blue chambray shirt, Crockett tucked his soiled suit under his arm and opened the small bathing chamber's door. A man with a tin star on the lapel of his dark gray coat stood waiting on the other side.

"Evening, stranger."

"Evening." Crockett adjusted his grip on his satchel and summoned a smile for the lawman as he stepped past him.

"Thought you might like to share a cup of coffee with me over at the office, so's we can get better acquainted." The man didn't lay a hand on him, but the authority in his voice gave his suggestion the weight of a command.

Crockett slowed his step. "That's mighty neighborly of you,

Marshal, but I've had a rather trying day. Perhaps we can visit tomorrow?"

"Won't take long, son." The barrel-chested lawman strode forward, firmly took charge of Crockett's bag, and extricated his clothes from beneath his arm. "Harold will secure a room for you at Bessie's place and see that your belongings are delivered." He handed the bag and clothes to the barber, a thin man with heavily pomaded hair. Then he dug out a coin from his vest pocket and pressed it into the barber's hand.

"Harold, have Miss Bessie clean and press our guest's suit. On me."

"Yes, sir, Marshal Coleson. I'll see to it." Harold spun around and headed to the front of his shop while the marshal gestured toward a side door.

"After you, mister."

Out of options, Crockett nodded and moved toward the exit. "Of course."

Once outside, the lawman steered him back in the direction of the livery, to a stone building boasting an uninviting small barred window high up the south wall. The glass-paned window at the front promised a warmer reception, but Crockett's chest only tightened as his promise to Joanna ran circles in his mind.

The inside of the marshal's office was dim but tidy, the man's desk empty except for an inkstand and a half-finished plate of food. Crockett frowned. The man had left his supper to chase him down. Such a man wouldn't be easily put off.

"What's your name, son?" the marshal asked as he dragged a chair from against the wall to a spot nearer his desk.

"Crockett Archer, sir."

"Brett Coleson." He offered his hand and shook Crockett's with an iron grip. "Have a seat, Archer."

The man's age and manner reminded Crockett of Silas Robbins, and an odd sort of recognition filled him as he took his seat. Marshal Coleson moved past him to the stove behind his desk, where a coffeepot sat waiting.

"Thanks for taking care of my laundry," Crockett interjected into the growing silence. "You didn't have to do that."

The lawman filled a chipped crockery mug, set it on the desk in front of Crockett, and then grabbed his own half-full one and splashed in a couple inches of fresh brew to reheat the dregs. "Glad to do it, son. You've had a trying day, after all." The marshal peered meaningfully at him over the top of the pot as he echoed Crockett's earlier words. "One I'd like to hear more about."

Crockett grasped the mug's handle and held it between the desk and his lips. "What would you like to know?"

"Is it true that you're the man those bandits took from the Gulf, Colorado, and Santa Fe this morning?"

"Yes."

Coleson lowered himself into his chair and took a swig from his mug as if he had all night to get the answers he sought. "What'd they want with you?"

A rueful grin slid into place on Crockett's face. "You wouldn't believe me if I told you."

"Try me."

Crockett shook his head, then met the lawman's eye without flinching. "I was supposed to be a birthday present."

Coleson held his gaze, assessing. Silence stretched, but Crockett didn't turn away. He left himself as open as possible, hoping to disarm the marshal with his honesty so that the vague answers he'd be forced to give later might cause less suspicion.

Finally Coleson blinked. "You know those fellers?"

"Nope. I was as surprised as anyone when they forced me from the train. I thank the Lord they decided they didn't need me after all and let me go. I'm supposed to be in Brenham tomorrow."

"That's right," Coleson said, lifting his cup. "The witness

accounts said the men were looking for a preacher. Seems like a strange request for a gang of outlaws."

"Doesn't it, though? They didn't even steal anyone's belongings, even when the passengers offered them up. I tell you, this adventure will make a great tale to add to a sermon. Jesus warned that he will return like a thief in the night. I experienced a thief in the daylight, but it was certainly no less unexpected. Goes to show one must always be ready to meet one's Maker."

"I reckon so." Coleson thumbed his hat back on his forehead. "You hear any names or see any faces you could identify?"

"They wore bandanas over their faces." Which was true—at least for the first part of the encounter. Crockett worked to change the direction of the conversation before Coleson demanded more details. "I appreciate your thoroughness, Marshal, but I won't be pressing charges." Crockett set his mug down, scraped the chair backward, and stood. "The men let me go, and except for a little inconvenience, no harm was done. Besides, what kind of parson would I be if I preached forgiveness from the pulpit but failed to extend it to those who do me wrong?"

"No charges, huh?" Coleson gained his feet, as well, his eyes narrowing slightly, as if he saw right through the conversational maneuver. "Well, I guess that's your right. The railroad might take a different stand, though, so your testimony is still needed."

"Of course." Crockett edged toward the door. "I'll be sure to leave my home address with the boardinghouse proprietress, in case you hear from the railroad." Praying that would prove sufficient, Crockett lifted a hand in parting. "Thanks for the coffee."

"You know, Archer," Coleson called out before Crockett could reach the door, "justice is a biblical concept, too. A man is to be held accountable for his crimes. To make restitution. Or don't you think the book of Exodus applies today?"

Crockett held his face carefully blank, despite the fact that every nerve ending in his body seemed to be sending alarms to his brain.

Marshal Coleson stepped around the desk. "It sticks in my craw when a criminal eludes justice. Reminds me of a gang I chased around Texas the first couple years I served as a Ranger. They were the only outlaws I chased that never gave in to greed. Smart, really, seeing as greed is what leads most thieves to their ruin. They never went after army pay wagons, government shipments, or banks. I'm guessing because they were too well guarded. They seemed content to rob stage passengers and an occasional railcar. And because no one was ever injured in the robberies, most lawmen saw them more as a nuisance than a serious threat."

He moved closer, his eyes locked on Crockett's. "They up and disappeared fifteen or so years back. Strange how your kidnapping is suddenly bringing them back to mind." He raised a brow. "Always bothered me that them yahoos didn't pay for their misdeeds. Thievin's wrong, no matter how little is taken."

"Indeed it is, Marshal," Crockett hurried to agree. "But remember, though all will be held accountable for their actions on the Day of Judgment, justice is not always achieved through men's efforts."

"Mmm," the lawman murmured noncommittally. "The witnesses had a sense the outlaws you encountered were older men." Coleson obviously wasn't ready to let the matter drop just yet. "Gray hair, stiff gaits. What did you obser—"

The door swung open, cutting off Coleson's question. "Howdy, Marshal." The telegraph operator rushed through the opening, oblivious to the tension filling the room. Crockett felt like kissing the little weasel—or at least bear-hugging him.

"A reply came from Brenham for you, Mr. Archer. Thought you'd want to see it right away."

8

Crockett reached for the slip of paper in the operator's hand and managed to sidle around the fellow, putting the little man squarely between him and the marshal. "You're a godsend, my friend." He tossed the operator a coin for his most timely interruption and turned back to Coleson.

"I'm afraid this is rather urgent, Marshal. Would you excuse me?" He reached behind him for the door frame, eager to make his escape.

Coleson crossed his arms over his chest, his expression none too pleased. "You really ought to press charges, Parson. If not for yourself, then for the poor fella they choose to kidnap next time. Do you want his fate on your hands?"

Recalling the way Joanna had taken her father to task over the day's shenanigans, Crockett felt certain Silas Robbins wouldn't be attempting any future clerical abductions. The train-riding preachers of the area should be safe.

"Your concern is well-meaning, Marshal, but unnecessary." Crockett backed fully into the doorway, pleased when the lawman made no move to stop him. "Today's events were instigated by a misunderstanding that has since been cleared up. These men pose no further threat. Therefore, I insist on extending forgiveness. I'll not be filing charges. Good day."

Crockett hesitated a moment longer, but the instant the marshal grunted and waved him off, he dashed through the door and made for the boardinghouse. He stuffed the telegram in his pocket as he went, afraid that if he paused to read it now, Coleson might corner him again. Better to save it for the privacy of his room.

Orange and red streaked the sky to the west, hailing evening's rapid approach. Crockett lengthened his stride as he rounded the corner where the now-darkened barber shop stood and searched for some kind of a placard to identify the boardinghouse.

The side street only boasted three homes, none of them very large. But the second one on the left had a porch lantern lit. Like a ship seeking safe harbor, Crockett aimed for the welcoming light, hoping his knock wouldn't disrupt a family's meal.

A woman tall enough to look him in the eye answered the door. "Yes?"

He doffed his hat. "Evenin', ma'am. I'm looking for Miss Bessie's boardinghouse."

"Ya found it." She turned and started off down the hall, leaving the door gaping behind her. "Scrape your boots afore ya come in. I don't abide no boarders trailing mud on my rugs." Her voice filtered back to him and smacked him into action like a wooden spoon across the knuckles.

Crockett darted to the edge of the porch. He'd polished his boots yesterday before boarding the train, and except for some dust, they'd survived his adventures relatively unscathed. But he didn't want to risk offending his hostess, so he gave them an obligatory scrape against the end of a floorboard and then hastened after Miss Bessie, taking care to close the door behind him.

"You'll be in the west room. Here." The woman pointed to a

doorway on the left of the hall but moved past without stopping. "Harold put your belongings in the room. Parlor's to the right."

Crockett barely spared the rooms a glance in his effort to keep up.

"I'm dishin' up supper now," she said as they entered the kitchen. "Breakfast's at six thirty. Food hits the slop bucket at seven, so don't be late."

"Yes, ma'am."

The woman marched up to the stove and ladled some kind of soup from the bottom of a small pot. As she poured it into a bowl, he thought he smelled chicken. But when she slapped the bowl onto the roughhewn table, all he could identify were a few orange chunks that he guessed might be carrots and a green bean or two. Nothing resembling meat floated in the pale broth.

"I don't eat with the boarders, so don't lollygag." She opened the door to the warming oven and brought out a pan of yeast rolls that smelled heavenly. Man might not live on bread alone, but Crockett suspected the rolls would do more to sustain him through the night than the watered-down soup.

That was unkind. Crockett harnessed the uncharitable thought and forced his mind onto a godlier path.

Miss Bessie hadn't been expecting company. She'd probably diluted her own small portion in order to share with the guest thrust upon her. He should be thankful for her generosity.

The woman covered the rolls with a dish towel and set them on the table along with a crock of butter. Then spoon and knife clattered beside the bowl. When she finally glanced his direction, it was to singe him with the heat of a perturbed glare.

"Don't just stand there sucking up the air. Get to eatin'."

"Yes, ma'am." Crockett took hold of the chair nearest him and pulled it out. Before he dropped into his seat, however, he favored his hostess with a bright smile. "Thank you for the fine meal, Miss Bessie."

The woman grunted and turned her back on him. "Just make sure you leave the night's payment on the table—it'll be two dollars." Then without another word, she disappeared into what he could only assume was a back bedroom and shut the door with a decisive thump—a thump followed by a click that sounded suspiciously like a key turning in a lock.

Did she think he would do her harm? Or was she simply protective of her privacy? He supposed the precaution wasn't wholly without merit. An unscrupulous man might attempt to take advantage. Although Crockett imagined Miss Bessie could hold her own with most. She'd probably have any disrespectful fellow hog-tied and booted out the back door before he could sneeze.

The woman was as no-nonsense as they came and seemed an expert at keeping folks at a distance. She'd never even asked his name. Nevertheless, she provided a roof over his head, food for his stomach, and a place to lay his head. If he'd wanted conversation, he could have stayed with the marshal.

Crockett laid his hat on the corner of the table and took his seat. After saying grace for the meal, asking the Lord's blessings on Miss Bessie, and thanking God for watching over him during the craziness with Silas Robbins, he took a few extra minutes to petition the Almighty on Joanna's behalf.

Provide the right man for her mission, Lord. Work through him to reestablish a flock of believers and assist Joanna in her efforts to win over her father. Soften Silas's heart to your message. Penetrate it with your truth.

As he mentally closed out the prayer, it occurred to him that he'd not mentioned the Brenham congregation. Adding a quick postscript, he asked that the elders be granted wisdom in their decision and that the members be blessed as a result.

His memory jogged, Crockett dug out the telegram from his trouser pocket and set the crumpled paper beside his spoon.

Too hungry to resist the call of the rolls any longer, he slathered one with butter, ate it in two bites, then buttered another before unfolding the message.

STAY IN DEANVILLE.
ELDERS WILL MEET AND SEND INSTRUCTIONS.

Crockett's jaw halted midchew. His eyes moved over the words a second time.

Stay in Deanville? Really? He'd expected them to encourage him to make all possible haste.

Well, if he were to be completely honest, he'd expected them to arrange a late afternoon service to accommodate his tardy arrival. Pretty vain expectation, now that he thought about it. People had farms to see to, families to tend. It would be unrealistic to ask them to stay in town all day or to make a long return trip. And in truth, that wouldn't be in his best interests, either. Surely only a handful of members would turn out for an evening service. Did he really want a decision to be made when the majority of the members had only heard the first candidate?

Crockett resumed his chewing, though he barely tasted the buttery bread any longer. His mind was fully consumed with generating convincing arguments as to why he shouldn't feel threatened or disheartened by the telegram.

While he slurped his soup, he lectured himself about how God was in control, how he knew what was best. During the consumption of his third and fourth rolls, he imagined scenarios where waiting for a later date to speak would actually prove beneficial. Perhaps a member of considerable influence in the congregation was currently out of town. Maybe an afternoon service would require preaching over wailing babies who'd missed naps. Or maybe the Lord knew that a tree was fixing to fall on the church roof at precisely 3:42 tomorrow afternoon, and keeping him away meant saving his life and the lives of dozens of church members.

All right, so that last one was a bit farfetched. But stranger things had happened. Like a preacher being stolen from a train instead of watches and jewelry. Who would've believed that would happen?

Crockett stood and carried his dishes to the washtub. As his bowl and utensils slid beneath the murky water, he cast a glance at the bolted door to his right. Washing the dishes himself might not do much to improve Miss Bessie's hospitality, but perhaps the small kindness would ease her burden a little. Crockett added some warm water from the kettle on the back of the stove, rolled up his sleeves, and got to work—not only on his dishes but on the few others he found in the bottom of the tub.

When he'd washed, dried, and stacked them on the counter, he hung up the damp towel and rolled down his sleeves. Then he covered the rolls he'd left on the table and collected his telegram. Scanning the kitchen to make sure he was leaving it as tidy as he'd found it, he placed two silver dollars beside the bread pan, where his hostess would be sure to find them, grabbed his hat, and headed for his room.

His travel satchel sat waiting for him on the end of a too-short bed atop a brown patchwork quilt that needed mending. He ran his finger along a frayed square that had come unstitched on one side. Miss Bessie would have his hide for sure if he snagged a satchel buckle on that and tore it further.

He hung his hat on the bedpost and moved the satchel from the bed to the small desk beneath the room's single window. A plain lamp with a slightly sooty chimney jiggled when the bag hit the desk, and its low flame flickered. Crockett adjusted the wick to allow more light to fill the dim room, then unbuckled the satchel and extracted his Bible. A page of sermon notes fell from inside the front cover and fluttered to the floor. Crockett bent to retrieve it.

That's when the idea struck.

An idea that would bless a particular young lady on her birthday while, at the same time, improving his chances at landing the Brenham job. An idea so perfect, it had to be inspired.

Blowing out a deep breath in an attempt to calm his suddenly racing pulse, Crockett ordered his notes, took his Bible in hand, and began preaching in hushed tones to the lacy throw pillows on Miss Bessie's bed.

9

Joanna huffed out a breath and watched her disobedient hair flutter in the mirror. Why did she even bother? The coils never stayed where she put them. Why couldn't she have lovely blond wisps like Holly Brewster? *Her* hair never pushed out of its pins or frizzed into an orange halo. Joanna had even overheard Holly complain to Becky Sue one time that it took her an hour to brush it out every night since it had grown past her hips. Joanna could barely keep hers long enough to reach the bottom of her shoulder blades. Any longer and the weight of it when piled atop her head induced headaches.

Maybe she should give up trying to look like a lady and simply wear it in a thick plait behind her neck. Heaven knew it would be easier to manage. But somehow the thought of giving up on arranging her hair felt like giving up on her chances of finding a husband. She was only turning twenty-one today. Surely that didn't qualify her for old-maid status yet.

Stiffening her spine, Joanna shoved another pin into the fluffy knot at her nape. Then, almost as if her mother were in the room, Joanna heard the echo of a tender voice soothing long-ago tears.

"A woman's hair is her glory, Joanna. And yours is truly glorious."

Joanna closed her eyes and recalled the feel of her mother drawing a brush through her thick tresses as the two of them sat on her bed.

"It's vibrant like a sunrise. Untamed like the most beautiful landscape. It reminds me of your father—wild, yet full of love. Your hair is a gift from God, Joanna. Don't despise it because it is different. See the beauty in his gift."

She opened her eyes and stared hard into the mirror. Her mother had taught her to examine the world through an artist's eye, to find splendor in a landscape where others saw only dirt and rocks. Under her mother's skilled tutelage, Joanna had learned to turn a dry creek bed into a beacon of hope through the stroke of her brush, portraying what could be instead of what was. Yet when she looked upon her reflection, her training proved ineffectual.

"'Tis a gift, Joanna." She scowled at the woman in the mirror. "To scorn it would be to dishonor the Giver."

So she looked again. Past the recalcitrant curls. Past the inadequate length. Past even the unnamable color that existed somewhere between ginger and cinnamon. She allowed her vision to blur slightly so that no details distracted. A minute passed. Then another. Until she realized her perspective had shifted. She saw not her own bright tresses, but the darker, russet tones of her father's hair. And not his alone, for her mind also recalled the light brown curls of her mother. The hair her father had always loved to touch, to twist around his finger when the two of them snuggled together on the settee during quiet evenings. Mama would lean her head against his shoulder, while Daddy wrapped his arm around her.

Joanna blinked, her gaze reluctant to focus on the present. *I see the gift now, God. Thank you.*

Wiping the sentimentality from the corner of her eyes, Joanna gave a little sniff and turned away from her mirror. She smoothed the wrinkles from her Sunday-best dress—a periwinkle polished muslin with indigo trim—and collected her Bible from the small table beside her bed.

She might not yet have a preacher, but she had a Lord who deserved her worship, and though her father and his men had made themselves scarce the minute breakfast ended, she intended to start her twenty-first year with a positive outlook. There'd be no quiet Bible reading in the parlor for her this Sunday. No, it was time to wake up the old chapel with hymns and brush the dust from the pews.

Joanna arranged her favorite straw bonnet upon her head, the one decorated with clusters of periwinkle blooms that made her eyes look more blue than gray, then tied the ribbons beneath her chin and tugged her mother's gloves over her hands.

Today she was going to church.

By the time Joanna neared the chapel, the sunny sky and quiet morning had restored her good humor. She hadn't encountered a single soul on the walk over, even with taking the road instead of the shortcut through the field. But she didn't mind the solitude. In fact, she welcomed it. She'd never been good at making idle chitchat. She much preferred to be alone with her thoughts. No one around to try to impress. No one to interrupt her musings. No one to hear should a song suddenly rise to her lips.

Grinning to herself, Joanna put voice to the hymn that had been running through her head since she left the house. "'For the beauty of the earth, for the glory of the skies.'" Timid at first, her breathy tones slipped softly into the morning air. She twisted her head to peer behind her, making sure no one was within earshot.

"'For the love which from our birth, over and around us lies.'" Joanna's voice grew stronger as she entered the churchyard. The words brought her mother to mind as well as her God, and her heart swelled as she moved into the chorus. "'Lord of all, to Thee we raise, this our hymn of grateful praise.'"

Her gaze caressed the trees by the church walls as she sang the second verse, the lyrics proclaiming God's glory in his creation. Joanna's voice grew bolder as she climbed the steps. Swept up in the moment, she turned around and truly raised her song to the heavens.

"'For the joy of human love; brother, sister, parent, child. Friends on—'"

"'Earth and friends above,'" a rich, masculine voice sang from behind. "'For all gentle thoughts and mild.'"

Joanna gasped and spun around.

Crockett Archer, eyes twinkling, stood in the chapel entrance.

Heat flooded her cheeks. Would she forever be embarrassing herself in front of this man? And how had he even come to be here? A dozen questions raced through her mind, but they all dissolved on her tongue as the handsome parson ignored her distress and continued singing, his deep baritone resonating through her.

"'Lord of all, to Thee we raise, this our hymn of grateful praise.'"

She expected him to stop after the refrain, but he continued unabashedly on to the final verse and turned to her, silently urging her to join him.

Unable to resist, and not really wanting to, Joanna shyly added her melody to his, while returning her attention to the sky, away from Brother Archer's all-too-penetrating stare.

"'For thy church that evermore lifteth holy hands above.'" Gradually, she increased her volume until she matched his, finding an amazing freedom in singing without reservation. "'Off'ring up on every shore her pure sacrifice of love.'"

When they came to the final refrain, she switched from the melody to a line of harmony and closed her eyes as the blend of notes reached into her very spirit. "'Lord of all, to Thee we raise, this our hymn of grateful praise.'"

The final chord hung in the air between them, the memory of its sound filling the silence. Neither of them spoke for a long moment, then Brother Archer murmured a quiet, reverent "Amen."

The Lord had blessed her with another gift, Joanna decided. A perfect moment to treasure in her heart.

Brother Archer turned to her then, a rascal's grin curving his lips. "Surprise."

That was stating it mildly.

Joanna darted a smile up at him, amazed at how comfortable she'd grown beside him as they sang. Usually her encounters with men left her acutely aware of her shortcomings, despite their efforts at politeness. But Brother Archer was different. Instead of kindly overlooking her flaws, he acted as if he were completely unaware of their existence.

"What are you doing here?" Joanna blurted, needing to change the directions of her thoughts before she could examine them too closely.

The parson winked at her. "Granting a birthday wish."

Joanna's breath caught. *Does he mean . . . ? Is he . . . staying?* Her heart hammered wildly in her breast until logic asserted itself. The man had a job waiting for him. Whatever his reasons for returning, she'd be foolish to read too much into them.

Brother Archer took her arm and led her into the small entryway. "After I wired the elders in Brenham, they responded by asking me to hold up in Deanville until they could meet and decide on a new plan. So, since I won't be delivering my sermon there this morning, I thought it might be nice to deliver it somewhere else. To someone who might appreciate it more than the pillows in my room at the boardinghouse."

He grinned at her with such sincerity and good humor that Joanna felt guilty over the pang of disappointment that shot through her at his words. He'd gone out of his way to give her a precious gift. The least she could do was show some appreciation.

Manufacturing a smile, she did her best to beam it up at him. "But how did you know I would be here?" she asked. "I usually conduct my Sunday devotions in my parlor at home."

Brother Archer glanced sheepishly at the floor, where a piece of rope lay huddled in the corner. "I'd intended to ring the bell as a call to worship, but the pull cord appears to have rotted." He brushed his hands together as if ridding them of leftover fibers. "I was fixin' to saddle up and ride to your place when your singing drew me to the front of the church. I'm sure Sunflower appreciates the reprieve."

Hearing her mare's name emerge from such masculine lips struck Joanna as quite ridiculous, and she found herself fighting down a giggle. Crockett Archer seemed the type to ride a steed named Hercules or Samson, not an animal named after the yellow blossoms that cover Texas fields in autumn. But since *she'd* been the one to offer him a horse, she hadn't felt right about assigning him one of her father's mounts. Therefore, she'd lent him her palomino. The mare was sturdy and strong and had enough fire in her to keep even a man like Crockett Archer on his toes.

"I didn't see her when I arrived." If she had, she never would have burst into song. Although, she had to admit, she'd rather enjoyed it when the parson had joined his voice to hers. It almost made her embarrassment worth it. Almost.

"I tied her up around back. Here . . ." He took her arm and led her down the center aisle. "I cleaned off the first few rows at the front. I wasn't sure where you usually sat."

"Third row on the left," she said as she surveyed the chapel.

The man had been busy. A broom stood propped against the edge of a windowsill on the far wall next to a pile of leaves, dirt, and something that looked like a nest. She prayed it was from a bird and not one of God's furrier little creatures.

Suddenly the quiet of the building registered. Her footsteps echoed loudly in her ears as she made her way down the aisle. The utter emptiness of the place soaked into her bones and left them cold. Abandoned. Like the pew she used to share with her mother.

Brother Archer handed her into the pew, and Joanna sidled along the edge of the bench and took her seat, bracing herself for the loneliness that would strike the moment he left her to take his place at the podium.

But the parson didn't leave. Instead he folded his tall frame into the pew beside her. Her coldness vanished.

"When my brothers and I worshiped together at home," he said, reaching over the back of the pew in front of them to collect a slender book, "Neill led the songs. As the youngest, his voice was the last to change."

Joanna smiled, imaging a younger version of Crockett Archer, his adolescent voice cracking while his big brothers looked on.

"When it did finally lower, it didn't deepen as far as the rest of ours did. As the only Archer who could sing a decent tenor, he got stuck with the job."

"Does he mind?"

"Neill? Nah. He's always had a hankerin' for music. Took to playing Pa's fiddle when he was about half grown. Made such a screeching racket, Travis banished him to the barn. But now folks actually pay him to play for their shindigs." Brother Archer shook his head as if such a thing was hard to believe, but an unmistakable gleam of pride shone in his dark eyes. "It gives him a reason to get off the ranch every now and again, which is probably a good thing."

The parson settled back into the pew, his shoulder brushing hers so slightly she doubted he was even aware of the contact, despite the fact that she found it hard to be aware of anything else.

"I found a couple of these behind the pulpit." He rubbed the cover of the hymnal he'd retrieved against his trouser leg, gave it a quick inspection, and handed it to her. "I'm no troubadour, but I'd gladly join you in a hymn or two before the sermon. If you'd like."

Taking the book, she thumbed through the pages, seizing the excuse to look anywhere other than his face. Because, really, how could she be expected to converse with any semblance of rationality when the warm kindness in his brown eyes was turning her insides to mush?

"This one," she managed to squeak as she smoothed the pages open.

He nodded, inhaled, and led her in the familiar strains of Charles Wesley's "Love Divine, All Loves Excelling."

She added her alto to his baritone, one song after another. Joanna would have been edified aplenty just staying in that pew with him and singing all morning. But all too soon he set the hymnal aside and strode to the front of the sanctuary.

"Brothers and sisters," he began, his gaze sweeping the invisible congregation before landing on her with a wink, "how blessed we are to come together on this Lord's Day, sanctified by the blood of Christ. But there are others outside these walls whose souls are perishing. Men and women, neighbors, friends, even members of our own families who are in desperate need of the living water that only Christ can provide. Their souls are parched and withering away, yet they don't admit their thirst."

The parson's eyes glowed with compassion as they met hers; however, the ache that usually came when she contemplated the state of her father's soul did not come. For there was passion in

Crockett Archer's eyes, too—fiery passion that filled her with hope, with purpose.

He didn't speak with religious rhetoric designed to impress and elevate his standing as a holy emissary of God. Nor did he shout out condemnation and dire warnings in order to frighten his listeners into obedience. No, Crockett Archer spoke in the same charismatic manner that had endeared him to her yesterday when he'd disarmed Jackson Spivey with friendly banter and genuine concern. His voice carried authority, but more than that, it carried authenticity. And it was the latter that held her enthralled.

She followed where he led, opening her Bible to 1 Peter and reading along as he quoted verses that brought evangelism into a new, more personal light. In chapter two he emphasized how all of God's people are a royal priesthood, not just the ministers in the pulpit or the missionaries in foreign fields. And as such, they are called to live holy lives so that others might see and be influenced. Like the wives in chapter three who won over their husbands, not with words but with chaste and reverent behavior. Yet verse fifteen also spoke of the need to always be ready to give an answer as to the reason for the hope evident in one's life.

The parson's words penetrated her heart on a level so personal, so deep, it was as if God himself were speaking truth into her soul. Crockett Archer might have written this sermon for a church dozens of miles away, but in that moment Joanna knew that the Lord had intended its message for her.

10

Silas Robbins reined in his gray, dismounted, and walked the beast to the barn. He and Jasper had gotten caught wrangling one of his heifers out of a mud pit in the far west pasture. Thanks to the stubborn gal's refusal to cooperate, it'd taken longer than expected to haul her sorry hide out of the mire, leaving him late for lunch and wearing more dirt than a wallowing hog.

Some prize of a father he was turning out to be. First his birthday present ran off to Deanville without granting his little girl's wish, then he'd run off himself this morning to avoid the daughter he loved more than life.

Silas's jaw clenched as he hefted the saddle from Marauder's back and slapped it onto the half wall that marked the edge of the first stall. After dragging the blankets off as well, he grabbed a strip of toweling and rubbed down his horse.

Why couldn't he have just sat in the parlor with her for once and let her read him a handful of those infernal verses she put such stock in? It wasn't as if they were gonna flay his skin or set fire to his heathen ears. He wouldn't even have had to listen, really. Just sit there and pretend for a few minutes. It was her birthday, for pity's sake. He coulda done it just this once.

He ran the towel in small, firm circles across Marauder's side, cleaning away the animal's sweat and wishing he could clean away his guilt as easily.

Jo asked so little of him. So little, yet so very much. More than she could comprehend. Martha hadn't understood, either. Probably 'cause he'd never had the heart to explain. She'd seen such goodness in everyone, especially her church folk. It woulda broken her heart to learn the truth. That those holy fellers sittin' beside her on the pew every Sunday were just as vile beneath their shiny veneer as any drunkard or thief. Worse, even.

No, he'd not had the heart to destroy his wife's illusions. And the same held true for his daughter. He'd thought he could set his memories aside for Jo's sake. Just for today. But across the breakfast table, he'd read the invitation in her eyes before she gave it voice. And in that moment, nausea had rolled so viciously through his innards that he'd nearly spewed the contents of his stomach all over the platter of toast Frank had just passed him.

He'd ridden out five minutes later.

Silas finished up with his horse and turned him loose in the corral. Then, straightening his shoulders, he gritted his teeth and marched up to the house.

Pulling the back door open, Silas stepped into the washroom and quickly divested himself of his mud-splattered shirt and pried his caked boots from his feet. His trousers would have to wait for the privacy of his bedroom. He washed his hands, face, and chest, and ran his fingers through his rusty hair before entering the kitchen. His stockinged feet made no noise as he shuffled across the floor to lift the lid and peek into the stew pot Jo had left simmering on the stove.

As he inhaled a tantalizing whiff of beef, onions, and potatoes, the sound of voices carried to him from down the hall. So sure he'd find his quiet little Jo waiting for him somewhat sullen and forlorn thanks to his hasty departure, he was shocked to hear her voice echo so animatedly through the house. Her subdued laugh even reached his ears, bringing a smile to his face.

That smile disappeared the instant a masculine chuckle hit the air. Silas reached for the gun at his hip.

Jasper and the others were still out wrestling cows. Which meant a stranger was in his parlor. Alone with Jo.

Silas cocked his weapon and charged down the short hallway, a growl rumbling in his chest. He burst through the open doorway, not taking time to do more than register the tall man's position by the mantelpiece.

"Touch my daughter and I'll be digging your grave before the day's out, stranger."

"Daddy!" Jo gasped and lurched protectively into the line of fire at the same moment the man turned from his perusal of one of Martha's landscapes. Recognition slammed into Silas like a well-aimed fist.

"Mr. Robbins," the preacher man said with a nod of calm acknowledgment as he stepped out from behind Jo's intended shield. "It appears I'm a little overdressed for Sunday dinner." Archer ran his hands along the lapels of his coat, leaving Silas all too aware of his lack of shirt.

"What're you doing in my parlor, preacher man?" Silas demanded. He held his gun arm steady, determined to regain the control that seemed to be sifting through his fingers. He'd not let this young pup put him on the defensive.

Before the man could answer, however, Joanna shoved herself into her father's face, forcing him to lower his weapon.

"Brother Archer rode in from Deanville this morning to deliver a birthday sermon for me." She threw the words at him. "A gift *you* arranged, I'll thank you to recall. I invited him to join us for dinner, as any hospitable person would. Now quit your barking and put some clothes on. The food will be on the table in fifteen minutes."

With that, she stormed out.

Silas glared at the parson, sure he was somehow responsible for his daughter's switch in loyalty. Archer met his scowl with an annoying degree of nonchalance. Silas holstered his revolver with a grunt. Honest living had apparently robbed him of his ability to intimidate properly.

"Thought you was in a hurry to leave, preacher man. Why'd ya come back?" Silas crossed his arms over his chest and braced his legs apart. He might be forty-six, but there wasn't a speck of flab on his frame. He didn't need a firearm to enforce his will. Archer would be wise to take note.

The parson's grip tightened on his lapels, but the man's eyes never wavered. Silas got the impression that Crockett Archer was fightin' hard against the urge to remove his coat and square off with him.

Curious. Preachers, in his experience, went out of their way to avoid confrontation and faced it only when trapped. This Archer fellow seemed exactly the opposite. He was itchin' for the chance to take him down a peg or two. Silas shifted his jaw, remembering the blow the parson had dealt him yesterday. But the man had been trapped then. What was driving him now?

"Due to my interrupted travels yesterday," the parson explained, "I missed my appointment in Brenham."

Ah, so the feller held a grudge. *Ha!* He might preach forgiveness, but he was as much a hypocrite as the rest of his kind.

"Since I had to wait for a new one to be scheduled, I thought I would spend my time in a worthy pursuit. And I could think of nothing more worthy than delivering a sermon as a birthday gift to your daughter."

Archer released his lapels and held out a hand to Silas. "I really ought to thank you, sir. You caused me no small amount of trouble yesterday, it's true, but you also brought a blessing into my life. Your daughter has a pure heart and a sense of spiritual purpose that humbles me. I am better for having known her. Thank you for giving me that opportunity."

Silas frowned down at the preacher's outstretched hand. What game was he playing? He lifted his focus to search Archer's eyes, hunting for any hint of sarcasm or sanctimony. He found none. Maybe the sermonizer was just better at hiding his motives than most. One thing was for sure, though, he'd not give Archer the satisfaction of thinking himself the bigger man. Silas unfolded his arms and grasped the preacher's hand.

The pressure built as both men tightened their grips. Their gazes met, challenge rife between them. Archer finally released Silas's hand, but Silas didn't kid himself by thinking it was due to any lack of stamina. The man's grip was like a vise. He'd let go as a matter of choice. What bothered Silas was not knowing what drove that choice.

"I think I'll see if I can lend a hand in the kitchen." The parson smiled and stepped around him.

Silas stared at the spot on the parlor rug that Archer had just vacated. Something about that man ate at his craw. He dressed like a preacher and spoke like one most of the time, but beneath that window dressing stood a man who acted more like a hardened cowman.

As Silas trudged to his bedroom to change his muddy trousers, he continued chewing over the Crockett Archer puzzle. He didn't fit Silas's expectations. He wasn't soft or overly scholarly. Although the man did carry more books and journals than clothes in that satchel of his, his hands boasted calluses, and his skin was tanned from the sun. Plus he spoke like a normal person, not with a bunch of highfalutin words that didn't mean nothin' to nobody but himself. The man was strong and willing to stand up for himself yet was not prideful or sanctimonious.

He'd fled yesterday to fulfill some private mission but came back this morning to give Jo a gift.

Silas gritted his teeth as he pulled a new work shirt over his head. The man didn't fit any of his tried-and-true notions for preachers. He was a riddle. Silas didn't like riddles. They were messy, unpredictable. And they forced a man to reconsider things that were better left alone.

Silas wanted him gone.

11

After enduring the weight of Silas's disapproval all through the tasty meal of beef stew, corn bread, and leftover chocolate cake, Crockett decided he'd worn his welcome thin enough and took his leave. Joanna insisted he keep Sunflower for his journey, so he and the little mare returned to Deanville, making good time.

Worshiping with Joanna Robbins had been a singular experience. Awkward at first, yet incredibly intimate as time went on. He'd never been one to believe the size of one's audience was an indicator of success. Shoot, for years his audience had consisted solely of his three brothers. God could impact hearers' hearts no matter the size of the congregation. And Joanna's heart thirsted like none other he had encountered.

As he'd stood in the long-abandoned pulpit, he'd made an effort not to stare directly at her for more than a few seconds at a time, not wanting to cause her discomfort. Yet he'd been continually drawn to her—her lovely face tipped up to meet his, her gaze intent and unwavering. He'd preached enough to know when a congregant was thinking more about Sunday dinner than the sermon and could easily recognize the glaze of sleepiness that numbed folks' attention after a too-long Saturday night.

Joanna's avid interest had inspired him, bringing words to his mouth that he hadn't rehearsed and fostering an energy that continued to hum through him even now. There had been times in the past where he'd felt the Spirit moving within him, granting him words beyond what he had prepared, but never before had he felt more like a vessel in the Lord's hand than he had as he stood in front of Joanna Robbins. It was quite humbling, yet exhilarating at the same time.

His mind busy mulling over the morning's events as he strolled from the livery to Miss Bessie's, Crockett nearly missed the frenetic waving of the telegraph operator scurrying across the street toward him.

"Mr. Archer! Mr. Archer!" The little man dodged two buggies and a mule cart before finally reaching Crockett's side.

"Yes?"

Slightly out of breath, the man leaned against the hitching post as he reached into his vest pocket. "I've been waiting for you for an age," he huffed. "This telegram arrived for you an hour ago. It's from that church in Brenham you been correspondin' with. It seemed real urgent, and I worried when I couldn't find you. Miss Bessie said you left early this morning but that your belongings were still in your room. I hoped that meant you was comin' back."

Crockett frowned and held out his hand to accept the paper. "I appreciate you tracking me down."

"It says you're to meet that fellow in Caldwell tonight."

"Yes. I can see that." Crockett looked up from the message to glare at the nosy operator. Mr. Hoffmann was taking the afternoon train from Brenham to Caldwell and asked Crockett to meet him at the hotel restaurant for supper at six so they could discuss the elders' decision.

An unwelcome heaviness settled in the pit of Crockett's stomach. Why were they sending someone to talk to him? Why not just have him come to Brenham?

"How far is the ride to Caldwell?" Crockett stuffed the telegram inside his coat and slipped a coin into the operator's waiting hand.

"About eight and a half miles if you take the northeast road. You got plenty of time to make it, as long as that horse of yours ain't too winded."

"I'll rent a fresh one from the livery." He wouldn't take Joanna's horse out of Deanville. She'd been kind to loan Sunflower to him, and he'd not abuse her generosity. Besides, he couldn't be sure he'd be returning. Despite the knots tightening in his gut, there was a chance he'd be taking the train to Brenham with Mr. Hoffmann after their meeting.

He needed to pack his things and get on the road.

"Thanks for your help, Mr. . . ." Crockett held out his hand as he searched his mind for a name to fit the little man with the big mustache.

"Stallings. Ed Stallings." The operator shook his hand and stepped back. "You better be on your way, Mr. Archer."

"Can't argue with that." Crockett smiled, feeling slightly more charitable toward the interfering fellow. He waved farewell to Mr. Stallings and made for the boardinghouse with long, purposeful strides.

Miss Bessie must have seen him coming, for her bedroom door was firmly shut with her behind it by the time he arrived in the kitchen.

Shaking his head, Crockett crossed the kitchen and raised his voice so that it might pass through the wooden barrier. "I'm checking out, Miss Bessie. Thank you for the room."

He turned to go, but the creak of a hinge stopped him.

"Will ya be comin' back?" His cloistered hostess emerged

through the small opening, an unreadable expression on her face.

"I suspect not, but one never knows for sure." The way he figured it, from Caldwell he'd be catching a train headed in one of two directions—either on to Brenham or home to Palestine.

"Well." Miss Bessie fiddled with her apron, not quite meeting his gaze. "Should ya ever wander back this way, you'll have a room waiting for ya." A touch of color stained her cheeks, and she immediately surged out of the doorway to start bustling about the kitchen. She collected pots and pans from where they'd been drying on the counter and piled them into her arms like homemade armor. "Unless I'm full-up, o' course."

"Of course." Crockett grinned and wondered what Miss Bessie would do if he plunked a thank-you kiss smack-dab in the middle of her cheek. The poor woman would probably suffer a heart seizure. He opted to tip his hat to her instead. "Thank you for the invite, ma'am. I'll be sure to stop by if I find myself in Deanville again."

She nodded, then turned her back, signaling she'd said her piece and didn't aim to expand upon it.

Oddly reluctant to say good-bye, Crockett held his tongue as he exited the kitchen. It took only a couple minutes to gather his things from his room and buckle the straps on his satchel. He glanced back into the kitchen on his way out but didn't see any sign of his hostess. Once outside on the road, however, he glanced over his shoulder at the small house and caught the motion of a curtain in the parlor window falling back into place.

"Bye, Miss Bessie," Crockett whispered, a smile tugging his lips upward.

He certainly wouldn't have chosen to be pulled from a train by a gang of retired outlaws, but at least he'd touched a life or two during his little side trip. It just went to show how the Lord could bring good out of any situation. And a reminder that his God was more than capable of working things out with the Brenham elders, as well.

Crockett sent a prayer heavenward as he stepped into the hotel dining room and spotted Brother Hoffmann at a table near the window.

See me through, Lord. See me through.

The Brenham elder caught his eye and stood to greet him as Crockett approached. "Brother Archer. Good to see you again."

Crockett nodded and accepted the man's hand. "Mr. Hoffmann. It was good of you to travel all this way to speak with me, though I would have been happy to meet you in Brenham."

"I know you would've, but I was headed this way on business, anyway, so it was no trouble." The older man waved him toward a chair, and the two seated themselves at the table.

After a waiter took Crockett's order, Lukas Hoffmann kept up a steady stream of friendly banter. He asked about the abduction and oohed and aahed in all the right places as Crockett recounted the adventure—minus a few key details. Crockett asked after the man's family and listened to several delightful anecdotes about Hoffmann's grandson and the scrapes the young lad seemed determined to get into.

Crockett liked Lukas Hoffmann—had since they first met a month ago. He was a jolly sort, always ready with a smile, a laugh, and a thump on the back when a man was feeling low. But as the waiter cleared away their empty plates and poured fresh coffee in their cups, Crockett knew the time for pleasantries had passed.

Hoffmann stirred a heaping spoonful of sugar into his coffee and stared at the swirling liquid, his face losing its cheerful mien. Crockett waited, his unease growing the longer the silence stretched between them. Finally, Hoffmann let out a heavy sigh and looked up from his coffee.

"We've decided to hire Stephen Middleton."

The suddenness of the statement hit Crockett like a fist to the gut.

"I see." The two words were all he could manage past the tightness in his throat.

This wasn't right. He deserved a chance to prove himself. Hiring his competitor simply because the man managed to survive his train travel without incident was grossly unfair! He'd fostered such hopes on this appointment, such dreams. God had been leading him to Brenham; he was sure of it. So how could they just cut him loose without a proper trial?

"You've got to understand, son. None of us took this decision lightly."

Yet you made it in a matter of hours without the benefit of hearing me preach.

"For weeks we have been asking for the Lord to make our path clear. To make our choice evident. When you failed to arrive yesterday, many of us saw it as a sign. A clearing of the path, you might say, leaving us one candidate for the position.

"When we learned of the abduction, however, we questioned our conclusion, considered that perhaps a force other than God was at work." Hoffmann paused to sip his coffee, but the fervor in his eyes didn't dim. "Then you wired that you were safe, and it brought to mind all the times the Lord worked his will even through the evil deeds of others. Joseph's brothers selling him into slavery. Pharaoh's oppression of the Israelites. The trickery that sent Daniel to the den of lions. Who were we to say that the Lord wasn't at work in a similar way with you?"

Hoffmann took another sip, his gaze challenging Crockett to ask himself the same question. "When Brother Middleton's sermon was well received by the congregation this morning, our conviction solidified. The Lord had made our choice."

If the Lord had made their choice, where did that leave him?

Unable to hold Hoffmann's scrutiny any longer, Crockett's attention fell to the coffee before him. He lifted the white china cup to his mouth and drank in the bitter beverage, its heat lightly scalding the back of his throat as it went down. Much like the painful truth he was mentally trying to swallow.

God had chosen another man to pastor the church in Brenham.

"I'm sorry it didn't work out the way you'd hoped, son." The genuine compassion in Lukas Hoffmann's tone soothed away a bit of the sting, though Crockett's heart still railed against the injustice of being removed from the running by an event so totally beyond his control.

"Me too." Crockett set his cup down, suddenly eager for some time alone.

"God has plans for you, Crockett Archer. Don't let this little setback sour your outlook." Hoffmann pulled a couple bills from his wallet and tucked them under the edge of his saucer, enough to cover the cost of both their meals. Then he pushed his chair back, tossed his napkin on the table, and rose to his feet. "His timing might not be our timing, but it is always perfect."

With that, he left.

Crockett lingered long enough to finish his coffee, then wandered to the hotel desk and rented a room for the night. There wouldn't be another train to Palestine until tomorrow.

The decision on his destination had been made.

Yet as he stood in his room discarding his suit coat and removing his boots, a vague disquiet nagged at him like the itch of a mosquito bite. And the more he tried to define it, the itchier it became.

Had his confidence been misplaced? He'd been so certain God was leading him to Brenham. How could he have mistaken the

Lord's purpose so completely? Or had this detour been God's plan all along? And if so, what did that mean for his future?

"What am I supposed to do, Lord?" Crockett whispered the question against the glass of the window that overlooked the dim side street below. He unfastened the buttons of his vest, undid the tie at his throat, and rolled up the sleeves of his shirt. None of the adjustments to his clothing made him comfortable, though. He reached for his watch, intending to set it on the small desk behind him, but when his fingers closed around the brass casing, Hoffmann's words echoed again in his mind.

"God's timing is not our timing."

Pieces of a verse flashed through his consciousness, a verse he'd read recently, during his study of Peter's epistles.

Crockett strode to the bed and unlatched his satchel. Taking up his Bible, he sank onto the mattress and flipped to the end of the second epistle. Pages crinkled as he searched for the passage. Then it was there.

"But, beloved, be not ignorant of this one thing, that one day is with the Lord as a thousand years, and a thousand years as one day. The Lord is not slack concerning his promise, as some men count slackness; but is longsuffering toward us, not willing that any should perish, but that all should come to repentance."

"'Not willing that any should perish . . .'" The whispered words fell from his tongue almost of their own accord. Crockett barely noticed, for at that moment other words bombarded his senses.

"I prayed for a preacher to come. To save my father's soul."

"I need help, Mr. Archer. I need a preacher to bring this old church back to life."

"I will help you find a new preacher. I promise."

Crockett rose from his seat on the bed, his finger sandwiched between the closed pages of the Bible he still grasped, and returned to his position at the window. Staring over the top of the building across the street, he found the steeple of a church a couple blocks away. A tiny smile touched his lips as the persistent nagging that had plagued him the last half hour suddenly dissipated.

"I'm not going home to Palestine, am I, Lord?"

12

Joanna whacked at the weeds daring to encroach her butter-nut squash plants as the late morning sun warmed her back through the fabric of her brown calico work dress. Once she finished her garden chores and ate a bite for lunch, she'd be able to escape to the barn loft for a few hours to paint. And, oh, how she needed that time away. After all the excitement of the last couple days, she craved the quiet serenity of her studio. Not even her father would bother her there. That sanctuary was hers alone.

The gentle thud of hoofbeats echoed in the distance. An ordinary sound on a ranch, but as Joanna tilted her head to listen better, she realized they were coming not from the pasture or barn but from the road. She straightened, resting her weight against the handle of the hoe. The floppy hat she wore blocked much of the sun, but it still took her a minute to recognize the approaching horse.

"Sunflower?"

Jasper had promised to retrieve her mare when he went to town tomorrow for supplies. Who would be riding . . .

Brother Archer?

Joanna recognized the black hat the preacher had worn the past two days, yet his clothes had changed. Gone was the black Sunday-go-to-meeting suit. Instead, the man riding her horse wore a pair of new denims and a tan work shirt. If it wasn't for the way he sat in the saddle, and the fact that she'd memorized that particular combination of man and horse yesterday as she watched him ride off, she probably would have mistaken him for a wandering cowhand looking for work.

As he dismounted near the barn, he must have caught sight of her, for he lifted a hand in greeting and strode toward the garden.

Her heart skipped a delighted beat, barely able to believe what she was seeing. Then her delight turned to horror as she realized the state of her attire.

Joanna bit her lip and spun around. *Good heavens!* She was covered in dirt. Probably had smudges on her face. And her nails? Joanna moaned as she examined the dark stains around her cuticles. Could his timing be any worse? Not only had he caught her in her ugliest dress with one of her father's old hats plopped on her head, but she probably smelled of the cabbage she had harvested before she checked on her squash. *Wonderful.* Just what a man wanted to smell when visiting a lady.

"Miss Robbins?"

Joanna pivoted and bit back a groan of despair. Crockett Archer was even more handsome than she'd remembered. Somehow his rancher's clothing made him seem more approachable, more . . . within her reach. And if that wasn't the most ridiculous notion, she didn't know what was. A man with his looks and kind heart could have any woman he chose. He'd never settle for a shy, freckly redhead with an ex-outlaw for a father. She was everything the ideal preacher's wife was *not*.

"Brother Archer. What a surprise." Joanna forced her lips to curve in welcome, praying there wasn't a big blotch of dirt on the end of her nose where she'd rubbed an itch a moment ago. "I didn't expect to see you again."

"I hadn't anticipated a reunion this soon, either, but it seems the Lord had other ideas."

His smile was so warm, it took a moment for his words to penetrate. "The Lord?" Joanna scrunched her eyebrows as she tried to puzzle out his meaning. "What ideas?"

The parson removed his hat and held it before him, worrying the brim as if he were actually nervous. "If you're still looking to fill the local pulpit, ma'am, I'd like to apply for the job."

"You'd like to . . . apply . . . ?" Joanna couldn't even form all the words. In fact, she barely managed to hold herself upright. No, truth be told, even that meager feat was beyond her, for she was listing dangerously to the right.

In an instant, Crockett Archer was by her side, steadying her elbow with a solid grip. He angled himself slightly behind her, as if he were a stake propping up a drooping bean plant. "Miss Robbins? Are you all right?"

When she continued teetering, he slapped his hat back on his head and wrapped his right arm around the back of her waist. Her knees quivered from the close contact and from the way his decadent brown eyes searched her face in concern.

His arms felt heavenly about her, and his attentive regard left her breathless, but she needed to clarify his words. Bracing her legs more firmly beneath her, she steadied herself and stepped away from his support. "Are you saying you'd like to . . . to preach here on a regular basis?"

His furrowed brow eased a bit as he nodded. "Yes'm. Every Sunday, if I can find work to support me until the church can pay my salary."

"But what about Brenham?"

From the moment he disarmed Jackson Spivey with nothing but a calm demeanor and a display of respect, Joanna had known in the depths of her soul that Crockett Archer was the minister she needed to reach her father. But she'd watched him leave—twice. Had God truly brought him back to stay?

"They apparently filled their vacancy yesterday."

"I'm sorry." And she was. For him. He'd been so excited, so full of plans when they spoke on Saturday. He must have been devastated.

And it was her fault.

If her father hadn't abducted him, he would have auditioned on schedule, and she knew firsthand how marvelously he could deliver a sermon. A day later, her heart still swelled when she recalled his passionate oration. The man had a gift. A gift she'd stolen from the people of Brenham.

Joanna pushed her father's floppy hat off her head, letting it dangle down her back from the string around her neck. She needed to see Brother Archer's face, his eyes. "How could you want to preach here when it is because of me that you lost your position?"

"Ah, Joanna." Her given name fell from his lips as his gaze melted into hers. "It was never my position to lose. If it had truly been God's will that I preach in Brenham, no abduction could have prevented my appointment. You are not to blame. And I know your rascal of a father's not, either—despite my carrying on the other day. God is the one in charge, and it is he who led me back here. Will you have me?"

Although she knew he only meant in an official preaching capacity, her heart fluttered with a little thrill at his words as she let herself imagine for the briefest of moments what it would be like to have Crockett Archer ask her the same question with a much more personal implication.

Foolish girl. She stood on the verge of having her dearest wish granted. Why did she have to go and start hungering for more?

Joanna resolutely turned her mind back to the gift Brother Archer was offering her, and a genuine smile burst across her face. "Of course I'll have you!"

As soon as the words left her mouth, heat sprinted to her cheeks. Heavens, that wasn't how she'd intended to answer. She cleared her throat, and dropped her gaze. "Having you here would do our community a world of good, Brother Archer. We'd be honored to have you serve as our minister."

There. That sounded better. More formal. Perhaps that would cover her earlier blunder. However, when she looked up, the parson's eyes twinkled with far too much merriment for her peace of mind.

"Wonderful!" he declared, and his enthusiasm eased some of her embarrassment. "Now, all I have to do is find sufficient employment to keep me in food and supplies until we can get this church of ours established."

This church of ours. It was amazing what that simple phrase did to her insides. Ours. This was *their* project. Both of them. Together. She wasn't alone in her mission anymore. And she'd make sure he wasn't alone in his.

"I can ask around. Introduce you to a few . . . " An idea struck her so hard while she was speaking, she almost felt the blow. "Wait! I know the perfect person to ask." Excitement buzzed over her nerve endings faster than a message on a telegraph wire. She'd taken three steps toward the barn before she remembered she was leaving a thoroughly bewildered preacher standing in the middle of her squash rows. She couldn't stop, though. Not now. Not when her mission was so clear.

"Go take stock of the parsonage," she called over her shoulder as she picked up speed. "See what you'll need to make it habitable. I'll meet you there in an hour."

Crockett watched Joanna dart through her garden like a rabbit fleeing a shotgun blast. Only it wasn't fear that drove her. It was purpose. She was definitely up to something.

Once she disappeared into the barn, Crockett broke out of his bemused stupor. He grinned over his own foolishness. What was it about Joanna Robbins that took his attention hostage whenever she was near? The expressive features that displayed her every thought? The delightful way she blushed when he teased her? Or perhaps it was the way she threw herself whole-heartedly into those things that were important to her. Whatever it was, it was certainly compelling.

Rubbing the back of his neck, Crockett glanced around. Apparently he wasn't the only thing Joanna had abandoned in the garden. Her hoe lay fallen atop the winter squash plants she'd been tending so carefully moments ago. And near the garden gate, a small burlap sack with a head or two of cabbage peeking out from between the folds sat forgotten.

Since Joanna was off to do him a kindness, it was only fair that he return the favor. Crockett retrieved the hoe and collected the cabbage on his way through the gate. He was halfway to the house, thinking to set the cabbage inside the kitchen door, when a brown blur thundered past him.

Joanna Robbins tore out of the barn astride a magnificent chestnut quarter horse. She leaned forward in the saddle, hat flopping against her back, hair streaming out behind her in a wild, curly mass as she urged her mount to a full-out gallop. Unable to do anything but stare, Crockett stood dumbstruck as she raced past.

She was the most amazing horsewoman he'd ever seen.

Joanna Robbins. The shy creature who claimed painting and reading were her favorite pastimes had just bolted across the yard like a seasoned jockey atop a Thoroughbred. She might have inherited her mother's grace and manner, but the woman rode like her outlaw father. Maybe better.

13

Sweat dripped down Silas's neck as he set his hatchet aside and signaled to Jasper. "Ease 'er back slow."

"You got it, boss." Jasper nudged his mount forward, and the rope that tethered the gelding to the fallen tree stretched taut.

Carl had discovered the deadfall on his rounds that morning. One of the post oaks had collapsed into the fence. Probably fell victim to the high winds they'd had last week. They'd been hacking at the branches the past half hour, trying to free it from the barbed wire so they could drag it away without taking half the fence line with it.

"Whoa!" Frank called out from the opposite side. "She's catchin' on my end." He groaned heavily as he forced his way past the outer branches to reach the spot where it had snared. "Confounded limbs, stabbin' a man like he was some female's pincushion," he grumbled as he strained forward. "I oughta just set ya on fire and let you burn your way free. Then I'd take my shovel and poke ya 'til there was nothin' left but ashes. Wouldn't be stabbin' me then, would ya?"

Silas rolled his eyes and reached for his bandana. After being partnered with the man for over twenty-five years, he knew better than to interrupt Frank during one of his rants. Not if he wanted to get the job done before sunset. So he held his tongue and swiped the bandana along the back of his neck, rubbing away his perspiration. He twisted his neck to the side to work out a kink, and caught sight of his daughter riding toward them as if a hangin' posse were in pursuit.

"Jo!" His gun clearing leather in an instant, Silas sprinted away from the tangled branches, planted his gloved palm against the rounded trunk, and vaulted over the tree that stood between him and his daughter. As he ran to meet her, his eyes scoured the landscape in search of whatever threatened her, but he saw nothing.

He held up his arms to slow the racing horse, but Joanna had the beast well under control. In a flash, she reined in the horse and bounded off its back.

"Daddy! I have the most wonderful news!" She jogged up to him and flung herself into his arms like she used to do when she was just a little bit of a thing. He caught her against his chest, and the laughter that bubbled out from her calmed his thundering pulse.

He embraced her tightly, a father's tenderness momentarily overriding his common sense. Then he shoved his weapon back into his holster and took her by her upper arms, setting her away from him as he schooled his face into a stern line.

"You scared a year off my life, ridin' in here like that. I thought fer sure a pack of coyotes must be on your heels."

"Sorry, Daddy." Her smile dimmed slightly, but not enough to count. The little scamp wasn't the slightest bit sorry. "I promise not to go over a trot on the way home. And I'll give Gamble a thorough rubdown when we get there. I swear. I was just too excited to hold him back, and you know how he loves to run."

Of course he did. He'd handpicked the animal for just that

reason. He just didn't expect his genteel daughter to be the one tearing across the countryside on his back.

Although he couldn't fully suppress his pride in seeing her do so. No doubt about it—his girl could ride.

"Everything all right, boss?" Silas turned to find Frank, hatchet in hand, a few steps behind him. Jasper and Carl stared in his direction, as well.

Silas waved him off. "Yeah." He lifted his voice to carry to the others. "Nothin' to worry about. Go on and see to that tree. We need it hauled off and the fence repaired before the end of the day."

Jasper saluted and started calling out instructions to Carl, while Frank let out a beleaguered sigh and muttered under his breath before plodding away.

Once the men returned to their duties, Silas steered his daughter back toward Gamble, using the horse's body to shield them from the curious looks he knew would be darting his way the moment he turned his back.

"All right, girlie. Spill it. What's got you in a dither?"

Jo bounced on her toes, fixin' to explode with her news. "Brother Archer wants to pastor our church! Can you believe it? I know I fussed at you for bringing him here against his will, but it's turned out to be the best birthday present ever. It's exactly what I wanted! Oh, Daddy. I'm so happy!"

That preacher man was worse than a bad penny. He just kept turnin' up. "What's he doin' back here? I thought he had some all-fired important engagement to get to."

"God changed his plans." She reached out and clasped his hand, and he swore he could feel excitement dancing through her veins. "He's back to stay. All he needs is a place to work until the church gets established. That's where you come in." She gave his hand a squeeze, and Silas's throat closed up.

"He's not working here," he choked out. Just the thought

of it gave him hives. "I ain't no charity house for out-of-work sermonizers. And you know how I feel about strangers. We've never had an outsider workin' on the Lazy R, and I ain't about to start now."

"But what about Frank's rheumatism and Jasper's bad knee? Just think of how much help Mr. Archer could be."

"The gal's got a point, Si," Frank said from a few paces away. The fool dropped a handful of twigs from the dead tree into a pile that had no business being so close to where he and Jo were talking. "My rheumatism *has* been flarin' up lately."

"Bah!" Silas snatched a fist-sized stone off the ground and chunked it at the man's head. "Your rheumatism flares whenever it suits your fancy, you sorry dog."

Frank ducked, narrowly avoiding the stone. "Watch it!" He glared at Silas, but there was no real heat behind the look. He knew he'd stuck his nose where it didn't belong. "I'm just sayin' that it wouldn't be so bad to have a young buck around to do the heavy lifting for a change."

Having said his piece, Frank held out a conciliatory hand and headed back to the fence line.

"He's right," Jo said, laying her hand on Silas's arm. "Crockett Archer grew up on a ranch, so it's not like he's some greenhorn who doesn't know a heifer from a steer. He'd be a help to you. I swear. Please, Daddy? Please? It would mean the world to me."

Consarn it! Why did it have to be a preacher that made her happy? It was one thing to have the feller at the church, but on his land? He'd rather house a cougar.

The denial of her request sprang to his tongue, but he just couldn't push it past his lips. Not when the sadness that had lingered in her eyes for more than a year had finally vanished.

"If he fails to do a proper day's work, I'll fire him on the spot." Silas scowled and jabbed a finger in Jo's face.

Unperturbed by his posturing, Joanna squealed in glee and

threw her arms around his neck. "Thank you, Daddy! You won't regret it. I promise."

He already regretted it. But after she smacked half a dozen kisses on his cheek and nearly squeezed the breath out of him with her huggin', the dread that had built inside him lessened to a tolerable level.

Looked like he and the preacher man were fixin' to get better acquainted.

Crockett opened the firebox on the stove in his new accommodations and winced as a pungent smell hit him in the face. Instinctively squinting and jerking his face to the side, he hastily identified the source of the stench. Some kind of rodent. Squirrel or mouse, most likely. Whatever it was, it was dead. His stomach churned, but he steeled himself against the compulsion to gag. Casting a desperate glance around for the stove shovel, he finally clapped eyes on the end of its handle protruding from behind the cobweb-strewn kindling bucket. He seized it and quickly scraped it along the base of the firebox, scooping up the indistinguishable furry mass and removing it from its tomb. Trying not to breathe, Crockett made for the door with all possible haste.

He'd be lighting a fire to sanitize that box just as soon as he ensured the stovepipe was clear of debris. No way would he be cooking on that thing tonight, though.

Once outside, Crockett moved toward the edge of the field that bordered the church and hurled the foul-smelling remains as far from him as he could.

"You treat all your visitors that way, Parson?"

Crockett did a brisk about-face. He'd been so intent on ridding himself of one varmint that he'd completely missed the arrival of another.

"Silas." Crockett tossed the stove shovel back toward the

church and pulled out a handkerchief to wipe his hands. Heaven knew there wasn't a clean spot left anywhere on his clothes after an hour of sifting through the rubble of his new living quarters.

Joanna's father glared down at him from atop his big Appaloosa. "I hear you're thinking about stickin' around these parts." He made no move to dismount, just crossed his wrists over the pommel, enjoying his position of power.

"That's right." Crockett tucked his thumbs into his suspenders and adopted a bored air, refusing to be intimidated.

All at once, Silas swung down from his horse and stalked up to Crockett, his eyes carrying deadly promise. Crockett freed his hands and formed them into fists, his muscles tense and ready.

"My little girl has her heart set on starting this here church up again. I ain't gonna try and stop her, but understand this, preacher man—I *will* see that nothing hurts her along the way. You already done left twice. If you're planning on leaving again, you best do it now. 'Cause if you leave after you get Jo's hopes up, I'll track you down and feed your liver to the buzzards. Got it?"

Crockett stiffened. "Keep your threats to yourself, Silas." He matched the man scowl for scowl. "You'll not be chasing me off. God brought me to this place, and I'll stay until the job he has for me is finished." And judging by the belligerent attitude of the hardheaded man in front of him, that job was going to take a while.

"What're you planning to do for food and supplies?" Silas challenged. "Don't look like the old parson left you much."

"The Lord will provide." Crockett crossed his arms.

"Ha! That's where you're wrong." Silas smiled, but the expression looked too much like a wolf eyeing his prey to be comforting. "The Lord ain't gonna do the providin'. I am."

"*You* are?" Crockett jerked, his arms unfolding.

"Yep. Startin' tomorrow morning, you'll be working for the Lazy R." He stated it as if everything had already been decided.

"Two meals and a dollar a day. Breakfast's at six. Come late, and you don't eat. Fail to handle the work I give you, and you're out on your ear."

Having delivered his dictates, Silas turned to leave. He made it all the way to his horse and had one foot in the stirrup when he stopped and shot a final hard look at Crockett.

"And no sermonizing. I'm hiring you to work cattle and tend to ranch chores, not spout nonsense at me all day. Understand?"

Oh, he understood. Better than Silas himself did. "Tomorrow at six," Crockett agreed, relaxing his stance. "I'll be there."

Silas muttered something under his breath, then mounted and rode off without another word.

Crockett watched him go, an odd satisfaction swelling in his chest. Silas had no idea what was in store for him. The Lord had indeed provided—provided not only a vocation for Crockett but also an opportunity for him to spend time with Joanna's father day in and day out. No wonder Joanna had lit out of the garden as if her skirts were on fire. She'd received divine inspiration. And it was brilliant.

He might be preaching on Sundays, but the rest of the week he'd be living out the message on a more practical level.

Help me make an impact, Lord. His heart is as hard as his head, but I know you are stronger. Work through me, and bring about your glory.

Crockett headed back to the mess that awaited him inside, a grin creasing his face. Silas might think he was coming to the ranch to work cattle, but in truth, he planned on fishing. Fishing for men.

14

Joanna adjusted her position on the high stool she had dragged to the loft window and studied her subject for several uninterrupted minutes before glancing away to add more details to her sketch. The way his hair brushed his collar at the back of his neck. The angle of his hat. The set of his chin. The way his rolled sleeves exposed muscled forearms.

His likeness was difficult to re-create exactly while he moved about the yard, but she hadn't been able to resist the lure of trying to capture him on paper when he'd driven the wagon in from the upper pasture and began stacking the split logs he'd transported into the woodshed.

Crockett Archer made an arresting artistic specimen.

When her father had ordered her to take Gamble home yesterday after her riotous ride and insisted on following up with the parson himself, she'd worried that he'd try to scare Brother Archer off. But the parson had knocked on her back door before six this morning and even helped her set out the platters of flapjacks and bacon.

She should have known better than to worry. Crockett Archer

had never yet allowed her father to cow him. It'd been foolish to think he'd start now.

Joanna stroked her pencil firmly against the tablet as she delineated Crockett's profile, bringing definition to the soft outlines of her preliminary sketch. She idly nibbled her tongue as she shaded in the black of his hat and the long, dark lines of his trousers. The more she worked, the more the drawing came to life beneath her fingers. When she finished and held it out for a final inspection, her heart fluttered at the image before her.

Careful, Jo. God brought him here for your father—not for you.

"Afternoon, Miss Robbins." Brother Archer's deep voice echoed directly below the loft window.

With a guilty start, Joanna slammed the cover of her sketch pad closed. "A-afternoon."

"What are you doing up there?" His hat shaded his eyes, saving her from the teasing twinkle sure to be in evidence otherwise.

Taking a moment to regulate her pulse, Joanna slid from her stool and moved to the window ledge, picturing an invisible book on her head just as her mother had taught her. However, she probably needed an entire imaginary library to ground the hopes that kept trying to take flight within her.

"This is where I paint," she said, proud that her voice sounded normal. Then, not wanting him to question her further about her activities, she hurried to redirect the conversation. "How's your first day at the Lazy R going?"

"It's been anything but lazy—that's for sure." He chuckled a bit, and the sound drew a smile from her. "I'm accustomed to working my family's spread and having a say in what my day looks like, so taking orders from your father will require some getting used to, but we're managing. He hasn't drawn his gun on me today. I count that a success." He tipped his brim back and winked.

"And how is the parsonage working out? I had intended to help you clean it yesterday, until my father placed me on horse duty."

"It'll do." His lack of explanation, more than anything, told her how bad it truly was. "I wrote to my brother and asked Jasper to post the letter for me the next time he goes to town. Travis can box up my things and ship them here. That will make it feel more like home."

"Well, don't worry about the sanctuary. I'll round up some of the ladies in the area, and we'll give it a good scrubbing."

"With all the work I'll be doing here during the day, having one less thing to do to get ready for Sunday would be a tremendous blessing. Thank you." All hint of teasing left his voice, and what remained seeped into her pores like warm bathwater. She wanted to close her eyes and sink into it, but good sense prevailed.

"I'm glad to help, Brother Archer. We're partners in this endeavor, after all."

His gaze held hers, shrinking the distance between them as well as her resolve to be sensible. "Call me Crockett. At least when we're not in church. We are partners, after all." He grinned as he echoed her words.

"Yes, we are." Her pulse started up those crazy flutters again. "And as such, I think we need to—"

A furtive movement near the chicken coop stole her attention.

"What is it?" Crockett asked.

"I'm not sure." The shadow vanished. She peered at the corner of the coop, searching for a clue to help her decipher what she had seen. Nothing. Except . . . There! A thin rod poked out from beneath the roof. A rod that looked suspiciously like . . .

Joanna spun away from her perch and clambered down the loft ladder as fast as her skirts would allow, ignoring Crockett's concerned calls. When she dashed into the yard, the parson dogged her heels.

"I know you're behind that coop, Jackson Spivey." Joanna eyed the rod as it twitched once, then disappeared behind the wall. "Show yourself."

She halted just short of the coop, wanting to give Jackson the chance to emerge on his own. He might be a boy, but he had his pride. And that pride was much in evidence when he marched around the corner, chin jutted, arms crossed.

"I ain't done nuthin' wrong, Jo. You don't have to lay into me like I'm some sort a criminal or somethin'."

"Didn't my father warn you about sneaking around the Lazy R? He told you not to do any more hunting on our land without permission."

Jackson blasted a puff of air out of the side of his mouth, as if her concerns needed shooing like some kind of pesky insect. "He just didn't want my rifle shots spookin' his cattle. Besides, I wasn't huntin'. I was fishin'. He ain't never said I couldn't do that." His glance shifted from Joanna to the man behind her, and his eyes widened as his belligerence drained away. "I made sure to stay clear of the pastures," he said, turning his attention back to her. "The best fishing holes and game trails are in the woods to the east, anyhow.

"I almost snared me a rabbit." This comment he directed to Crockett, a touch of excitement creeping into his voice. "He slipped the noose, though."

It irked a bit to know that a virtual stranger could inspire such a change in Jackson without saying a single word, while all her efforts to help the boy stay out of trouble seemed only to provide fodder for arguments. It must be a man thing—some kind of code. Her father could do the same thing with his men. She often left the dinner table feeling like an entire secondary conversation had taken place with nothing more than glances and grunts.

"You use fishing line for the snare?" Crockett asked as if there weren't more important issues to pursue.

"Yep. But I didn't have much time to set it up and got the knot tangled. It didn't close right."

"I can show you a quick knot my brother Jim showed me when we were kids. He was in charge of our meals, so he had the most practice—"

"Can we discuss this later, please?" Joanna glared a warning at Crockett. The rogue had the grace to look slightly abashed, but the way Jackson cocked a grin left her feeling as if the two had somehow allied against her.

"Jackson." She lightly gripped his shoulder to get his attention. "It's not just about scaring the cattle. My father has strict rules about knowing where each of the hands are, and he makes sure to always let me know where I can find him should there be a need. What if you were injured? No one would know where to find you."

"I could get injured in the wild lands behind my house and no one would find me there, either." The boy straightened his shoulders and stepped away from her mothering touch. "I'm man enough to know how to take care of myself, Jo. You don't have to worry about me."

The kid was all bravado, but she didn't have the heart to call him on it. "Would you please just ask permission first? I'm sure my father wouldn't mind letting you fish or snare small game in our woods now and again."

Jackson made no response, but the way his gaze darted toward the trees and back, she got the feeling he made more than the occasional foray through the Lazy R woods. Joanna swallowed a sigh. He probably had a hard time finding much game on that barren patch of land his father owned. And there was no telling how often Mr. Spivey actually remembered to bring home supplies after his drinking binges in Deanville. Taking access to the woods away from Jackson might mean taking away his food supply.

Before she could come up with a decent solution that would soothe Jackson's pride without riling her father's temper, Crockett voiced a suggestion.

"If you've got time to go fishing in the afternoons, I would guess you'd have time to put those muscles of yours to more profitable use."

Interest immediately lit Jackson's face. "You talkin' cash money, profitable?"

"Yep." Gone was the twinkle from Crockett's eye. The parson approached Jackson with all the seriousness and respect of one man doing business with another. "With me working at the ranch now, I'll need someone to run errands for me and help with repairs around the church. And since I don't know the area yet, I'll need someone to show me around and introduce me to folks. You interested?"

"How much you payin'?" Jackson crossed his arms, but not before Joanna noticed the trembling in his fingers.

Most people ignored Jackson, their lack of respect for his wastrel of a father leading them to keep their distance from him, as well. His penchant for trouble didn't help much, either. Yet as he stood there trying so hard to act as if he didn't care about Brother Archer's offer, Joanna could almost feel his hunger to prove himself worthy of the respect that had been denied him.

"Fifty cents a week."

Jackson's eyes doubled in size. She doubted the boy had ever had more than a couple pennies of his own to rub together.

"You got yourself a deal, Preacher." He held out a slightly shaky hand, and Crockett grasped it.

"Excellent. Can you meet me at the parsonage tonight around seven? We can discuss more of the details then." He slapped the boy on the shoulder, but then a small frown crept across his brow. "Unless you're needed at home, of course," he said. "I don't want you to neglect your other responsibilities."

"I ain't got none when Pa's away. And when he's home he's always shooing me out so he can do his leatherwork in peace. His head pains him a lot," Jackson added by way of explanation, "and noise makes it worse. As long as I leave him something to eat before I head out in the morning and show up long enough to fix him supper in the evening, he don't care what I do the rest of the time."

Joanna caught Crockett's quick glance and knew he felt the same sympathy she did for the boy. Thankfully, he did a good job of hiding it.

"Well, I'll plan to see you tonight, then, Jackson."

"I'll be there, sir." He spun away to collect his fishing gear and a string of three small catfish and a carp. "Tell your pa thanks for the fish, Jo." He winked and dodged out of her reach when she pretended to give chase, then set off for the road.

"Having a job will be good for him," Joanna said, stepping closer to Crockett. "Keep him out of trouble."

"Maybe it will keep him out of your hair for a while." The skin around the parson's brown eyes crinkled slightly when he smiled. She'd have to add that detail to her sketch later.

Joanna returned his smile, then dragged her thoughts back where they belonged—on Jackson. "I really don't mind having him around. In truth, some days I want to tie him to a chair and feed him 'til he fattens up. Other times I want to hug him until that chip on his shoulder falls off. That boy needs some serious mothering. Unfortunately, I don't think I'm the right one to do it."

"Because he's sweet on you." She could feel Crockett's eyes on her when he spoke, but she didn't turn. What she *did* do was wonder what he saw when he looked at her.

Perhaps she'd be better off not knowing.

"I just don't want to give him the wrong idea and end up being one more adult who lets him down." She kicked at the dirt with her foot. "He has an abundance of those already."

"So you harp at him like a big sister instead."

That brought her head up, along with an affronted gasp. Until she saw the teasing gleam in his eyes.

"You show all the classic signs," he said. "You order him about, take him to task when he misbehaves, and bake him chocolate cake on your birthday because you know it's *his* favorite. All because you care and want to protect him." He shook his head in mock despair. "Yep. You've got a bad case. I've seen it before. My brother Travis still exhibits the symptoms, despite the fact that all the siblings who were in his care are now grown men."

Joanna pondered his observation, the revelation clicking things into place in a way that made sense. "I guess I do rather think of him as a younger brother." Somehow, knowing how to categorize her relationship with Jackson made it easier to define their boundaries.

Now she just needed Jackson to see it the same way. Maybe his spending time with Crockett would help with that.

"I suspect I need to be getting back to work." The parson ambled toward the emptied wagon. "Silas will be looking for me."

Joanna nodded, disappointed that he had to leave so soon but not wanting anything to cause friction between him and her father.

Crockett led the horses around, then climbed onto the driver's bench, took up the reins, and released the brake. She lifted a hand to wave.

"You've a good heart, Joanna Robbins," he said from his perch on the wagon seat. "It's easy to see why Jackson admires you."

He touched the brim of his hat in farewell and slapped the reins to get the team moving. As the wagon rolled out, his words lingered, tempting her to ponder other ideas. Like . . . if he could see why Jackson might admire her, did that mean *he* could come to admire her, as well? Or was he just playing big brother, unaware of the growing attraction she felt?

Perhaps she and Jackson had more in common than she'd thought.

15

It'd been three days since that conversation by the barn. Three days since she'd seen Crockett outside of mealtimes. Three days of staring at that silly sketch and wishing for things that would surely lead only to heartache.

Joanna exhaled a long breath and sat up enough to rub the perspiration from her forehead with her rolled sleeve. Her knees throbbed from being pressed into the wood floor for so long, but the dais supporting the pulpit glistened as if it were new.

Earlier in the week, she had arranged for several ladies to meet her at the church this afternoon for a cleaning spree. Together they'd been sweeping floors, washing windows, oiling pews, and even ridding the rafters of cobwebs, thanks to a large crate, a long-handled broom, and Mrs. Grimley's unfashionable height.

"Mother, is it time to go yet? We've been here for *hours*." Holly Brewster's woeful moan cut through the sounds of industriousness to grate on Joanna's nerves.

Grant me patience, Lord. Her mind sent the prayer heavenward while her eyes rolled the same direction. At least Holly had shown up to help. That's what she kept telling herself. But really, all she'd done was flick a dust rag haphazardly over a handful of windowsills—windowsills her mother had made a point to surreptitiously clean a second time when she came through with a bucket of vinegar water for the glass. The girl's apron was still as white and pressed as when she'd arrived and her hair flowed in beautiful blond waves down her back—unlike the rest of the women, who had clothes covered in grime and heads covered with kerchiefs.

"I think we're nearly finished, dear," Mrs. Brewster soothed. "Why don't you see if Joanna has anything that needs doing?"

Holly trudged over to the front of the church and twirled a hair ribbon around her index finger as she smiled prettily down at Joanna. "You don't need me to do anything—do you, Joanna? The angels themselves couldn't make this place any cleaner."

Joanna set aside her scrub brush and pressed her hand into the small of her back as she sat back on her heels. "Actually, if you could dump this lye water out in the field for me, I would really appreciate it. That way, I can start mopping up the excess moisture from the wood right away."

Holly eyed the dark brown water with obvious distaste. "Why, I don't think I could carry that heavy thing without sloshing its filthiness all over this beautiful clean floor. I would just feel dreadful if I caused a mess after everyone's diligent work."

And she'd probably feel even worse about sloshing the dirty liquid on her clean hem, but Joanna kept that opinion to herself. "I'm sure you can manage, Holly. Just walk slowly."

"I don't think you understand." Holly's smile never dimmed, but her eyes hardened. "I'm *sure* to spill. And I know you don't want that."

The not-so-veiled threat hung between them just long enough for Joanna to fantasize about turning the bucket over Holly Brewster's lovely head. In the end, Joanna simply shrugged and asked Holly to hand her the toweling piled in the front pew. She didn't have the energy to deal with a confrontation.

Holly tossed the rags to her with a triumphant grin and meandered over to one of the windows. Joanna had just started mopping up the first small puddle on the dais when Holly's quiet gasp brought her head up. The young woman's face was plastered to the window, her arms braced against the sill to give her a higher vantage point as she peered out toward the field.

"Joanna," she hissed, tossing a quick glance over her shoulder before pressing her nose back to the glass. "Is *that* the new parson? The man walking with Jackson Spivey?"

A curl of unease wound through Joanna's chest at Holly's obvious interest. "I reckon so," she admitted, despite her irrational desire to hoard the information. "Jackson does odd jobs for Brother Archer, so I wouldn't be surprised to see them together."

Holly spun from the window, tidied her already pristine apron, pinched some color into her cheeks, and then did the one thing Joanna never thought to see her do. She picked up the bucket of grungy lye water and started hauling it toward the door. *Without* spilling a drop on her pretty, ruffled hem, Joanna couldn't help but notice.

The girl had impeccable timing, too. She managed to reach the door at the exact moment Crockett did.

"Oh!" she exclaimed, as if coming upon him in the doorway had surprised her. "Pardon me. I hope I didn't get any of this dirty water on you."

Was it possible to hear eyelashes bat? Because Joanna could have sworn she heard heavy fluttering as Holly gazed adoringly up at Crockett.

"No harm done, miss."

Did he have to smile at her with the same twinkling grin she'd come to think of as hers? *Come now, Joanna, you can't really see his eyes from here.* Maybe not, but she could hear the charm oozing in his voice. All right, so maybe it wasn't oozing, but he certainly gave no indication that he saw through Holly's ruse. She'd thought him smarter than that. Really. Could the man not see that there was not a single smudge of dirt anywhere on her person? Nor was there even a hint of perspiration on her brow. Yet as Joanna watched, Holly raised a hand to her forehead as if to blot that nonexistent sheen.

"I'm so glad I didn't get any on you," she said, using that same hand to touch Crockett's arm. "After all the work I've done this afternoon, I'm quite fatigued, and I feared my grip might not be as steady as it should be."

"Why don't you let me dispose of that water for you?" Crockett shifted to take the pail, forcing the hand Holly had laid on his arm to fall back to her side. Joanna's lips curved slightly in satisfaction. Until his fingers encircled Holly's around the handle.

"Oh, thank you, Parson." Holly made no move to extract her hand. "That's ever so kind of you."

"It's the least I can do after all the work you ladies have done." He raised his eyes to glance about the sanctuary, directing his appreciation to everyone present. "The place looks marvelous. I can't thank you all enough." His gaze rested briefly on Joanna, and her breath caught. Had his smile deepened just then? But before she could decide the answer, Crockett turned his attention back to Holly.

"I'll be right back." He gently pulled the pail away, but Holly held on as long as possible.

"I'll come with you," she said. "I could do with some fresh air. My name's Holly, by the way. Holly Brewster."

And with that, the two of them disappeared through the doorway.

Joanna fought the urge to dash to the window and press her own face to the glass. The only thing restraining her was the fear that the other women would notice and comment upon her strange behavior. That, and the fact that her knees had been bent so long, her feet were numb.

"I think Holly's taken a fancy to the new preacher, Sarah." Etta Ward elbowed Mrs. Brewster and favored her with a match-maker's smile.

"Heaven help us all," Mrs. Grimley muttered, turning her back on the scene.

Joanna amened the sentiment wholeheartedly.

"I'd steer clear of that Brewster gal if I were you." Jackson gave Crockett a man-to-man look as he handed the parson another nail.

Crockett hammered it into the new step he held in place while fighting to keep a smile from his face. "Oh? Why's that?"

Ever since the women left that afternoon, Jackson had been filling him in on all the pertinent details of the families that had been represented. Which ones came from farms versus ranches. How many young'uns they had. The names of their husbands. He'd efficiently rattled off the facts as the two of them repaired the church steps, but this latest comment seemed more personal.

"She acts real sweet and all, as long as things are going her way. But the minute you cross her, she turns meaner than a swarm of fire ants."

Crockett wondered what experience had led the boy to that conclusion, but he knew better than to ask. "I appreciate the warning," he said, reaching for another nail. "However, we need to be careful not to say anything unkind about her when she's not here to defend herself. All right?"

Jackson frowned and looked as if he wanted to argue, but eventually he nodded, and they resumed their work.

Yet thoughts of Holly, now resurrected, stubbornly refused

to die. The young lady was certainly pretty. And even though he could tell she'd been exaggerating the tale of her cleaning exploits, the fact that she'd done it to impress him was rather gratifying. What man wouldn't enjoy the overt attentions of a beautiful woman? And while he could easily imagine her turning her lips out in a pout or storming off in a huff if she didn't get her wish, he could hardly picture her turning venomous. Maybe it would seem so to a boy, but it wouldn't be more than an irritant to a man.

Crockett drove in the last nail and straightened, visions of another young woman entering his mind, one who'd conversed with him on these very steps. Joanna's quietly intent nature contrasted sharply with Holly's vibrancy. While Miss Brewster's flirtation stroked his ego, the spiritual maturity Miss Robbins exhibited commanded his admiration and respect. Of course, to be fair, the ten minutes he'd spent in Miss Brewster's company this afternoon offered scant opportunity to form more than a surface opinion. A masculine smile tugged at Crockett's lips. He had to admit, though, his opinion of her surface was quite favorable.

"You want me to start sandin' the steps?" Jackson's question broke Crockett free from the dueling female images wreaking havoc on his concentration.

He cleared his throat. "Yes. They'll need a coat of paint, too, but it will be a while before I can make a trip to Deanville to pick some up."

"You gonna get enough to do the whole buildin'?" Jackson asked, assessing the peeling white clapboard with a critical eye.

"It sure needs it, doesn't it?" Crockett tipped his hat back, braced his right foot on the edge of one of the steps, and leaned his forearm across his thigh as he examined the neglect.

Jackson mirrored his stance from the opposite side. "Yep. But I ain't never painted a building afore. And if we gotta wait for you to get done at the Lazy R every day, it'd take us a right long time."

"I've got an idea about that."

Jackson stared at him expectantly, but Crockett said no more—partly to pique the kid's curiosity, and partly because he wasn't sure he could pull it off.

But if he could, he just might succeed at taking the first major step toward bringing the community together, and—even better—the first major step in bringing Silas Robbins into the fold.

16

Sunday arrived, and with it came an abundance of nervous energy that Joanna could not dispel. Unable to sleep, she'd risen before dawn and dispatched all her chores in record time. She'd even fussed over her appearance longer than usual, wrestling her unruly hair into a soft chignon and trying on both of her Sunday-worthy dresses so many times it was a wonder the shine hadn't worn off the brass buttons. Despite her lengthy attire deliberations, though, when she checked the mantel clock in the parlor, the hands hadn't progressed nearly as far as she had hoped. Services weren't scheduled to start for another hour.

A tiny moan escaped her lips. She couldn't stay here and wait. She'd go crazy.

Joanna entered the kitchen, thinking to check on the roast she'd put in the oven. But what was there to check? She'd already done everything that could be done ahead of time. The roast, onions, carrots, and potatoes were baking. The spinach greens were washed and ready for boiling. Bread baked yesterday waited in the pie safe, and the hard-boiled eggs to top the spinach were already peeled and sitting in a covered bowl on the counter. So what was she to do?

Her gloves and Bible beckoned to her from where they lay on the table. It had been about this time last Sunday when she'd decided to walk down to the church. Of course, that was before services were officially being held. Yet even then, Crockett had been there. He was probably there now, strolling up and down the center aisle, making sure everything was ready for his inaugural service, perhaps going over his sermon a final time. Was he nervous?

He always seemed so calm and in control, but he had no way of knowing if his presence would be readily accepted. *She* had no way of knowing. Starting the church back up had been *her* dream. What if the community failed to embrace the idea of a new minister? What if no one came?

Joanna's eyes rolled at her melodramatic thoughts. Of course they'd come—out of curiosity, if nothing else. After all, the ladies had shown up to help with the cleaning. They wouldn't expend such an effort if they didn't plan to attend. Still, it wouldn't hurt to offer Crockett some moral support, a friendly face to soothe away any anxiety he might be feeling.

She wouldn't mind the chance to be alone with him again, either.

And wasn't *that* an improper thought to be having on a Sunday morning.

Blowing out a breath, Joanna shoved her hands into her best pair of gloves, grabbed up her Bible, and resolved to purify her motives before she reached the church.

Never one to enjoy stringent lectures, even mental ones instigated by herself, Joanna delighted in discovering a familiar figure a few paces ahead of her when she joined the main road. She quickened her step to catch him.

"Jackson Spivey. Don't you look dapper, all cleaned up," she said by way of greeting as she pulled abreast of the young man. He slowed his step and kicked at a tuft of grass at the side of the road.

"Yeah, well, I ain't been to church since my ma left," he said, a dull red rising up his neck, "but I remember she always made me wash behind my ears afore we came. So I figured I ought to scrub real good today."

A soft smile tugged at Joanna's mouth. It seemed Crockett's presence was already working miracles. The boy's damp hair had been combed into submission and he sported a clean shirt, though the sleeves hung past his wrists. He'd probably borrowed it from his father. Tenderness welled inside her for the young man so eager to please his new mentor.

"I think you look quite fine."

Jackson's face jerked toward hers. "You do?"

The vulnerability he usually tried to hide flashed to the surface for a moment, and Joanna couldn't help but offer the reassurance he so obviously craved. "Yes, I do."

"Fine enough for me to escort you to services?" Just that fast, all hint of self-doubt fled from his expression, leaving only adolescent male swagger in its wake.

Even so, Joanna couldn't ignore the plea for acceptance that lurked behind the cocksure words. "I'd be happy to accept your escort," she said, "as a friend." She gave special emphasis to the word *friend* and breathed easier when Jackson nodded in understanding.

He offered her his arm, and Joanna slipped her fingers into the crook of his elbow.

"If you're gonna walk with me, Jo, you gotta pick up the pace." Once he had hold of her, Jackson lengthened his stride, nearly dragging her in his hurry. "Crock promised I could ring the bell if I got there early enough. We can't be late."

Joanna stifled a chuckle and quickened her steps. It seemed

escorting her to services wasn't quite as big a coup as ringing the church bell.

"God loves us all individually," Crockett pronounced as he strode across the dais, making eye contact with imaginary church members seated in the pews, "and he has blessed each of us with talents and spiritual gifts as unique as the shape of a face or the sound of a voice. Yet it is not God's will that we exist solely as individuals. He desires us to be in community with him and with each other. For it is only when individual members unite as a single body under Christ that the fullness of his love can be demonstrated to the world. It was for this unity that Jesus himself prayed in John's gospel, chapter seventeen."

Crockett paced back to the pulpit and his notes, uncertainty stealing his voice as he moved into the next section of the sermon, the part that had kept him up until midnight last night writing and rewriting. Praying over and worrying over. He wanted to call the community together, to bind them, to challenge them. But what if he alienated them or offended them? Would his ministry be over before it began?

He shifted his papers and cleared his throat. He couldn't remember ever being this unsure over a lesson. Ever. Since the time he was a boy, confidence in his calling had always been the foundation that gave him the courage to speak with boldness, more concerned with the message God wanted him to impart than pleasing itching ears. So why was that foundation shaking?

Grant me wisdom to speak what you want spoken, Lord, and nothing more.

Glancing over his notes a final time, Crockett inhaled a cleansing breath, released it, and continued where he had left off.

"For too long, this community has consisted of individuals. Individuals drawn together by geography, or perhaps friendship, or even family. But it has not been united as fully as God desires. It has not been one body under Christ. Today we can change that. Today God has brought us together in a way that pleases him, as the text we read a moment ago from 1 Corinthians 12 attests.

"We don't simply meet together in this building because it is a convenient place to worship. We meet in order to rejoice together and mourn together. To uplift and encourage one another. To gain strength from the strong and humility from the weak. To experience the artistry of the Master Weaver who brings all of our individual gifts together to create a tapestry more beautiful than any one person can achieve alone. A tapestry that proclaims God's glory to every eye that beholds it. A tapestry that is incomplete without you . . ."

His gaze crossed from a pew halfway back on the left to the second one from the front on the right. "Or you . . . or . . ." His gaze slid toward the back of the sanctuary and collided with Joanna, standing silently in the doorway. "You. . . ." Crockett's voice tapered off.

For a moment, all he could do was stare. Her rapt attention, the tiny smile that brought into relief the freckles dusting her cheekbones, the way the light passed through the doorway behind her to set her hair ablaze beneath the prim straw bonnet she wore. Yet it was her inner light that captured him most. The serenity of her features. The glow in her blue eyes. This was a woman of authentic spirituality. No wonder the Master Weaver had chosen her to be the central thread to anchor his new tapestry.

Crockett had no idea how long he stood there gawking. It would have been longer, he was sure, had Jackson not bounded past her and down the aisle, severing the connection that had held him enthralled.

"I'm ready to ring the bell, Crock. Is it time?"

Joanna dipped her head, further releasing him.

"Not yet. Ah . . ." He coughed a bit and dug in his vest pocket for his timepiece as he stepped off the dais and strode down the aisle. "Here," he said, handing the watch to Jackson. "At a quarter 'til the hour, you can ring the call to worship."

The boy cupped the watch in his hand as if it were a piece of fine china. "I'll be careful with it. I swear."

"I know you will." Crockett thumped him on the shoulder. "Go on, now. Take up your position and prepare the rope like I showed you."

The boy traipsed to the back of the sanctuary, leaving Crockett all too conscious of the woman who had moved down the aisle to join him.

"If you win over the rest of the folks the way you have Jackson," she said in a quiet voice that suggested she had no doubt he would, "you'll soon be in need of a larger building."

Crockett darted a glance at her, then directed his attention to the floorboards, an unseen band tightening across his chest. "He's a good kid." A lonely kid who needed a friend. Easy enough to handle. Crockett understood loneliness. Seclusion. He'd lived it. It was no hardship having Jackson around. He kind of reminded Crockett of his kid brother, Neill.

But meeting the spiritual needs of grown men and women was different. More complicated.

Crockett stared at the notes still in his hand. How inadequate they seemed. What did he know about shepherding a flock? *I'm not ready. I—*

"Everyone is looking forward to the services today." Joanna's innocent comment only fueled his doubts. "I told the women when we were cleaning about the sermon you preached last Sunday—how powerful it was, how it moved me."

"You shouldn't have done that," he muttered, his clothes starting to itch against his skin. He paced behind a pair of pews to the window that overlooked the road and scratched a spot on the back of his neck near his collar. "They'll expect too much of me." *You'll expect too much of me.* "I'd practiced that sermon for weeks. This one . . ." He held up the notes and waved them dismissively in the air. "This one I didn't even finish until late last night."

"But I heard you when I came in," she argued, her footsteps echoing on the floor behind him. "Your words touched me the same way as before. Such wisdom and confidence. I know the others will hear it, too."

Confidence? Ha! What confidence? It had deserted him along with his clarity and focus.

She had no business building up people's expectations. He was just an ordinary preacher, self-taught for the most part. Who was he to bring a community together? Who was he to break through to her father when neither she nor her mother had been able to? It was too much to ask. *I should have never agreed to—*

A gentle hand suddenly covered his fisted one where it ground into the windowsill. Crockett closed his eyes as her calm soaked into his spirit.

"Moses doubted he could lead God's people," she said, her voice as gentle as her touch. "Jeremiah thought himself too young and inexperienced to speak for the Lord. It was only when they realized that success was not up to them but up to God that they were able to accomplish what the Lord asked of them."

Slowly, her fingers worked their way into his until his fist loosened and his hand lay relaxed, cradled within hers. "I, more than anyone, know how heavy the burden can become when we feel incapable of coping with the calling set before us. But as my mother used to remind me, I now remind you. Our only job is to be obedient to the call, to scatter the seed. It is God's job to give the increase. Don't try to carry that load. No human can."

Finally he turned. His eyes met hers, and the confidence that had abandoned him in such haste began trickling back.

"Speak the words God has given you, Crockett. Let him worry about the rest."

At that moment, he wanted nothing more than to pull Joanna into his arms and hold her against his chest, to absorb her strength and refuel his depleted stores. But such an act would be neither proper nor prudent, so he settled for squeezing her hand and smiling into her sweet face—a face that hid the heart of a warrior.

"Thank you." Crockett prayed she could read the depth of his gratitude through those paltry words. "God must have known I'd need you to bolster my confidence this morning."

"So it's *your* fault that ornery rooster sounded off an hour early." She startled a laugh out of him with that sassy retort, and all at once, it seemed as if the earth shifted back onto its normal axis.

Crockett straightened away from the window and reluctantly released Joanna's hand. "Seems only fitting that a rooster would help me get my swagger back." He winked, and she cuffed him lightly on the arm, her own eyes dancing.

"Seems to me, you have swagger to spare." Her voice was playfully prim, but the quick glance she shot at him over her shoulder as she moved away left him fighting the urge to engage in some very rooster-like strutting.

The chiming of the church bell saved him from any barnyard theatrics—that and the fact that his little chick had flown the coop to check on Jackson. Crockett tipped his head back and grinned up at the rafters.

"Impeccable timing—as usual, Lord."

His optimism and good humor restored, Crockett sauntered

down the aisle and vaulted back up onto the dais to return his notes to the pulpit before taking up his place at the door to greet his congregation.

Let them come, he thought as the first wagon appeared around the curve in the road. *I'm ready.*

17

Joanna's heart swelled with satisfaction as the service neared its close. Crockett's sermon had been delivered flawlessly, as she'd known it would be, full of the same passion and sincerity that stirred her soul the first time she'd heard him speak. And if the few amens that had echoed in the rafters earlier were any indication, she wasn't the only one who'd been moved.

In truth, the only thing that would have made her happier was if her father were sitting in the pew beside her and Jackson. But she wouldn't get ahead of herself. One step at a time.

"One day is with the Lord as a thousand years, and a thousand years as one day." The familiar verse ran through her mind as Crockett invited the congregation to stand for the final hymn, "Trust and Obey"—a fitting selection, as well as a fitting reminder. Joanna joined her voice with the others as her heart prayed for greater patience and trust in the Lord's timing.

Once the song concluded, Crockett asked the members to retake their seats. "I have a few announcements to make before we dismiss," he said, his smile apologetic. "I promise not to take long."

He waited for the shuffle of bodies settling to quiet before he continued. "I wanted to give special thanks to the ladies who worked so diligently on Friday afternoon scrubbing, sweeping, and shining things up in here." His focus rested briefly on each of the women who'd helped with the cleaning, including Holly Brewster, who was leaning so far forward in her pew to preen that for a moment Joanna thought the girl would rise and take a bow.

When Crockett's eyes finally met Joanna's, the twinkle she loved was in full force, as if he could read her thoughts and was sharing a private laugh with her. Wishful thinking, most likely, but pleasant warmth spread through her nonetheless.

"Now that we have the inside refurbished, I'd like to enlist your aid in fixing up the outside."

One man grumbled something under his breath from a row or so behind Joanna, then another from across the aisle. She had to fight the urge to glare some courtesy into them. This building belonged to all of them. It was only right for everyone to contribute to its upkeep. Especially since Crockett had yet to draw a salary.

"I know everyone is busy," Crockett conceded, moving out from behind the pulpit, "so I thought we would turn our work-day into a celebration with games and activities for the whole family. Horse races and shooting contests for the men, pie-baking contests for the women, and maybe a greased pig for the kids."

An excited buzz now hummed through the chapel.

"Instead of a barn-raising shindig, we'll have a church-painting one. I'll need some help in organizing the activities, so if there is anyone who would like to volunteer to chair a planning committee, please speak with me after we dismiss. We'll take the funds collected from the offering today and next Sunday to purchase paint and supplies. Then, two weeks from Saturday we'll gather for the event. Everyone in the community will be welcome to participate, whether they attend services here or not." Crockett looked directly at her as he imparted this last bit, and her pulse leapt at the implications.

Her father. He couldn't resist a chance to show off his marksmanship. And she doubted he could keep from entering Gamble in the races, either. He'd been itching for a chance to pit his new horse's speed against mounts offering more competition than the Lazy R cow ponies. This event would be the perfect enticement.

"Did you know about this?" she whispered to Jackson when Crockett turned his attention to the rest of the crowd.

The boy bent his head close to hers. "Nah. I knew he wanted to paint, but I never guessed he'd throw a party. You think it'll work?"

"We'll just have to make sure it does. Deal?" She extended her gloved hand to shake on it.

Jackson fit his hand to hers, his jaw set. "Deal."

Her mind suddenly swirling with ideas, Joanna reached for the small tablet she carried with her for taking notes during the sermon and flipped to a clean page. She'd never planned any kind of community event before, but she'd attended them. Surely she could figure out what needed to be done. Crockett would help.

Joanna bit her lip as her pencil hovered above the paper. The thought of having an excuse to spend more time with the parson set her stomach to dancing. So distracted was she by the image of the two of them huddled together on the settee in the parlor, that she failed to hear Crockett's dismissal. When Mrs. Grimley stopped by her pew, it startled Joanna to realize that everyone was up and milling around and probably had been for several minutes.

Clutching her Bible and tablet to her chest, she lurched to her feet. "Oh, Mrs. Grimley! I didn't see you there."

"Well, now that you do, what do you think of the preacher's plan?" The stern-faced woman raised a brow at her, but Joanna had known her too long to be fooled into thinking the dour expression actually indicated what was in her heart.

"I think it's a wonderful idea. In fact, I was thinking of volunteering to help with the planning committee."

Mrs. Grimley tilted her head toward the pulpit. "Better get a move on, then. That Brewster gal's already got a jump on you."

Sure enough, Holly had Crockett blocked in at the front of the church. She and Becky Sue stood side by side, barricading the center aisle while Holly gushed all over the parson.

Crockett smiled and nodded politely, but there was a tension about his eyes that Joanna hadn't seen since the day her father brought him to the ranch with a lariat around his middle. Clearly, the man was crying out for rescue.

"Excuse me, Mrs. Grimley," Joanna said as she started backing toward the outer aisle. "I believe I'm needed at the front."

She had already turned and had nearly reached the end of the pew when Mrs. Grimley's quiet chuckle met her ear. "Yes, dearie. I believe you are."

Strengthened by the thought of having at least one ally in her corner, Joanna skirted a pair of farmers discussing the worth of a particular mule another man had for sale, and made her way along the wall to the dais. There wasn't much room to maneuver, what with Holly's mother and Etta Ward working hard to eavesdrop from their position in front of the first pew, where they pretended to converse. Joanna supposed she could walk over the dais to get to Crockett, but somehow it seemed wrong for her to step up there, despite the fact that she'd crawled across it on her hands and knees not two days ago. So instead, she twisted sideways and inched along the edge of the stage until she stood a few feet behind Crockett.

"I have so many wonderful ideas," Holly was saying, "and I know simply *everyone* around here, so you won't have to worry about a thing with me in charge." Holly laid her hand on Crockett's arm, and Joanna had to fight the sudden urge to slap it away.

"I'm grateful for your assistance, Miss Brewster. I have no doubt that you are the perfect person to head up the planning committee."

The perfect person? The words cut a surprisingly deep gash in Joanna's hide. Of course he'd think she was perfect. Perfect hair, perfect figure, perfect smile, perfect connections. Perfect veneer for that perfectly horrid temperament she hid so well from the male population.

"Becky Sue and I can arrange decorations for the tables, and I'm sure Mother would be happy to oversee the food arrangements. Wouldn't you, Mama." Holly finally tore her gaze away from Crockett to draw her mother into the conversation, but when she saw Joanna, she immediately turned back to the parson.

"Mama's the best cook in the county. And she knows what every woman's specialty is. She'll organize a feast like you've never tasted. And I'm sure her dear friend Mrs. Ward would volunteer to plan the pie-baking contest. Her husband would be the perfect judge. Nelson Ward's sweet tooth is legendary in these parts."

"That sounds splendid. I'm sure they'll do a fine job. Now, if—"

"Oh, but what about the games?" Holly interrupted, determined to monopolize his time. Didn't she care that she was keeping him from speaking to the other members? It was essential for a new minister to get to know the people of his congregation. All he needed was for one or two crotchety souls to get their dander up because he didn't speak to them before they left.

Joanna frowned. Her own hurt feelings no longer seemed so important. The important thing was ensuring Holly didn't sabotage Crockett's chance to make the best possible first impression.

"I'll need your input on the arrangements for the men's sporting events," Holly insisted.

Crockett backed away, and began looking past her to the rear of the building, where people were slipping through the door. "I'll be happy to assist you, Miss Brewster, but now is not the time."

"Of course." Holly must have sensed that she'd pushed him too far, for she immediately changed tactics. "How silly of me. I just got so excited. We can discuss it over dinner. Mother insisted that I invite you to join us after services."

Joanna's heart fell. She'd been hoping Crockett would dine at the Lazy R. Did Holly have to beat her at this, too? Apparently so, judging by the triumphant smile the blond beauty shot her when Crockett wasn't looking.

"That'll be fine," he said, his attention more focused on the door than on the woman before him. But even that was small comfort in light of the knowledge that Holly Brewster would have him all to herself this afternoon. "Now, if you'll excuse me?"

Holly beamed at him, successfully drawing his notice once again. Then, like the Red Sea of old, she and Becky Sue parted to let Crockett pass through on dry land.

He hadn't even realized she'd been standing behind him.

"It's too bad Brother Archer had to dash off before you had a chance to speak with him, Joanna." Holly sashayed back toward the pulpit, waving the edges of her royal blue skirt like a jay showing off its wings. No, not a jay. With that predatory gleam in her eyes, she was definitely a hawk. A hawk marking her territory and fluttering her wings to keep another female from chasing after her mate of choice.

Well, she could flutter and glare all she wanted. Joanna wasn't about to scurry away like a frightened mouse. "That's all right," she said. "I can speak with him at breakfast tomorrow."

For a fleeting moment, Holly's mouth twisted into a grimace. It didn't last long before being smoothed away, but Joanna experienced a little thrill of satisfaction, nonetheless. It felt good to score a point.

"If it has anything to do with the church picnic, you can ask me. Brother Archer put me in charge of the event." Her brows lifted slightly, as if checking off a point in her own score column.

"I see." Joanna hated to ask the girl for any favors, but helping Crockett was worth more than her pride. And so was her father. "I *had* intended to volunteer my services for the painting day. Perhaps I could assist with some of the games or sporting contests?"

"Definitely not the sporting contests," Holly barked, then immediately softened her tone. "Your father is sure to enter those. He always does. How would it look if Silas Robbins's daughter was in charge of laying out the racecourse or placing the targets? If he were to win, some disgruntled contestant might cry foul. I'm sure you would never do anything to grant your father an unfair advantage, but we don't want there to be even a hint of impropriety. Why, it could reflect poorly on Brother Archer, and I know you wouldn't want that."

"Of course not, but—"

"And I've already decided on committee members for the food and baking events."

"What about the greased pig for the kids?" Joanna couldn't imagine the always pristine Holly wanting anything at all to do with that event. "I could—"

"No." Holly shook her head. "I've already decided that Jackson should be in charge of that. You know how the parson dotes on him. I'm sure he'd want the boy to be involved."

Jackson *would* be a good choice, Joanna thought sourly, and naming him to the committee was just the kind of action that could endear Holly to Crockett. Which no doubt was the girl's motivation for suggesting it. But that left Joanna without a way to participate.

"How about the paint?" Becky Sue spoke up for the first time, darting a quick glance at Holly before continuing. "You know, since she and her mother were always painting those pictures, she'd probably know what kind of paint to buy."

"Any ninny would know what kind of paint to buy," Holly huffed.

"But if she were in charge of the paint, she'd have to travel to Deanville to pick it up and would probably be gone most of the day . . ."

"And that would free Brother Archer up to help me with any last-minute details. Excellent idea, Becky Sue."

The brunette grinned like a puppy that had just been rewarded with a scrap of jerky.

"I'd be happy to take charge of the paint." Joanna hurried to claim the responsibility before Holly changed her mind. Any opportunity to help was better than none.

Besides, it'd been ages since her father had let her travel to Deanville. Maybe if she made the trip soon enough, she could pick out some fabric for a new dress and actually have time to make it up before the picnic. Something pretty. Something to catch a certain gentleman's eye before the blond hawk of doom swooped down and sunk her talons into him.

18

Rain pounded Silas's shoulders as he pulled Marauder to a halt under a large oak. The branches above him did blessed little to ease the downpour, but it was more cover than the man in the flats below him had. Out in the open, his new hand's only protection was a borrowed yellow pommel slicker and a hat that had been pulverized too long to adequately hold its shape.

The others had had the good sense to come in an hour ago and were drying out by the stove in the bunkhouse. Silas had hunkered down with them for a while, too—until Frank's belly-aching wore on his nerves—but the house was no better, what with Jo's fretful glances and pestering questions about Crockett Archer's whereabouts. Silas's only chance for peace was to head back out into the storm and find him.

He'd expected to find the preacher man holed up in one of the line shacks or limping back after being thrown from his horse. He hadn't expected to find the man knee-deep in mud trying to wrestle a cow out of a washed-out gulley.

A frown tugged on Silas's mouth as he nudged Marauder

down the hill to lend a hand. What made the man work so hard for one cow? A cow that wasn't even his?

Over the last three weeks, Silas had worked Archer hard— gave him the worst jobs, demanded he stay late, knowing full well the fella needed every spare minute he could wrangle to plan his silly church-painting shindig. He'd seen the dark circles under the parson's eyes, noted the drag in his step, but still he'd pushed—practically dared the sermonizer to quit.

Not only did the preacher man not quit, he worked harder than any of the other hands.

Frank and Carl were lazy cusses who only did what was required of them, but they'd run with Silas in the early days, so turning them out would be like turning out family. Jasper was capable enough to run things on the ranch, should the need ever arise, but he shied from the responsibility of the place. His loyalty was to Silas, not the ranch.

Archer, on the other hand, worked the ranch as if he were personally vested in the outcome. He worked it like an owner. Like Silas himself. No job was beneath him, because all had to be done. He never complained. Always completed his tasks. And if he saw something that needed doing, he did it, whether it was his assignment or not. Which probably explained why he was out in this downpour instead of inside, where anyone with half a brain would be.

Silas reached the gulley and quickly unstrapped the lariat from his pommel. With ease of practice, he lengthened the noose, twirled it a couple times to get a feel for how it would fly in the rain, and let it sail over the cow's head. Archer's hand flew to his sidearm as his face came around. Silas raised a hand in greeting, knowing any words would get lost in the deluge. Archer released his weapon and returned the wave. Silas wrapped the end of the rope around the saddle horn, patted Marauder's neck, and then dismounted and strode to the edge of the wash.

Archer slogged over to meet him, the mud sucking at his boots. "Her forelegs are stuck," he yelled to be heard above the storm. "I was afraid she'd strangle if I roped her neck. I've been trying to dig her out, but the mud is so soft, it slides right back in."

"I'll work the head, you work the legs," Silas shouted. "Maybe we can get her out together."

Archer nodded.

After twenty minutes of pushing and pulling, digging and squirming, and three armloads of twigs, branches, and leaves to add stability to the mud, the bawling cow finally managed to crawl out.

Silas removed the rope from her neck, mounted Marauder, and herded the heifer back to the group of strays that were huddled front-to-end beneath a stand of pines a short distance away. Once he was sure the ornery thing didn't intend to wander toward the gulley again, he turned his horse and headed back to meet up with Archer. Only the man wasn't on his horse. He was sitting on the edge of the wash, hunched over with his head against his knees.

A pang ricocheted off Silas's conscience. The man had given all he had on that final push, practically lifting the stupid beast onto his shoulder as he strained to free her legs. Silas hated to admit it, but without the parson, he probably would've lost that beeve. He never thought the day would come when he'd feel beholden to a preacher man or, worse, actually respect one.

With a grunt, he swung down out of the saddle and carved his way through the rain and mud until his feet stood boot tip to boot tip with his new man. He waited for Archer's head to tip up and then held out his hand. The parson's gaze moved from his hand to his face, and something in Archer's eyes gave Silas the impression that he recognized he was being offered more than just a hand up.

Archer's stare held his without wavering, and when his hand clasped Silas's, the grip was strong and sure. And as he hauled the parson to his feet, a burning need flared to life in Silas's gut—a need to understand what drove this man. What compelled a rancher who co-owned a family spread to work for another man just so he could preach in a small country church in the middle of nowhere?

Joanna paced back to the kitchen window for what must have been the hundredth time in the last twenty minutes. Crockett should have come home with the rest of the hands hours ago, but he hadn't. Was he hurt? Had his horse broken a leg in a mud hole? No one could work in this rain. She couldn't even see past the edge of the porch.

Her daddy had rolled his eyes at her worrying, but he'd eventually gone out to look for Crockett. As always, Silas Robbins knew exactly where each of his men would be working, and he'd promised to drag the parson back within the hour. Only that hour had become two. Now she had two men to fret over.

Joanna's nails dug into her palms as she strained to see through the downpour. It was barely three in the afternoon, but it was dark as night out there. The cascading rain drowned out all other sounds, so she couldn't depend upon hearing the horses when they returned. All she could do was stare into the torrent and hope to spy the shadowy outlines of Crockett and her father.

Bring them home safely, Lord. Please. Bring both of them home.

She'd already made coffee and laid out towels and blankets— had even fetched two sets of dry clothes from her father's room, knowing all of Crockett's spares were back at the parsonage.

She turned away from the window long enough to retrieve a pair of earthenware mugs from the cabinet, then resumed her vigil.

The sheets of rain were so thick she could barely make out the barn, but she probed the darkness anyway, desperate for a sign of . . . There! Movement. Definitely movement. Joanna pressed her palm to the glass and angled her face so she could see farther to the east. Lightning flashed overhead, followed immediately by a loud clap of thunder. But the noise didn't matter, for in those brief seconds of light, the mustard yellow of the men's slickers signaled her like a beacon.

Needing to get closer to them, she bolted out to the porch to watch their progress. Jasper must have been keeping an eye out, as well, for the bunkhouse door slammed open and his stiff-legged, poncho-covered form darted out into the yard and met them at the barn entrance. The men dismounted and handed their reins to Jasper. When they turned, Joanna waved to them in large sweeping motions, hoping they'd see her through the rain. She moved as close to the edge of the covered porch as she dared and cupped her hands around her mouth.

"Come to the house!" she shouted when Crockett started trudging toward the building Jasper had just vacated.

The parson lifted his head and stopped but made no move to change direction.

"Don't make me come out there to get you!"

Crockett would probably accuse her of taking on the bossy big-sister role again, but there was nothing sisterly about the concern she felt for him. And if he turned away from her again, he would see just how bossy she could be. She had no qualms about going after him. Her father's men wouldn't take care of him the way she would, and she aimed to see that he suffered no ill effects from this day's work. The poor man had to be drenched to the skin. He'd easily catch his death if not properly tended.

Thankfully, her father saved her from having to chase the

man down. He came alongside Crockett and said something while jerking his head toward the house. After that, Crockett followed him, and soon the two men joined her on the porch.

Her father hung his hat and slicker on a peg and bent to kiss Joanna's cheek. His whiskery face was cold against hers. Crockett had been out twice as long. He must be nearly frozen.

"You got coffee going, Jo?" Her father asked as he made use of the bootjack.

"Yes, and there's plenty of hot water for washing." She wanted to hug his neck but knew he wouldn't want to get her wet, so instead she took charge of his boots once he had them off and stood them up against the wall.

"Thanks, darlin'." He grinned at her, then turned to Crockett. "Don't dawdle, Archer. You won't be any use to me if you start ailin'."

The kitchen door closed behind her father, and still Crockett made no move. "I shouldn't come in," he finally said. "I'm covered in grime and will drip mud all over your floors."

"I'd rather worry about the floors than about you. Come on, now. You're trembling from the cold, Crockett. Come in and get warm."

He was pale, too, and sluggish in his movements. After watching him struggle with the fasteners on his slicker for a long, agonizing minute, Joanna stepped close and took over the task herself.

Even with his weakened condition, standing close to him tickled her insides. Her heart thumped wildly in her chest, but she kept her head down, hiding his effect on her with a mask of efficiency. Once the metal buttons had been worked free, she stepped back to allow him space to pull the slicker off. His trembling became more violent as he hung up the coat and reached for his hat.

Her father's shirt had been damp, and his trousers had been

soaked from the knees down, but Crockett looked as if he'd just pulled himself out of the river fully clothed. He was sodden, dripping.

Joanna clasped his arm to steady him when he tried to use the bootjack, then quickly arranged his footwear next to her father's before half pushing, half pulling him into the kitchen and steering him toward the stove. One of the mugs was missing from the table, so she knew her father had grabbed some coffee before heading to his room to change.

Crockett just stood where she'd placed him, as if he couldn't figure out what to do next. Gone was his playful, teasing manner. Gone was the twinkle from those deep brown eyes. Truly, he was starting to scare her. She reached for the coffeepot, thinking that getting something hot and bracing inside him would help. But then she heard his teeth chatter, and she immediately changed tactics. She grabbed one of the blankets she'd set out earlier and threw it around his shoulders, like her mother used to do for her after her baths when she'd been little. Then she began rubbing his arms, trying to warm him with the friction. Frowning at his continued shivering, she stepped closer and wrapped her arms more fully around him, rubbing his shoulders and his back. Only he was so broad she couldn't reach all the way around.

His chin bumped the top of her head as she slanted in for a better vantage. She glanced up and froze. His eyes were anything but lifeless now. Intensity glowed from within their depths, the type of intensity that made it impossible to look away. Or breathe.

The type of intensity that whispered possibilities. If she hadn't trapped his arms with the blanket, would he circle them around her and draw her into a real embrace? Would his face bend to hers and sear her lips with a kiss?

Would her father catch them and tear the parson limb from limb?

This last thought brought sanity. Joanna dropped her gaze and stepped back. Eyeing the table, she grabbed the towel sitting so prim and tidy on the corner and shoved it at him.

"For your hair," she mumbled.

He stretched a hand out from under the blanket and took it from her. Unable to resist the temptation of seeing if that intensity still burned in his eyes, she chanced a quick glance at his face. His features had indeed changed, but the heart-stopping half smile he sported, and the resurgence of the twinkle that had earlier been dormant, left her equally giddy.

As she aimed her attention at the coffee once again and turned her back to the soggy parson with the dancing eyes, a secret smile curved her lips.

"Ain't you poured the man his coffee yet, Jo? He's gotta be half froze." Her father's booming voice nearly startled her out of her skin.

"I wanted to dry off first," Crockett quickly interjected, scrubbing the towel against his hair. "At this rate, I'm going to leave a lake-sized puddle in your kitchen." His teeth still chattered slightly as he spoke, but he was starting to sound more like himself—a fact that soothed Joanna considerably.

"Well, since Jo went to the trouble of laying out a second set of clothes, and seeing as how I don't plan to wear both, I suggest you step into the back room and put those on." Her father jabbed a finger toward the shirt, pants, and socks folded tidily on the tabletop.

Crockett stilled. "Thank you, sir. I will."

But he didn't seem to know how to collect the clothes while holding both the blanket and towel. He couldn't exactly tuck them under his arm. They'd be soaked in seconds.

"Here." Joanna grabbed the dry clothes and reached for the coffee she'd just poured him. "I'll show you the way."

She led him to a small guest room at the back of the house

and set his coffee on the edge of the bureau near the door. "Just wrap your wet things up in the blanket when you're through and bring them out to the kitchen. I'll string a clothesline near the stove."

Crockett squeezed through the doorway beside her. Slowly. So slowly that when his eyes met hers and held, she felt as if time had halted altogether. Neither of them spoke, but something was definitely being communicated. Joanna just wished she understood what it was. Her untutored, rapidly pounding heart wanted very much to believe it was two souls recognizing they belonged together, yet her head warned it was probably nothing more than friendship and gratitude.

So when Crockett murmured a quiet "Thank you" and moved into the room, proving her mind wiser than her heart, Joanna hid her disappointment with a gracious smile and a hasty retreat.

She slid into a chair at the table next to her father, drawing in the comfort of his solid, dependable presence. It was too bad she couldn't climb up into his lap like she used to as a child. She eyed his shoulder longingly, took in his pensive demeanor as he stared into his half-empty coffee mug, and finally decided to ignore her head and listen to the urging of her heart. Without saying a word, she scooted her chair closer to his and laid her head on his shoulder.

He didn't turn his head or say a word. The break in the pattern of his breathing was the only indication he was aware of her actions. But then a measure of tension drained from his muscles, and his head tipped toward hers in an armless embrace.

"He's a hard worker, this preacher of yours," her father said after a long minute. He straightened his head and rearranged his fingers around his cup. "If he's not careful, I might actually start to like him."

"Oh no." Joanna sat up, her heart lightening. "Don't do that, Daddy. Just think of your reputation."

"Scamp." Her father chuckled and playfully bumped his shoulder against hers. "It does make me wonder what he's up to, though." His voice turned serious, contemplative. "Why would a man work so hard, going beyond what is asked, when this job is clearly nothing more than a stepping-stone for him."

"Because everything I do reflects upon my Lord."

Joanna and her father swiveled as one toward the sound of Crockett's voice.

He dropped his soggy bundle into the washtub where her father's clothes lay heaped and took a seat at the table across from them. "Scripture instructs God's people to give our best to whatever task we turn our hands to, to conduct ourselves as if we work for the Lord himself, not for man." His focus never wavered from her father.

"I've known plenty of *god-fearing* men who were lazy no-accounts—men who'd rather beat a child than spare him a loaf of bread." Her father spat the accusation at Crockett, but Joanna was the one who flinched. She'd never heard such anger from him, such pain. When had he witnessed such cruelty? Her stomach clinched suddenly. Had *he* been the child?

"And that poisons your view of God, doesn't it." Crockett's words were softly spoken, but the weight behind them was staggering.

Her father gave no response beyond tightening his jaw.

"God desires his people to be abounding in love and good works. To be people of integrity and honor. People who reflect his character. But we are human—sinful people capable of evil deeds."

A snort of disgust erupted from her father, but he quickly pressed his lips together, as if shutting a gate to keep anything else from escaping.

"Sometimes those mistakes have far-reaching effects," Crockett quietly intoned, "ones that can be used by the enemy to drive others away from the God who loves them."

Joanna's pulse stuttered. Would her father actually open himself to what Crockett was saying? Was he softening?

But as she watched, a shutter fell over his face, and he pushed away from the table. "I thought we agreed to no sermonizing, Archer." He turned his back to the table and strode over to the window, staring out at the rain that had finally started to lessen.

"That we did, Silas. That we did. Forgive me." Crockett immediately lightened his tone and leaned back in his chair. "I'm not immune to making mistakes myself, I'm afraid. Just ask my brothers. They'd gladly regale you with tale after tale, I'm sure."

Crockett shot her a wink from across the table, and Joanna found herself smiling despite the forfeiture of the previous topic of conversation. *Give it time*, he seemed to be saying with that wink. *A new seed has been planted. Don't churn up the soil before it can take root.*

For several minutes, no one spoke. The rain spattered against the roof. The parlor clock struck the quarter hour. The stovepipe creaked.

Then her father broke the silence. "You still want to go to town tomorrow if the weather clears, Jo?" He addressed his question to the window glass instead of to her.

"Yes, I would." She shared a look with Crockett before turning to regard the back of her father's head. "Brother Archer gave me the money from the offering to buy the paint for the church, and I'd like to get everything purchased as soon as possible." *Including that dress fabric.*

She'd hoped to get to town before now, but there had been too much work on the ranch for a hand to make a trip solely for workday and picnic supplies.

"I don't think I can spare Jasper," her father said, and Joanna's hopes withered. "But after his hard work today, I'd thought to give Archer some time off. If you can convince him to make the trip, I'd not be opposed to letting him drive you."

Joanna's gaze flew to Crockett's, her breath catching in her throat.

"I'd be honored to escort you, Miss Robbins." He dipped his head in a gentlemanly gesture, but it was the twinkle in his eye that set her heart aquiver.

Had her father really planned to reward Crockett with a day off, or was this simply a ploy to keep the parson and his arguments away for a time?

Did she really care, since it meant she'd be spending an entire day in Crockett's company? The bubbles of delight effervescing in Joanna's middle provided her answer.

19

Crockett arrived at the Lazy R bright and early the following morning, despite his supposed day off. He'd much rather eat Joanna's cooking than his own, and truth be told, he was half afraid Holly Brewster might somehow discern that he'd been granted time off and show up on his doorstep with more ideas and plans for him to consider. The woman's constant need for attention and affirmation drained energy out of him faster than water ran through a sieve.

Unlike Joanna, whose very presence seemed to pour strength into him.

Watching her bustle about the kitchen, making sure the men had plenty to eat and coffee mugs that never ran dry, memories of yesterday flooded his mind. The way she'd fussed over him when his fingers were too numb to unfasten his own slicker. The way she'd warmed him with her hands through the blanket. The way her hair smelled and the softness of it as it brushed his chin. He'd wanted to pillow his head against it. More than that, he'd wanted to throw the blanket aside, take her in his arms, and taste her lips. Not the most parson-like instinct.

He'd never experienced such strong desire before. He enjoyed the company of women, had even flirted a little, but never had he been stirred to any deeper emotion. After fourteen years of being secluded with only brothers for company, he'd found women a delightful experience—their smiles, their softness, their lilting voices. Each encounter had been like a bee flitting to a new blossom—every bloom beautiful and sweet in its own way. But the more time he spent with Joanna, the more addicted he became to her particular nectar. It was as if the rest of the flowers had begun to fade, losing their attraction.

"Honey, Mr. Archer?"

Coffee nearly exploded from Crockett's mouth. Had the woman somehow divined his thoughts?

Joanna arched her brows, a line of puzzlement crinkling her forehead. "For your biscuit." She lifted the small crock in front of her, nothing but innocent inquiry in her eyes.

He managed to choke down his coffee, only too aware of the strange looks he was garnering from the other men around the table. He dipped his chin in a desperate bid to compose himself and found a lone biscuit sitting uneaten on his plate.

"No . . . uh . . . thank you. Butter will suffice." He immediately picked up his knife and set about the task of buttering said biscuit, throwing in a mental lecture on the dangers of undisciplined rumination for good measure.

Thankfully, breakfast soon concluded. Silas and the others scattered to their chores, and Joanna cleared the table. Crockett offered to help her with the dishes, but she shooed him to the parlor, claiming it was his day off and insisting she wasn't going to let him lift a finger until it came time to drive the wagon to Deanville.

Determined not to give his mind a chance to wander into perilous territory again, Crockett picked up one of the three books stacked on a small table between a pair of armchairs. Taking a seat, he opened the book to a random page, only to come face-to-face with the skeletal anatomy of a horse. He twisted the volume to examine its spine. *The Diseases of Livestock and Their Most Efficient Remedies* by a Dr. Lloyd V. Tellor. Well, it could have been worse, he supposed. It could have been a treatise on beekeeping.

Chuckling to himself, Crockett turned to a section that explained how to properly diagnose the source of a horse's lameness.

He'd always enjoyed studying medicine. As youngsters, his brothers came to him with aches and pains as well as their more serious injuries—probably due to the fact that his bedside manner was sunnier than that of Travis, who preferred barking orders. Whatever the reasons, Crockett had embraced his role as family healer and studied every medical text and home-remedy manual he could get his hands on. Admittedly, there hadn't been many, but he made good use of the ones he'd found. Much like he was doing today, although veterinary science didn't hold the same allure for him as the treatment of human ailments. Yet a rancher couldn't expect to be successful without at least a rudimentary knowledge of how to doctor his stock. So with a determined tilt to his head, Crockett turned back to Dr. Tellor's symptomatology.

Unfortunately, he was only a few pages in when a light melody drifted into the parlor, effectively stealing his attention from the discussion of splinting shins and diseased knee joints.

Joanna was singing.

He thought of the first time he'd heard her sing, the morning he'd surprised her with a birthday sermon. At the time, he'd contemplated hiding his presence in order to listen longer to the sweetness of her voice, to the emotion she projected be-hind the words. In the end, however, he'd been unable to resist joining her. Even now, the lure was strong. Setting aside his book, Crockett leaned back in his chair and softly hummed a companion harmony.

His gaze idled about the room, taking in the little feminine touches that warmed the place. The lacy handkerchief beneath the lamp. The bow in the curtain sash. The embroidered sampler perched on the table near his elbow. Were they evidence of the late Mrs. Robbins, or had Joanna contributed to the styling?

He examined the framed sampler more closely. Noah's ark floated atop a wavy blue line of floodwater, beneath which had been stitched the following verse: "*Now faith is the substance of things hoped for, the evidence of things not seen.*" An olive branch and a dove served as a divider between the verse and the next line of text. "*1874—Joanna Robbins—age 10.*"

Crockett grinned, imagining a little red-headed girl bent over her needlework, her tongue caught between her teeth as she concentrated on getting the stitches just right. What pride she must have felt at having her efforts deemed worthy of such a prominent display. Not as prominent as the large oil painting above the mantel, however.

Crockett pushed to his feet and walked to the hearth to get a closer look at the magnificent rendering of a picturesque river vaguely reminiscent of the one that ran behind the chapel. The work was extraordinary, really, the way light glowed throughout. It was as if the sun had purposely broken through the clouds to beam upon the land in honor of the artist's visit.

"One of my mother's finest," Joanna said beside him, and Crockett turned to face her.

"Your *mother* painted this? It's masterful." His eyes veered back to the landscape searching out the signature in the bottom corner. *M. E. Robbins.* "I did wonder how Silas came by such a piece."

Hearing how that sounded, Crockett pivoted, an apology on his lips. "I didn't mean to imply—"

"What? That my father had stolen it?" Joanna's mouth quirked, and her eyes danced with delightful mischief. "Yes, because stage passengers are so apt to cart around bulky framed art when they travel."

Crockett smiled, gracefully accepting her teasing censure.

"No," she said, a wistful expression softening her features. "He didn't steal the painting, just the artist. Or at least her heart." Joanna stroked the edge of the frame with a reverence that came from deep affection. "Of course, she stole his right back."

Silas seemed like such a hard man; Crockett had difficulty picturing him as a lovesick swain.

As if she had guessed his thoughts, Joanna stepped closer and whispered like a conspirator in his ear. "You should see his bedroom."

Crockett arched a brow, which only served to deepen Joanna's smile.

"You won't find one inch of open space on those walls. Other than a few hanging about the house, every canvas Martha Eleanor Robbins ever painted is in his room." A little sigh escaped her. "They used to only hang four at a time. Mama would rotate new ones in every few months and keep the rest in storage. But after she died, Daddy hung every last one of them up. I think it helps him feel closer to her, to be surrounded so completely by her work."

Silas Robbins had more depth to him than he liked to let on. Crockett clutched his hands behind his back and rocked onto the balls of his feet as new thoughts took shape in his mind. A man who loved his wife and daughter with such fervor would love the Lord with similar ferocity. If he ever gave his heart in that direction.

An hour later, Crockett steered the wagon around a particularly ominous-looking mud puddle as he and Joanna slowly made their way to Deanville. The sun had broken through the clouds to warm the air, but the road remained decidedly soggy in places. He'd looked forward to this outing too much to risk being mired to a halt.

He glanced over to the woman at his side, all buttoned up in her Sunday gloves and bonnet. *Entrancing* was the word that came to mind. If it was possible for a face to sparkle, hers did as she drank in the scenery. He imagined her cataloguing the rise and fall of the land, the position of the trees, the way the yellowed grass bent with the breeze. Is this what she painted in the barn loft?

Silas had left strict instructions naming the makeshift studio off limits. Even he never ventured into his daughter's sanctuary. That was where she could express herself through her art without fear of censure, where she could truly be free. And where, Crockett assumed, she felt closest to her mother.

"Do you paint landscapes, as well?" he asked, hoping she'd open the door just a bit and let him peek inside those secret places.

She turned toward him and smiled. "A few, though I find myself more drawn to human subjects." Her eyes traced the lines of his face for a moment, and Crockett found himself wondering what she saw. Did she simply perceive angles and shadows, or did she truly see *him*?

"My mother tutored me in the style of the Hudson River School," she said, aiming her attention back toward the road, "the style she fell in love with after viewing a Thomas Cole exhibit as a young girl. The paintings idealized nature in such a way that it built a craving within her to someday explore the untamed wilderness in the West."

"Is that how she met your father?"

Joanna peeked at him from beneath the brim of her bonnet. The look would have been coquettish had it not been for the fact that her features were alight with little-girl eagerness. He sensed he was about to be regaled with a well-loved Robbins family tale.

"She was considered quite a spinster back in New York," Joanna began. "Not handsome enough to catch a society beau but too educated to attract the average working man. So she dedicated herself to teaching. Art mostly, though she also gave instruction in music. Each year she rewarded her top students with a trip to Frederic Edwin Church's latest exhibit. He was her favorite contemporary artist, you see."

She mentioned the man's name almost reverently, so Crockett quickly nodded in response, as if he comprehended the significance. He hadn't a clue who the fellow was, of course, but Joanna didn't need to know that.

"Church would travel to far-off exotic places and then return to New York in the winter to paint. Mama longed to follow in his footsteps. She knew, as a woman, she'd never cultivate the type of investors who would allow her to travel to South America as he had, but she'd gained a small inheritance from her father's estate and saved every spare penny of her earnings, hoping that one day she'd be able to take her own wilderness excursion."

"What made her finally leave home?"

"A painting, naturally." Joanna winked at him. Crockett was so charmed to be on the receiving end of the gesture for once that he nearly laughed aloud.

"*Twilight in the Wilderness*," Joanna said, as if that explained everything. "Church had captured a rugged landscape of tree-covered mountains embracing a quiet river, all beneath a darkening sky swept with clouds still colored with the lingering pink of a sunset that had just passed. Once she saw that painting, Mama knew she had to go west—had to capture her own piece of the wilderness before civilization swallowed her for the rest of her days.

"So she finished out her school term, packed her sketchbook and supplies, and set out to find her wilderness."

"And found your father instead." Although a young outlaw like Silas Robbins was bound to be wilderness enough for anyone.

"Yep." Another sideways peek from under her bonnet. "He held up her stage."

Crockett did laugh then. It was too perfect.

"She'd been traveling for several months and had made it as far west as Texas when her funds ran out. The stage was to take her to Galveston, where she planned to board a ship for home. When Daddy and the boys held it up, she handed over her few valuables without a quibble. But when one of the men—Frank, I think—took the satchel that held her sketchbook, she fought like a wildcat to get it back.

"Jasper tried to restrain her while Frank dumped the contents of the bag. They all thought she had a hidden stash of jewels or something. Daddy was the one who first took hold of the sketchbook. He opened it and gazed upon her work. He told me later, that was the moment he fell in love with her—said any woman who could see such beauty in an unforgiving land had to have a pure soul. And Mama said that when the outlaw leader returned her sketchbook to her, his blue eyes glowed above his mask with an admiration she'd never seen in any man back east. It was as if he'd seen her heart when he looked at her sketches, and that glimpse made her beautiful in his eyes."

Joanna turned to look at him then, a wistful smile curving her lips. Crockett's gut clenched. He didn't have to see her sketchbook. She was already beautiful in his eyes.

Clearing his throat, Crockett adjusted his grip on the reins and adjusted his thoughts in a less dangerous direction. "So did he abduct her?"

Joanna laughed, a light, airy sound that wrapped itself around his heart. "Of course not. He did follow her, though. And that evening, he risked his life by coming to town to court her. Mama recognized him immediately but was too enamored to turn him away. They took a table in a dark corner of the café and talked for hours. When he learned she was set to leave in the morning, Daddy proposed that night."

"And she agreed?" Crockett couldn't quite keep the incredulity out of his voice.

"Not at first. She was worried about the difference in their ages. She was four years older than him, you see, and she worried that such a young, spirited man would grow weary of her as she aged. But Daddy convinced her that once his loyalty was given, nothing could sway him. So she agreed. But she gave a condition—he had to stop his thievery."

Crockett did some quick figuring. "But you told me he's been a rancher for the last sixteen years, so he must not have stopped robbing stages until after you were born."

"That's correct. Unfortunately. It was the only spot of contention between them in the early years. Daddy had promised to go straight as soon as he had enough money to buy a ranch and provide a home for her. He and his gang had always played it safe by stealing only enough to provide for their immediate needs, so he hadn't stored up much of a cache. They never pulled heists large enough to draw significant attention from the authorities. And they *never* harmed anyone." Joanna gave special emphasis to this last point.

"My mother continued to plead with him to stop, insisting she didn't need a large house or fancy things. He could hire on at a ranch somewhere or take a job at a mill or a mine. But Daddy refused to work for anyone other than himself, so he continued with his gang until he'd saved up the money to buy a ranch of his own."

Her description of her father's exploits sounded eerily familiar. Crockett frowned as he looked ahead to the outskirts of Deanville. Hadn't Marshal Coleson said much the same thing when he'd questioned him about his abduction?

"Oh, you don't need to frown, Crockett." Joanna gave his shoulder a playful nudge, clearly misinterpreting his concern. "Mama and I got him on the straight and narrow soon enough."

"What role did you play?" he asked, not wanting her to guess his thoughts about the marshal.

A light blush pinkened her cheeks. "Well, according to Mama, I captured Daddy's heart the moment I was born. Whenever he was home, he'd tote me around with him—teaching me how to ride, showing me animal tracks, and carving me wooden toys. I adored him, having no inkling of the secret life he lived. All I knew was that he was my father and he loved me.

"Then one day, he and his gang held up a coach heading for Bremond. When he opened the door to demand the passengers' valuables, he found a woman traveling with her daughter. The little girl was about my age, with red hair and freckles. When she saw him, she screamed in terror and nearly tore her mother's skirts in a desperate bid to get away from him. Daddy slammed the door closed and rode away without taking a single penny from anyone that day, or any day after. He told me later that all he could see that day was my face on that little girl. My terror. Of him. And he couldn't bear it."

Crockett absorbed her words. "Your father might be a stubborn man," he said after a moment, "but he loves fiercely and has proven capable of radical change. Your story gives me hope for our other endeavor."

"Do you think so?" Her eager face shone up at him as if he had just given her a handful of gold.

Crockett nodded, and her answering smile was glorious.

As he steered the team toward the general store, Crockett

couldn't help but wonder what stories Joanna would someday tell her own children about how she met their father. Would it be a rousing adventure tale to rival her parents' story, or would it be an ordinary account of a gentle romance that developed over time? Somehow the latter just didn't seem to fit.

Crockett set the brake, climbed down, and turned to assist Joanna. His hands clasped her waist, and an unbidden image of Silas dandling a grandchild on each knee filled his mind—children who were begging to hear the tale of how Grandpa stole their daddy from a train as a birthday present for their mama.

He jerked his hands away from Joanna's waist as if she'd burned him. *Slow down, Crock*, he warned himself. Admitting his attraction to Joanna was one thing. Imagining their future children was quite another.

"Let's . . . uh . . . let's go find that paint." Crockett took Joanna's arm and quickly steered her toward the boardwalk before the quizzical look on her face had time to become an actual question.

Selecting the paint didn't take long, and when Crockett offered to cart the canisters out to the wagon, Joanna urged him to get out and explore the town afterward, thereby granting her some time for personal shopping.

"It's so rare that I get the chance to wander through the store myself," she explained when he offered to wait. "I usually just give Jasper a list and have him pick up the necessary items when he comes into town, but since I'm here, I'd love the chance to linger over the pretty ribbons and sweet-smelling soaps."

Surely *that* would scare him off. What man wanted to be caught up in a cloud of perfumed soaps and toilet water?

"I'll just stroll down to the livery for a bit," Crockett said, his easy agreement rankling a bit, despite the fact that he was doing exactly what she wanted.

Botheration. Why did her feelings always have to be in such a jumble whenever he was around?

"When you're finished," he continued, "we can have lunch."

Joanna forced her mind back to the task at hand. *Fabric.*

"That would be lovely." She smiled and shooed him toward the door. "I'll come find you when I'm finished here."

"I'll keep an eye out for you." He winked and dipped his head to her before taking the last of the paint outside.

She hovered by the window, waiting until he'd situated the paint cans in the wagon bed and started making his way down the street toward the livery. Then she made a beeline for the fabric display along the back wall.

Dean's Store didn't boast a very wide selection, and most of it was simple calico, but Joanna eagerly fingered every bolt of cloth, imagining what each might look like done up into a dress. The golden brown material dotted with tiny maroon roses might work well with her coloring, but it was too subdued, too safe. For once, she wanted to stand out instead of blending into the background. A hard enough task when Holly Brewster was prancing around. It'd be even worse now that the woman had actually set her cap for Crockett. Joanna sighed as she considered the choices before her. All the tans and dark greens weren't going to help much.

Taking the gold calico in hand, she reached for a bolt of deep russet, thinking it might be close enough in color to the rose pattern to make a pairing, but when she tugged it loose, she discovered a length of blushing pink polished muslin hiding underneath. Joanna sucked in a breath, the russet bolt falling from her hand to thud against the table.

She carefully extracted the pink fabric from the bottom of the pile. The sheen of it caught the light, drawing a sigh from her as she stroked her hand along its length. It had probably been left over from last spring; the color was far too pastel to be fashionable this time of year, but Joanna didn't care. In fact, the lighter color suited her purposes precisely. Even better, it would pair well with the chocolate brown underskirt her mother used to wear with her lemon polonaise. The pale yellow hue had always turned Joanna's complexion rather sallow, so she'd never remade the gown, but the underskirt was a different story. It would add an elegant touch to the cheery pink muslin. Not to mention saving her a great deal of time in the sewing.

Joanna gathered the bolt into her arms and turned to walk to the counter, only to find a woman blocking her path. The lady's hair was pulled back into a rather severe knot, her charcoal dress clean but nondescript. Yet it was her assessing stare that stirred Joanna's unease.

"I seen you with him." The accusation lacked heat and was almost conversational in nature, but Joanna still did a quick scan of the store to make sure she had a clear path to the exit should a mad dash become necessary.

"Who?" she asked, drawing the fabric bolt closer to her chest.

"The parson. Archer."

"Yes. He works for my father and was kind enough to drive me to town." Joanna pasted on a grin and retreated a step, thinking to make her escape down another aisle.

"He's a good man." The woman blushed slightly and fidgeted with the cuff of her sleeve as her gaze slid to the floor. "If ya ain't in too big a hurry, I'd be pleased to have the two of ya lunch with me at the boardinghouse. Archer knows where. Just tell 'im Bessie said come."

Joanna halted her retreat, touched by the awkward invitation. This woman was no threat. She was simply uncomfortable around strangers, a trait Joanna understood all too well. What must it have cost her to initiate the conversation? It was obvious she held Crockett in high esteem—which proved her a woman of good sense.

"How kind of you, Bessie. We'd be delighted to join you for lunch. I'm Joanna." She extended her hand.

Bessie nodded but barely touched her fingers to Joanna's. As if she'd suffered through all the socializing she could manage,

Bessie spun around without further word and left Joanna alone with her new dress fabric.

"Care for some more greens, Parson?" Bessie held the bowl out to him, and Crockett accepted it, still in a daze over actually having the woman seated at the table with him. The presence of another female apparently made socializing a less threatening endeavor.

"Thank you, ma'am." He placed a small spoonful on his plate and passed the bowl on to Joanna. "I'll take another one of your yeast rolls, too, if you don't mind."

The woman couldn't have blushed more prettily if he had named her the fairest maiden in the land.

"I remembered how much you liked 'em," she said as she reached for the towel-covered basket.

"They are truly a piece of heaven, Miss Bessie." As he reached under the towel to claim a roll, Crockett winked playfully at her. But he regretted his unthinking gesture when his hostess nearly toppled out of her chair from the shock of it.

Thankfully, Joanna quickly attempted to smooth things over. "You must meet a lot of interesting people, running a boardinghouse. Do you enjoy it?"

"Not particularly."

Crockett ducked his chin and fixed his attention firmly upon his plate, intending to shrink from the conversation so that Miss Bessie could regain her footing.

"It must be hard work," Joanna said, impressing him with how quickly and sensitively she adjusted to Bessie's blunt response.

"It ain't the work. I been tendin' house since I was old enough to wrangle a broom." She shifted in her chair, and her thumb tapped restlessly against the tabletop. "It's havin' strangers showin' up uninvited and expecting me to wait on 'em hand and foot that puts me in a foul mood."

Crockett stuffed the roll in his mouth before she could catch him grinning. He could certainly attest to the truth of that statement.

"If it were up to me, I wouldn't take on boarders at all." Bessie leaned back in her chair and crossed her arms with a huff.

"Why do you do it, then?" Joanna's voice held no censure, only curiosity. It didn't surprise him at all when Miss Bessie's arms relaxed. Joanna's calm manner invited openness. Though not the social whirlwind that Holly Brewster was, she had a way of reaching out to those society missed, those most in need of compassion and a listening ear.

"It was my brother Albert's idea. All because of that wife of his. She wanted him to sell this place, our parents' house, so that she and Bertie could move into a nicer one themselves up in Caldwell. He assured me I'd be given a room of my own—a room off the kitchen, I'm sure, so I can do all the cookin' and cleanin'. Heaven knows that's what I end up doin' every time I go for a visit. At least here I can keep my independence and don't have to put up with Francine's hostility."

Crockett gave up all pretense of eating and sat back to watch the two women, who seemed to have forgotten his presence.

"So how'd you convince your brother to let you keep the house?" Joanna asked.

"I think he knew what a disaster it would be to have me and Francine under the same roof, so he offered to let me keep the house if I would agree to take in boarders so that he could lower my monthly stipend. It was his way of tryin' to make both of us happy, I guess."

"Do you attract enough business to make up the difference?"

"Some months are better than others, but I got extra put aside, so—"

A loud knock cut off the rest of her explanation.

"Miss Bessie?" A gruff masculine voice echoed through the hall as the front door eased open. "I hear ya got comp'ny."

A start of recognition hit Crockett, followed by a jolt of apprehension.

"Yep," Bessie hollered, making no move to greet the visitor in person. "We're in the kitchen, Marshal. You're just in time for a piece of pie."

Crockett looked to Joanna, his pulse growing a bit erratic. Had Marshal Coleson come to question him again? Or had he somehow figured out Joanna's connection to a particular ex-outlaw? Was she in danger?

His eyes raked her face. She surely wasn't acting like she considered herself to be in danger. After Bessie got up to retrieve another plate and cut the pie, Joanna simply wrapped her hands around the delicate china cup in front of her and lifted it to her lips for a sip, the picture of serenity. What she didn't do, however, was meet his gaze, so he had no way of judging whether her composure was legitimate or strictly an act.

He had the oddest urge to grab her and dash out the back door.

Then common sense prevailed. He was pretty sure Silas couldn't be arrested for crimes committed sixteen years ago, especially without witnesses or evidence. But when Brett Coleson strode into the kitchen, pulled his hat from his head, and sat in the vacant chair next to him, it dawned on Crockett that there *was* a crime for which Silas Robbins could be prosecuted—kidnapping.

Joanna eyed the marshal over the rim of her cup. She had too much of her father in her to be comfortable around lawmen, but too much of her mother in her to let it show. Slowly, she lowered her cup to the table and smiled a welcome to the newcomer.

He nodded politely and took his seat. "Brett Coleson, ma'am," he said by way of introduction.

She dipped her chin in return. "Joanna Robbins." Thankfully, the marshal seemed more interested in Crockett than her. After he mumbled something perfunctory, he turned his full attention to the man beside him.

"I didn't expect to see you 'round these parts again, Parson. You decide to take my advice and press charges against those yahoos that abducted you from the train?"

Her pulse bucked like an unbroken horse. Joanna darted a glance at Crockett, knowing even as she did so that the gesture would be telling if the marshal happened to notice. Crockett apparently had better self-control, for he kept his attention on the lawman. She told herself she was glad even while she ached for his reassurance.

"No, sir," Crockett replied, and the denial soothed Joanna's ragged nerves. "That misunderstanding was worked out weeks ago. I'm here because I took a job in the area. Came into town for supplies. That's all."

"Mmm." The sound carried a decidedly unconvinced tone.

Thankfully, Bessie arrived with dessert before the marshal could say much else. "Stop interrogatin' my guests, Brett, and eat your pie."

She plopped an extra-large piece in front of the marshal and slid a slightly smaller one toward Crockett.

"Yes, ma'am, Miss Bessie," the marshal replied, all smiles as he picked up the fork she'd laid out on the plate. "A man'd be foolish to waste his mouth on talkin' when he could be chewin' on your de-lectable blackberry pie."

The woman grunted, unimpressed by the compliment. She

retreated to the counter to collect the remaining plates, served Joanna, and returned to her place at the table.

A blessed few minutes of silence fell upon the room as everyone ate their dessert. Joanna loved blackberry pie, but she didn't taste a single bite. How could she when the marshal kept looking at her? She felt as if the truths of her heritage and her father's past sins were rising to the surface under the lawman's perceptive study. If she didn't leave soon, she feared they'd emerge through her skin like a tattoo inked upon her forehead.

"I don't think I can eat another bite," Joanna declared, pushing her half-finished pie away from her. "Bessie, thank you for a wonderful meal. I truly enjoyed getting to know you, but I'm afraid I have several tasks needing my attention back at the ranch. We really must be on our way." She stood.

Crockett took his cue. He pushed to his feet and collected his hat. "Miss Bessie, it was a pleasure to see you again. I'll be sure to stop by and say hello the next time I'm in town."

"You do that." She grabbed the roll basket from the table, tied off the towel around the bread inside, and handed the soft bundle to him. "Take these with you. You might get hungry later."

"Thanks." He accepted the gift, then ushered Joanna toward the front door.

"Hey, Parson?" The deep drawl brought them to a halt.

Crockett pulled slightly away from her in order to pivot and regard the marshal.

"I got a sermon idea for you," the lawman said, his dark eyes narrowed slightly. "Proverbs 21:3. 'To do justice and judgment is more acceptable to the Lord than sacrifice.' Might want to spend some time ponderin' that one."

"I've been leaning more toward Proverbs 16:6," Crockett answered without so much as a blink. "'By mercy and truth iniquity is purged: and by the fear of the Lord men depart from evil.'"

Before the lawman could respond, Crockett took Joanna's arm and led her out of the house.

As he steered her to where their wagon waited, Joanna hid her concern over the odd conversation. She doubted either man had actually been talking about sermons. They'd definitely been tugging on opposite ends of a doctrinal rope, though, and she could only deduce that her father was somehow at the center of it.

21

Sitting in the kitchen where the light was best, Joanna bent over the pile of shiny pink fabric in her lap and pushed her needle in and out of the seemingly never-ending yardage that made up the hem of her new polonaise. She'd taken her mother's yellow brocade apart and used it as a pattern for cutting the pink muslin after she and Crockett returned from Deanville on Wednesday. Then yesterday, she'd kept the treadle machine whirring for hours, only stopping when she had to cook meals for the men. Fortunately, none of them complained about the simple fare of vegetable soup at midday or the only slightly more substantial beef hash at supper.

Now, if she could just finish the handwork in the hems and trim today, she might actually have her dress ready for the picnic tomorrow. Little frissons of excitement skittered along her nerve endings, energizing tired fingers and blurry eyes. The men wouldn't be back for another couple hours. Surely that would be enough time to complete the hem on her overskirt and add the lace she'd taken from her mother's gown to the sleeves and neckline. Joanna straightened her posture for a moment in order to stretch the kinks from her back, then exhaled a determined breath and set back to work.

When her thread grew too short to easily work with, she knotted it and snipped off the end. As she unwound another length for her needle, the sound of a wagon approaching the house brought her head up.

Had one of the men returned early? What if it was Crockett? She didn't want him to see her working on the dress. It would spoil the surprise. Joanna grabbed up the folds of pink fabric, lace pieces, and thread spools and scurried to her room. She tossed her armload onto the bed, closed the door, and hustled back to the kitchen. Stabbing her needle into the pincushion, she looked for a place to hide her sewing basket. Not finding anything overly promising, she shoved her scissors, pins, and needle case inside the basket and covered the top with a bread cloth. She hurriedly brushed the tabletop with her hand to clear it of cut threads and fabric scraps, gave it a couple blows to send the residual fuzz flying, and spun toward the door. As she stepped onto the back porch, she gave a quick pat to her hair to make sure her mad rush hadn't loosened her pins. She might not want Crockett seeing her dress just yet, but neither did she want him seeing her looking like a frazzled ragamuffin.

That thought set her to dusting off her apron, so it took a moment to realize the wagon had pulled to a stop. She didn't recognize the team, or the man climbing down from the bench seat—although there was something about his long-legged stride that seemed oddly familiar. When he drew a little closer and smiled a greeting, recognition toyed with her, itching the back of her brain like a mosquito bite she couldn't quite reach.

"Afternoon, ma'am." He touched his hat brim. "This the Lazy R?"

"It is." Joanna sensed no threat from the man, who couldn't have been much older than she, judging by his unlined face and slender build. But her father didn't like her welcoming strangers when he and the hands were away, so she kept her place on the porch and addressed him with caution. "Do you have business here?"

She didn't see how he could. Daddy never invited anyone to the ranch without telling her, and Jasper always took care of town business himself, never arranging for deliveries. Joanna eyed the two trunks in the wagon bed with suspicion.

"Yes, ma'am. I do."

Her eyebrows lifted.

The young cowboy shifted his weight and snatched the hat from his head, as if his hands needed something to fiddle with. "My brother wrote that he hired on here. Crockett Archer? I brought his things."

She could have smacked herself in the forehead for not recognizing the resemblance earlier. Of course he was an Archer. The strong chin. The rich sepia hair. The smile that made his eyes light. He was much too young to be Travis, though, the brother Crockett spoke of most often. She searched her memory for the correct name and mentally pounced as she recalled a discussion about a youthful song leader whose voice was the last to change in the Archer household.

"You must be Neill." She poured all the warmth and welcome she'd been holding back into her burgeoning smile as she stepped off the porch. "I'm Joanna Robbins. Crockett works for my father."

Relief flashed across the young man's features. He swiped his palm down his trouser leg, then held his hand out to her, his grin as wide as the sky. "Pleased to meet you, Miss Robbins. Crock mentioned you were the one who arranged his new preaching position. That sure was kind of you."

Joanna clasped his hand briefly and then stepped back. "He's doing *me* the favor, I assure you. Our little church has been in need of a preacher for far too long, and your brother fills the pulpit better than I dared hope. He's done more to bring this community together in three short weeks than most could accomplish in a year. Why, he's even organized a church picnic to reach out to those who don't regularly attend services. You should stay. See your brother in action."

Neill peered at her oddly, tilting his head just a bit, as if to look behind her words for some deeper meaning. Only then did she realize how she'd been gushing about Crockett's accomplishments.

"But then you've seen him in action all your life, haven't you." She gave a little laugh to cover her embarrassment. "Why don't you come inside? I'll fix you a glass of spring water and treat you to some leftover fried pies."

"I don't want to put you to any trouble, miss." Yet his eyes had gone quite wide when she'd mentioned pies.

"They're apple . . ." she teased.

"Well, if you're sure it wouldn't be no hardship." A huge grin stretched across his face, and for a moment his eyes danced just like Crockett's.

Joanna found herself caught up in his enthusiasm as she led him into the kitchen. The sewing basket on the table brought her up short, though. Ruthlessly, she swept away the reminder of her unfinished dreams, whisking the basket from the table and dropping it on the floor against the wall.

There'd still be time to work by lantern light after supper. And if not, well, there'd be other picnics, or so she told herself as she set about fetching the water pitcher.

She had just reached into the pie safe to retrieve the leftover pastries when someone knocked on the back door. Before she could take a step in that direction, though, the door cracked open and a golden-brown head popped into view.

Joanna grinned. "Come on in, Jackson. There's plenty for

you, too." How the boy knew she'd been about to serve pies, she couldn't fathom, but then Jackson had always had a sixth sense about food. He had a talent for showing up whenever it was being handed out.

"Saw this stranger roll up your drive and thought I better check it out." Jackson straightened to his full height and eyed Neill. "He ain't botherin' ya, is he, Jo?"

She shook her head and moved the platter of pies to the table. "No. He's a guest, Jackson. Neill Archer. Crockett's brother."

The boy snagged one of the small pies as his attention veered sharply back to Neill. "No foolin'? The one who plays the fiddle? Crock told me all about how you used to scare away the barn cats with your screechin' before you got the hang of it."

"Jackson!" If she'd had a spoon in her hand, she would have smacked his knuckles. As it was, she gave serious consideration to yanking the half-eaten pie from his mouth and banishing him from her kitchen. But that would only compound the already poor impression they were making.

Neill, however, didn't seem to take offense at Jackson's insulting comment. He chuckled good-naturedly as he rubbed the back of his neck. "Yeah, Travis wouldn't let me play in the house, so the barn critters made up my audience. Fortunately, our mule and milk cow couldn't escape as readily as the cats."

Jackson laughed and reached for a second pastry, leaving three on the plate for Neill. "Crock says you're pretty good now, though. Played at a barn raising last year, right?"

"Yep. The cats even stuck around." Neill turned to smile up at Joanna when she reached past him to set his water glass on the table. "Thanks."

She dipped her chin in acknowledgment and moved back to the stove.

"Hey," Jackson said, speaking around cheeks bulging with apple filling. Joanna groaned inwardly and tried to pretend she hadn't noticed. "If I can scrounge up a fiddle, would you play at our shindig tomorrow?"

"You wouldn't have to scrounge one up." Neill winked at him. "I brought my own. Never have liked the quiet around a campfire at night. But we best not get ahead of ourselves. I'm supposed to meet up with a friend of mine later, and I haven't even talked to Crockett yet."

Jackson's eyes lit with purpose, and she knew the boy would do everything in his power to see that Neill stayed for the picnic. "I'll go fetch Crockett." He pushed back from the table so fast the chair nearly toppled. "Where's he workin', Jo?"

She bit back a grin. "In the north pasture. Why don't you take Sunflower?" she said, knowing how rarely he got to ride. "You can meet up with the men in the large clearing. They're cutting out the calves for weaning and driving them into the lower pasture."

"You mean it, Jo? You'll let me ride Sunflower?"

"Sure."

Jackson was sprinting for the door the moment the word left her lips.

"Just make sure you saddle her properly," she called after him. "I don't want to have to cart a pile of busted bones back to your pa's house. Understand?"

"Yeah, yeah." He waved her off and disappeared through the door. His excited footsteps clomped across the porch floorboards in a rapid staccato, then quieted into softer thuds as they hit the packed dirt of the yard.

Joanna shook her head and smiled. It took so little to make the boy happy. She poured a second glass of water from the pitcher and joined Neill at the table.

"I could have sworn the two of you were brother and sister," he said, his eyes alight with humor. "My brothers used to scold me the same way. Still do from time to time."

"You aren't the first Archer to accuse me of taking on the bossy big-sister role with Jackson." Joanna chuckled. "I guess that's what happens when a gal doesn't have real siblings to practice on. She badgers poor, unsuspecting neighbor boys."

Neill grinned. "He doesn't seem to mind."

Joanna ducked her chin, his tone bringing a touch of heat to her cheeks. Eager to turn the conversation in a different direction, she questioned him about growing up as the youngest of the Archer pack. He regaled her with stories that made her laugh and some that made her ache for the four boys who'd been forced to raise themselves in the harsh Texas landscape.

"And then there was the time I thought it'd be a hoot to trick my brothers into eating fish bait. I threw a handful of worms into Jim's squirrel stew when he wasn't looking. But somehow Crock must've figured out what I done because when it was suppertime, he insisted I eat my bowl first. They all just sat there watching me until I finished every last bite. Then they gave their portions to the dog and took out some cold ham and stale biscuits instead. Watching them eat, I was sure I could feel those worms wigglin' around in my stomach. It was enough to send me runnin' for the outhouse. I tell you, I never pulled a prank involving food again."

Joanna grinned at the tale, easily imagining him as a boy running wild and getting into one scrape after another. Before she could ask if he ever discovered how Crockett had outsmarted him, the sound of pounding hooves announced his brother's arrival.

Neill's eyes brightened with an excitement that could only be inspired by deep affection. He launched to his feet and was halfway to the door when he recalled his manners. "Excuse me, miss."

But she was every bit as excited as he, and dashed past him when he paused, beating him to the door. "Come along, Neill," she said with a smile. "Your brother's here."

She opened the door and hurried out, but she halted at the edge of the porch and allowed Neill to race down the steps alone. Wrapping her arm around the support post, Joanna watched the brothers embrace. And when Crockett lifted his gaze to include her in his pleasure, a longing struck her with such force she had to tighten her grip on the post to keep herself from trotting down to join the reunion.

Neill said something that set Crockett to laughing and drew his full attention. When his gaze left hers, Joanna turned and slipped back into the house. Back to the dress that would hopefully help Crockett see her not only as a partner but as a woman.

22

Crockett thumped Neill on the back as he embraced his brother a second time. It was just so good to see him, to reconnect with family. As eager as he'd been to leave the ranch and start his ministry, he'd never imagined how hard the separation would be. Forged through trials and survival, trust and mutual respect, the Archer bond went deeper than blood. Having Neill here was like regaining a piece of himself that had been missing.

He glanced up to the house, intending to invite Joanna to join them. Yet when he scanned the porch, all he saw was the back of her skirt disappearing through the kitchen door.

"It must be rough working for such a pretty lady." Neill lifted his chin toward the house.

His brother's knowing stare penetrated a place Crockett wasn't ready to expose. Doing his best to cover his reaction with his usual wink and grin, he draped his arm over Neill's shoulders and steered him toward the wagon. "You haven't met her father yet."

"I still can't believe you took a job with the man who

kidnapped you." Neill shrugged out from under his brother's arm when an approaching rider broke through the trees on the far side of the house. "Of course, now that I've seen his daughter, it makes a little more sense."

Avoiding his brother's scrutiny, Crockett turned to greet Jackson as the boy barreled into the yard on Sunflower. Crockett strode back to his own mount and gathered the reins he'd left draped over the saddle horn.

"Do you mind seeing to my horse as well as Sunflower?" He drew his bay's head up from where he'd been nibbling on a tuft of grass near the corral fence and paced over to where Jackson had dismounted. "Silas gave me the rest of the afternoon off, and I'd like to show Neill my place at the church."

"Sure." Jackson collected the reins from him and patted Sunflower's neck. "I'll rub 'em down and turn them out in the corral for a bit." He started to lead the animals to the barn, one on either side of him, but stopped to glance back. "You want me to come by when I'm done? We still gotta set up the shootin' targets and lay out the racecourse tonight, 'cause the gals expect us to help with the decoratin' in the morning. Although why they think they gotta hang ribbons and bows on everything is beyond me."

Crockett shared a grin with Neill over the boy's youthful disdain. The Archer brothers couldn't claim much understanding of females, either, but they had enough sense to know when to go along with one.

"Well, we want the ladies to enjoy the picnic, too," Crockett said in conciliation. "And if dressing the old churchyard up adds to their pleasure, I suppose we can handle decoration duty."

"I guess." Jackson sighed heavily and plodded on into the barn.

"He reminds me a lot of you," Crockett said, returning to Neill's side at the back of the wagon. "He runs wild with little or no supervision, but he's got a heart that's eager to please and a work ethic that, when properly motivated, can be quite impressive."

"Are you calling me impressive?" Mischief danced in Neill's eyes.

Crockett shoved his brother's shoulder, pushing Neill around to the left side of the wagon as he strode to the right. "Only when properly motivated."

Stifling a chuckle, Crockett jammed a booted foot onto a wheel spoke and hefted himself onto the wagon seat. Neill flashed a grin, joined him on the seat, and took up the reins.

On the way to the parsonage, Crockett answered questions about the church, the upcoming picnic, and the work at the Lazy R. But once there, he turned the conversation toward home.

"I'm surprised Travis let you come all this way alone." Crockett hopped over the seat into the wagon bed and scooted the two trunks toward the open end.

"He didn't." Neill hauled one of the trunks up onto his shoulder. "Josiah's waiting for me in Deanville. The lady running the boardinghouse hired him to fix her roof when she heard he had carpentry experience. Said her attic was gettin' musty and insisted he find the leak causing it."

"Ah. Miss Bessie." Crockett jumped to the ground and took up the second trunk. "If he finds that leak, she'll treat him like a king." He led the way to his living quarters, wincing slightly at the weight of his trunk. Travis must've packed his books in this one. No wonder Neill had claimed the larger one.

As they entered, Neill cleared his throat. "Frankly, I was surprised she asked Josiah to stick around. She hardly said two words to him and never sat at the table with us during meals. Made me kinda mad, to tell the truth."

Crockett lowered his trunk to the floor at the foot of his bed and motioned for Neill to place his against the wall. "I'm certain it has nothing to do with the color of Josiah's skin. Miss Bessie's just a little afraid of strangers, men especially. When I stayed with her, she locked herself in her room instead of eating with me. Yet the other day, when I took Joanna to town, the woman insisted we come for lunch and actually stayed in the room. I'm pretty sure having another woman as a buffer precipitated the change."

Neill planted himself in the one chair the room boasted while Crockett opened the first trunk. His gun belt and revolvers lay on top next to his rifle wrapped in flannel. He reached for the rifle, pulling away the protective cloth.

"I've missed having my own guns," he said as he stroked the familiar barrel and tucked the stock into his shoulder, the oiled walnut sliding into place as if it had never left. "Silas lent me a sidearm for working on the ranch, but it's just not the same as having a weapon that's more companion than tool."

Neill nodded. "Yeah. Travis packed the guns. Meredith packed the books."

A fond smile curved Crockett's lips at his sister-in-law's name. He set the rifle on the cot and reached for his copy of D. L. Moody's *The Gospel Awakening*, the volume she'd given him for Christmas last year. "How is Meredith?"

"I've never seen her happier. Or fatter."

Crockett cuffed his brother on the side of his head. "She's pregnant, you dolt, not fat."

"Ow." Neill rubbed the spot where Crockett had smacked him, but his eyes glowed with humor. "Travis is the one you should be worried about, not Meri. After losin' Ma the way we did, he ain't too keen on letting Meredith go through childbirth."

"As if he has any say in the matter at this point."

Neill smirked. "You know Travis."

Yes, he did. His brother had always been one for controlling things. Meredith had helped him mellow over the last few years, but Crockett could imagine those old habits creeping back now that he had a baby on the way.

"Travis asked Josiah's ma to move out to the ranch for the last weeks of Meri's lying-in."

"Weeks?" Crockett sputtered. "I can't picture Myra agreeing to that. Not with the school to run and her own brood to see to."

"No, but she did promise to make regular visits." Neill stretched his long legs into the middle of the room. "That combined with me swearing to fetch her at Meri's first twinge seems to have satisfied him for now."

"And Jim?" Crockett set aside all pretense of unpacking. He craved news from home more than anything stowed in his trunks. Leaning his shoulder blades against the wall, he gave Neill his full attention.

"He's fine. Finally got around to trimming back those oaks around the old homestead last week. I think he and Cassie are planning another trip down to Palestine to visit her folks soon."

Crockett winced in sympathy. "Poor Jim." The man's mother-in-law was a harridan of the first order, but Jim put up with her in the same stoic manner he handled everything else in life, and somehow they made it work. Cassie's happiness obviously meant more to him than his own.

That's what love did to people. It prompted sacrifice. Crockett suppressed a sympathetic chuckle. And helped you endure disagreeable in-laws.

Like stubborn-minded ex-outlaw kidnappers?

"Yoo-hoo," a sing-song voice called from outside. "Are you in there, Brother Archer?"

Still a bit rattled from the picture of his future being tied to Silas Robbins—he could almost feel the lasso tightening around his middle as it had when the man had stolen him from the train—it took Crockett a minute to gather his wits and respond.

When he did, he pushed away from the wall and lurched

for the door. About the same time, Holly Brewster's delicate little fist rapped against the wood and sent the unlatched door swinging gently in on its hinges.

"Oh, there you are," Holly said, an almost too perfect smile shaping her lips. "I saw the wagon outside and hoped that meant you were here. I was just delivering the last of the decorations for tomorrow. They're all in the back of the chapel, as you suggested." Her lashes lowered at a languid pace before lifting to reveal a heated stare that sent a shiver of warning down his spine. She took a step closer, and he could have sworn her eyes pleaded with him to invite her in. But that couldn't be right. Surely she knew how improper it would be for her to enter his private quarters.

Taking no chances, Crockett took her arm and steered her out to the yard. The heat in her eyes turned a bit more snappish until she caught sight of Neill coming up behind them.

Her eyes widened, and she latched onto his arm. "Who's your friend, Crockett?"

His name slipped off her tongue as if she'd used it a hundred times. Familiar. Possessive. Far too presumptive.

"My youngest brother, Neill," Crockett ground out, using the introduction as an excuse to extricate himself from Holly's hold. "Neill, may I present Miss Holly Brewster."

"Miss Brewster." Neill touched his hat brim and bent his head. "What's a pretty lady like you doin' hangin' around with this ornery old cuss?" He jerked his chin toward Crockett.

Holly's tinkling laugh filled the air. "He's not *that* old."

"Positively ancient." Neill rolled his eyes in exaggeration. "And don't let those smooth sermons fool you. He can be as ornery as a coyote when he's riled."

Crockett tightened his jaw, restraining the wolfish urge to smack the teasing grin right off his brother's face. He was only twenty-eight, for crying out loud, not exactly in his dotage. And he was the sweetest tempered of all the Archers. Everyone said so.

Yet as he listened to Holly giggle and flirt with his brother, the gulf between their ages seemed to widen. He hadn't felt this old with Joanna. Of course, Joanna had left him and Neill to reunite on their own. Even so, there was a depth to Joanna that lent her a mature air, despite the seven years difference in their ages. Until this moment, in fact, he'd never even thought to calculate it.

"Miss Brewster is the picnic committee chair," Crockett interjected, dispelling the lingering laughter with his impassive tone. "She's been a great help in planning the events and organizing the food and decorations."

Holly preened under the praise, like a cat being stroked in its favorite spot.

"Impressive," Neill said. "It's too bad I won't be able to see the results of such fine handiwork."

"You're not staying?" She pouted prettily. "Crockett, you must insist he stay. With all the young ladies sure to be in attendance, we need all the handsome young men we can get."

Crockett didn't care a hill of beans about the ratio of men to women at the picnic, but he *had* hoped to visit with Neill longer. "Are you sure you can't delay your departure for a day? It would give us more chance to talk."

Neill regarded his brother with serious eyes. "I told Josiah our visit might last overnight, if you had a place for me. I could swing another day, if you don't mind the imposition."

"Of course he won't mind," Holly enthused. "Will you, Crockett?"

"Not one bit." Although he did mind Miss Brewster speaking for him when he was perfectly capable of forming his own sentences. But she was probably just excited about the picnic and got a little carried away.

"I'll have to leave around midday, though." Neill favored Holly with an apologetic look before turning back to Crockett.

"You know how Travis worries. And with Meredith expecting, it's even worse. I best not leave him alone too long. Josiah and I need to get on the road to Caldwell before dark. That way we can catch the early train back to Palestine."

"Well . . ." A cracking adolescent voice echoed behind them. "As long as you're here, you might as well help us set up the shooting targets."

The three turned to find Jackson manhandling a set of large wooden discs with white Xs painted in the middle. Crockett reached out to grab one as it slid from the boy's grasp.

Then, unable to resist the boyish urge, he flung the oversized disc directly at his brother's gut. Neill reacted in time to catch it but not before an *oomph* of air forced its way from his lungs.

Satisfied that his place in the Archer ranks was once again secure, Crockett grinned and slapped Neill on the back. "Looks like we're putting you to work, little brother."

"Well, let's get going, then . . . old man." Without batting an eye, Neill slapped the flat side of the disc against Crockett's rump and raced past.

Jackson guffawed.

Holly gasped.

Crockett grinned and gave chase.

23

"Come on, Jo." Silas rapped his knuckles twice against his daughter's door. "You're the one who wanted me to go to this shindig. At this rate, it's gonna be half over afore we get there."

Dressed in overalls and an old flannel work shirt for painting duty, Silas stalked down the hall to the kitchen and snatched up the knapsack that held the clean trousers and fancy shirt Jo had pressed for him that morning. He swung the strap over his shoulder just as a door creaked open down the hall.

"It's about ti—"

The vision walking toward him stole his speech as well as every thought in his head save one—his little girl had grown into a full-blown woman right under his nose.

Ah, Martha. Can you see her, darlin'? You'd be so proud.

The fancy pink dress Jo wore swished when she walked. A matching blush stained her cheeks, and she refused to lift her gaze from the floor as she entered the kitchen.

Silas swallowed the lump that had swollen in his throat. "Jo." His quiet rasp of her name rumbled almost too low to be heard.

Nevertheless, she lifted her face, her teeth catching the edge of her bottom lip. "You're the spittin' image of your mama in that dress. She looked just like you do on the day I met her. All frilly and lacy and more beautiful than a woman had a right to look." He stepped closer and ran a light finger down the edge of her sleeve. "It's a good thing I'm takin' my rifle for the sport shooting later. I'll need it to run off all the young men."

"Don't be silly, Daddy. You know Jackson's the only young man to ever pay me any attention, and he's too young. Save your bullets for your targets." Jo tapped the bib on his overalls and moved past him to drape a piece of cheesecloth over the large bowl of potato salad sitting on the table.

Silas frowned. It was true that no young man had ever paid court to her. 'Course she'd never hinted at harboring feelings for any of them, neither. So who was the dress for? Because one thing was for certain—she hadn't gotten this gussied up just for a picnic. They had picnics every Fourth of July, and never once had she donned such a fancy getup. Was she trying to attract a beau? His fingers curled into a fist around the strap of his knapsack.

He had known the day would come when some fella would strike her fancy. He just hadn't expected it to be *now*. Watching her graceful movements as she packed plates and flatware into a crate, a sense of inevitability prompted a bittersweet ache in his chest. He wanted her to be happy, to find a love like he had found with her mother. But there was no way he was gonna stand by and let some sweet-talkin' cowhand make off with his Jo before the fella proved his worth to Silas's satisfaction.

So who was he?

The only new man around these parts was . . .

The parson? Absolutely not!

If Jasper and the boys hadn't already ridden down to the churchyard with Gamble in tow, Silas would have leapt on the beast's back and raced in the opposite direction.

How could his daughter . . . *his* daughter . . . fancy a preacher man? He never should have brought Crockett Archer to his ranch. He shoulda left him on that train where he belonged. He should fire him tomorrow. Send him packing.

"Everything's ready, Daddy." Jo turned that sweet smile of hers on him, and Silas bit back a groan. "Would you carry this crate out to the wagon? I'll get the potato salad."

Not daring to open his mouth for fear of what might come out, Silas gave a brisk nod and snatched up the crate of dishes. His jerky motion rattled the crockery, and he had to remind himself to be gentle—with more than just the dishes.

Once outside, he inhaled a calming breath, settled the crate in the wagon bed alongside the two small kegs of cider he'd loaded earlier, and tossed his knapsack on top of the pile. Jo met him near the front of the wagon, hope shining in her eyes. A hope that made him want to snarl like a trapped cougar.

Careful not to let her see his inner turmoil, he took the salad from her, tucked it into the crook of one arm, and gave her a hand up with the other. After she gained her seat and arranged her skirts, he returned the bowl and scrambled up beside her.

They didn't speak much during the short drive, but when they pulled up to the churchyard and that scoundrel of a parson moved to greet them, the pleasure on Jo's face spoke loud enough to ring his ears.

"Miss Robbins." Crockett Archer couldn't take his eyes off her. The bounder. He practically ran up to the wagon, so eager was he to get his hands on Jo and assist her to the ground. His grip on her waist didn't linger long enough to be improper, but his fingers took their sweet time disengaging. "You look lovely, Joanna," the man said so low Silas doubted anyone but he and Jo heard it.

Silas stared a hole in the parson's head until the fella finally remembered someone besides Jo existed. Tempted to upend Jo's potato salad on the man's head when he finally looked back to the wagon, Silas restrained the impulse and contented himself with a glare that would melt iron.

Archer blinked, then smiled up at him as if he hadn't just been scorched. "Silas! So glad you could come. I understand you're the man to beat when it comes to target shooting."

"You needin' some lessons, Preacher?" He was more than willing to do some teaching. Especially if Archer was the target.

"No, sir." The parson's smile widened, but determination glittered in his eyes. "I'm needing some competition."

"Ha!" Silas surprised himself with the shout of laughter. "If you think you can beat me, preacher man, you best save some room after lunch for the humble pie you'll be eating."

"You're probably right, but it will be interesting to see, won't it?" Challenge radiated from Archer as he reached up to the wagon seat and took hold of the potato salad.

Silas tried to glare him down, but the man didn't even flinch. He simply turned and offered Jo his arm before leading her over to the food tables.

Dratted sermonizer.

The crazy thing was, if Archer were just a cowhand, Silas would probably favor a match between him and Jo. The man worked hard, lived up to his word, and refused to be intimidated, even by Silas. He was the kind of man who would be a good provider, a good protector, and if he truly loved his girl, a good husband.

But how could he trust his daughter's future happiness to a preacher? To the type of man who knew how to trick the world into believing his holy façade while wielding a cruel rod of tyranny behind closed doors? His gut told him Archer was different, that he would never strike down a woman or a child, but the vision of little Andy Murdoch, broken and battered, flashed an unforgettable warning in his mind.

His gut had been wrong before.

It seemed the entire community had turned out for the church painting and picnic. Joanna was amazed at how quickly the men had the exterior white-washed. Jackson and some of the older boys even scrambled up the hackberry trees and onto the roof in order to paint the steeple.

She had brought an apron and planned to carry water around to the workers, but Holly commandeered the bucket and ladle from her before she could move past the food tables, insisting that she and Becky Sue had been assigned that task. Holly even went so far as to suggest that Joanna should round up the younger children for a game of hide-and-seek or other entertainment.

"Their mothers so rarely get a chance to sit and visit without having to worry about the little ones getting into mischief," Holly had said. "Just think what a boon it would be to have you tend them for an hour or so."

Then she and Becky Sue had sauntered over to the men. Holly inserted herself between Crockett and his brother Neill, sidling close as Crockett gratefully accepted the refreshment she offered. She turned to Neill next, and the man must have made some teasing comment, for she threw her head back and tittered a laugh that grated worse than fingernails on a schoolroom blackboard.

Holly loitered and lingered while Becky Sue dashed from one thirsty man to the next, and when she finally moved on, she made a point to arch a superior brow in Joanna's direction before approaching the next gentleman.

The vile woman. She'd done everything in her power to keep Joanna away from Crockett while insinuating herself into the very position Joanna coveted. And all Crockett did was smile at her. Stupid man.

Yet despite her raging jealousy, Joanna had recognized the

truth in Holly's earlier statement. The young mothers really could be blessed by having someone else tend their children for a while. Deciding it would be better to focus her energies in a positive direction instead of sitting around brooding over missed opportunities, Joanna spent an hour organizing footraces, a pinecone toss, and a game of leapfrog for the boys and hopscotch for the girls.

When the church bell finally rang, the signal for everyone to gather in the yard for lunch, the children whooped and scampered back to their mothers. Joanna lagged behind, savoring the quiet of the uninhabited field, and steeling herself for more of Holly's machinations.

She arrived in time to hear Crockett's prayer of thanksgiving for the food and for all the neighbors who had worked so hard that morning. She halted on the fringe of the crowd to bow her head, but not before catching a glimpse of her father across the way, head uncovered, eyes respectfully closed. Her heart swelled in her chest.

I have so much to be thankful for, Lord. Forgive me for forgetting that there are more important things at work here than my own desires.

The men had all washed up and changed into their picnic attire behind the church's shuttered windows. The painting done, now their only concern lay in piling their plates as high as possible with the feast Mrs. Brewster had organized.

Crockett stood in the center of it all, smiling and chatting. Bowing to the ladies. Clasping men on the arm. Ruffling a boy's hair as he dodged between the adult legs to get closer to the food. His face gradually turned in her direction, and she lifted a hand to wave, her lips curving upward in anticipation. But Mrs. Grimley snagged his attention by pushing a plate into his hands and steering him over to the food.

The woman could be a force of nature when set to a task,

so Joanna knew Crockett had no choice but to follow. Yet that knowledge did little to keep the disappointment at bay.

Focus on what's important, Joanna.

Squaring her shoulders, she sought out her father and his men. They'd spread out the blankets she'd packed under one of the hackberry trees near the back of the chapel. Thinking to make sure they had everything they needed before claiming a plate for herself, she skirted the edge of the crowd, pressing as close to the building as she dared without brushing up against the wet paint.

She had just come even with one of the shuttered windows, when Becky Sue's distinctive nasal voice echoed from within the church.

"The parson *kissed* you? However did you manage that?"

Shock stopped Joanna midstep.

"I just created the opportunity for him to do exactly what he's been wanting to do for the last several days."

Holly Brewster? Crockett kissed Holly Brewster? No. It had to be some kind of mistake. He wouldn't. Would he? Joanna's palms pressed against her stomach as she fought to find a breath.

"We've grown quite close, Crockett and I."

The sound of his given name on Holly's lips bruised Joanna's sore heart.

"We spent long hours talking in the evenings on my mama's porch, and not always about picnic business—if you know what I mean."

"But how did you get him to kiss you?" Becky Sue pressed. "Here. At the picnic."

Holly's voice grew quiet and conspiratorial. Joanna had to strain to hear. "While the men changed out of their work clothes, I snuck around to the back of the church and waited for him to show up. I figured he would drop his painting clothes off in his living quarters before rejoining the group over by the food.

He's the tidy sort, you know." She imparted this last bit as if she were a relative or sweetheart, someone intimately acquainted with the nuances of his preferences and personality. It made Joanna want to scream. Or sob. Or yank Holly's shiny blond hair out by the fistful.

"Well, just as I suspected," Holly continued, "he came around the corner and disappeared into his room. I ran up to the door and met him as he came out. Finding me there, he wrapped his arms around me, and his lips caressed my forehead. He couldn't risk anything more since someone could have come by, but it was enough to assure me that his feelings are indeed engaged."

"His feelings are indeed engaged." The words echoed in Joanna's mind like a death knoll.

Biting back a wounded cry, Joanna spun around and sprinted back the way she had come. She couldn't let her father see the tears streaking her cheeks. She couldn't let anyone see. Plunging back into the field where she'd romped so cheerfully with the children, she headed for the one place she could hide.

The river.

24

Mrs. Grimley bulldogged her way through the crowd, dragging Crockett in her wake. The woman could have given Moses instructions on sea parting. She refused to rest until she had him firmly planted at the head of the line. Not used to being mothered, Crockett shrugged apologetically at the men whose places were being usurped, but none of them seemed to mind. They just grinned and slapped his back as he passed.

Once the lady had shoved a plate at him and ordered him to heap it full, she apparently considered her duty accomplished, for she left his side in order to shoo away a pair of boys who were trying to stuff extra cookies into their trouser pockets down at the dessert table. Crockett recognized the scamps from the group that had been playing with Joanna earlier.

She'd been so good with the kids. Laughter and squeals had carried to the work crew from the field, bringing smiles to many of the fathers' faces. He'd smiled, too, though not because of the children. Because of Joanna.

His eyes had followed her all morning. He'd been aware of her when she assisted at the food tables, and again when she helped unload an elderly couple's wagon and set up their rockers beneath the shade of a large oak. He'd noticed, too, when she lingered to visit with them so they wouldn't feel excluded from the activities. More than once, his arm had gone slack, leaving paint to drip unused from his brush before he roused himself and got back to work. He couldn't seem to stop himself from searching her out. Even when he'd opened his eyes after offering the blessing, a flash of pink in his periphery told him she was near.

Crockett glanced back to the place where he'd last seen her, hoping to meet her eye or share a smile. This was *their* day, their success. Something inside him stretched toward her, needing to connect, to share the moment in whatever way possible.

But she wasn't there.

He craned his neck to see over the heads of the people milling about the yard. There. Was that her by the chapel? Where was she . . . ?

A red-haired pixie in a fancy pink dress bolted down the side of the church and disappeared around the corner, swiping a hand across her cheek as she ran—the way a woman would swipe at a tear.

If someone had hurt her . . .

Crockett's gut hardened to stone.

He turned to the man behind him in line and forced his lips to curve enough to pass for a smile. "Go ahead of me, brother. I just realized there's something I need to attend to." He set the plate Mrs. Grimley had given him well out of the way of the lunch traffic, and squeezed between the men huddled around him and the food.

"Can't it wait, preacher?" one of the men he was pushing past asked. "You're gonna miss the best pickin's."

"I won't be long," Crockett said. "Besides, the way the women around here cook, they're all good pickin's."

"You ain't tried my Maybelle's corn pone, then. Stuff's drier than a dust storm in August."

That set the men to cackling, and Crockett used the distraction to make his escape. He stretched his stride as long as the crowded yard would allow, but the minute he reached the far side of the chapel, he broke into a loping run.

He crossed the field in the direction he'd assumed she'd gone but had to halt when he couldn't find her. He scanned east, then west, his heart thudding against the wall of his chest. Where was she?

Fighting the urge to cup his hands around his mouth and shout her name, Crockett bit the edge of his tongue and scoured the landscape again. As his head turned south, a red cardinal shot into the air above the water oaks that lined the river and chirped an alarm.

Joanna.

Crockett made for the trees.

He found her beneath the branches of a pecan, her back to him. Her left arm was braced against its trunk, her head hanging low, her shoulders heaving with quiet sobs. The sight broke his heart.

He stepped forward, every instinct screaming at him to take her into his arms and soothe away the hurt, but she must have heard his approach, for she gave a little squeal of distress and dodged behind the tree.

"Jo, wait. It's me." He hurried after her, reaching out to capture her hand and draw her to him, but she recoiled. She scooted farther around the tree, forcing more distance between them and keeping her face averted.

"Go away, Crockett." Her voice hitched as she struggled to subdue her tears. "You should be at the picnic. You'll be missed."

He dug a handkerchief from his pocket and handed it over

her shoulder, careful not to crowd her. "You're more important to me than the picnic."

She clasped the white cotton but offered no thanks. "I know we've been friends," she said between sniffs and a delicate blow, "but you shouldn't say things like that to me. Not when you're courting someone else."

"Courting?" The idea jarred him so thoroughly that his response shot from his mouth like a bullet from a gun, throwing him back a step. "What are you talking about? I'm not courting anyone."

At least not yet. And certainly not someone other than the woman standing before him.

"Maybe not officially," Joanna allowed, "but from what I heard, the young lady in question seems to believe that a certain understanding has been established."

"What young lady? I swear to you, Joanna, any *understanding* this person believes she has is a *mis*understanding. I've made no promises. I've not even hinted at promises."

She spun around to face him then, her eyes the dark blue-gray of a stormy sky, her chin jutting, her reddened nose sniffing in disdain instead of distress. "A kiss is more than a hinted promise, Crockett Archer. At least for an honorable man. But maybe you're not as honorable as I thought."

"Now, hold on a minute." Crockett raised a hand to ward off her accusations, his clenched jaw clipping the ends off his words. "Before you go impugning my honor, let me make it perfectly clear that I have kissed no one."

"So you deny being with Holly outside your personal quarters less than an hour ago?"

Crockett's brow furrowed. What did that have to do with anything? "No . . ."

"I heard her describe the encounter to Becky Sue in vivid detail." Joanna advanced on him, hands fisted at her sides. "The way you wrapped your arms around her and pressed your lips to her forehead."

"Heaven help me!" Crockett's arms sliced upward through the air like twin sabers, then slapped down against his thighs. "If she considered that a kiss, the woman is deranged."

"Deranged? Just because you're too ill-mannered to consider such a gesture a kiss doesn't make her deranged. How dare you toy with a woman's affections in that manner? You . . . you . . . toad!" She flung his soggy, crushed handkerchief directly into his face along with her ridiculously innocuous insult.

Suddenly Crockett wanted to laugh. Either that or show the little firebrand exactly how he defined a kiss. But he dared not let his mouth so much as twitch for fear she'd assume he was belittling her pain. For he saw now that that was exactly what it was. Her pain. Not Holly's. Hers.

And though he hated himself for finding joy in her distress, that pain gave him hope. Hope that her feelings might run deeper than friendship.

Stepping over the handkerchief that had bounced off his nose and fallen to the ground, Crockett gently clasped her upper arms. He'd not let her back away from him this time.

She trembled at his touch, and a tiny gasp echoed in the air between them.

"Joanna," he said as he stroked the bottom of her shoulder with his thumb. "The contact I made with Holly was nothing personal. I ran into her—almost sent her tumbling to the ground, in fact. That's why I put my arms around her. To keep her upright. Nothing more."

The skin between her brows scrunched, and her eyes searched his. "But—"

"Shh. Let me finish, sweetheart." Her damp lashes blinked in surprise at the endearment, bringing a smile to his face. "When we collided, my chin banged against Holly's forehead. That's it. I separated myself from her as quickly as I could, made my apologies, and hurried back to the gathering. There was no rendezvous. No embrace. And definitely no kiss."

"So Holly was wrong about your feelings being engaged?" She tilted her head farther back to examine his reaction to her question. Of course, that only strengthened his reaction to *her*. Joanna's face was at the perfect angle for a kiss. Her lips parted ever so slightly as she awaited his answer.

Oh! His answer.

"I have no feelings for Miss Brewster beyond gratitude for her help with the picnic." That and a bit of suspicion of her motives. Holly had a way of twisting the truth to suit her purposes, and he was leery of what exactly those purposes might be since they seemed to involve him. He needed to keep her at a distance from now on.

"You don't intend to court her, then?" Joanna's soft mouth curved ever so slightly, and his stomach clenched in response. Heaven help him, but he wanted to kiss her.

"No." The hoarse reply came out so low, he added a slight shake of his head for clarification.

"I'm glad," she whispered. At least he thought she whispered. It might just have been the increased thudding of his heart against his rib cage that kept him from hearing.

"If I were going to instigate a courtship with a kiss," he murmured, "it wouldn't be a quick peck on the forehead." He tightened his grip on her shoulders as he spoke.

"It wouldn't?" She swayed toward him slightly.

Crockett shook his head, his eyes never leaving her upturned face.

"What would it be?" Her breathy question dissolved the last of his reserve.

"This." Crockett drew her toward him and lowered his head. He stopped a fraction of an inch from her mouth. Gave her a final chance to change her mind and pull away. When she made no move beyond shifting her focus from his eyes to his lips, he closed the last of the distance.

His mouth covered hers. Instinctively, he tugged her closer. She came to him—her hands on his waist, the feathery touch speeding his already charging pulse.

Releasing her shoulders, he slid his palms around to her back. She felt so good in his arms, so right. He wanted to hold her there forever, to kiss her until they both forgot everything else.

He deepened the kiss.

She startled at the change, then softened against him. But her momentary shock was enough to bring him back to his senses.

Swallowing a groan of reluctance, Crockett lifted his head. Joanna rose up on her tiptoes as if to follow, but his greater height kept her from her goal.

His hands shook slightly as he released her. Merciful heavens. He'd never experienced anything so intense. So exhilarating. And terrifying. It was as if some element of his very being had been altered.

Had she felt it, too?

Joanna's eyes flickered open, and a pretty pink blush washed over the pale freckles bridging her cheeks. Her eyes, now more blue than gray, gazed at him with a wonderfully bemused expression—one that filled his heart with tenderness.

And protectiveness.

"Joanna."

She blinked, her eyes slow to focus. "Mmm?"

"You need to get back to the picnic, sweetheart. Before someone notices that both of us are missing."

"Oh . . . yes . . ." She stepped back and darted a glance behind her. "But you better stay here for a while. Daddy is probably looking for me by now, and we wouldn't want him to get the wrong idea."

Crockett imagined Silas would get precisely the *right* idea, but it wouldn't do to have the man jumping to unsavory conclusions before Crockett had a chance to declare himself. And to do that, he and Joanna needed time to explore this new direction their relationship had taken. Not to mention the time still needed to break through Silas's distrust of preachers. As long as her father held on to his prejudice, Joanna would be caught in the middle. Having to choose would tear her heart out, and Crockett refused to put her through that. No, he'd have to win Silas's favor first. Only then could he ask Joanna to be his wife.

25

Somehow Joanna navigated the busy churchyard and ended up at her blanket with actual food on her plate. Her father brushed the crumbs from his lap and stood to assist her, taking her plate and then her hand as she lowered herself to the ground.

He started to hand the plate down to her but stopped halfway, his brow furrowing. "Playin' with them kids sure stirred up an odd appetite in you, girl."

Joanna accepted the plate from him, puzzling over his comment. Until she got a fresh look at what sat upon her dish—three carrot sticks, a spoonful of pickled beets, a slice of chocolate cake, and two helpings of Maybelle Parker's atrocious corn pone. She had to press her lips together with extreme force to keep a burst of laughter from exploding into the air. She had no recollection whatsoever of serving herself such a strange assortment. Beets? Really? She hated beets.

"Things were rather picked over by the time I went through the line." Not that she remembered, but it was bound to be true since nearly everyone had already eaten. Although why she'd taken beets, she couldn't possibly imagine.

Her daddy raised an eyebrow at her, so she stabbed one of the magenta circles with her fork and popped it into her mouth. The briny taste assaulted her tongue as she chewed, puckering her face against her will. She managed to swallow, though, and considered that a great triumph until her father hunkered down beside her and felt her head with the back of his hand.

"You feelin' all right, Jo? You look a little flushed."

Which, of course, only made her flush more. Especially when his mouth curved down in a frown, and his eyes narrowed as if he could see the truth of what had happened to her written across her features.

"I'm fine, Daddy." Except that she wasn't. She was better than fine. *Much* better. So much better, in fact, that even a plate of pickled beets couldn't sour her mood.

Her father let out a noncommittal grunt as he settled back on the blanket beside her, but Joanna ignored the sound along with the scowl that accompanied it and stuck a carrot stick in her mouth to keep from smiling too big.

Crockett had kissed her. Well and truly kissed her. On purpose. Joanna fought down a giggle as she pictured the awkward tangle that must have resulted from Holly's manufactured collision—the one Crockett had scrambled to escape. He hadn't scrambled to escape *her* down by the river. No. He'd taken his time. And what a lovely time it had been.

She could still picture the intent look on his face as he bent his head and waited for her silent permission. His eyes had roamed her face as if he yearned for her, his mouth curving just enough to let her know she pleased him. *She* pleased him. Her—the shy little wallflower with the ungovernable hair and freckled skin; the woman no one ever looked at twice; the daughter of the man who'd kidnapped him. She pleased him.

And heavenly stars, how he pleased her.

Unable to resist the lure, Joanna turned her head to scan the crowd for a glimpse of him. Just a peek, she promised herself. It wouldn't be wise to let her father catch her mooning over the preacher. But when she finally caught sight of him horsing around with Jackson and Neill over by the greased pig enclosure, his smile was so bright, she couldn't help staring. He was so handsome. And kind. And fun-loving. And . . . courting her!

Crockett must have sensed her attention, for he lifted his face. His gaze found hers, and a subtle change crept into his expression. His grin never dimmed, but somehow it deepened, became personal, private, between the two of them. She couldn't have looked away had a herd of longhorns stampeded through the churchyard.

Then he winked and turned back to his brother, freeing her to look elsewhere. But what else could possibly capture her interest after that? Joanna dropped her attention to her lap and held the moment close to her breast, as if it were a kitten begging to be stroked and snuggled for a little longer before squirming away.

"I would've thought a smart gal like you would have better taste."

Joanna jerked her head up at her father's grumbled comment, her stomach clutching. He was staring at her just like he used to when she was a girl and he caught her doing something she oughtn't have.

He'd never been one to throw out verbal accusations. He didn't have to. All he had to do was stare at her until she recognized the error of her ways and confessed everything. Even now she could feel the truth about Crockett's kiss creeping up her throat and knocking on the back of her teeth.

But then her daddy let out a ragged sigh and nodded his chin toward her plate while he pushed up to his feet. "Even I know to avoid Miz Maybelle's corn pone, Jo."

Air whooshed from her lungs, turning unspoken admissions into harmless giggles. "Somebody's got to eat them, Daddy," she said, lifting one to her mouth. "It would be an embarrassment for her to take a full platter back home."

"You got a bigger heart than I do." He grunted and adjusted his suspenders, his attention briefly captured by something behind her and at an angle very much in line with where she'd last seen Crockett. Then he shook his head and gathered up his rifle from where it leaned against the hackberry's trunk. "I'm gonna go check on Gamble, make sure he's ready for the race."

"All right." Joanna smiled up at him, guilt pricking at her conscience for the relief she felt at his departure. "I'll pack up our things."

He waved a hand to let her know he'd heard, then ambled off toward the rope corral that had been strung in the trees behind the church for the horses. He muttered something under his breath as he strode past her, something that sounded an awful lot like *Archer* and *shooting*.

Not a good combination.

Abandoning the beets, carrots, and pone, Joanna went straight for the cake. Somehow a suspicious father armed with a gun seemed less threatening when chocolate was melting on her tongue.

Crockett made a point to keep his distance from Joanna during the afternoon activities. At least in body. In mind, well, that was a different matter. She constantly crept into his thoughts, despite his best efforts to concentrate on the discussions and people around him. Thankfully, once the games started, everyone's attention turned to the children and their bumbling efforts to tackle the greased pig, leaving laughter to outrank conversation.

After little Joey Anderson successfully captured the pig, Neill took out his fiddle and played a set of sprightly songs that had the crowd toe tappin' and hand clappin' in rhythm. Some of the kids even swung partners around in an impromptu dance full of elbows and knees that kept getting tangled together.

One fellow pulled a mouth harp from his pocket and took up a position next to Neill, and another grabbed a pair of spoons and added some percussion to the ensemble. The audience began throwing in whoops for musical emphasis and urged the musicians to a faster tempo by quickening the pace of their clapping.

Neill's bow flew over the strings, his fingers moving to capture all the notes. Then all at once, the crescendo climaxed, and he stabbed his bow into the air with a final flourish. The crowd roared its approval. Neill bowed.

The kid had gotten better since the last time Crockett had heard him play.

Smiling to himself, Crockett hung back, allowing Neill to accept the appreciation that was his due without big brother hovering. Once the back slaps and handshakes concluded, however, and the crowd dispersed to witness the pie-baking contest, he made his way to his brother's side.

"You sure you can't stay longer?" Crockett asked, even though he knew the answer.

Neill placed his fiddle in the carrying case that lay open atop one of the emptied food tables and carefully fastened the lid. "Yep, but I imagine I'll be back before long."

"Oh?" Crockett raised a brow. "Why's that?"

Neill slanted a sly look at his brother. "Well, with as hard as that blonde is working to draw your attention away from your boss's redheaded daughter, I figure one of the two will end up leg-shacklin' you before too long, which means I'll be returnin' for a wedding." He paused to tuck his fiddle case under his arm, then leaned close. "My money's on the redhead, by the way."

Mine too, Crockett thought, yet he hid his opinion behind a scowl of displeasure. "Mind your own business, pup," he growled.

Neill laughed and clapped a hand on Crockett's shoulder. "Now, where's the fun in that?"

Incorrigible kid. Crockett cuffed him on the arm. "Yeah, well, someday some woman will run *you* around in circles, and we'll see who's laughing then."

The two of them walked to the wagon that waited across the churchyard, close to the road. Neill set his fiddle in the back and turned to Crockett. "It was good to see you, Crock."

"You too. Thanks for making the trip out here."

Neill shrugged off his gratitude. "You know me. Always ready to use any excuse to escape the ranch for a few days."

Crockett yanked him into an embrace. "Give everyone my love." He pounded Neill on the back a time or two, then stepped back.

"Will do." Neill climbed up onto the bench, gathered up the reins, and released the brake. "Take care, brother."

Crockett nodded and watched the wagon roll away.

A gunshot cracked through the air. Crockett's pulse skittered. He whipped his head around, instinctively searching out Joanna for the brief seconds it took his mind to recall the reason for the sound. The horse race. Crockett chuckled at himself and hurried to the edge of the designated course. He arrived just in time to see a blur of horses approaching the first turn. He glanced across the way and found Joanna with the Lazy R hands. She was bouncing up and down and shouting encouragement to her father. Her delight ignited his own.

Someone nudged his side as the horses thundered past. He scooted aside to allow whomever it was to pass, but the person pressed closer to him instead and even slipped a hand into the crook of his elbow.

"I'd say our picnic is a rousing success," a warm feminine voice purred.

Crockett fought down the urge to yank his arm from Holly Brewster's grasp. The woman had a tendency for boldness and far too creative a manner of reading meaning into situations where there was none, but she was still a lady and deserved his kindness. Digging deep, he found a polite grin for her.

"You organized a fine event, Miss Brewster."

Was her thumb stroking the inside of his arm?

"After all the hours we put in together during the planning, Crockett, I think you know me well enough to call me Holly." She smiled so sweetly at him it was hard to believe she was purposely being forward, yet the way she leaned into him made him blasted uncomfortable.

He patted her hand and gently disengaged it from his arm, subtly removing her hold on him without drawing any attention from the spectators crowded around them. "We wouldn't want anyone to get the wrong idea, Miss Brewster," he said, emphasizing the more formal name. "That's how rumors get started."

She pouted prettily, then glanced sideways at him. "If you think that's best." Her gaze drifted slowly downward from his face to his chest, dipped nearly to his waist, then gradually lifted again. "I'll be careful to address you as Brother Archer when we're around others."

But not when we're alone. He wasn't so naïve as to miss the message hanging unspoken between them.

And in that instant, he knew the time for polite consideration had passed. Like Joseph in the clutches of Potiphar's wife, it was time to flee.

He muttered a brief "Pardon me" and without further explanation darted through the dispersing crowd, spotted Jackson giving a smaller boy a leg up into the hackberry tree that stood closest to the front of the church, and broke into a jog.

"What's going on over here?" he asked, hoping the flimsy excuse of checking up on the boys would be viewed as reason enough for him to have scurried across the yard like a lizard who'd just had his rock overturned.

The younger boy paid Crockett no mind, immediately scrambling up to a higher branch. He planted his feet, grabbed the trunk for balance, and pushed to his feet. "They're coming up to the halfway marker!" he shouted. "Three of 'em are bunched together at the front. The rest are falling behind."

Excitement buzzed through the crowd as anticipation built to see who the leaders would be.

"I bet Robbins wins again," one nearby man commented. "That new chestnut of his looked to be even faster than his gray."

Another turned to Crockett. "You work out at the Lazy R, don't ya, preacher? Ever seen that horse run?"

The magnificent image of Joanna bursting out of the barn on Gamble's back came immediately to mind. "Yep. He's got the speed for sure, but I'm not sure how he'll hold up under Silas's weight. Some of the other riders are much smaller. It might give them an advantage."

"Not against Silas," the first man said. "He races all out—like a bandit tryin' to outrun the law."

The men chuckled over the comparison. Crockett choked.

"You all right, Crock?" Jackson pounded his back until Crockett held up a hand to assure him he was fine.

"They're comin' round the bend!" came the announcement from the treetop.

Crockett welcomed the distraction. The top three horses pounded toward the churchyard, the largest starting to pull away.

"Yeehaw. Get 'em, Silas!"

Crockett grinned, recognizing Carl's voice. Jasper and Frank were walking toward the finish line with Joanna in tow, her eyes alight. She glanced across the yard, her gaze finding his as if she'd known precisely where he was all the time. A smile of pure joy beamed from her face, leaving Crockett helpless to do anything but smile in return.

At the last minute, she turned back to the race and applauded as her father plunged to victory two lengths ahead of the next horse. A loud cheer rose from the crowd. Silas's arm shot into the air in triumph. Crockett added a hurrah to the chorus, then waited for the rush of congratulations to fade before joining the Lazy R crew gathered around their leader.

"Great race, Silas," Crockett said, taking hold of Gamble's bridle. "I'd be happy to cool him down for you while you celebrate."

"Oh, I ain't celebratin' too much just yet, Parson." Silas swung down from the saddle and handed Crockett the reins but didn't release his own grip. "Not 'til I beat you in the shooting contest." His eyes held something more than friendly challenge, and when Crockett tugged on the reins, Silas held on. A look passed between them—a look that Crockett suspected had little to do with horses or shooting.

The line between respecting Silas as an employer and the father of the woman he wished to court, and proving himself a man equally worthy of respect was growing thinner and more precarious by the minute.

Crockett made no move to tug the reins away, but neither did he release his own grip. "You don't expect me to go easy on you, just because you're my boss, do you?" He injected humor into his voice, though he was only half teasing.

"You do and I'll fire you on the spot," Silas growled. "I ain't no charity case, boy. And I ain't afraid of your best. Shoot to win, and I'll still beat ya."

"We'll see." Crockett winked at a wide-eyed Joanna, who stood beside her father. Jasper and the other hands looked at him as if he'd lost his mind.

Silas's face took on a red hue, but he kept his temper in check. He tossed the reins at Crockett and smacked his shoulder with the force of a small grizzly. "You're a big talker, Parson. But we already knew that, didn't we? Time to see if your actions match up."

26

Nearly everyone at the picnic turned out for the shooting contest. Man after man stepped up to the line and took aim at the first target. The crowd held its collective breath until a shot was fired and then either cheered or groaned, depending on whether or not the bullet hit the scoring disc.

Nelson Ward, still waddling a bit after tasting all the pies during the baking contest, served as referee. Following each shot, he emerged from one of the safety positions, circled the mark where the bullet struck the target with a carpenter's pencil, and wrote the shooter's initials below it. Only shots that hit within six inches of the center of the painted X would qualify to move on to the next round, where the distance would be increased.

Crockett eyed Silas as he came up to the line. The man strolled forward with the swagger of a marksman confident in his abilities. Previous contestants had taken the time to check the wind or bend their bodies into the perfect stance before raising their rifles. When Silas reached the line, though, he simply lifted his weapon and fired a shot in one continuous motion. The whole exhibition was over in an instant.

A twinge of unease settled in Crockett's gut. It *was* a rather impressive display. Of course, the first target stood only one hundred yards away, so it didn't require excessive finesse to place a shot near enough the center to continue in the competition. At least not for a skilled shooter. And Silas was definitely skilled.

"You're up, Parson." Silas regarded him with such a superior air that when Crockett stepped up to the line he had to close his eyes for a moment to clear his head of the raging voice that demanded he shoot even faster and straighter in order to wipe the smug grin off his employer's face.

But only a fool would play the game on his competitor's terms instead of his own. Crockett waved to the onlookers who were busy shouting encouragement, most of it none too flattering. It seemed no one expected a preacher to be able to hit the broad side of a barn.

Well, it was time to open the eyes of the blind.

Silas might be a sharpshooting ex-outlaw, but Crockett was no slouch. The Archers had lived by the gun since they were boys. Life on their secluded ranch required it, both for protection and for food. If he could outshoot Travis, which he had done on more than one occasion, he could outshoot anyone, even a stubborn, middle-aged kidnapper turned rancher.

Inhaling a calming breath, Crockett raised his rifle, sighted down the barrel, and squeezed the trigger.

Wood splintered in gratifying fashion as the target vibrated with the force of the strike.

"You hit it, Parson!" The boy who had scampered up the tree to call out the racers' positions earlier looked up at him with a mixture of shock and awe.

"He did more than that, boy," his father said, coming up behind him, his own rifle draped through the crook of his arm. "If I don't miss my guess, he hit it dead center." The man held his hand out to Crockett. "Best shot of the round."

Crockett grinned and accepted the man's hand. It didn't take long for others to follow suit. Men who had respected his position as minister now suddenly seemed to respect him as a man—as one of them.

Jackson ran in from the target range, the scoring disc held out before him like a giant serving platter. "You won the round, Crock!" he shouted. "Here, look." He held out the target for all to see, then pointed to the mark at the center of the white X with the initials CA printed beneath.

"Looks like I'll have plenty of company in round two," Crockett said in answer, noting the number of markings within the designated advancement area. "Must be at least fifteen qualifying shots there."

"Yep." Jackson pulled a piece of crumpled paper from his pocket. "Mr. Ward gave me the list."

As he started calling out the names of the men moving on in the competition, Crockett checked to see where Silas's shot had landed. It was only about an inch away from his own, up and to the right. For a fellow who'd done such little preparation, the result was impressive.

"Don't get cocky, Archer." Silas slid in beside him while everyone else circled around Jackson to hear the reading of the names. "We still got us two rounds to go."

Crockett clapped his boss on the shoulder with the same degree of force Silas had used on him earlier. "Should make for a good contest." With that, he edged away from the center of the crowd so the other competitors could examine the scoring disc.

Joanna caught his eye from where she stood among the spectators. She lifted her hand in front of herself, just enough for a small wave. No one else would notice, but the tiny gesture went straight to his heart. She was rooting for him.

Of course, she was probably rooting for her father, too, but right now her smile and encouragement were solely for his benefit.

The target in the second round had been nailed to a tree approximately two hundred fifty yards from the shooting line. Carl was the only Lazy R hand who'd failed to qualify. While he grumbled under his breath about nature's cruelty in stealing his eyesight, Jasper and Frank both took their turns at the line. When Silas was up, he demonstrated greater care and deliberation in taking aim, but he still fired faster than any previous competitor. And put his shot directly in the center of the X.

Crockett's bullet veered a little to the left, leaving Silas the winner of the round.

Only six names graced round three's list. Half of them belonged to the Lazy R.

"Your last shot went a bit wide back there, preacher man," Silas said as he tucked the stock of his weapon into his shoulder and sighted an imaginary target somewhere among the trees that lined the river. "Too bad. I thought I might finally have some competition."

Crockett grinned, recognizing the intimidation tactic for what it was. "Oh, I won't let you down, Silas. Don't worry. We're fighting for Lazy R pride, after all. If you and Jasper both miss, I'll be there to clinch the victory."

Silas raised a sardonic brow.

"Might even be worth an extra afternoon off, huh?" Crockett gripped the man's collarbone in a friendly squeeze.

"You beat me, boy, I'll give you two afternoons off."

Crockett winked and released his hold. "Deal."

Two afternoons to spend with Joanna. Now he had even more incentive.

"'Course, if I win, you'll be giving me an extra hour after supper each night for a week. We got plenty of harness that needs mendin' and saddles in want of oil."

"Fair enough." He wouldn't mind a little extra work, especially if Joanna found reasons to come visit him out in the barn.

"You want in on the action, too, Jasper?" Silas nodded to the quiet man standing a few steps away.

"No thanks, boss." Jasper shrugged. "I still remember the contest last Fourth of July. You were the only one who even hit the final target. I'd rather keep my evenings free, thank you."

Crockett lifted his head and searched the trees along the river for the third scoring disc. *There.* It was easily five hundred yards out. The X on its face had been painted twice as large as the previous ones, but he still had to squint to make it out. Not quite the same as shooting cans off the woodcutting stump with Travis. Eager to outdo each other over the years, he and Trav had worked their way past the barn all the way to the tree line, which was a fairly comparable distance to today's target. But even as men, they'd missed those cans as often as they'd hit them.

Winning today would be no small feat.

The first man was called to the line. Crockett's belly started aching. Each marksman had his own ritual, and these rituals seemed to grow ever longer as the men set and reset their stances, waiting for the perfect conditions to shoot.

The first two missed the target. The crowd groaned in sympathy and offered polite applause for their good showing. The third man nicked the rim of the scoring disc. The spectators roared their approval.

Jasper stepped up to the line next. The onlookers hushed. He fit his rifle into his shoulder and searched for the best line, making tiny adjustments to his grip. Once satisfied, he stilled. And waited. And waited. The instant the gentle breeze swirling around them died, he pulled the trigger.

The scoring disc jerked as the bullet struck near the top.

"Great shot." Crockett slapped Jasper on the back as whistles and applause rose from the crowd. "Maybe you should have joined in on the wager after all. You might end up with the best mark."

Jasper shook his head, though a smile lit his face. "Nah. Silas will find a way to beat me. The boss man don't know how to lose. Never has."

Crockett could well believe that. The man exuded confidence and skill in everything he did. Whether he was working the ranch or leading a group of bandits on an abduction mission, one thing remained constant—the man fought hard to accomplish his goals. And never failed.

Could it be that the very self-sufficiency that allowed him to be such a successful rancher and leader of men was also his biggest barrier to accepting Christ? A man who needed only his own strength and wits to succeed in life would be blind to his need for a Savior.

Conviction settled in Crockett's gut as he watched Silas stride up to the line. The man's face showed nothing beyond concentration. No perspiration beaded his forehead. No tremors seized his hands. His legs stood solid beneath him; not even a heel dared swivel for better purchase. The *crack* of his shot rent the air, followed quickly by a distant *thunk* as his bullet collided with the target.

As a shout exploded from the crowd, Crockett's attention turned inward. If he could hand Silas a loss, would it put a chink in the man's armor? A chink that could weaken his defenses, giving truth a better chance to find its way inside?

If so, Lord, I ask that you steady my hand. Make my aim true. And grant me victory today, so that you can claim the victory tomorrow.

Silas backed away from the line, and gestured with a sweep of his arm for Crockett to take his place. Crockett hesitated, then slowly moved forward. The knot in his gut tightened with each step. He braced his right foot behind him, digging his boot into the dirt for better balance. He eyed the scoring disc and tried to picture a can on a tree stump. Well-wishers called out encouragement and advice, but their words were nothing more than a faint buzzing in his ears. He lifted his Winchester into position, and the buzz faded into silence.

Crockett inhaled. Sighted the center of the target. Adjusted for the breeze that ruffled his hair. Exhaled just enough air to relax his lungs. Then with a prayer in his heart, he squeezed the trigger.

The rifle butt kicked into his shoulder. A touch of smoke leaked from the muzzle. The shot blast rang in his ears.

But what made his heart sing was the telltale jerk of the scoring disc as his bullet lodged into its wooden surface.

Mr. Ward wandered out to mark the shot and take the necessary measurements. Then Jackson retrieved the target and ran ahead, collecting spectators as he went. By the time he reached the firing line, the entire community swarmed at his back. Everyone pressed forward, eager to hear the results, but Jackson held the large disc flat against his midsection as he struggled to catch his breath after the long jog.

A cool hand slid into Crockett's overheated palm. The light touch only lasted a moment before it pulled away, but a moment was all he needed to recognize its source. *Joanna.* He twisted his neck in the direction of the touch and found her at his side, her shy smile throwing his heartbeat into an erratic rhythm.

"The winner of the shooting contest," Jackson shouted, tearing Crockett's attention away from Joanna's sweet face, "with a mark only two and a half inches from dead center—" he paused, then twirled the scoring disk around for all to see— "is Crockett Archer!"

A loud cheer arose, but it was the pride glistening in Joanna's eyes that reverberated loudest in his heart. She smiled and clapped, but when others moved in to offer their congratulations, she quietly retreated. While he appreciated the handshakes and good-natured back thumping, what he really wanted was to sweep Joanna into his arms and twirl her around until her laughter spilled over them both. Then he'd kiss her and take that laughter inside himself as together they reveled in the joy of the moment.

But when the next hand firmed around his and Crockett found himself staring into Silas's face, he remembered that this moment was not about him at all. It was about what the Lord had done through him.

"Looks like you earned yourself some time off, Archer."

For once, Crockett offered no grin, just a slight nod of acknowledgment. "It was a fine match. One that I can't take credit for."

"What do you mean, you can't take credit for it?" Silas's grip tightened, grinding Crockett's fingers. "You find some way to cheat?"

"No," Crockett said with a little chuckle as he eased his hand out of Silas's vise. "I just meant that my abilities are not my own—they come from God. He provided the training during the hardship of my youth and helped me hone them as an adult. He deserves the credit."

"But he wasn't the one standing here pulling the trigger. You were."

"Oh, he was here," Crockett said, taking encouragement from the confusion that pushed past the defiance in Silas's eyes. "I visited him in prayer before raising my rifle and felt his presence throughout."

"Why would he care about a stupid shooting contest?"

"He doesn't, Silas. He cares about *you*."

27

Two days later, Silas was still puzzling over Crockett Archer's declaration as he rubbed Marauder down after a long ride through the woods. Crazy preachers. Always talkin' in riddles. He drew the currycomb through the gray's coat, wishing he could use the same method to untangle his thoughts.

What in the world did a shooting contest have to do with God? And why would his losing be a message that God cared about him? More likely God was showing favoritism—helping Archer win. Silas wanted no part of a God who cheated. But then, he'd always known the Almighty didn't play fair. For if he were truly interested in justice, Andy Murdoch would still be alive and that Bible-totin', child-bashin', sermon-spewin' step-father of his woulda had his brains fried by some holy lightning.

Instead, God had turned a blind eye to the preacher's faults and let an innocent suffer.

Silas blew out a harsh breath, stormed out of Marauder's stall, and flung the currycomb onto the shelf. He kicked the wall hard enough to jangle the tack above, then bent over the half wall that sectioned off the milk cow's quarters and pressed his forearms against the wood.

"Daddy?"

Silas bit back an oath at the sight of his daughter climbing down the loft ladder.

"Are you all right?" she asked, wiping her hands on the painting smock that protected her dress. "I heard a crash."

He turned to face her, rubbing the dents out of his forearms. "I'm fine, Jo. Just had some bad memories sneak up on me and stir my temper. Nothing to worry about."

She glided toward him, a penetrating look in her eyes that reminded him so much of her mother he wanted to spin on his heels and run. Martha had always been able to see past his bluster to the doubts and pain beneath. But he didn't want his sweet Jo exposed to that darker side. It was his duty to protect her, to shield her from the ugly part of the world, even to the point of preserving her illusions about a loving God.

Jo halted in front of him and touched his arm. "Can I pray about it for you?"

He flinched.

"If it'll make you feel better," he grumbled. Silas turned away from the compassion in his daughter's eyes. He knew she was only trying to help, but doggone it, prayer was the last thing he wanted. The very idea chafed like a pair of sandpaper drawers.

"I'm not the one who needs to feel better, Daddy. You do. God can heal those old pains if you let him. He loves you."

"Ha!" Silas shoved away from the half wall and glowered at his daughter. Maybe he'd kept her too sheltered. Maybe it was time for a dose of reality. Something to protect her from the wiles of smooth-talkin' preachers.

"If your God was interested in sparin' me pain, he shoulda restrained the evil that caused it in the first place. You and Archer can go around spoutin' off about how God cares, but all I've ever seen from him is cold indifference. So forgive me if I'm not too eager to deepen our acquaintance."

"Did he feel indifferent toward you when the soldiers stripped the clothes from his only Son's body and plied him with whips until flesh was torn from bone?" Jo's quiet voice knocked him back. He wanted to discount her example. God had sent his Son for all mankind, not for him individually. It wasn't personal.

Yet somehow, when Joanna murmured the words, it felt personal.

"Did he feel indifferent when they pierced his Son's hands with nails and spat upon his face? Was it coldness he felt when his Son's tortured cry punctured the heavens, accusing him of forsaking him? It must have been agony for the Father to turn his back. Yet he could not gaze upon the sin clinging to Jesus. *Your* sin. *My* sin. Was it indifference that kept him from intervening? No, it was love. Love for you."

Silas couldn't answer. He couldn't look at her, either. Why wouldn't she just leave? He wished she would quit muddying the water. He was entitled to his opinions, to his anger—justified in them.

So why was he still listening?

She stepped closer. He could feel her, though she didn't touch him again. "Evil exists in this world, Daddy. When people choose that path, there are harsh consequences. Innocents are hurt. Once in a while God chooses to intervene. Many times he doesn't. Why? I don't know. But what I do know is that he promises to work things out for good for those who love him. He finds ways to create blessings even in the wake of disasters."

"I've never seen any such blessings." Silas muttered this observation more to himself than her, but Jo must have heard, for a sad little laugh fell from her lips.

"Oh, Daddy. You blame God for the bad in your life, yet you refuse to acknowledge his hand in the good. How many times have you bragged about the fact that you never get sick and can outwork any man? Who do you think blessed you with such a strong constitution? And Jasper's always talking about how smart you are, how you can lay out plans to perfection."

"Jasper should keep his mouth shut."

"God gave you that intelligence," Jo continued, determined to ride this train all the way to the end of the track. "And what about Mama?"

That brought his head around. "What about her? Your God had nothing to do with Martha. I found her on my own."

"Did you?" She raised a doubtful brow. "So it was nothing more than chance that placed Mama in the very stage you were set to hold up. A woman who would eventually convince you to leave your life of crime, who would bring you joy and comfort. A godly woman who prayed for your salvation every day of her life, and whose last wish was for her daughter to take over her spiritual vigil so that she might one day see her beloved husband again in eternity."

"She asked that of you?" Something rasped the back of his throat. Martha had always been a religious woman, but he never realized his lack of faith was such a burden to her. A burden she passed on to their daughter.

"She did. But she didn't have to ask. I would have done it anyway. I love you too much to give up on you."

Silas leaned his arm against the half wall behind him, suddenly unsteady. "I . . . I don't understand."

"Why do you think I wanted a new preacher so desperately? I didn't have Mama's support any longer. I needed help. And God answered my prayer by sending me a parson who is so much like you that he's probably the only preacher in the country you could come to respect."

Archer was in on this, too? Of course he was. Suddenly his comment at the end of the shooting match made sense. It was all a plot, a plan. They were ganging up on him, herding him places he didn't want to go.

"The best part of all, Daddy, is that God used *you* to bring him here. I never would have found Crockett if it hadn't been for you."

"I'll send him back," Silas threatened, panic setting in. He needed space to breathe, to think. He hated being chased, cornered.

"God's pursuing you," Jo pressed, relentless. "He wants you as his own. All you have to do is stop run . . ."

Her words died away as he sprinted out the barn door.

28

A cool breeze ruffled Crockett's shirt as he rode onto the Lazy R at the conclusion of his afternoon visits. He'd borrowed Joanna's mount to pay calls on the folks who'd not attended services following the picnic and to check in on the few he'd heard were ill. Everyone welcomed him warmly, although most had been more eager to discuss the shooting contest than church attendance. But he wouldn't complain. A foot in the door was a foot in the door, no matter how it came to be there.

The only true disappointment of the day came when he realized how much time those visits had consumed. He'd intended to spend only two or three hours paying calls and instead had spent nearly four. That didn't leave much time for courting.

Crockett grinned as his mare trotted toward the barn. It was a good thing Archers knew how to make the most of limited resources.

Frank was washing up at the pump near the corral trough. Crockett waved, thinking it might be a good idea to freshen up a bit himself before searching Joanna out. He had just tugged the reins to steer Sunflower in that direction when Silas burst out of the barn like a cat with his tail on fire. The mare reared, her shrill neigh a scream in Crockett's ears. He instinctively tightened his knees and leaned forward in the saddle to keep his seat.

"Easy, girl. Whoa now." He patted her neck, and Sunflower finally returned her forelegs to the ground.

Frank hobbled after his boss as fast as his stiff gait would allow. "Silas?" he called.

The fleeing man ignored his shout and soon pulled so far ahead, Frank was forced to give up the chase. He shuffled back to Crockett and ran a hand through his damp, graying hair. "What in tarnation was that all about?"

"I have no idea," he said, staring after his employer's retreating back. "It was like he didn't even see us." Which was odd. The man prided himself on his detailed awareness of all of the ranch's workings.

"Didn't hear us, neither." Frank grunted and crossed his arms over his chest, obviously put out by Silas's callous dismissal. "Something musta got him riled."

Crockett dismounted, continuing to stroke Sunflower's neck as she snorted and tossed her head. Her chest heaved, and a large breath expelled from her lungs. "That-a-girl," Crockett crooned. He kept a snug grip on the reins, still leery of the mare trying to bolt.

Bolt. Crockett turned to where Silas was disappearing into the trees out past the corral. "He's not mad," he murmured. "He's scared."

"Scared?" Frank scoffed. "You're out of your gourd if you think that. I've known Silas Robbins for more than twenty-five years, and I can promise you that man ain't afeared of nothin'."

Nothing but preachers and religious discussions, Crockett thought with a smile. Then all at once, a picture of what must have happened crystallized in his brain, and his gut lurched.

"Joanna!" Her name echoed across the yard ahead of him. He spared only a moment to toss Sunflower's reins to Frank before breaking into a run.

He found her huddled against the tack wall, arms wrapped around her middle, shoulders trembling. Her eyes lifted to meet his, her teeth digging into her bottom lip as she fought to contain the tears that swam in her eyes.

"I've ruined ev-everything." The hitch in her voice broke his heart. "I pressed him too hard. Said too much." A fat tear crested the dam and rolled slowly down her cheek. "He ran from me, Crockett." She swallowed a sob. "He ran from *me*."

He opened his arms and caught her as she staggered toward him. Folding her into his chest, he laid his cheek against her hair and stroked her back. "Shh, sweetheart. He didn't run from you. He ran from the truth."

"I never should have said anything." She tipped her head back, gently dislodging him. Her eyes shimmered, but she held the remaining tears at bay. "I thought it was the right time. He actually seemed to be listening. But then I went too far. I told him about my promise to Mama and the real reason you came here. I even pointed out how he'd unwittingly played a role himself by abducting you from that train."

Joanna braced her palms against his shirtfront, her touch ricocheting through him as she leaned backward against his hold. "He threatened to send you away, Crockett. And heaven knows if he'll ever let me speak of this again. You warned me to be subtle, to be patient, but I just blundered forward and made a mess of everything."

Crockett released his hold on her waist with one hand and moved to cup her chin with his other. "There's a time for subtlety, and a time to be bold. If the Spirit was moving you to speak, it would have been a sin not to."

"But what if it wasn't the Spirit? What if it was just me?"

Crockett sighed and snuggled her head back into his chest. "I battle the same question every time I write a sermon."

"How do you know?" She mumbled the question against his shirt, leaving her head where it rested in the hollow between his shoulder and neck. The place that seemed to be made for her.

Crockett rubbed her arm and dropped a gentle kiss on the top of her head before answering. "I don't always know. Not for certain. The best we can do is ensure our hearts are right, our motives pure, and then listen for God's guidance, praying that he will correct our path if we veer off course."

"Do you think I veered off course?" The quiet question tugged at his heart.

"No." The memory of Silas's agitated dash convicted him. "I know you, Jo. For years, you've prayed for your father, wanting only what is in his best interest. If you believed the time was right for you to speak, it was right."

"Then why did he run?" She didn't pull away, but she did tilt her head to meet his gaze.

For a moment her upturned lips distracted him. Steeling himself against the ill-timed surge of desire, he dragged his focus back up to her eyes.

"He needs time to think," Crockett said, "to examine his beliefs. You can't make the choice for him. He has to choose it on his own. We'll give him some time, see where the Lord leads next."

"But what if he makes you leave?" Her fingers wrinkled the cotton of his shirt as if she meant to hold him captive.

If she only knew how captivated he already was.

Crockett smiled down at her, his heart full of promises as he covered her hand with his own. "He might fire me, darlin', but he can't make me leave the area. I've got a church to run, you know. Besides"—he winked—"I get the feeling the woman who hired me might fancy me a little. I think I can convince her to let me stay on."

At last the clouds cleared from her eyes, and her mouth curved flirtatiously. "Oh, you do, do you?"

Crockett waggled his eyebrows. "I'm not above using my masculine wiles for a good cause." He shifted his grip on her hand and raised it toward his lips. "Do you think she'd let me stay in exchange for a kiss?" He lowered his head and lightly caressed the skin just below the bend of her knuckles, in the valley where her first two fingers met.

Her breath caught, and a tremor passed through her, a delicate version of the one pounding through him.

"You know, Archer," a gruff voice rasped behind them, making Joanna jump, "I don't reckon the boss's mood would improve much if he were to come home and find you dallyin' with his daughter."

Crockett squeezed Joanna's hand before slowly pivoting to face Frank.

The older man dropped Sunflower's reins, his right hand moving to hover above his holster. "Can't say I like it much, either, seein' as how Jo's practically my niece." His steely stare moved to Joanna and examined her from head to toe, assuring himself she was unharmed.

"I'd never take sinful advantage of a woman, Frank," Crockett ground out, his jaw clenching as he strove to keep a lid on his temper. He took a step closer to his accuser. "Especially not one whom I respect and care for as much as Joanna."

Frank's bow-legged stride closed the remaining distance between them. His eyes latched onto Crockett's, his palm resting on the butt of his pistol. "You telling me you got honorable intentions toward our gal?"

Crockett gave a clipped nod. "Yes, sir, I am—I do."

Instantly the man's face cleared, and the old grump actually smiled. "Hot diggity!" He cackled and slapped his thigh with his empty gun hand. "I knew it! Wait'll I tell the boys. Jasper's gonna owe me twenty bucks."

"Frank?" Joanna slid around Crockett's side, her fingers trailing down his arm until her slender hand nestled into his palm. "I don't understand." She tipped her face up to Crockett, puzzlement evident in the lines upon her brow.

He shrugged slightly, then closed his hand around hers and stroked his thumb over her knuckles.

"I ain't so old I can't remember what it's like to be young. I ain't blind, neither. I seen the way you look at her across the supper table when you think no one's watching." Frank jabbed his bony elbow into Crockett's ribs. "Why do ya think I waited so long to follow ya in here? Didja think Sunflower and I were out in the yard shootin' the breeze? Ha!"

Truth be told, after finding Joanna, he hadn't thought of anything but how best to comfort and reassure her. Now his little pixie was blushing up a storm and doing her best to hide her face behind his shoulder. It was all he could do not to grin.

"You mind keeping this information under your hat for a bit, Frank?" If the old buzzard went squawkin' to Silas about his and Joanna's courtship, her father would have him hog-tied and thrown off the Lazy R before he could blink. It wouldn't keep him away from Joanna, of course. Crockett had meant what he'd said about hanging around no matter what. However, Silas was at a crossroads. The fewer distractions he had to deal with, the better. "We'd like Silas to hear about it from us. When the time is right."

"All right," Frank grumbled, his usual grim demeanor reasserting itself. "But don't take your sweet time about it. I ain't met the man yet who can pull the wool over Si's eyes for long. In fact, it wouldn't surprise me if he already suspects something's afoot. Ever since the picnic, he's had a peculiar look about him when he watches you work—like he can't decide if he should keep you around or send ya packin'." Frank socked him in the arm. "Might be a good idea to stay upwind of him when we go huntin' tomorrow."

The man cackled at his own witticism, then finally moved on, leading Sunflower to her stall near the back wall.

"You're going hunting tomorrow?" Joanna's soft question pulled him away from the complications mushrooming in his mind.

"Your father grumbled something about putting my rifle skills to use for the Lazy R before I take another afternoon for myself." Crockett winked. "If you ask me, though, I think he just wants to see if I can hit a moving target."

A teasing smile lit up Joanna's face. "Can you?"

"I've been known to take down a squirrel midleap between trees." The Archer ranch had crawled with the little rodents. As kids, he and Travis used to have contests to see who could bag the most—until Jim threatened to quit cooking if they didn't start giving him some variety. Of course, Jim wouldn't be the one cooking this time. Crockett grinned at Joanna. "I think I can manage to bring something home to your table."

It was her turn to wink as she slipped from his hold and headed back toward the loft ladder. "I'll look forward to it."

29

Silas veered west through a stand of post oaks, separating himself from the rest of the hunting party. He knew these game trails as well as the Tonkawa Indians who roamed the area a hundred years ago had, and frankly, he wasn't in the mood for company. The conversation he'd had with Jo yesterday had replayed over and over in his mind during the course of the night, robbing him of sleep and leaving his temper dangerously ragged. Worst of all, it'd made things awkward between him and Jo.

He hadn't been able to look his girl in the eye this morning, not after running out on her like some kind of coward yesterday. He hated himself for that. She was his baby girl. His Jo. And he couldn't look at her.

Not without seeing her mother and recalling the promise Martha had extracted from her.

All those years they were together, she'd never harped at him about God. She had invited him to services once in a while and insisted on praying before meals, but she'd never nagged him about it. Probably 'cause she knew it wouldn't do any good.

Had she really prayed for him every day? Fought some kind

of unseen battle for his soul that he'd never even been aware of? Apparently she'd passed the duty on to Jo, leaving their girl to take up the fight. A fight that drained her so much, she'd felt she had to call in reinforcements.

Archer.

Silas spat at the ground as he trudged deeper into the woods. What kind of man let his womenfolk fight his battles? So what if he'd known nothing about it. He did now. And that meant he had to make some changes. What exactly those changes were supposed to entail he hadn't quite figured out. Tightening his grip on his rifle, Silas squinted up at the sky.

"Why do you care about an old reprobate like me?" The harsh whisper rasped in his throat. "Did you tangle me up with a God-fearin' woman just to lure me in? 'Cause I ain't biting. It don't make no sense for you to go to such lengths to lasso my soul when you wouldn't lift a finger to stop one of your own sermonizers from caning Andy to death. So you can just quit chasin' me."

I love you too much to give up on you.

The words had been Joanna's yesterday. Yet the voice ringing in his head now sounded nothing like his little girl and everything like the roar of rushing waters.

Silas gritted his teeth and halted in the shade of a hickory tree—away from the early morning sun forcing its warmth onto the earth. Silas didn't want to be warm. He wanted the numbness the cold offered. A numbness that would keep him from thinking, keep him from feeling.

A rustle to his right brought his senses to alert.

Finally. A distraction.

Moving deliberately, so as not to make a noise that would give away his position, Silas shifted his rifle into a ready position and stole a careful glance around the hickory's trunk. About two hundred yards downhill and to the south, a white-tailed deer stepped out from the trees to nose the grass of a tiny clearing.

Sunlight glinted off the buck's rack. The beast was strong. Mature. And easy pickin's.

A smile of triumph curved Silas's lips. The others were safely to the north—too far away to poach his find. He'd be the one with the first kill of the day. And judging by the size of the specimen in front of him, he'd be bringing in the best of the day, as well.

Silas eased into a secure stance and took aim. Drawing a line up from the buck's front leg, he sighted the center of the chest. A lung shot. He'd take no chances on the head or spine. Anything less than an instant kill would send the deer bounding into the trees, never to be found. No, this was his chance to prove his marksmanship. To prove his self-sufficiency. To regain the control Jo had shattered in him yesterday.

A tiny sound echoed somewhere downhill from him, between his position and the buck. Some varmint with bad timing, blast it all. The buck lifted his head and blinked, poised to leap away, but Silas wouldn't allow it. Without a second thought, he squeezed the trigger.

But it wasn't the buck that fell.

A slender figure had emerged from the brush fifty yards downwind at the same moment Silas's rifle cracked its shot. The buck bounded away. The figure crumpled.

No! Silas's mind screamed the word his constricted throat couldn't voice. How . . . ? Where had he . . . ? It wasn't possible. All of the men were farther north.

But it wasn't a man.

Acid churned in his stomach as the truth dawned in horrifying clarity. "No. Please, God. No!" Leaping forward, Silas sprinted down the hill, stumbling over tree roots, slipping on sandy soil. Thick shrub branches tore at his face and hands. He shoved them aside.

He forced his way through the last bramble and fell to his

knees beside Jackson Spivey's writhing form. The boy was belly down, moaning, trying to reach behind his shoulder to the place where blood oozed from a bullet-sized hole. A bullet Silas had put there.

"Easy, Jackson." Silas snatched the bandana from his neck, wadded it, and pressed it hard against the boy's wound.

Jackson cried out, the sound lacerating Silas's soul.

"Don't worry, son. I'm gonna get you out of here. You're gonna be fine." He *had* to be fine. Silas couldn't be responsible for another boy's death.

Holding the dressing in place, Silas rolled him over. A whimper echoed in the air between them, but Silas wasn't sure if it emanated from Jackson or himself.

Muddy streaks marred the kid's face, where tears had coursed over his cheeks. His breaths came in shallow little pants as he struggled to keep a brave front. "It hurts, Mr. Robbins."

"I know, boy. But you're tough. You'll pull through." Maybe if he said it enough times, one of them would start to believe it.

Silas searched Jackson's chest for an exit wound. He found none. Biting back an oath, he scanned the hillside for any sign of his men. *Where are they?* They should have headed his way after hearing his gunshot—if for no other reason than to see what type of game he'd bagged.

His grip tightened on Jackson, remorse hitting him so hard, his head spun. He squeezed his eyes shut and gathered his wits. Regret wasn't going to get the boy home. A strong back was. Silas slid his hunting knife from the sheath at his waist and yanked the tail of his shirt free from his trousers. Slicing the flannel with the blade, he tugged and tore until he had a strip long enough to wrap around Jackson's chest. Trying not to jostle the boy too much, he wrestled the bandage until it securely bound the dressing to the wound.

When he finished, Jackson's eyes had closed. The fight seemed to be draining from him along with his blood. Silas swallowed the growing lump in his throat. He couldn't let another minute pass without saying what needed to be said.

"I'm sorry, Jackson." He hugged the boy gently to his chest and squinted away the moisture pooling near his lashes. "So sorry."

"It ain't your fault." Jackson's eyes cracked open a slit. "Jo fussed at me 'bout not hunting without permission. I was . . . too stubborn to listen. Guess . . . she was right, huh?" He tried to chuckle, but the weak sound turned into a cough.

Silas winced.

He'd been too stubborn to listen, too. What if she was right again? What if God really did care?

Jackson's head lolled to the side as the boy lost consciousness. His face ashen, his body limp, he was knockin' on death's door.

Silas lifted his face to heaven. "I know you and I ain't seen eye to eye for quite some time, and I know I'm to blame for this predicament. But if you could see your way to intervening on the boy's behalf, I'd take it as a personal favor."

The sky didn't open. No angelic chorus started singing. No beam of heavenly light fell across Jackson's face. The kid just lay there as broken as before.

Fine. He'd handle it by himself. It'd been crazy to think God would listen to him anyway. Maybe he listened to people like Jo and Martha, but to bitter old outlaws with blood on their hands? Not likely.

"All right, kid," he grunted as he shifted to take Jackson's weight. "Let's get you out of here." He collected the fallen rifles and hoisted the boy over his right shoulder like a gangly sack of potatoes. Using the rifles as if they were a cane, Silas levered himself up to a standing position and quickly braced his legs. Once he had Jackson's weight distributed evenly, he set off for the trail using the arm with the rifles to shield the boy from the worst of the brush as he pushed them through.

A pair of shots echoed some distance to the north, drawing a scowl from Silas. If the men were off chasing their own game, there'd be no one to help him with Jackson. The kid would never make it.

"Why won't you do something?" Silas groaned beneath his labored breath. He would have shouted his frustration to the sky, but he had no energy to spare. The vegetation thinned as he neared the edge of the gulley. He struggled to put one foot in front of the other, the ground beneath him growing increasingly steep.

His boot slipped. He tightened his one-arm hold on Jackson and leaned into the hill, digging his toes into the sandy soil. Silas rammed the rifle butts into the ground to help him stabilize. His gaze lifted to where the hill leveled out above him. Still twenty yards to go.

Sweat beaded his forehead despite the cool morning breeze. Silas set his jaw and took another step. He'd get the boy home or die trying.

Ten yards. Five. Something caught the toe of his boot. A root, maybe? He staggered to the right, Jackson's weight nearly toppling him sideways. Not now. He was so close. Just a few more steps.

He thrust the rifle butts into the earth as he corrected his balance. Once steady he started onward, but the sandy slope shifted beneath his boots. As his feet struggled to find purchase again and again, his defenses weakened. Determination alone wasn't going to save Jackson. Nor would stubbornness or strength of will.

The next slip took Silas to his knees. As his legs absorbed the impact of his collision, his soul absorbed the realization that relying on himself was hopeless. A forty-year-old grudge against God had no place on this hillside nor in his heart. Not when a boy's life hung in the balance.

Arms shaking, he clung to Jackson while his pride and bitterness crumbled to dust. "I need your help." Though God knew he didn't deserve it. "Please. No favors. No bargains. I'm just a sinner on his knees beggin' for mercy. Beggin' you to spare the life of this boy. Please. I ain't demandin' a miracle or a flock of angels to swoop down and flutter their wings around him. I ain't got no right to ask for such things. All I ask is that you give us a fighting chance."

His breath shuddered as he inhaled. "I'm done running. If you want me . . . I'm yours."

Silas made no effort to get up. He *did* make an effort to trust—to trust in a God he didn't understand. Leaning on the faith of his daughter and his wife . . . he waited.

Barely a moment passed before the sound of his name being called met his ears.

"Here!" Silas yelled in response. "Hurry!"

Footsteps pounded faster, louder.

Silas struggled to stand, bracing himself against the slope and clasping Jackson's legs tight to his chest.

"Give me your hand," a voice called from above.

Silas lifted his head as he swung the rifles up over the ridge. "Archer. Thank God." Never had he meant two words more.

The parson's solid grasp encircled his wrist, and with his strength counterbalancing the downward slope of the hill, it only took two long strides for Silas to regain the trail.

"Is that Jackson?" Archer paled, taking in the kid's limp form.

Silas swallowed hard, guilt tearing at his throat. "He jumped in front of my bullet when I tried to take down a buck. I never knew he was there." Moisture pooled in his eyes, but for once he didn't care. His pride no longer mattered. All that mattered was Jackson.

He braced himself for Archer's disdain. It was what he deserved. But the man met his gaze head on, nothing more than concern etched on his face. "Come on," he said, slinging his rifle strap over his shoulder and gathering up the other two. "I'll help you get him to the house."

Each man took one of Jackson's arms and wound it about his neck. Their greater height kept all but the toes of the boy's boots from scraping the ground as they stretched their stride in the rush to get home.

"How'd you know to come?" Silas huffed out between steps. "I heard the others hunting farther on."

"It's hard to explain," Archer replied, his own breath heaving between the words. "As soon as I heard your shot, my gut reacted. The guys assured me you were fine, but I couldn't shake the feeling that I was supposed to check on you."

God brought him back. Archer didn't make the claim, but Silas knew it was true. God had intervened. Even before Silas had been aware of the need.

Silence fell between them again as they concentrated on putting one foot in front of the other as quickly as possible. Finally, the barn came into view. And with it another slew of problems. They might have gotten the boy home, but the doctor was miles away. Fetching one from Deanville would take at least a couple hours—if they could even find the man.

Silas regarded the preacher from the corner of his eye. "You prayin', Archer?" Heaven knew the boy needed someone with more pull than he had with the big man upstairs if the kid was gonna have a shot at surviving this mess.

"With every step, Si," he grunted out, twisting his neck to meet his gaze. "With every step."

Silas nodded, the vise around his heart loosening just a touch. "Me too."

30

Joanna plucked another weed free from around the new carrot tops that had recently pushed through the soil, her mind far from her task. Crockett had invited her to go riding with him when he returned from hunting. Just the two of them. A flutter of anticipation danced in her belly. She planned to show him some of her mother's favorite painting spots, and if she could muster the nerve, she might even ask permission to sketch his likeness. Not that she hadn't sketched him already. She'd completed at least a dozen drawings, but they'd all captured Crockett from a distance.

What would it be like to study him up close? To take her time with each feature of his face in order to replicate it on paper? The strong line of his jaw. The sparkle in his eyes when he teased her. The curve of his mouth when he smiled.

The way his lips softened right before they met hers.

Joanna's hands stilled. Would Crockett kiss her again? Mercy, but she hoped so. Her breath caught in her throat as her eyes slid closed to savor the memory of the kiss they'd shared down by the river. Would their second kiss be as heavenly as the first?

She blinked against the sunlight, and a smile bloomed across her face—until she noticed three men limping toward her from the edge of the woods.

Instantly alert, she shot to her feet and lifted a hand to block the sun's glare.

Someone was hurt. She couldn't tell who from this distance, but she knew what her father expected of her in such a situation.

Dashing through the open gate, Joanna abandoned the garden and ran for the house. She bounded up the back porch steps and grabbed the metal rod that hung from the large metal triangle she used for calling the men to supper. She circled the inside of it again and again, striking metal against metal with a strength borne of fear. The clamor nearly deafened her, but she kept it up until the ache in her arm forced her to stop. She prayed the others were within earshot. If so, the alarm would have them running for the house.

The entire time she rang the dinner bell, her focus remained locked on the trio of men approaching from the north. The one on the right had the build of her father, but he was so hunched over from the weight of the injured man, she couldn't be sure. The one on the left was slightly taller, and her heart wanted so badly to believe it was Crockett—that both he and her father were unharmed.

She longed to sprint out to meet them and see for herself who'd been hurt and how bad the injuries were, but practicality drove her into the house instead. Rushing out to them would only assuage her curiosity, but it wouldn't actually help anyone. She'd be of better service gathering medical supplies and preparing a sickroom.

Working the pump at the sink, Joanna quickly scrubbed away the garden dirt from her hands and under her nails, then ransacked the linen closet for the rolls of bandages and wads of cotton wool she always kept on hand. By the time she'd gathered the medicine box and the shears from her sewing basket, and stripped the quilt from her bed, heavy footfalls from the porch announced the arrival of the men.

She'd purposely left the back door ajar, and as she rounded the corner into the kitchen, a male boot kicked it wide.

"Bring him around to my room," Joanna instructed before she'd even gotten a look at the men. "I've got things set up for him in there."

She held the door open as the threesome finagled their way through. A breath she hadn't known she'd been holding whooshed from her lungs when she recognized her father and Crockett.

Thank you, Lord, for keeping them safe.

Crockett dropped the rifles he'd been toting to the floor. The injured man didn't even flinch at the racket. That's when she noticed the sandy hair and the slender build.

"Jackson?" The name escaped her in a strangled cry.

How had this happened? He was just a boy. A boy who should be pestering her with inappropriate marriage proposals, not drooping lifelessly across her daddy's shoulders. She moaned, pressing her hand over her mouth to mute the sound. Was he dead already?

"Is he . . ." She couldn't quite voice the question as the men shuffled past her into the hall.

"He's still breathing, but there's a bullet in him," Crockett answered, his grim expression offering her little comfort.

She followed the men into her room, and when she realized they meant to lay Jackson facedown, she darted to the head of the bed to remove the pillow. Better not take any chances. If he survived the bullet, she didn't want a pillow suffocating him.

The men grunted as they slowly lowered Jackson to the bed, taking care not to jostle him too much.

"Hand me those shears," Crockett said from the far side

of the bed and immediately set to work extricating Jackson's shirttails from his trousers.

Joanna grabbed the scissors from the bedside table and held them out handle first.

"Thanks." He barely spared her a glance, so focused was he on Jackson. He snipped through the makeshift bandage that held the blood-soaked dressing in place and then started in on the shirt, cutting it from tail to neck.

She retrieved the discarded bandage from where he'd tossed it on the sheet. Only then did she recognize the fabric as being from her father's shirt.

"Daddy . . . ?" Joanna turned, intending to ask what had happened, but the haunted look etched into his features dissolved her words.

He stared at Jackson as if he didn't really see him, as if his mind recalled another horror. She held her hand out to him, but he backed away until his bootheels hit the wall on the opposite side of the room. Then he slowly lowered himself to the floor. His hat knocked against the wall and tumbled to the rug. He never even blinked. He just covered his face with his hands and bowed his head over his knees.

She'd never seen him like this—defeated. It frightened her.

"I'm going to need water, Jo," Crockett said, bringing her attention back to the boy on the bed. "Warm if you have it. And sponges or rags to clean the injured area."

She met Crockett's gaze over the top of Jackson's prone form. Compassion glowed there, along with a rigid determination that helped her own spine stiffen. They would fight this. Together.

"You can start with the water in the pitcher." She hurried to the washstand and filled the porcelain basin with water, then carried it to Crockett's side of the bed, setting it on the edge of the dresser at his elbow. "The stove reservoir should have warm water, and I'll put on a couple of kettles, too."

He caught her hand before she could dash off to the kitchen. "Heat some of the reservoir water nearly to a boil and bring me the strongest lye soap you've got. Oh, and a knife. A thin, sharp one. And tweezers if you have 'em." He spoke softly, as if he didn't want the unconscious boy to overhear and start fretting.

His gentleness nearly brought the tears she'd been battling to the surface, but she blinked them back and nodded her understanding before slipping out to the kitchen.

She had just set the second kettle on to boil when the rest of the hands burst into the house.

Frank and Carl bent double as soon as they saw she was unharmed and started wheezing as they gulped air into their lungs.

"What happened?" Jasper demanded, apparently the only one who had enough breath to talk.

"Jackson's been shot. We'll need to fetch a doctor." She glanced back at the hall, expecting to see her father emerge. There was no way he couldn't have heard the thundering herd arrive. He'd snap back to his usual self, start barking orders, and set everything to right. But he never came.

"The boss?" Jasper asked, obviously at as much of a loss as Joanna.

"He and Crockett are in with Jackson." They didn't need to know what state he was in at the moment. It would only rattle them, and right now Jackson needed them at their sharpest.

"What do ya want us to do?" Frank wheezed.

Joanna straightened her shoulders and spoke with authority. "Jasper, you and Frank ride to Deanville. One of you fetch the doctor. The other better track down Sam Spivey." After years of watching her father lead his men, she easily mimicked his manner and tone. "Search the saloons first. Sober him up before you bring him back here, though. The last thing we need is someone yelling and knocking things around when we're trying to save his boy's life."

Jasper and Frank nodded, then spun and headed out the door without another word.

"What about me, Jo?" Carl stepped forward. He dragged his hat from his head and scrunched it up in his fist. His eyes barely met hers. "I ain't much good around sick folk." His Adam's apple bobbed as he leaned close. "The sight of blood makes me woozy."

The poor fellow's face burned deep red at the admission, and his feet shuffled as if he couldn't wait to leave.

"That's just as well," Joanna said. She twisted to check the steam on the kettle, hoping to relieve his embarrassment by acting as if she hadn't noticed. "With my father and Crockett tending to Jackson, and Frank and Jasper gone to Deanville, the care of the ranch falls to you. I need you to see to the stock and handle all the regular chores while we're short-handed."

"Yes'm. I can do that." He slapped his hat over his thinning hair and dashed for the back door before she could change her mind.

Judging the water in the first kettle to be close enough to boiling, she palmed a folded dish towel and removed it from the fire.

After pouring the hot water into a small dishpan, she balanced the tray containing the lye soap, her two sharpest knives, and clean towels atop it and carried the materials to the sickroom.

Disheartened to see her father still huddled on the floor, Joanna tried not to look at him as she circled the bed to set the dishpan on the dresser top. She could only imagine one thing that could have brought her father this low.

"It's his bullet in Jackson, isn't it?" she whispered when Crockett turned toward her and started rolling up his sleeves.

His eyes met hers. "An accident."

She nodded. It could be nothing else. Her father would never intentionally harm Jackson. But, oh, how her heart ached for both of them, and she worried that neither would recover.

Bring healing, Father. Please. For both of them.

Crockett's breath hissed out of him as he dunked his arms elbow deep into the near-scalding water.

"Do you want me to cool it down a little?" Joanna moved to collect the pitcher from the washstand.

"No. I can handle it." He latched onto the cake of soap and started scrubbing. "How long until the doctor arrives?"

"I don't know. A couple hours, at least. Jasper and Frank are fetching him from Deanville." She returned to his side and held a towel out for him.

His head jerked toward her. "Deanville? There's not one closer?"

"No."

He hung his head for a moment, eyes closed, shoulders hunched forward. She thought she heard him murmur, "Not again, Lord." Then his back straightened and he spoke more distinctly. "Grant me strength and skill."

Opening his eyes, he accepted the towel from her. "I need you to go to my room at the church, Jo, and fetch my medical books. They're in the trunk that Neill brought me. Do you remember it?"

She frowned. "Yes, but why . . . ?"

"I might have need of them, and I'll feel better having them on hand." His jaw hardened and his brown eyes darkened with resolution. "We can't wait for the doctor. I'm going to have to get the bullet out and patch Jackson up myself."

"You . . . you can't do that, can you?" What could he possibly know about surgery? He would just make things worse. No, they should wait for the doctor.

She started shaking her head, but his answer stopped her.

"I've done it before."

A short bark of laughter erupted from her father. "Of course he has."

The comment puckered her brow, but Joanna was too stunned by Crockett's claim to respond. "I-I don't understand."

"Pulled a bullet out of my brother Jim's shoulder when we were kids. He was about Jackson's age. I wasn't much older. But there was no one else to do it." He sighed, then bent his mouth in a crooked half grin. "He's got a nasty scar, but he lived through it."

She steadied herself with a hand on the dresser top. Heavenly stars. He had dug a bullet out of his own brother when he was just a child. How was that even possible?

"After that day," Crockett continued, "I was in charge of all the doctoring on the Archer ranch. I read every medical book I could get my hands on and memorized most of them. I can do this, Jo. I have to."

She couldn't seem to move. Or speak. She just stood there staring at him.

Then her father's voice broke her stupor. "Have faith in your man, Jo, and go fetch his books. The Lord brought him here. Remember?" The words were slightly mocking as he flung her earlier comments back at her, but there was an edge to them she'd not heard before. Resignation? Or maybe bewilderment, as if someone had just solved an impossible puzzle in front of him, leaving him no longer able to discern between what could and couldn't be done. "Might as well let the two of them get to work."

So consumed was she in trying to decipher the change in her father, she was halfway to the barn to collect Sunflower before the full impact of what he said hit her. He'd called Crockett *her* man. And heaven be praised, he'd actually acknowledged not only God's presence but his involvement in their lives.

Tears of thanksgiving clouded her vision, and new energy surged as she raced the rest of the way to the barn.

31

Crockett blew out a prayerful breath as he gently removed the dressing from Jackson's back and started cleaning around the wound. His fingers shook. He paused, clenched them into a fist a couple times, and then continued.

Could he do this? His hands were so much larger now than when he'd dug that bullet out of Jim. What if he caused more damage than good?

Don't let me hurt him, God. Help me save him. I can't do it alone.

Crockett swished the dishrag he was using in the hot water to rinse away the blood and dirt, then set back to work on the wound.

The sound of Silas adjusting his position against the far wall drew Crockett's attention. He wished he could somehow ease the man's burden. Guilt and worry seemed to have cut the man's legs out from under him.

Silas raised his head slightly, the glazed look in his eyes giving Crockett serious cause for concern. "It's Andy all over again," he muttered.

"Who's Andy?" Crockett spoke softly, giving Silas the opening to answer or not, whichever he chose. Jackson wasn't the only one in the room with wounds that needed tending.

"A kid I knew back in Missouri before I lit out for Texas." Silas stared straight ahead, as if he were peering through a window into the past. "He died."

The stark words hit Crockett like a blow. He turned back to Jackson. It wasn't right for children to die. Jackson should be scampering all over the countryside—poaching fish, climbing trees, snaring rabbits—not lying here with a hole beneath his shoulder blade.

"An accident?" Crockett washed some fabric fibers from the entry wound.

"Nope," Silas answered, his voice flat. "His preacher step-father beat him to death with a cane."

"What?" Crockett's near shout destroyed the calm he'd worked so hard to maintain in the room. Jackson's body flinched, and he let out a muffled moan. Crockett whispered an apology and steadied the boy by clasping his uninjured side until he stilled.

How could a man of God thrash a child to death? It was unthinkable. No wonder Silas held such a deep-seated revulsion of preachers. Crockett felt soiled by association.

"It was my fault." Silas rambled on, unfazed by Crockett's outburst. "I was always getting Andy into trouble. I was a year older and had a talent for mischief. I didn't have no folks to steer me straight. All Mr. and Mrs. Washburn cared about was how much work they could wring outta me on their farm. And when Mr. Washburn got a hankering for the corn whiskey down at his still, I'd sneak away to town.

"Andy was a sickly kid. Scrawny. An easy mark for the bigger boys to pick on. Three of them ganged up on him one day out behind the schoolhouse, and when I came across 'em, something inside me snapped. I launched myself at the biggest one and blackened his eye before he even knew what hit him. Knocked out another kid's tooth, and bloodied the third one's nose. I made it clear that anyone who messed with Andy in the future would get more of the same."

Crockett listened intently as he finished cleansing Jackson's wound. Only a tiny amount of blood seeped from the hole now, but Crockett worried more was leaking inside. At least the boy's breathing seemed normal, if a bit shallow. Surely if the bullet had punctured a lung he'd be in a lot more distress. Maybe things weren't as bad as they'd feared.

Or maybe the damage was hidden. Like the damage inside Silas. Perhaps he could cleanse that wound a little more, too.

"I imagine you earned Andy's loyalty that day."

Silas snorted. "Kid followed me around like a puppy after that. I acted all put out, like having him around was a hassle, but in truth, he'd become the little brother I'd always wanted.

"So when we sneaked down to the creek for a swim one afternoon and I saw the bruises on his back, I was livid. I demanded he tell me who had hit him so I could pound some decency into him. He made up some excuse about tripping on the church steps, but I didn't buy it. Finally he admitted his stepfather had punished him for lying about Mrs. Carson's bloomers."

Bloomers? A smile edged its way onto Crockett's face as he placed a clean dressing over the torn flesh of Jackson's back. He took the whiskey bottle from Joanna's medicine box and poured a portion over the blades of the knives she had brought him, thinking he'd need to pour some in the wound, too, eventually. His smile dissolved.

"I was the one who'd stolen the bloomers, of course, and tied them to the weathervane atop her house," Silas rattled on. "Andy was just the lookout. But the old man didn't care. All that mattered was making someone pay for the crime. He insisted that Andy stay away from me, but Andy refused. He snuck out every chance he got. And every chance *I* got, I plotted how to get even with the old man for hurting my friend."

Crockett bent over Jackson, peering intently into the wound. Now that the bleeding had slowed, he could judge the bullet's path more readily. The angle seemed to head outward, toward a spot under the boy's arm. Thank God. He hoped that meant no major organs had been hit. There were some bone chips that would need to be cleared out from where the bullet appeared to have grazed the ribs, but as long as the bullet wasn't lodged behind bone, he shouldn't have too much trouble extracting it.

Silas had grown quiet again. Crockett decided he'd done all that he could for Jackson until Joanna returned. He'd need her help swabbing the blood when he went in, or he'd never be able to see what he was doing. Her father was in no shape to assist.

As a precaution against infection, Crockett poured a generous splash of whiskey in and around Jackson's wound, holding the boy down when he screamed and tried to raise up off the bed. Once the initial shock passed, Jackson collapsed against the mattress, and Crockett managed to apply a fresh dressing without further reaction.

Crockett's gut told him Silas wouldn't continue his story if Joanna was around, and expecting she'd be back in minutes, Crockett said a quick prayer over Jackson, then strode across the room to seat himself next to Silas on the floor.

"So what'd you end up doing?" He directed his question to the air in front of him, though he watched Silas from the corner of his eye.

A sad crooked smile turned the corners of Silas's mouth. "I dropped a snake on his head from the rafters of the church during one of his sermons."

Crockett bit back a grin.

"The fella squealed and flailed as if the brimstone he'd been calling down had set his hair afire. I dropped from the rafters to a spot in the aisle right in front of him—wanted to make sure the lout knew it was me that done it so his anger would have the proper target. Then I lit out of there and raced for the farm.

"I was only gone a couple hours. Just long enough for church to finish and Sunday dinner to be eaten. But by the time I got to Andy's house ready to take my punishment, the parson had already spent his rage. I could hear Andy's mom wailing and begging her husband to let her fetch the doctor. Then a loud crash echoed through the front room, and the wailing stopped.

"I shimmied up the tree that shaded Andy's window and forced my way inside." Tears rolled down Silas's cheek as he spoke, but he made no move to brush them away. Crockett wasn't sure he was even aware they were there.

"He looked so tiny in that bed. Tiny and battered beyond recognition. I was afraid to touch him. Afraid I'd hurt him more. He made horrible rasping sounds when he breathed, and his chest barely moved. But when I came closer, the less swollen of his eyes cracked open a slit, as if he knew I was there.

"'It doesn't hurt, Silas,' he told me. 'It doesn't hurt to go to heaven.' After that, he didn't rasp anymore."

Silas's legs fell flat upon the floor and his arms circled closed in front of his chest as if he were clutching Andy's broken body to his breast.

"All this time I blamed God for not protecting him, for siding with one of his own and abandoning Andy to the brutality of a madman. But I was the one to blame. I was the one who prodded the bull and left Andy to face the horns alone."

Silas's voice grew husky. Eyes still straight ahead, he cleared his throat. Crockett wanted to lay a supporting hand upon his shoulder, to console him with assurances that it wasn't his fault, either, that the blame rested solely with the fiend who vented his rage on a child. But Crockett sensed his touch would jar Silas from his vulnerable state and possibly bring his walls back up. He didn't need pity. He needed to finish his story.

"God didn't abandon Andy. I see that now." Silas swallowed long and slow. "I remember the peace that settled over his face as he took his last breath. The smile that touched his lips as the angels welcomed him home. It was the same look Martha had when she . . ."

Crockett couldn't stop himself this time. He put his hand on Silas's shoulder and squeezed. The man finally turned to look at him.

"I been running from God for forty years, Archer. Today I stopped."

Moisture collected in the corner of Crockett's eye as his soul shouted praise for the lost sheep that had finally been dragged home.

"Something happened out there while I was trying to get Jackson home. I still don't understand it, but I guess God don't need me to understand everything. He just needs me to trust."

The simple statement of faith seared Crockett's heart. His hand tightened reflexively on Silas's shoulder as the man's gaze burned into his with a conviction Crockett had never witnessed in him before.

"God brought you here, Archer. Brought you here for this moment." Silas reached out his hand and clasped Crockett's shoulder. "A preacher with doctorin' skills." He grinned and shook his head as if he still couldn't quite believe it. "I might've pulled you off that train, but God was the one who put you there. Put you there for Jo. For me. And for Jackson."

Silas shoved up to his feet, then held out a hand and yanked Crockett up, as well. "The boy's going to be fine, Parson. I trust you. But more importantly, I trust the God who brought you here."

He slapped Crockett on the back, his vigor returning in force, causing Crockett to stagger forward a step.

"Now, show me what I can do to help."

32

Joanna tossed Sunflower's reins to Carl and slid from the horse's back, all while cradling the two medical books she'd found in Crockett's room. It had taken her longer than she'd expected to find the volumes, since they were mixed among two dozen or so other books in a small trunk under his bed. She prayed the delay would not prove too costly.

After sprinting across the yard, she burst through the back door, dashed down the hall to the sickroom, and careened to a halt.

Her father and Crockett, sleeves rolled to their elbows, fingers covered in blood, stood over Jackson, their heads only inches apart. Discarded wads of cotton wool stained bright red littered the floor around her father's feet. A strong metallic tang filled her nostrils, and she fought against the urge to gag.

Too much blood. Too much . . .

Crockett glanced up. "Good. You're back. I need tweezers and a needle and thread."

A wave of dizziness hit her, but she pushed through it to

concentrate on his words. Needle and thread. Her sewing basket. The kitchen.

Slowly, she bent at the waist and lowered the books to the floor. Then she backed into the hall and hurried to escape . . . er . . . fetch the items. Grabbing up the entire basket, she thrust it over her arm and turned to face the hall.

You can do this, Joanna. Crockett needs you. You can be strong for him. Strong for Jackson.

Setting her shoulders, she marched on to the sickroom. Keeping her gaze averted from Jackson, she rounded the bed and placed the sewing basket on the dresser top.

"I have the needle and thread," she said, tugging a needle free from the pincushion. She always kept two or three of them threaded and ready to go for mending projects. She'd plucked out the one with black thread. Somehow it just seemed a sturdier color than white or blue.

"Soak it in the whiskey in the tray over there." Crockett didn't even look up. He didn't have to. His tone said everything for him—complete assurance that she would accomplish whatever he asked of her. "Then wash up yourself. You need to be clean before you handle any of the instruments."

She hadn't planned on staying long enough to handle any instruments. Surely her father could see to that task. He seemed recovered and back to his usual capable self. Joanna opened her mouth to say just that, then closed it. If Crockett had need of her, she'd stay.

The smell of the whiskey wrinkled her nose as she dropped the needle and thread into the shallow puddle on the tray. She couldn't decide if that smell was better or worse than the blood. Maybe if she kept her back turned, her stomach would stay where it belonged and not jump into her throat again.

Breathing more through her mouth than her nose, Joanna unbuttoned her cuffs and rolled her sleeves. She had just finished scrubbing to her elbows with the lye soap when Crockett's voice cut through the quiet.

"Hand me the tweezers. I can see the bullet, but I can't quite reach it." Crockett held his bloody hand out in expectation.

Joanna stared helplessly at the tweezer-less tray. "I . . . um . . . don't have any tweezers."

Crockett finally glanced her way, a frown scrunching his brow. His eyes raked the tray as if hoping she'd overlooked them. Not finding them, his scowl deepened. His gaze traveled over the entire dresser top, then narrowed in on her. All at once the lines cleared from his forehead.

"Towel off and bring me your hands. Your fingers should be slender enough."

"Slender enough for *what*?" But she knew the answer. She shook her head even as she reached for the towel. She stared at Jackson, at the hole in his flesh, at the blood. "I-I can't."

"Joanna." The firmness in Crockett's voice brooked no argument. She forced her eyes to meet his. "Come here." He spoke in the same authoritative tone he used from the pulpit, and before she consciously chose to obey, her feet carried her to his side.

"The more I cut, the more chance there is of damaging something that can't be repaired. The top of the bullet is exposed. All you have to do is pull it out." He circled his left arm around her, careful not to touch her clothing with his hand, and gently nudged her into position directly in front of him. He pressed close, his heat warming her back. Then his cheek came alongside hers, and he spoke directly into her ear. "You can do this, Joanna. I wouldn't ask it of you if I didn't believe you could do it."

She glanced across the bed to her father. He winked at her and nodded. "Easy as cleaning the innards from a chicken before throwing it in the pot."

The comparison was absurd, but somehow it grounded her.

If she could reach into a chicken to pull out its gizzard, surely she could pull out a bullet.

Only Jackson didn't look a thing like a chicken, and that tiny circle of lead Crockett was pointing out to her was no gizzard.

"As soon as we blot away the excess blood, reach for it." Giving her no time to formulate an adequate reason to delay, Crockett signaled her father with a nod of his head. "Silas."

The two of them patted the area with clean cotton, then held the wound open for her. Biting her tongue, Joanna reached for the bullet. The warm squish around her finger and thumb set her legs to trembling so fiercely, it was only by God's grace she stayed upright.

As if sensing her weakness, Crockett braced her with his own frame, surrounding her, steadying her.

Her fingertip brushed against something solid. Metal. So close. She just needed to get a grip on it. All thought of where her hand was faded away as she concentrated solely on retrieving the bullet. She burrowed deeper, twisting her wrist to get her thumb nearer the target.

She could feel it. Almost there. Just as her thumb and forefinger closed around it, it slipped away. A frustrated grunt echoed in her throat. If only she could push it toward her from the other side.

Well . . . why not? Joanna pulled her fingers out and reached around to press on Jackson's side, estimating where the exit wound would have been if his rib cage hadn't slowed the bullet's progress. Easing the fingers of her left hand into the wound, she searched again for the bullet. Once she could feel it, she experimented with different angles and pressures with her right hand until she found one that lifted the bullet ever so slightly. She reached with her fingers, praying the metal ball wouldn't slip away again.

Her thumb was too short, but she managed to trap the bullet

between her first two fingers. Holding her breath, she clasped the hunk of lead between her fingertips and slowly tugged it toward her. Movement! Ever so slight, but it definitely moved. She tugged again. Gently. Afraid the slightest jostle would steal it from her grasp. Again, it moved with her.

"I think I've got it," she whispered.

Crockett's arms seemed to firm around her, though in truth he barely touched her. He drew in breath as she did, their chests rising together.

Joanna maneuvered her thumb into the small opening and secured her grip on the piece of lead. She pulled her arm back, and the bullet finally slid free of Jackson's flesh.

Staring at the mangled lead between her fingers, not quite believing she'd really removed it, she dropped it into her palm and pivoted to face Crockett.

"It's out." A tremulous smile lifted the corners of her mouth.

Crockett's answering grin was tender yet beaming with satisfaction. "That it is." He lifted the bullet from her palm and bent his forehead close to hers. "I never doubted you." His lips brushed against her hair as he spoke, and his cheek rested against the top of her head for a single precious moment before he stepped aside.

"Why don't you get cleaned up while I finish things here." Crockett nodded toward her hands as he reached for the needle soaking on the tray.

Joanna glanced down at her bloodstained fingers and staggered a bit as light-headedness assailed her. Now that the bullet had been retrieved, her queasy stomach was back in full force. "I think I'll . . . um . . . wash up in the kitchen."

Holding her hands awkwardly in front of her, she circled the bed and headed for the door. Before she reached it, her father's voice stopped her.

"You did good, Jo." His eyes glowed, and Joanna stood a

little taller. Her stomach settled a bit, and her head no longer felt as if it were going to roll off her shoulders.

All her life she'd strived to please him, whether it was with her riding skills, her painting, or even just the way she cooked his beefsteak. Never a great dispenser of flattery, her father rarely spoke his approval aloud. Yet when he did, she treasured the words as if they'd been crafted from the finest silver.

Not trusting her voice, Joanna simply nodded in response and exited.

It didn't take long to wash up, yet even after cleaning away Jackson's blood, her hands continued to shake, causing her fingers to fumble with the button at her cuff.

Maybe tea would help. Joanna refilled the empty kettle, set it over the hottest part of the stove, and dug in the cabinet for her tea tin. She grabbed the coffee, too, thinking of the men. As she worked the handle on the grinder, her mind returned to Jackson. So pale. So still. So young. Too young.

"Please, Lord," she whispered under her breath. "Please bring him through this."

Once her tea had steeped, she poured a cupful and stirred in a teaspoon of honey, hoping the sweetness would serve as an extra balm to her ragged emotions. She sat at the table, circled her fingers around the heated cup, and blew gently across the brew's surface. Inhaling the flavorful steam, she closed her eyes and let her head loll forward. The tension she'd carried in her neck for the last hour finally loosened.

"Is that coffee I smell?"

Joanna jerked her head up to find Crockett approaching the table.

"Yes," she answered, scrambling to her feet. "Sit down. I'll pour you a cup." Joanna grabbed a towel to protect her hand, then lifted the coffeepot from the back of the stove and filled a mug. She turned to place it on the table in front of his usual place, but he wasn't sitting at the table. He was standing two feet from her, his eyes drinking her in as if he needed her more than any hot beverage.

Crockett Archer was the strongest, most capable man she'd ever met. Never once had he projected anything less than confidence as he dealt with Jackson's injury—with her father, as well. She was no fool. Something had happened between the two men while she'd been gone. Something that had restored her father's wilted spirit.

Yet as Crockett stood before her, she saw the toll it all had taken. The weariness etched into his forehead, the vulnerability in his eyes.

Without a word, she set the ceramic mug on the table, then stepped up to Crockett and wrapped her arms around him. She held him fast, laying her head upon his chest and squeezing him close, her only thought to give him the comfort he so readily gave others.

He stiffened at first, then with a strangled sound that could have been a swallowed sob, he clutched her to himself and buried his face in her hair.

Tremors coursed through him. Joanna gathered him closer, as if she could protect him from the storm running its course. After a long moment, the tremors subsided and his hold on her changed. His grip loosened slightly, allowing his hands to roam her back. One traced the line of her spine up to her nape, the light touch of his fingers bringing on another case of light-headedness.

The softness of his lips pressed into her scalp, and his warm breath fanned across the edge of her brow. "I love you, Joanna Robbins."

Everything inside her froze for a single moment, only to be followed by a deluge of reactions that nearly buckled her knees. Her heart pounded. Her stomach danced. And her mind swirled so fast, she could barely keep a grip on the words she thought she'd heard.

Tilting her face up, she searched Crockett's face for the truth she so desperately wanted to believe. She found no teasing smile, no laughing eyes. Only an intensity that stole her breath.

"I love you, Jo."

Then his lips were bending to hers, and all thought scattered. She stretched up to meet him, thrilling at the way his arms tightened around her. His mouth was soft, insistent. A little bit desperate yet achingly gentle. Joanna melted into him, tasting the promise in his kiss. The hope.

She wanted to linger, to savor, to stretch the kiss into forever. But they weren't alone. Her father could come in at any moment. And Jackson . . . Well, Jackson should be their focus now.

Slowly she pulled away. The hand Crockett held at her nape slipped around to cup her cheek, and for a moment she didn't think he would let her go. But then he seemed to remember their circumstances, as well, and lifted his head.

Her breathing ragged, she looked up into the deep brown eyes she loved so well. With a hand that was none too steady, she reached up and combed a bit of his unruly hair off his forehead. Then, as if her fingers were one of her paintbrushes, she stroked the lines of his face, tracing his eyebrows, his cheek, his jaw.

Suddenly shy, she dropped her gaze. Her hand followed, coming to rest against his chest, the beat of his heart thudding against her palm.

"You're a dream for me, Crockett," she whispered. "A dream I never imagined would come true. I love you so much my heart aches with it."

His arms encircled her again, drawing her firmly against him. She laid her head in the hollow beneath his shoulder, her arms wrapping around his waist.

Neither spoke. They simply absorbed strength and comfort

from one another, silently rejoicing in the precious gift they'd found.

But they couldn't stay as they were forever, not with all that was going on around them. So after lingering as long as her conscience would allow, Joanna eased away from Crockett's hold.

"How's Jackson?" she asked in a soft voice, reluctant to completely break the spell that had been woven over the two of them. "Do you think he'll recover?"

Crockett cleared his throat as he stepped away. He bent to pick up the forgotten mug of coffee, then took a sip before answering.

"I'll feel better after the doctor examines him," he said, finally meeting her eye. "But yes, I think he'll recover. The bullet didn't strike any vital organs as far as I could tell." He paused for another sip. "There's always a danger of infection, though."

"Maybe when his father comes to collect him, I should try to convince him to leave Jackson here so I can tend him. Sam Spivey's not the most dependable sort."

Crockett dipped his chin in agreement. "If he does take the boy home, it might be a good idea for one or both of us to make periodic visits."

"I'm sure Mr. Spivey would welcome a meal or two if I was to come by. I could make some broth for Jackson and leave his father a heartier soup."

"That's a good plan." He winked at her, and her heart turned a flip. It was such a little thing, yet his approval warmed her inside and out.

Silence crept back into the kitchen, but it was a comfortable one. One that allowed Joanna's thoughts to flow from one to the next unheeded.

"Is Daddy sitting with Jackson?" She traced the edge of the table with her finger as she moved toward the stove. "I should probably take him some coffee." She reached for another mug and filled it with fragrant brew.

Hesitating at the edge of the table, she turned back to Crockett. "How's he doing? He looked more like his old self when I came back from your place, but I know he still feels responsible."

"If you ask me," Crockett said, a slight smile touching his lips, "he looks more like his new self than his old one."

Joanna's brow furrowed. "His new self? I don't understand."

"He's praying, Jo." Crockett reached out and clasped her hand. "Truly praying. I think for the first time in forty years, he's letting go of the past and opening himself to the Lord."

Her knees did buckle then. She thunked the coffee mug she held onto the table—not caring about the liquid that sloshed over the brim—and all but fell into the nearest chair. Her vision blurred as tears pooled in her eyes and rolled down her cheeks.

Crockett moved behind her, his hands massaging her shoulders. "Those seeds you and your mother planted are coming to fruition, Jo. He's finally stopped running."

Joanna leaned her head back against Crockett, her mind too overwhelmed to pray anything more than *Thank you.*

33

Crockett clasped Jackson's good arm above the elbow and levered him to a sitting position. It'd only been four days since the accident, but the boy was already itching to return to his free-spirited ways.

"Easy does it," Crockett cautioned as Jackson tried to stand on his own. "Let me help you." He adjusted his hold, moving his hand to grip the boy's upper arm.

"Aww, come on, Crock. Quit treating me like an old woman." He tugged his arm free and staggered a bit at the sudden loss of support. "The doc came by yesterday and said I was mendin' just fine. I ain't got a fever no more, and so long as I wear this stupid sling, I can go about my business."

"Within reason." Crockett raised a brow until Jackson squirmed sufficiently to let him know he'd caught the message. "If you try to do too much too soon, it could set you back."

"Yes, *Ma*." Jackson rolled his eyes.

Crockett chuckled and gently ruffled his hair. "You're a mess, kid." But he was improving, praise God. This was the second day he'd been out of bed, and he seemed stronger.

Jackson made his way gingerly across the one-room Spivey cabin and lowered himself into a chair at the rickety table in the corner by the stove. He reached for the towel-covered plate Crockett had brought.

"What'd she make this time?" He peeked beneath the cloth. "Mmm. Oatmeal cookies." He grabbed one and shoved it into his mouth. "I should get shot more often," he said around a mouthful of cookie, "if it means Jo will keep sending me treats."

"It might be less painful if you just stopped by the house every once in a while." Crockett winked, and Jackson, cheeks bulging, grinned.

Helping himself to a cookie as he joined Jackson at the table, Crockett took a bite, then surreptitiously surveyed the cabin. Cooking wasn't all Jo had done. The cabin glowed with a cleanliness that must have taken her hours to accomplish, even with the room's small size. The walls looked as if they might crumple like a pile of sticks if the wind blew too hard, and the furniture was a broken, mismatched mess, but there wasn't a speck of dirt to be found.

He frowned as he surveyed the cot Sam Spivey used. Apparently dirt wasn't the only thing scarce around here.

"Your father's saddlebags are gone." Crockett strove to keep his voice free of condemnation. "He light out again?"

"Yeah, well . . ." Jackson shrugged, the reddish tinge creeping up his cheeks belying his air of nonchalance. "Three days is about his limit, you know. And with the doc's good report, he figured I'd be all right. Said he had a job lined up with one of the ranchers closer to Deanville and was worried the man would give it to someone else if he didn't show up soon." He jutted his chin forward as he grabbed another cookie from the plate. "All his hoverin' was driving me batty, anyway. We're both better alone."

Crockett met Jackson's skittery gaze and waited for the boy's attention to settle. "You're not alone."

Jackson swallowed the bite he'd been chewing. "I know."

A confirming silence passed between them before Crockett pushed to his feet. "Why don't you let me take you back to the Lazy R? If nothing else it would save Joanna from having to drag food over here twice a day."

"Nah. Tell Jo I got enough to tide me over for a while. Pa laid in supplies before he left. She don't have to keep coming."

"She will anyway. You know how she is."

"Yeah. But a man don't want his lady to see him weak. If I were to stay there, she'd probably coddle me like some kind of baby or something." His face screwed into a comically disgusted expression.

At his words, though, memories assailed Crockett of the way Joanna had held him after he'd emerged from Jackson's sickroom. She seen him at his weakest, yet instead of diminishing him, the sharing of the burden made him stronger. Her love made him stronger.

Jackson's heavy sigh from across the table pulled Crockett from his thoughts. "You're gonna marry her, aren't ya?"

A pinprick of guilt poked Crockett's conscience for depriving the boy of his infatuation. Nevertheless, he straightened in his seat and nodded once. "Yes."

"Figures." Jackson leaned back in his chair. "Well, if I had to lose her to somebody, I'm glad it's you."

"No hard feelings?"

The boy looked more resigned than pained, but Jackson was good at putting up fronts, so it was hard to tell.

Jackson sat a little straighter, his demeanor changing from boy to man as he eyed Crockett with surprising maturity. "If I didn't think you'd be good for her, I'd fight you for her. But I trust you, Crock. I been around you enough to know that you don't just spout nice words from the pulpit—you live 'em. She'll be in good hands."

For once, Crockett had no words at the ready. Humbled by the boy's faith, all he could manage was a gravelly "Thanks."

"'Course, you still gotta get through Silas." The smile that twisted Jackson's face made it clear he wouldn't mind witnessing his friend endure a little fatherly torture.

And Crockett fully expected to suffer some. Silas might have opened up to him in a moment of weakness after Jackson's injury, and he might have even worked through some of his issues with preachers, but the man was still an ornery cuss who wouldn't give away his precious daughter without demanding his pound of flesh. Crockett hid a grin behind his hand. He actually looked forward to the challenge.

"Well, anything worth having is worth working for, right?" He winked at Jackson.

"Yep." Jackson grabbed the towel that had guarded the cookies and wadded it in his good hand. "Don't worry." He launched the towel at Crockett's head. "I'll put in a good word for you. Silas promised to bring his checkerboard over tomorrow to entertain me while you and Jo are off at church."

Crockett hid his disappointment. He'd hoped Silas would attend services. According to Joanna, he'd been reading her mother's Bible the last few evenings and even asked a question or two. But Silas was a man used to making his own way—a leader, not a follower. Nagging him about attending church would only create friction. The man needed to come to his own conclusions and decide for himself whom he would serve. Like Joshua, all Crockett could do was offer the invitation and proclaim his own allegiance through his words and deeds. It was up to Silas to do the rest.

"You think you can manage to ring the bell without me?" Jackson interjected into the silence.

Crockett shook off his ponderings and smiled. He snagged the towel from where it had fallen across his shoulder and tossed it back at Jackson's face. "Maybe. But just this once." He crossed his arms over his chest and spoke with his best mock-lecture tone. "You don't need two arms to pull the bell rope, you know. I fully expect you to be back at work next Sunday. No more lazing about, you hear?"

Jackson chuckled. "You got it."

As it turned out, Crockett missed Jackson for more than his bell ringing skills the next day. With the boy at home, Crockett had no one to run interference for him when it came to dodging Holly Brewster. The gal seemed to be constantly circling like some kind of hungry buzzard, swooping in every chance she got to pick at his flesh. She arrived early and offered to ring the bell in Jackson's place. Yet when he unhooked the rope for her, all she did was bat her eyelashes and plead with him to help her.

What if the rope slipped through her fingers? What if she did it wrong? Wouldn't it be better for him to hold the rope, too? Preferably by holding her in the process.

She hadn't said that last part aloud, but it projected through the sultry glances she kept aiming in his direction. He'd finally instructed her to yank on the rope however she liked, then left her to her own devices and strode away to the podium to review the sermon notes he'd finished reviewing not five minutes before.

Thankfully, Joanna arrived soon after, saving him from Holly's more blatant machinations. But all through the service, Miss Brewster continued her subtle attack. She sang a touch too loudly from the pew behind his, ensuring he heard her voice above any other. He strained to hear Joanna's gentle lilting from across the aisle, but Holly's brassy tones drowned her out.

During the sermon, Holly stared at him with a far-too-enraptured expression. As much as he would've liked to believe that his message could hold her so in thrall, not even his pride could swallow that much rot. Then she started toying with the buttons on the bodice of her dress, and that's when he gave up all pretense of acting as if he didn't notice her. He locked his focus on the left side of the congregation from that moment on and never veered to the right again.

Her brazenness had gone too far. It was no longer just a matter of his being uncomfortable with her forward manner; it had progressed to the point where he worried about moral implications. He couldn't simply strive to avoid her. He needed to confront her. Not only as a man who wished to discourage her interest but also as a minister who needed to caution her about the slippery path she was walking.

But he hated confrontation. Growing up, he'd been the keeper of the peace in the Archer household. If Travis got too uptight, Crockett would tease him into a better frame of mind. If Jim wanted to pound Neill into a pulp for ruining his stew, Crockett intervened with a funny anecdote to diffuse the tension. He was an expert at charming people back onto the honorable path. Unfortunately, charm wouldn't work with Holly. It would only inflame the problem.

So he had no choice. He had to confront her directly. Which meant he'd have to hurt her, because the truth was not what she wanted to hear.

Is there any other way, Lord? Couldn't you just change her heart? I have little experience in talking to women. I'm bound to muck this up.

No peace came with the prayer. Only a recollection of a verse from James. *"He which converteth the sinner from the error of his way shall save a soul from death, and shall hide a multitude of sins."*

Apparently, he couldn't charm God, either.

As Crockett stood at the rear of the church, shaking the hands of departing members, he forced himself to smile and make polite conversation despite the sick mound of dread swelling in his stomach. A confrontation with Holly was sure to be awkward, possibly even volatile. But he'd been called to minister to all the members of his flock, not just the easy ones.

So when Holly and her mother made their way toward him, he steeled himself for what needed to be done.

"Another wonderful sermon, Brother Archer," Sarah Brewster gushed. "As always." She tittered like a young girl as she held her hand out to him. "Won't you come for lunch? I'm frying chicken, and Holly baked a wild blackberry cobbler that will melt in your mouth."

"It sounds wonderful, ma'am," Crockett said as he clasped her hand, "but I'm afraid I'm already promised elsewhere today."

"At the Lazy R?" Holly interjected, her lips puffed into a pretty pout. "Pish. You eat there all the time. I'm sure Joanna wouldn't mind sharing you."

Actually, he figured she'd probably mind quite a bit.

The possessive thought cheered him considerably. "I'm sorry, ladies. I've given my word. However . . ." He drew the word out to keep Holly from arguing further, then turned his attention to her mother. "I would like to ask your permission to call on Holly tomorrow evening. Perhaps around seven? There is a matter of some urgency I need to discuss with her."

He'd tried to make it clear that his visit would not be a courting call by his last remark, but judging by the way Holly's pout disappeared beneath the onslaught of a beaming smile, she hadn't caught on.

Pressing the issue with so many parishioners within hearing distance didn't seem wise, and he supposed she'd understand soon enough, so he held his tongue.

Mrs. Brewster squeezed his hand and nearly bounced in her delight. "Of course you can pay a call, Parson. We'll be sure to hold back a serving of cobbler for you."

"Thank you, ma'am."

She finally released his hand and grabbed hold of her daughter. "Come along, Holly. Let the man get to his lunch. You'll see him tomorrow."

Holly captured his hand despite the fact that he hadn't extended it to her. "I'll be looking forward to it."

He wished he could say the same.

34

The following afternoon, Joanna steered her wagon through the Lazy R gate after a visit with Jackson and spotted Crockett striding out of the barn to meet her. He halted by the edge of the building and rubbed a bandana over the back of his neck before stuffing the blue cloth back into his pocket. He stood so tall; his long legs braced apart, the fabric of his shirt outlining the breadth of his shoulders and arms. Her heart fluttered as she rambled closer.

This man loved her. This strong, handsome, godly man truly loved her. It didn't seem possible.

She bit her lip, yet her mouth stretched into a wide grin anyway when he raised his hand in greeting. Joanna returned the gesture, keeping one hand on the reins as the team plodded toward the barn.

"How's Jackson today?" Crockett's eyes danced as he waited for her to set the brake.

Joanna wrapped the harness straps around the brake lever and bent to retrieve the food basket from the floorboards. "Oh, as ornery as ever," she said as she gathered her skirts to one side. "He was outside trying to chop wood one-handed when I got there."

Crockett's warm hands circled her waist as he lifted her from the wagon, and they lingered even after her feet were solidly aground.

"I chopped a pile for him two days ago." One of his brows arched, nearly disappearing beneath the rim of his hat. "Surely the kid hasn't depleted it already. Especially with you doing all the cooking."

"The woodpile was still stacked high in the shed. I think he was trying to prove something to himself," Joanna said, finding it hard to concentrate on the conversation with Crockett's fingers stroking her sleeves. "I don't mind him testing his capabilities; I just wish he wouldn't use such sharp implements until he's sure of what those capabilities are."

His fingertips had worked their way up to her shoulders and she abandoned all hope of coherent thought and leaned into the caress. His thumb brushed the edge of her jaw, and her eyes slid closed. The feel of his breath on her face was the only warning she received before his lips met hers.

Joanna reached up to stroke his cheek. Crockett tugged her closer and began to deepen the kiss, then suddenly drew back.

"Sorry." His voice shook a little, then turned into a soft chuckle. "I hadn't intended to do that when I came to help you down."

Joanna lowered her lashes, not quite able to meet his gaze after the sweetness of the kiss. "I didn't mind."

He laughed outright. "Heavens, Jo. That's not the thing to say to a man when he's battling to hang onto his self-control and good intentions." His words were lighthearted, but she didn't miss the way he stepped back and released his hold on her.

Did she really tempt his self-control? Red hair, freckles, and all? If she'd ever needed proof that he really loved her, he'd just given it to her.

"You're a good man, Crockett Archer. I trust you."

"That's good, because I need to tell you something you're not going to like."

She frowned at the change that came over his features. Gone was the teasing suitor. Like a storm cloud blowing in to cover the sun, Crockett's eyes darkened with a seriousness that immediately set her on edge.

"The horses will be all right for a minute," he said, relieving her of the basket and taking her arm. "Let's go sit on the porch."

She didn't want to sit on the porch. She wanted him to spit out the bad news. He wasn't leaving, was he? If he was, would he take her with him? And what about her father? They'd been making such progress. And Jackson. He would be devastated.

By the time Crockett led her up the porch steps and into one of the rockers, Joanna felt as brittle as a week-old cookie, ready to crumble at the slightest tap.

"What is it?" She scooted to the edge of the seat and braced her feet against the porch floor to keep the chair from rocking. Her neck craned up to gauge Crockett's expression, and her gaze followed him as he took the seat next to hers. The chair creaked as it accepted his weight, and Joanna feared she might scream right along with it if the man didn't hurry up and end her suspense.

Finally he turned. He ran his palms down his pant legs and took a breath before looking up to meet her eyes. "I'm paying a call on Holly Brewster tonight after supper."

Joanna frowned and blinked several times. Did that mean he wasn't leaving? Relief whooshed the air from her lungs until the rest of the message sank into her brain. "Why are you going to see Holly?"

She fought to control the alarm rising in her breast. Just

because he was going to see Holly didn't mean he had feelings for her. He couldn't and still kiss her the way he had down by the wagon, right? "Are the two of you planning another church picnic?"

A picnic. That's probably all it was. Holly always loved to be at the center of any event, and she *had* done a decent job with organizing the last one—even if she did stick Joanna with babysitting duty to keep her away from Crockett.

"No. We're not planning another picnic."

Not a picnic? Then what was he going there for? "Is she . . . uh . . . ill?"

She'd looked fine at church yesterday. Better than fine, actually. The lavender dress she'd worn had shown off every one of her feminine curves to perfection, and her pretty blond hair had practically shimmered beneath her stylish matching bonnet. She'd seemed in disgustingly good health.

"No, she's not ill, either. I'm going to talk to her about a personal matter that I'm worried might soon have some serious spiritual implications." The corners of his mouth pinched, and lines appeared on his forehead. This wasn't a call he was looking forward to making.

Somehow that made everything better.

He ran a hand over his face but didn't quite manage to erase his grimace. "I'm afraid I can't give you any specifics since it's a private matter. However, I didn't want to keep my visit a secret from you. After Holly twisted events at the picnic to make you think something happened that actually didn't, I worried that something similar might happen with this situation." He bridged the space between them, covering her left hand with his right. "I love you, Joanna. I don't want you to doubt that for a moment. No matter what anyone says."

The fact that he knew her well enough to recognize her weaknesses and cared enough to help her fortify them spoke volumes. "Thank you for telling me. Is there anything I can do to help?"

"Pray." Crockett's eyes bored into hers. "Pray for the Spirit to provide me with the right words. And for Miss Brewster's heart to be receptive."

"I will," she vowed, and started that very moment.

Lord, I don't know what has happened or what the ramifications are, but I ask that you guide Crockett tonight. Give him the words you wish him to say and the courage to say them. May they find fertile ground in Holly's heart.

Crockett must have been praying, too, for though his eyes were open they lacked focus. Not wanting to disturb him, Joanna simply held his hand and silently repeated parts of her own prayer until the sound of an approaching horse brought her head around.

A single rider trotted down the drive. From a distance, Joanna recognized neither the mount nor the man, but as the rider neared the porch, an awful tightening wound about her chest. Surely not . . .

Crockett slipped his hand from hers and pushed to his feet, sending his rocker into a gentle creaking motion. "Marshal Coleson. What brings you out to the Lazy R?" He stepped to the edge of the porch and leaned against the support beam. Tipping his hat back, he grinned a welcome that set Joanna's teeth to grinding.

"Came to see Mr. Robbins. He around?"

Joanna's hands fisted in the fabric of her skirt. What did the lawman want with her father? Had he figured out who Silas Robbins used to be? Or had this visit been prompted by something else? She'd been uneasy about the marshal ever since that odd exchange between him and Crockett at Miss Bessie's place, and now he was here. At the Lazy R.

Crockett glanced up at the sky, then back at Coleson. "Silas and Jasper are checking on one of the heifers out in the eastern pasture. She's fixin' to drop a calf."

Saddle leather groaned as the marshal brought his mount to a halt and crossed his wrists over the horn. "Mind fetching him for me?"

"I'll go." Joanna sprang from her chair, her mind racing. She could warn him. Maybe even take him some food if he decided to run. There was cheese in the kitchen. And apples. She could pack the bread she'd baked this morning, too. She could have it together before the marshal even dismounted. All she had to do—

"If it's all the same to you, miss, I'd prefer the parson fetch him."

She swallowed nervously, looking from Coleson to the barn and back again. She couldn't just stand by and let this man take her daddy away. He'd changed. He was a good man. A good father.

"Joanna." Crockett's voice echoed quietly in her ears. He was facing her now, his hands massaging her rigid shoulders. "It will be all right. Do you hear me? God is in control. It will be all right."

She dragged her attention from the lawman and found Crockett's face. He smiled. She latched onto that smile, desperate for a taste of the peace it offered.

"We don't even know why the marshal's here." He brushed a stray curl off her forehead and back over her ear. "Just invite him in and give him some of that great coffee you make. Treat him like any other guest."

But he wasn't any other guest. He was a lawman. A lawman who wanted to talk with her father. She didn't want to pour him coffee, she wanted to send him packing.

Yet a more rational part of her brain had her nodding agreement.

"That's my girl." Crockett started to pull away. Joanna grabbed his hand.

"Promise you won't leave for Holly's until we work whatever this is out. Please?" If he left, she'd shatter.

Crockett, his hand still trapped in her death grip, raised her hand to his lips and kissed her whitened knuckles. "I promise. You're my top priority, Joanna. Everything else but God comes second."

Finally, she let him go, clinging now to his vow instead of his hand. The marshal dipped his chin to Crockett when he strode past, then touched the brim of his hat in a salute to her.

"If you don't mind, miss, I'll water my horse."

She forced a smile to her lips, hoping it didn't look as quivery as it felt. "Of course, Marshal. Help yourself."

"I'll see to your team, as well." He dismounted and took hold of his horse's bridle. "It's only right since I'm the reason Archer won't be around to do it." He turned and led his horse toward the corral trough.

"Thank you." The words fell automatically from her lips as she watched him go. Then she remembered Crockett's instructions and called after him. "Come up to the house and get some coffee when you're finished. I'll make a fresh pot."

"I'll do that, miss. Thanks."

As Joanna walked into the kitchen and set about tossing out the old coffee and making up new, she couldn't shake the feeling that she'd just invited Disaster to dinner.

Silas reined in Marauder and stared down at the roof of the ranch house. He'd always enjoyed the view from this small rise. Many a time he'd ridden in from a long day on the range only to pause at this spot and absorb the vision of home. Martha had always seemed to know when he was there. Maybe she watched for him; maybe she just sensed his nearness. Either way, she'd usually come out into the yard and wave.

Man, how he missed those waves.

I got the law waitin' on me, Martha. Waiting in our home. At our table. There ain't no runnin' this time.

He closed his eyes and tried to visualize his wife, but her face didn't appear. His gut clenched. Martha had always been his rock. His support. His conscience. Even after her death. She couldn't abandon him now. Not when he needed her most.

"'Fear thou not; for I am with thee.'"

Silas swiveled and stared at the man behind him. Archer sat peacefully atop his mount, not even looking in Silas's direction, just spoutin' verses into the wind.

"'Be not dismayed; for I am thy God: I will strengthen thee;

yea, I will help thee; yea, I will uphold thee with the right hand of my righteousness.'" Finally Archer turned to look at him, and his gaze seemed to penetrate to the very marrow of his bones. "Whatever happens, Si, God is with you. Lean on his strength, and you'll get through."

Then the parson nudged his horse and headed down the rise.

Silas watched him go, a prickle in his chest. What if *gettin' through* meant enduring a prison term? He'd been reading about that Paul feller, the one Jo told him had written so many of them church letters. Seemed he wrote most of 'em from jail. Not exactly the way Silas wanted to spend his twilight years. But what if that's what God had in mind for him? Heaven knew he deserved it.

"I can't say as I trust where you're leadin'," Silas said, squinting up at the clouds as Marauder pranced beneath him, eager to follow Archer's mount, "but I gave my word to stop running, and that's what I aim to do. If you're . . . uh . . . of a mind to send some of that help the preacher was yammerin' about, I'd not turn my nose up at it. . . . Just so you know."

The clouds offered no reply, so Silas gave Marauder his head and plunged over the rise.

The marshal stood waiting on the porch, hip cocked against the rail, coffee cup in hand.

Silas scowled. The man looked downright comfortable.

"I hear you're lookin' for me," Silas said, swinging his leg over Marauder's back. Archer appeared at the horse's head and led the beast away, giving Silas an unobstructed view of the lawman trespassin' on his porch.

"Need to ask you a few questions, if you don't mind."

Silas got the distinct impression it wouldn't matter if he minded or not. The man's casual pose failed to soften the steel in his eyes.

"I reckon I can spare the time to answer a few." Silas climbed the porch steps and eyed the marshal from head to toe, taking in the gun slung low on his hip, the badge pinned to his vest, and the hard lines of everything in between.

The lawman straightened to his full height and met Silas's stare with one of his own.

Silas deliberately turned his back and stepped to the door. Pulling it wide, he waved the marshal ahead of him into the house. "I hear you're an ex-Ranger. That true?"

The man paused halfway over the threshold. "I hear you're an ex-outlaw. *That* true?"

Years of living by his wits kept Silas's expression bland as milk toast. "Marshal, if that's the kind of question you plan on askin', this is gonna be a real short visit."

"We'll see." The marshal held his gaze for a long moment before continuing into the kitchen.

Yep. He'd been a Ranger all right. Silas could see it in his eyes. Jasper had suspected as much, even warned Silas about him five years ago, when Coleson had taken over as town marshal.

Now that he'd stared the man down, though, an eerie feeling of destiny crawled up Silas's spine. Coleson knew who he was.

"Daddy?" Joanna's blue eyes rounded with concern as she skirted the kitchen table and hurried toward him.

Something caught in his throat when he thought about the possibility of being dragged off in front of his little girl—of never seeing her again. He opened his right arm and pulled her into a half hug.

"Everything's all right, Jo." His voice sounded like gravel under a wagon wheel, but she burrowed closer anyway. He patted her shoulder once and dropped a quick kiss against her forehead, turning slightly so the marshal wouldn't catch the gesture, and stepped away. "Ya got some of that brew for your old man?"

She nodded, blinking the moisture from her eyes. Then she stiffened her spine, lifted her chin, and marched past Coleson as if he were nothing more than a new piece of furniture in the room.

Pride in his Jo would have brought a smile to Silas's face if he hadn't been so determined to keep his features schooled. Couldn't give Coleson even the smallest advantage.

"There a place we can talk, Robbins?" The lawman barely waited long enough for Jo to put the mug in his hand before starting in.

"Here's as good a place as any." Silas deliberately moved to the head of the table and took a seat. "Pull up a chair, Marshal."

Coleson glanced meaningfully at Jo. "You sure you want your daughter hearin' all I got to say?"

Jo scraped chair legs against the floor and plopped into the seat to Silas's right. "I'm staying."

Silas's mouth curved a tad at the corners. Family stood by family.

The marshal shrugged and chose a chair near the stove, probably so he could keep an eye on the door. "Suit yourself."

Coleson set aside his coffee and pushed his hat brim up onto the high part of his forehead with a bent knuckle. His focus never wavered from Silas's face. "I understand there was a shooting here a few days ago."

Somehow Silas managed not to flinch. *That* was what this was about?

"Yep. Hunting accident." He paused to take a sip of coffee. "Scared the beans right outta me when I saw Jackson go down."

Coleson's eyes widened a bit at his ready answer. Silas stifled a grin. Nothing like knocking a lawman off his high horse with a little straight shootin'. They never expected it.

"Sam Spivey claims you're the man who shot his son."

The accusation jabbed him right in the sore spot of his heart. Silas winced and dropped his chin. "It's true." Regret clogged his voice. He coughed a bit to clear it. "I wish it weren't."

Triumph flashed in Coleson's eyes. "So you admit to back-shooting the boy in cold blood."

"Now hold on a cotton-pickin' minute, Marshal. I ain't no back-shooter!" Silas slapped the flat of his hand against the table with a loud crash. If Coleson thought he could twist a horrible accident around into a hangin' offense, this friendly chat was gonna end up with Silas introducing the business end of his boot to the lawman's backside.

"Doc Granger confirmed that the bullet entered the boy from behind." Coleson narrowed his eyes. "You saying the doc's wrong?"

"You're making it sound like my father shot Jackson on purpose!" Jo sprang to her feet, her voice quivering. "It was an accident. Daddy was aiming at a buck and had no idea Jackson was even there until after he pulled the trigger."

Coleson raised an eyebrow at her. "Were you there, miss?"

"No, but Crockett told me—"

"If you didn't witness the shooting yourself," the marshal interrupted, "then I'll thank you to refrain from spoutin' opinions and hearsay. I'm interested only in facts."

"If you're truly interested in facts, Marshal," a deep voice echoed from the doorway, "perhaps you should interview the only other person who was there at the time of the shooting."

Archer.

Silas never thought he'd actually be glad to have the man around, but when the parson crossed the room to stand directly behind Jo and placed his hands on her shoulders in a show of support and protection, an odd sense of relief washed over him. If this sorry excuse for a lawman managed to drag him out of here, Archer would take care of his little girl.

"Jackson's recovering quite nicely thanks to Silas's quick actions in the field as well as his assistance with the surgery." Archer's usually polite tone carried an undercurrent of iron as he addressed the marshal. "I'm sure the boy would be happy to answer your questions with all the facts you need. I could even escort you to the Spivey place myself, if you'd like."

"Thank you, Parson. But I prefer to interview the boy without anyone around who might feel obliged to influence his testimony."

Silas grunted. "You interested in finding the *truth*, Marshal? Or you just lookin' for someone to confirm the assumptions you already made?"

"Usually my assumptions aren't too far off, Robbins. Lucky for you, though, this badge keeps me from acting on them without proof." He slowly unfolded his lean frame from the chair and rose to his full height. "I was planning on payin' Jackson a visit anyway. His pa asked me to look in on the boy—maybe even stay a night or two. So you can count on me takin' my time gettin' to the bottom of this. I intend to be real thorough."

His hard expression lent credibility to his threat, but Silas stared right back, refusing to be intimidated. Finally the marshal turned away. He found a smile somewhere behind that iron wall of his and tipped his hat to Jo. "Thanks for the coffee, miss." He lifted his gaze to Archer next. "Parson," he said, and then ambled to the door.

"I'll see you out, Marshal." Jo followed the man to the porch and accompanied him across the yard, all those manners her mother had drummed into her coming into play.

Keeping his eye on Jo and the marshal through the open door, Silas got down to business, not knowing how much time he'd have.

"I've seen the way you look at my daughter, Archer." The words came out as much of an accusation as any of the statements Coleson had unleashed. "You intend to do right by her?"

"I do." The parson came up alongside him, his focus, too,

on the redheaded angel beside the barn. "I aim to make her my wife if you'll give us your blessing."

"Swear to me you'll look after her if this mess goes south."

"You have my word." Archer's voice rang with conviction, and the pressure gripping Silas's chest eased slightly. "She's my heart, Silas. I'd give my life for her."

Silas nodded and extended his hand toward the preacher. Neither of them looked the other in the face, but as Archer's hand moved to clasp his, understanding passed between them.

The pact had been sealed.

36

Supper at the Lazy R that evening was a somber affair. Brett Coleson's earlier presence lingered over the room like a burial shroud. The ranch hands picked at Joanna's baked beans instead of wolfing them down with their usual gusto and even failed to finish off the corn bread she'd browned to perfection. Not that she'd noticed.

Crockett eyed Joanna from across the table. Spoon tipped downward, she listlessly dragged a bean from the edge of her dish to the pile in the center, the same way he would've driven a stray calf back into the herd. The comparison tempted him to smile, but the fact that he couldn't recall any of the little critters on her plate, stray or otherwise, actually making their way to her mouth stole his frivolity.

"Well, aren't we a bunch of sorry hangdogs?" Silas scraped his chair back, yanked his napkin from his shirt collar, and chucked it onto the table. "Enough of this moping. Frank. Carl. You boys have saddles to oil and harnesses to mend. Get to it. Jasper, meet me in the barn. We need to talk about Henderson's bull and start makin' plans.

"Archer?"

Crockett met his employer's gaze while the men around him shuffled to fulfill their assigned tasks.

"Don't be late for your appointment." Silas glanced briefly at Joanna and then back at Crockett before pivoting away and striding for the door.

"Your appointment?" Joanna paused in the middle of collecting the dirty dishes from the table. "Oh, that's right." Crockett hadn't thought it possible for her eyes to dim any further. He'd been wrong. "I had forgotten about Holly."

He wished he could forget about her, too. All he wanted was to hold Jo in his arms and lay tiny kisses on her head until she smiled again.

Crockett moved to her side and took the stack of plates from her hands. "I don't have to go just yet," he said, setting the dishes on the table and tipping her face up with the crook of his finger. "Come sit with me in the parlor for a minute?"

She responded with only a nod. Crockett slid his palm into the slight indention of her back and gently guided her toward the sitting room. He led her to the small sofa and took a seat beside her.

"It's going to be all right, Jo." He cradled her hand in his. "Who knows? This trial might be just what your father needs to solidify his faith."

"But it's so new to him!" Her fingers dug into the flesh of his hand with almost painful force. "What if he sees this as proof that God doesn't care about him? He rejected God for so long. What if this gives him the excuse to revert back?"

"What if God delivers him and thereby reveals his mercy?" Crockett stroked his knuckles along her cheek, needing to touch her, to soothe her. "Or what if Silas needs adversity to grow? He started out as an orphan without a penny to his name, and now he's an established rancher supporting four men and a beautiful daughter. Who's to say his spiritual maturity won't be forged in the same fashion? We can't know what is best for him. Only God knows. What we *can* do is stand by him, support him, and love him through it all."

An unexpected lump suddenly lodged in Crockett's throat. That's what he wanted to do for Joanna. Stand by her. Support her. Love her with every fiber of his being. Forever.

He gazed into his love's sweet face and knew. Now was the time. She was nodding and saying something about needing to trust God more, but in all honesty he could barely hear her over the thudding of his heart and the urgent demand ringing in his mind.

"Jo, I . . . er . . ." He stumbled. He *never* stumbled over his words. Never. Yet his tongue seemed to have swollen to twice its normal size in the time it took him to suck in a single breath.

She glanced quizzically up at him, her mouth slightly parted. Only then did he realize he'd interrupted her. Heat crept up his neck.

She nodded and gave him a brief smile. "Yes?"

Crockett cleared his throat and tried again. "I know this might seem like an inappropriate time, but everything in my heart is telling me it's exactly the *right* time. For you. For me. For the two of us together."

The furrows in her brow deepened, and her head tipped at an odd angle. She stared at him as if he were spouting gibberish.

Which, of course, he was.

A laugh exploded from his chest. He shook his head at his complete ineptitude and tunneled his fingers through his hair, hoping to stimulate some cohesive thoughts. "Just my luck," he muttered, "the one moment a man wants to be his most eloquent, and I fumble around like I haven't a thought in my head."

"Crockett? What's wrong?"

"You." He groaned. "No, not you." He was making a complete

muck of this. Desperate to find some way to salvage the situation, he surged to his feet, paced a couple steps, and turned back to face her. Drawing in a deep breath, he dropped to his knees by her feet and reclaimed her hand.

"We can't know what the future holds, but what I *do* know is that I want to share my future with you."

The frown lines on Joanna's brow smoothed, and her eyes grew misty. She caught her lower lip between her teeth, her body going completely still.

Crockett lifted her hand to his mouth and pressed his lips to the soft skin above her knuckles. "Joanna Robbins, you've stolen my heart. I've fallen in love with your quiet smile, your tender soul, your compassionate nature. I love the way you rush to defend those you care about and stand and fight when danger threatens."

He lifted his hand to brush at a stray ringlet that had fallen to frame her face, marveling at how it wrapped itself around his finger as if it belonged there. "I love the way your hair curls with unleashed abandon." He cupped her cheek in his palm, and she leaned into his touch. A surge of desire pulsed through him as her eyes warmed beneath his gaze. "And I adore those tiny freckles dancing across your cheeks."

Joanna dipped her chin and lowered her lashes as a pretty pink blush stole over her skin. But she didn't hide herself for long. Her lashes lifted, revealing eyes rimmed with anticipation and love. The intensity nearly knocked the breath from his chest.

"Marry me, Jo?" The simple words were all he could manage.

She nodded, shakily at first, then with growing vigor. "Yes, Crockett. Oh, yes!"

In a flash he was on his feet, catching her as she sprang up from the sofa and into his arms. His mouth found her sweet lips, and triumph sang in his veins.

She was his.

Crockett's arms tightened about her as he drew her close and buried his fingers into the curls at her nape, luxuriating in their softness as they spiraled around him. He broke away from her lips to feather kisses across her cheeks and the bridge of her nose, not wanting to miss a single freckle.

"I never dreamed I could be so happy," Joanna whispered, her breath warm against his chin.

He was kissing a line past her ear when he felt her stiffen. Lifting his head, he forced his attention from the pale expanse of neck that he longed to explore and instead focused on her face. "What is it?"

"Do you think Daddy will give his blessing?" Her fingers clasped his shirt. "I want to be your wife more than anything, Crockett. Truly I do. But the thought of defying my father to do so . . . it . . . well, I fear it would leave my heart in shreds."

"Shh." He tucked her head beneath his chin and rubbed gentle circles over her back. "I would never make you choose between your father and me, darling. I know how much he means to you, and frankly, he's rather grown on me, as well."

She tilted her head and locked on his gaze. He winked, and the smile that creased her face, though small, made his heart swell.

"Silas and I came to an understanding a short time ago. He approves my suit."

The last of the tension leaked from Joanna's body, and when she raised up on her toes, he met her halfway, sealing their commitment with a kiss so deep and joyful that when he finally brought it to a close, his breathing was ragged and his hands trembled as he struggled to release his hold on the woman who would soon be his wife.

Later, as he hiked up the rutted drive to the Brewster homestead, Crockett replayed that moment in his mind. The way

Joanna's face brightened. The way she sought his kiss. The way she felt pressed up against his chest when her arms circled his waist. Such memories put a man in a right cheerful frame of mind, even when embarking on a distasteful task.

Why, he actually found himself whistling as he trudged past the Brewsters' corral and bending to pat the head of the old hound dog that trotted out from under the house to sniff his boots.

"Leave the parson alone, Clancy." A large man rumbled the order as he stepped down from the front porch. He thumbed his drooping suspenders back onto his shoulders in a well-practiced motion as he strode across the yard. "Go on, now. Git!"

He kicked at the dog halfheartedly. Clancy evaded the strike with a quick stutter step and scampered off to investigate the mud by the water trough.

"Parson." Holly's father offered his hand in greeting, though his expression remained rather closed. Crockett smiled anyway and clasped the man's hand.

"Alan. Good to see you, sir."

The two slowly made their way up to the house.

"Your visit's got my womenfolk all in a dither," Alan complained. "Kicked me out of my own kitchen. Sent the boys to the barn as if this were some kind of special occasion. It's not like you haven't been here before with all those plannin' meetings and such." He halted at the porch steps and eyed Crockett with a wary glance. "Unless this call you're payin' tonight is different somehow." His eyes narrowed even further. "Is it, Parson? Different?"

Dread tickled his nape as he faced Holly's father, but he strove to keep his voice steady with no hint of apology. "I'm not here to plan another church event, but I am here in an official capacity."

"What kind of official capacity?" Suspicion darkened the man's features.

Crockett met his stare without a blink. "I'm afraid it's a

private matter between Holly and me, but your concern does you credit, sir. In fact, I would welcome your supervision should you care to keep an eye on things."

"Plan on it."

Crockett nodded. Having Alan Brewster chaperone the visit might not be terribly comfortable with the grizzly-bear stare the man was aiming at him, but he'd rather suffer that discomfort than the type Holly dished out.

"Sarah!" Mr. Brewster yelled up to the house. "Parson's here!"

Holly's mother burst out of the door like a plump quail freshly flushed from her nest. "Well, for heaven's sake, Alan. Quit your hollerin' and show the man up here."

"He can find his own way," Alan groused. "I'll be out by the corral. Keepin' an eye on . . . things." He shot a meaningful glance at Crockett.

Crockett stepped aside to let the man pass, feeling the heat of that glance between his shoulder blades as he climbed the steps to the front porch. Removing his hat, he dipped his chin to Sarah. "Ma'am."

"Brother Archer, we're delighted to have you pay a call on us this evening." The woman's hands fluttered about like a pair of birds that couldn't decide where to alight. "Holly could talk of nothing else all day."

"Mother," a second feminine voice chided from just inside the door, "you're going to embarrass him *and* me with talk like that."

Crockett crossed the threshold and found Holly standing just inside the door. A fading sunbeam fell through the westward facing window to dance upon her blond hair, making it glow like a golden halo. She smiled prettily and held out her hands to take his hat, but she waited for him to come to her, as if she knew the sunlight in that particular spot showed her beauty off to its best advantage and was loath to leave it.

"We saved you some cobbler," Holly said, finally abandoning her sunbeam to take his arm and lead him to a chair. "I'll dish some up for you."

"Only if you ladies will join me." Crockett aimed his smile at Sarah, but Holly was the one who answered.

"Oh, Mother has some mending to attend to in the parlor. Don't you, Mama?"

"Ah . . . yes. That's right. Mending. Big pile."

Crockett felt himself being maneuvered into a corner. Time for a quick dodge. "Well, in that case, why don't you and I enjoy our dessert out on the porch, Miss Brewster?" He favored Holly with his most charming grin. Two could play this game. "The swing would make a cozy place for our talk—private yet still proper."

"That's a wonderful idea, Parson," Sarah gushed. "I'll dish up the cobbler while you two get comfortable."

She shooed them out the front door, and Crockett escorted Holly to the wooden swing that turned out to be a bit narrower than he had originally thought. It didn't help matters when Holly seated herself several inches away from the arm on her side, leaving barely enough room for him to sit without having his leg rub up against hers.

Reminding himself of his reason for coming, he aimed an apologetic grin her way. "I'm sorry, Miss Brewster. Would you mind scooting over a bit? I don't have quite enough room."

Her lips tightened in a disgruntled expression before quickly softening into a smile. "Of course." She shifted a negligible amount. "Is that better?"

"A little more please."

Something unpleasant flashed in her eyes, but she complied. "Thank you."

The cobbler arrived, saving Crockett from having to say anything more, and he welcomed the reprieve. He tucked into the dessert, the sweetness of the sugared blackberries helping to improve his mood. He scraped every last bit of the deep purple syrup from the inside of his bowl before finally setting the dish on the floor to his side. The reprieve was over.

"You're a fine cook, Miss Brewster. That cobbler was delicious."

Her cheeks pinkened at his compliment, her lashes lowering demurely. "Thank you. But please, Crockett"—her lashes lifted as she drew his given name across her tongue as if it were the dessert—"call me Holly."

"No, ma'am. I don't think I will."

She blinked. "What?"

"This is what I wanted to talk to you about, Miss Brewster." Pressing his back against the swing arm, Crockett turned to face her more squarely as he tried desperately to ignore the jittery surging of his pulse. He needed to present a strong, confident front, not prove himself a bag of nerves. Clearing his throat, he forced himself to meet her gaze. "I'm concerned that you are playing a game that could lead you to serious harm."

"Why, I-I have no idea what you mean." She put up a good front, but when her fingers started plucking at her skirt, he knew he'd unsettled her.

"Miss Brewster, I'm not unaware of the special attention you've been paying to me. It is quite flattering, but I fear, not . . . appropriate." Crockett spoke slowly, thinking over each word as he strove to find the proper balance of gentleness and reproof. *"Restore in the spirit of meekness,"* Scripture admonished. "I do not wish to injure your feelings; however, I must make my position clear. I will *not* be pursuing a courtship with you. My heart is already engaged elsewhere."

Deep lines marred the pale perfection of her brow. "But you're here . . . now. Didn't you come to see me?" Slowly the lines eased, replaced by the pout she had perfected.

"I came as your minister, not as a beau." Crockett leaned forward, willing her soul to heed his warning. "You are young and lovely, but some of your behavior of late has been shockingly forward. To tell the truth, it has made me quite uncomfortable. I worry that if you continue in this manner, other men might get the wrong idea and attempt to take advantage of you."

"But I'm not interested in any other men, Crockett. I'm interested in *you*." She reached between them and placed her hand on his knee.

Frowning, he took hold of her wrist and dropped her hand back onto her lap. "You see, Miss Brewster? This is exactly what I mean. I have told you that my heart belongs to another, yet you continue to press yourself upon me, despite my warnings. I really must insist that you stop."

Crockett stood, setting the swing in motion. "I'm sorry to have to be so frank, but you need to understand and accept that the only relationship I am interested in having with you is that of preacher and parishioner."

Holly stopped the swing's motion with the sole of her shoe and launched to her feet. Her blue eyes crackled like a midday sky after the hiss of lightning. "Who is this woman who claims your heart? Someone you knew before?" Gone were the pretty pout and the languid lashes. Fire was all that remained when she jammed her fists onto her hips and stood toe-to-toe with him.

"Her identity doesn't matter. What matters is that you curb your forward behavior. It attracts the wrong kind of attention from the wrong kind of man and has no place in a Christian woman's life. Hold yourself to a higher standard, Miss Brewster, and accept the truth that there will never be anything between us."

"You know what I think?" She poked him in the chest. "I think there *is* no other woman. I think you're just frightened by what I make you feel. I tempt you, don't I? I make you feel things you think a preacher ought not feel."

"Miss Brewster." Crockett growled the warning, barely keeping his ire leashed. But Holly took no heed as she rushed on.

"Passion is not evil, Crockett. It's a gift from God. Haven't you read Solomon's Song? And what about Paul? Didn't he say that marriage is the godly solution for those who burn for one another?"

"Enough!"

She jumped at his bark, but Crockett no longer cared about her comfort. The time for gentleness had passed. He longed to throw Joanna's name into her arguments like a stick of dynamite and blow them all to bits. Holly would hear the news soon enough anyway. However, a shred of caution stayed his tongue. He'd be doing his love no favors if he dragged her into this ugliness.

Instead he forced other words through his teeth, spitting out one at a time. "I am not now, nor will I ever be, interested in a relationship with you, Miss Brewster, and I'll thank you to never speak of this again."

With that, he strode across the porch to the front door, opened it, and leaned inside to collect his hat from the hook on the wall. Slapping it on his head, he marched down the steps into the yard, his only goal to escape this place and the irrational woman who refused to take no for an answer.

He didn't miss the wail that pierced the evening air nor the slam of the door that echoed behind him, but neither did he turn to look. He wouldn't have stopped at all had not a shadowy figure emerged from the barn.

"I don't know what your game is, Parson," Alan Brewster murmured in a lethal voice not two feet away, "but if you hurt my little girl, the only preachin' you'll be doin' is from six feet under. Understand?"

Crockett nodded with a sharp downward thrust of his chin and without a word continued his march home.

37

The following evening found Crockett equally weary as he trudged home. Silas had taken it into his head to show Crockett the ins and outs of the ranch in excruciating detail—everything from riding the borders of the property to going over the account ledgers to discussing his plans for breeding and future expansion of the herd. Silas hadn't stopped once all day, even discussing business through lunch and supper. Crockett feared his head would explode if he tried to squeeze one more piece of information between his ears.

Silas had tried well to hide his desperation, but Crockett had felt it with every instruction he gave, every plan he shared. He was like a condemned man talking over the sound of sand rushing through his hourglass. When Crockett reminded him that Coleson had made no move to pursue an arrest after speaking with Jackson, Silas had just clasped his shoulder and told him that once he and Jo were married, he would be a partner in the Lazy R anyway, so there was nothing to lose in showing him the ropes now.

Crockett grinned as he crossed the field to the churchyard.

The man who'd hated preachers for forty years was not only welcoming one into the family but handing over the reins of his ranch. If anyone doubted the existence of God, they'd have only to witness Silas Robbins's turnabout to be convinced. No other explanation would suffice.

Thank you, Father, for your patient wooing, for never giving up on any of us. Keep working on Silas. Guard his newfound faith through whatever trials may arise, and help him to fully accept you as Lord. Give Jo and me wisdom as we walk alongside him and—

A clanking noise from inside his rooms interrupted his prayer as he approached the rear of the church. Had a coon found its way inside? He hoped the little bandit hadn't gotten into his books. Most were safely stored in his trunk, but he'd left a few sitting out on his table last night, including his Bible. He'd had to read all three epistles of John to calm down after his run-in with Holly. He'd gone to bed meditating on 1 John 4:11—"Beloved, if God so loved us, we ought also to love one another"—before he'd finally reclaimed enough peace to sleep. Some people were a trial to love, but with God's help, he'd find a way.

Having reached his door, he yanked it open and scanned the interior for signs of a furry intruder. The intruder he found, though, was neither furry nor likely to scamper away with a stomp of his foot or a wave of his hat.

Crockett stiffened. "What are you doing in my house?"

Holly Brewster smiled sweetly and held out a cup of coffee and a plate bearing some kind of wedge-shaped dessert. Crockett didn't take the time to assess if it was pie or cake. All of his attention, and fury, were focused on the woman making herself at home in his personal sanctuary.

"I came to apologize for that little misunderstanding we had last night and to bring you a peace offering." She lifted the plate toward him again, but Crockett just scowled at her, not about to accept anything she offered. "Come on," she cooed. "It's my vanilla cream cake, guaranteed to bring a smile to even the grumpiest of faces."

"You need to leave. Now." Crockett strode forward and swiped the plate from her hand. He dumped the dish, cake and all, into the ribbon-covered basket sitting on his table.

Finding a shawl that could only be hers draped across his bed, he snatched it up and tossed it at her, not caring if the coffee she held splattered the fine wool.

"Do you have no care for your reputation?" He growled the question, barely restraining the shout clawing its way up his throat. "Or mine? You can't be in my rooms."

She set the coffee cup aside and folded her shawl over her arm as if his reaction didn't perturb her the slightest bit. "You're overreacting, Crockett."

"It's Brother Archer," he ground out between clenched teeth. "I am your minister, not your beau." He clasped her elbow, maintaining enough self-control to keep his grip only firm, not painful, while he *encouraged* her toward the door.

She tried to yank her arm free from his grasp, her eyes finally widening in alarm, but he refused to release her.

"How dare you treat me this way," she sputtered. "You have no right!" She fought his hold yet was no match for his strength.

"I not only have the right," he said, grabbing the basket from the table as they passed, "I have the obligation as a Christian man to protect your virtue." He reached the door that still hung ajar from when he'd entered and pushed it fully open with the toe of his boot. "You're like a child who keeps wandering too close to the stove. You won't heed my warnings, so my only choice is to put you out of the kitchen."

"A child?" Holly screeched. "Why, you condescending, man-handling barbarian! You think you're so noble, but you're nothing more than a bully. A bully!"

With a swing of his arm, Crockett set her forcibly out of his home, thrust the basket at her, and then stepped back and closed the door in her disbelieving face.

Something crashed against the wall. Probably a plate, by the sound of it. Crockett leaned his back against the door, some part of his brain wondering if the cake had still been on it when she threw it.

"You'll pay for this, Crockett Archer! Do you hear me?" Something else thudded against the side of the building. The basket, perhaps? "You'll pay for this!"

Another screech. Then something that sounded like tearing fabric, followed by feet stomping in rapid succession. He'd never witnessed a grown woman throw a temper tantrum, but Holly Brewster seemed to have a definite knack for such things.

Through his window he caught a glimpse of her back as she huffed off. She'd worked herself up to such an extent, half her hair was coming out of its pins. Crockett shook his head, pitying the man she did finally wrangle into marriage. She'd either walk all over him or shred him to pieces with those claws whenever he did something she didn't like.

"'It is better to dwell in the corner of the housetop, than with a brawling woman in a wide house.'" Crockett chuckled to himself as his anger cooled. "Now I know why Solomon saw fit to record that particular proverb twice."

Thanking God for his providence in providing a peace-loving woman like Joanna for him to share a house and life with, Crockett pushed away from the door and headed for the table. Lighting the lamp to chase away the encroaching darkness, he settled in his chair and reread that passage from 1 John before starting in on his evening prayers.

He prayed over a different household from his congregation each night. However, instead of moving on to the Wards as he had originally planned, he decided to return to the Brewsters.

Heaven only knew what kind of upheaval they'd be facing once Holly got home. And Holly herself needed prayer, too. Prayers for wisdom, for a forgiving heart, and for comfort. Now that he had his own emotions back under control, he could see that her tantrum was driven by hurt. He'd rejected her quite adamantly. Probably bruised her pride as well as her heart.

Guilt pricked his conscience. Had he been too hard on her? Too forceful? Had he acted more in anger than admonishment? Crockett bowed his head again and added a plea for his own forgiveness to his list of petitions.

An hour later, Crockett had a completely different petition on his lips when Alan Brewster kicked in his door and started throwing punches.

Crockett barely had enough time to throw a hand up to ward off Alan's meaty fist before the enraged man grabbed him by the shirtfront and slammed him into the wall. Crockett twisted his body at the last second to take the force of the collision on his shoulder instead of his skull, sending shards of pain down his arm.

"You call yourself a man of God? You wretch!" Alan's fist slammed into Crockett's gut as his left hand pinned his shoulder to the wall. "You're a demon who preys on the trust of young women!" Another blow came, but Crockett hardened his muscles to deflect the force while knocking away Alan's hold with an upward thrust of a stiff arm.

He ducked and spun toward the door. "What are you talking about?"

Alan roared and charged like a bull. Crockett braced his legs, but the man's weight and momentum were too great. Alan wrapped his arms about Crockett's middle and drove him through the open doorway, taking him to the ground.

The air rushed from Crockett's lungs as he hit. The back of his head bounced against the hard-packed earth, stunning him.

Arms from behind hoisted him to his feet, dragging him out from under Brewster. Crockett was about to thank whomever had stepped in, when those same arms tightened like manacles around his biceps. Crockett strained against the hold, but the men on either side of him gave no quarter.

"I haven't done anything!" He swiveled his head from side to side to plead with his captors, men who seemed slightly more rational than Holly's father. He recognized them as kin to Alan and Sarah. He'd met them at the picnic but had never seen them at church.

Brewster staggered forward, winded but still packing plenty of rage to fuel another attack. "Are you saying that you never laid hands on my girl?"

Crockett hesitated for a split second, thinking of the way he'd grabbed Holly's arm and ushered her out the door. That second was all it took to reignite Alan's fury. His fist crashed into Crockett's jaw, knocking his head into the chin of one of the men holding him.

"I didn't harm her," Crockett insisted, desperate to insert some reason into this situation before things got any worse. "She was in my house when I arrived home from the ranch, and I escorted her out. I was concerned for her reputation and made her leave. That's all."

"That's all?" Alan bellowed and landed a blow to his ribs. Crockett groaned. "My Holly comes home bawling her eyes out, her dress torn clear off her shoulder, her hair falling down around her ears, leaves and sticks poked every which way, dirt in her nails as if she had to claw to get away from you, and you dare to tell me you were protecting her reputation?" A volley of punches to Crockett's midsection punctuated the accusation.

Crockett's legs sagged, but his captors held him upright to accept the blows. He tasted blood in his mouth. Agony throbbed in his side. His strength was nearly gone.

Thankfully, so was Alan's.

The man took a step back, his chest heaving from his exertion.

Crockett slowly lifted his head and met Alan Brewster's glare with the fierce dignity of one unjustly accused. "With God as my witness, I did not harm your daughter. Holly was upset when she left me but unharmed. Perhaps she fell on her way home. Perhaps someone else attacked her. I don't know what happened. All I know is that it wasn't me."

No one spoke. Crockett's avowal simply hung in the air like a righteous beacon. And he started to hope.

"Did Holly actually *say* the parson attacked her?" one of the men at Crockett's back dared ask.

Please, God, let them see the truth.

"You think I'm gonna ask for all the gritty details?" Alan snapped, his eyes dark as the surrounding night. "The evidence spoke for itself. My baby girl threw herself into my arms and sobbed her heart out. 'Make him go away, Papa,' she said. 'Make Brother Archer go away and never come back.' I aim to do just that. To make sure this man never hurts another young girl like he did my Holly. Do you boys stand with me or not?"

The arms holding Crockett tightened, hefting him nearly off the ground.

"We're with you, Alan."

"Good," Brewster said. "Then, let's string him up."

38

Joanna stood before the canvas she'd been working on for the last several months and gazed into the beloved eyes she missed so keenly.

"Oh, Mama. I'm going to be married. Can you believe it?" A thrill coursed through her at the thought of becoming Crockett's wife.

Her mother's likeness smiled back at her, serene and loving, just the way Joanna remembered her. She hoped she'd captured her the way her father remembered her, as well, for the portrait was to be his birthday present. If he was still at home and not in prison somewhere when his birthday came around next month.

Don't think about that. It was much more pleasant to think about Crockett. Her betrothed. Joanna grinned as she stepped to her worktable to rinse out her paintbrush. She swished the bristles in the small Mason jar of turpentine, the pungent smell familiar and well loved, one that never failed to bring her mother to mind. But at the moment, a handsome man with twinkling eyes and strong arms consumed her thoughts.

Those thoughts drew her to the barn loft window and lifted

her gaze over the trees to focus on the church. Would Crockett be in his room composing his next sermon or crawling into bed after a grueling day of ranch work? Her heart leapt at the thought that she wouldn't have to wonder much longer. Soon she would be there with him, perhaps mending quietly in a corner while he worked on his notes, or maybe rubbing the soreness from his shoulders as they readied for bed.

Joanna nibbled on her lip, her stomach fluttering in a way that sent delightful shivers through her core. But then something caught her eye in the direction of the churchyard. Were those lights? She braced a hand against the frame of the window and squinted into the night. It looked like two—no, three—lights. Lanterns.

Crockett hadn't mentioned any appointments. Could there be an emergency of some kind? An illness or injury? Word had gotten around about his skill in tending Jackson's wound. Yet something didn't feel right. An odd urgency prodded her, turning those belly flutters into needle pricks. Reaching behind her back to untie her painting smock, Joanna whirled from the window and dashed to the loft ladder.

Once her feet hit the ground, Joanna ran for the bunkhouse. "Jasper!"

Her father's most trusted man had the door opened and was several steps into the yard, his pistol in hand, by the time she met up with him.

"Saddle Sunflower and Gamble. There's trouble at the church."

He didn't waste time on words, just nodded once and jogged toward the barn.

"Jo?" Her father must have heard her shout for he was crossing the yard with long strides, buckling his gun belt as he went.

She ran to him and grabbed his arm. "Daddy, something's going on at the church. There are lights in the yard. I can't explain it, but I just know something's wrong. Will you ride with me to check on Crockett?"

Silas wrapped his arm around her shoulder and steered her toward the barn. "I don't see the harm in payin' Archer a little visit."

"Thank you, Daddy."

He gave her a firm pat and rushed forward to take over Gamble's preparation, freeing Jasper to see to Sunflower.

The instant the cinch was fastened on her mount, Joanna stuck her foot in the stirrup and hoisted herself astride. Without waiting for her father, she kicked Sunflower into an easy canter. The deepening darkness kept her from the gallop her heart demanded. By the time she crossed onto the main road, her father was at her side, urging Gamble to take the lead.

"Stay mounted until we know what's going on," her father ordered.

She knew better than to argue.

Cutting through the field would be too treacherous for the horses at night, so Joanna and her father kept to the road. As they approached, she could make out a handful of men in lantern light under one of the large, spreading oaks that had shaded the crowd during the picnic. She leaned forward in the saddle, trying to get a better view of what was going on. A pair of horses stood ground-tethered nearby, but there seemed to be one in the middle of the men.

Had it been injured? Is that why they all huddled around it? But their attention didn't seem to be on the horse directly. No, they seemed to be focused on something else. Something writhing against them. They were beating it; she could see that now. Beating it and throwing it on top of the horse.

That's when a snake fell down from among the tree branches. A snake whose tail was looped at the end. Her stomach dropped. Not a snake. A rope.

And the thing on the horse was . . .

"Crockett!" She screamed his name at the top of her voice and urged Sunflower to a gallop. But her father cut in front of her before she could race into the fray.

"Stay behind me." His voice was harsh. Harsher than she'd ever heard it. Then he pulled his rifle from his scabbard without breaking stride and fired a shot in the air. Once fully upon the men, he pulled Gamble to a halt and aimed his weapon at the belligerent fellow in the front of the pack—Alan Brewster.

"What's going on here?" Her father's voice echoed calmly in the night, as if meeting a neighbor at an impromptu hanging was nothing out of the ordinary.

Joanna reined Sunflower in a few paces back as her father had instructed but close enough that she could see Crockett. And the sight wasn't pretty. His beloved face was beaten and bloody, his hair dusty and disheveled, his hands bound behind his back.

Oh, Crockett. She moaned and had to restrain herself from running to him. Fear for his safety rooted her to the earth, however. For while they'd ridden in, one of the men had slipped the noose over Crockett's neck and tightened the knot. If the horse he sat on spooked, or if one of the men gave the beast a slap, Crockett would be left dangling.

"This is none of your concern, Silas." Mr. Brewster planted his hands on his hips—hips that supported a gun belt with a revolver at the ready.

"You're about to string up one of my ranch hands, and my future son-in-law. That makes it my concern."

"Son-in-law?" Mr. Brewster turned his head to spit, then lifted the back of his hand to wipe his mouth. Only then did Joanna notice that he sported several cuts and bruises of his own. "Seems to me I'm doing you and that girl of yours a favor, then. When you hear what this skunk did to my Holly, you'll be beggin' to help instead of asking me to stop."

A sick feeling churned in Joanna's stomach. *Holly.* No doubt that girl had twisted the truth into something ugly and vile. But surely not even Holly could be so cruel as to crave a man's death.

"What is she accusing him of?" Her father shifted slightly in his saddle, laying his rifle across his lap as if he no longer saw a need for it.

Joanna longed to snatch the weapon from him and demand Crockett's release . . . until she noticed her daddy's finger hovering over the trigger. He'd not surrendered. He'd just removed the appearance of the threat to put Brewster's men at ease.

"My girl stumbled home tonight with her dress torn, hair a mess, sobbing about how she hated Brother Archer and wanted me to make him leave and never come back. If your Jo had done the same, what would you have done?"

"Beaten the man responsible to a bloody pulp."

"Exactly." Mr. Brewster nodded in satisfaction, righteous indignation glowing in his eyes.

"But I wouldn't hang him. That's the law's job."

Mr. Brewster's face darkened, his jaw working back and forth as if it were in danger of locking. "There ain't no law around these parts, Silas. A man's gotta see to his own justice."

"But there is law around. Marshal Coleson's up at the Spivey place."

Joanna shot a look at her father. Would he actually bring the law in on this, put himself in the marshal's path to save Crockett?

"Let me go fetch him."

Apparently he would. Moisture clouded Joanna's eyes. Never had she loved her father more.

"You sure bringin' in the law is the best idea, Alan?" the man holding the horse's head asked.

Mr. Brewster hesitated.

"You hang that man, you're doing it out of anger and vengeance, not justice." Joanna's father slowly brought his rifle back around and aimed it at Alan Brewster's chest. "Besides, as sure as you are that Archer's guilty, I'm equally sure he's innocent. I know this man. I've worked with him day after day. You think I'd trust him with my daughter if I wasn't completely convinced of his character?"

"Every man's got secrets, Silas. Even you." The threat hung in the air. Joanna peered at the man, her pulse erratic. Did Mr. Brewster know something about her father's past?

"I'm getting the marshal, Brewster." Her father's voice had hardened to stone. "He'll sort this out. If I'm wrong, Coleson will take care of Archer. But if I'm right and you hang him before I get back, you'll be the one the marshal carts off to prison. For murder."

"Fine," Mr. Brewster shouted, spooking Crockett's horse.

Joanna gasped, her knees tightening around her own mount, causing Sunflower to sidestep. Thankfully, the man tending Crockett's horse held the beast steady.

"Fetch the marshal," Mr. Brewster conceded. "While you do that I'll send Buck after Holly." The man who had been up in the tree securing the rope slithered down and hurried to his horse. "We'll see who Coleson believes."

"That we shall." Joanna's father reined Gamble around and came up alongside her. "Take my rifle, Jo." He pushed the weapon into her shaky hands.

"Shouldn't I be the one to fetch the marshal?" Joanna eyed the angry men around her. She hated the idea of leaving Crockett, but of the two of them, her father would prove the bigger deterrent. Alan Brewster wouldn't consider her much of a threat, even with the rifle.

Her father shook his head. "No, stay here. I know Archer didn't lay a hand on Holly, but somebody else might have. I don't want you riding alone in the dark." He clasped her shoulder and gave her one of those looks that made it clear the discussion was over. "Watch over your man."

Joanna steeled her spine and nodded. "I love you, Daddy."

His lips turned up in a strained smile. "I love you, too, darlin', and I swear to you that I'll make this right."

All she could do was nod in response.

Taking up the reins, her father brought Gamble's head around and touched his heels to the animal's flanks. Gamble leapt forward and the two of them raced up the road that led to Jackson's cabin.

"Hurry," she whispered.

39

Silas's heart pounded as fast and hard as Gamble's hooves while he raced up the path to Jackson's home. When he caught sight of the marshal's horse sheltered under the broken-down lean-to west of the house, a heavy exhale released the pressure that'd been building in his chest.

If Coleson had already returned to Deanville, Archer would have been in a world of hurt. Not that he was all that dandy now.

Silas had spent most of his younger years doing everything possible to keep his neck out of a noose, but when Joanna screamed Archer's name as if her heart were being torn from her body, all he could think was that it should be him wearin' that rope necktie, not the parson.

Reining Gamble in, Silas leapt from the saddle, not surprised in the slightest when the marshal shoved the door open and came out to meet him, pistol in hand.

"Mount up, Coleson." Silas paid the gun no heed, just rounded Gamble's head and faced the lawman straight on. "You're needed down at the church."

"The church?" Coleson scoffed. "That's rich coming from you,

Robbins. Don't think I'm fool enough to go haring after you in the dark on some manufactured pretense. I know you want me gone."

"What I want is your butt in the saddle." Silas's hands clenched into fists, but he kept them at his sides as he marched up to where the lawman lounged against the doorframe. "An innocent man's gonna be lynched unless you put a stop to it."

"And who's the poor soul I'm supposed to save?" Coleman straightened a bit at Silas's approach but gave no indication he intended to follow him to the churchyard.

"The parson."

"Archer?" Laughter sputtered out of the lawman. Silas's right hand twitched. He ached to shut the man up with a quick jab to the mouth.

Coleson pushed his hat back on his forehead. "I guess I'm supposed to believe he stepped on the wrong toes in one of his sermons, huh? Come on, Robbins. I expected better of you. At least come up with a tale that's remotely believable."

Silas was debating the merits of forcibly installing the man on his horse when Jackson pushed past Coleson, his face whiter than milk on snow.

"Who's got Crock?"

"Alan Brewster." Silas focused on the boy, letting the marshal fade from his vision entirely. "He's got it in his head that the parson attacked Holly."

Color surged back to Jackson's cheeks. "Crock would never hurt a woman. Never!" The kid stomped over to Silas's side, then hopped from one foot to the next as if he couldn't quite contain his outrage. "Holly Brewster's been chasing after him for weeks, always throwin' herself in his path and makin' eyes at him in church. I kept telling him he needed to set her straight, but you know Crock. He's too nice. Every time he tried to discourage her, she doubled her efforts. She must've cornered him, pushed him so far that he stopped worryin' about her feelings

311

and finally told her flat out to leave him be. That woulda made her madder than spit."

"Well, right now the only thing standing between Archer and a stretched neck is Jo and my promise to fetch a lawman to sort things out." Silas glared at Coleson. "So, you comin'?"

The marshal glared back, holding his answer hostage.

"I am." Jackson shoved his foot into Gamble's stirrup and reached for the saddle horn.

"Watch that arm, boy." Worried Jackson would damage his still-healing wound, Silas hurried over to give him a leg up. "You sure you're ready to ride?"

"Crock's the best friend I got. I'm goin'." Jackson's mulish expression as he settled into the saddle kept Silas from arguing. He nodded instead and swung up behind the boy.

Coleson approached the pair and laid a staying hand on Jackson's leg. "You really believe Archer's in trouble, son?"

"Yes, sir, Marshal." Jackson glanced over his shoulder at Silas, then turned back to Coleson. "I know you think he used to rob them stagecoaches, and maybe he did way back when. But that don't make no never mind to me. I've known Mr. Robbins for near half my life, and I trust him."

"Even after he shot you?"

"On accident—how many times do I have to tell you?" Jackson corrected, his defense a salve on Silas's conscience. "And yes, I still trust him."

Coleson's gaze narrowed as it slid from the kid to Silas. "Maybe I'd trust him, too, if he stopped hiding his past."

"Come with me now, and I'll tell you everything you want to know." The words surprised Silas as much as the lawman, but something inside clicked into place with the saying of them. He'd vowed to let God have his way with him, but that couldn't happen if he was still holding on to the sins of his past, could it? Time to put the old to rest and take up the new.

After they saw to Archer.

"I plan to hold you to that, Robbins," the marshal said as he strode toward his horse.

Silas maintained his stoic mask despite the rapid thump in his chest. He'd face what he had to face when the time came, but for now what mattered was keeping his promise to his little girl.

Touching his heels to Gamble's flanks, he set off for the church, praying he'd find Archer still breathing when he got there.

Joanna's arms ached and had begun to shake, but she refused to lower her rifle, despite the fact that Alan Brewster was no longer paying her any mind. It was the only thing she could do for Crockett, and she had to do something. She couldn't tend his wounds, couldn't hold him, couldn't even get that foul rope off his neck. All she could do was watch, pray, and keep her rifle trained on the man who threatened his life.

She spared a quick glance toward the road. *Where are you, Daddy?* Had the marshal moved on? What would happen if he wasn't there? Would they be able to stop Mr. Brewster without the law to intervene?

A bead of sweat rolled down her spine, slowing over each bump of her backbone. Joanna felt each rise and fall of the droplet as if time had slowed. And when the trail ended at the small of her back, she couldn't escape the morbid sensation that Crockett's time had reached its end, as well.

"This is taking too long," Alan Brewster grumbled. He stopped his agitated pacing and strode over to Crockett. "I shouldn't have sent Buck after Holly. She's been through enough tonight without being forced to see this scum again. I say we just take care of business now and spare her the ugliness."

"No!" Joanna jumped from Sunflower's back and raced

toward the men. She raised her rifle like a club, fully prepared to swing it at Mr. Brewster's head, but he turned, and with a mighty sweep of his arm, knocked the weapon out of her hands. She cried out in surprise and despair, staggering slightly from the blow, while the second man dashed over to collect the rifle.

"Jo!" Crockett jerked against his bonds, fighting to get free. But his struggles only served to upset his horse. His body stretched dangerously backward, the rope pulling taut as his mount skittered forward.

"I'm fine, Crockett," Joanna rushed to assure him. She attempted to dodge Holly's father in order to get to the horse, but he grabbed her about the waist and set her aside.

"Not so fast, girlie. You ain't getting near my prisoner."

"Then get your man to control that horse," Joanna demanded.

"Walt?" Mr. Brewster didn't even have the decency to glance at Crockett's predicament, so intent was he on glaring her into submission.

"I got him, Alan." The man reclaimed the reins and backed the horse up a step, then two. Finally, Crockett sat at a normal angle, and Joanna breathed easier.

"Please, Mr. Brewster." Joanna grabbed his sleeve in supplication. "Undo the rope. Marshal Coleson will make sure justice is done when he arrives. There's no reason to risk an accident taking Crockett's life in the meantime."

Holly's father shook off her hold. "You know, a decent woman would have more compassion for the female who'd been hurt instead of pleading for the release of her attacker."

Joanna's spine stiffened. She straightened to her full height and stared the man directly in the eyes. "A decent woman stands by the man she loves no matter what vile lies are used to condemn him."

"Are you calling my Holly a liar?"

Joanna said nothing. She just stared back at him, letting her certainty do the talking for her.

"Why, you . . ." He raised his hand, his intent clear.

Joanna braced herself but never took her eyes from his.

"Lay a hand on that woman, and you'll be the one I cart off to jail tonight, mister. No questions asked."

Marshal Coleson. Joanna spun to face the lawman, not surprised to see two guns trained on Mr. Brewster, the second belonging to her father. What did surprise her was the blond beauty peering over the marshal's shoulder from the back of his horse, and the truly horrified expression marring her usually lovely features.

"Papa! What are you *doing*?"

40

Alan Brewster lowered his hand, and the wildness rising to a fever pitch inside Crockett subsided.

"Holly?" Alan stepped away from Joanna and took a step toward his daughter.

Joanna took advantage of his distraction and ran to Crockett. She grabbed hold of his leg and laid her cheek against the bend of his knee. Crockett's eyes slid closed as he absorbed the feel of her, wishing his hands were free to caress her face and stroke her glorious hair.

"Are you all right?" he managed through a tight throat, the rope keeping him from bending his chin enough to see more than the top of her head. "He didn't hurt you, did he?" Crockett hated the helplessness of his position. He could deal with the bonds and the noose and the stupidly skittish horse when he was the only one in danger, but when Brewster turned on Joanna, he'd nearly gone out of his mind.

She raised her head and leaned back enough to allow him to see her eyes glittering in the lantern light. "I'm fine as long as you are alive and well."

"I love you, Joanna. No matter what happens, know that."

A fierce look swept over her face, much like the expression she'd worn when she confronted Alan Brewster with nothing but her faith in his innocence—a faith that made him want to shout in triumph and kiss her senseless all at the same time. "The only thing that's going to happen, Crockett Archer, is you getting out of that awful rope and off this horse so you can marry me like you promised. You got that?"

A grin pulled against his split lip, but Crockett welcomed the prick of pain. "Yes, ma'am."

"This your daughter, mister?" Coleson called out, drawing Crockett's attention as the marshal gave Holly an arm down from her perch behind him. "We found her walking along the road with some fella named Buck. She seemed surprised to hear what was transpirin' down here at the church. Asked if she could ride with me the rest of the way."

Holly slid to the ground and rushed to her father. She had changed her dress and repaired her hair, and Crockett prayed her improved appearance would play in his favor.

"Papa, this is wrong," she murmured, her voice quiet after the booming tones of Marshal Coleson, but it still managed to carry through the night air. She cast a guilty glance toward Crockett, and then her gaze fell on Joanna and her eyes widened before shooting a look back at Crockett's face. She bit her lip and turned back to her father. "Let him go, Papa."

"But he hurt you, darlin'. I can't let him get away with that." The tender way he spoke did nothing to dim the hostility in his stance. "Either the marshal takes him in or I mete out the justice myself, but I ain't leavin' here tonight without making sure he pays for what he done to you."

"He did hurt me," Holly began, and Joanna stiffened beside Crockett.

"Easy," he whispered. "Give her a chance to do what's right."

He'd seen the way Holly looked at Joanna. She knew now—knew that Joanna was the woman he'd spoken about, knew that he'd told the truth about being promised to another.

"He hurt me," Holly said, her gaze dropping to the ground, "but not in the way you think. He only hurt my pride."

"But your dress," Alan sputtered. "Your hair. The dirt and leaves. I know what I saw when you came home, and the damage was to more than your pride, girl. Don't let this lawman intimidate you and keep you from speaking the truth."

Holly's head snapped up. "When have I ever let a man intimidate me?"

Crockett nearly choked on the sudden urge to laugh.

"Are you sayin' you lied to me, girl?" Brewster growled, grabbing onto Holly's arm.

"I never lied," she shot back. "I just let you draw your own conclusions."

Brewster shoved his daughter away and clasped his hands behind his back, as if afraid of what they might do if he didn't rein them in. "Land sakes, girl! I nearly killed a man, and you're tellin' me it was all some kind of game?" He strode toward Crockett, muttering under his breath.

Holly followed on his heels. "I never asked you to hang him, Papa. I just wanted you to make him leave."

"Why?" Brewster spun to face her. "Because he chose to court Joanna Robbins instead of you?"

Holly drew up short, her eyes going wide. "What?"

"Don't think I haven't heard you and your mama scheming. I knew you were anglin' after the parson, but I never believed any child of mine could be so spiteful as to mar a good man's reputation just because she didn't get what she wanted from him. You're a spoiled, deceitful girl, Holly, and I'm ashamed of ya." Brewster turned his back on her, pulled a hunting knife from

318

the leather sheath at his waist, and reached behind Crockett to slice the ropes binding his wrists.

Crockett's arms sprang apart, and hundreds of needle-sharp pricks stabbed into his hands as blood began to flow back into his palms and fingers. Without giving his flesh time to recover, he reached to his neck, grasped the rope chaffing the underside of his jaw, and flung it over his head. In the next instant he was off the saddle—clutching Joanna to his chest and wiping the tears of relief from her cheeks while trying to keep his own from falling.

Her arms wrapped around his middle and drew his bruised body up against her softness. "Thank you, God," she whispered. "Thank you. Thank you. Thank you."

His heart echoed her sentiment while his face buried itself in her hair. Inhaling deeply, he exulted in the clean, sunshiny scent of her. He was going to live. Live to be a husband, a father. To love Joanna for however many days the Lord granted them together.

So lost was he in the woman in his arms, that when another feminine voice clamored, he startled.

"Papa! How can you say such horrible things?" Genuine shock and hurt laced Holly's voice. Crockett lifted his head and winced when Brewster yanked his arm away from his daughter's attempted touch. "I never once uttered anything untrue," she insisted. "It was you who drew the wrong conclusion, your rage that put Brother Archer's head in that noose."

Brewster's shoulders slumped, and his hand trembled as he rubbed it over his face. "It's true that I let my rage spin out of control, and when I think of what almost happened, it turns my stomach. I can only pray that God and the parson will forgive me."

Holly stood straighter, a smile brightening her face. But when her father saw that smile, he stiffened.

"I got a scare today, Holly. A scare that will keep me from making a mistake like this again. What have *you* learned?"

She blinked and tipped her head sideways, as if trying to puzzle out her father's meaning.

"You're not innocent of wrongdoing," Alan said, his voice heavy, tired. "It was you who instigated these events with your manipulations and deceitful ways."

Her brow scrunched, and she opened her mouth as if to protest, but he cut her off. "You don't have to lie with your tongue to be deceitful. Satan himself tried to tempt Christ with the truth of Scripture twisted to his own purposes."

"Are you comparing me to . . . to *Satan*?" Holly reared back as if he'd struck her.

Crockett's heart stirred with compassion, and he thought to intervene, but Joanna squeezed his hand. "Easy," she whispered, echoing his earlier words to her. "Give him a chance. He knows her better than we do."

Crockett smiled down at the beautiful woman looking at him with wise blue-gray eyes and squeezed her hand in return. "You're going to make me a fine wife, Miss Robbins."

She favored him with the wink he would have given her if his left eye hadn't swollen nearly shut. "I vow to do my best, Mr. Archer."

He wanted nothing more than to tug her close again, but Alan Brewster had turned his back on Holly in order to face them.

"I owe you an apology, Parson." Brewster lifted his chin and met Crockett's stare head on.

Crockett nodded quickly and without reservation. Then he held his hand out to the older man. Brewster hesitated a moment, then shook it with a firm grip.

"I promise you that I'll be taking the girl firmly in hand after this. And I'll be havin' a talk with her mother, as well." The man didn't wait for a response, just barked at Holly to get herself on his horse and marched back toward the church where his mount waited.

Walt collected the lanterns without uttering a word, and Holly scampered after her father, keeping her attention glued to the ground in front of her.

Once they rode out, Joanna sagged against Crockett's side. "Praise God that's over," she sighed. Maintaining her grip on his hand, she swung around to regard him more fully. Her eyes scanned his face, and her lips pursed in displeasure at what she saw. "Those cuts are going to need some attention."

"You volunteering for the job?" He did his best to waggle his brows in a rakish manner, and was thoroughly enjoying the bloom of her smile when Jackson came running up from across the churchyard.

"Crock! Crock, come quick." The boy waved his good arm in frantic motions above his head. "The marshal's arrestin' Silas!"

41

"What?" Joanna's already frayed emotions shredded like a piece of antique lace being dragged across a thistle patch.

This can't be happening. Not now. It had to be some kind of mistake.

She looked past Jackson to her father. His hands were outstretched, wrist-over-wrist before him while Marshal Coleson secured them with a strip of leather, as if her father were a horse to be hobbled.

"Wait!" She lurched forward, her legs nothing but trembling sticks as she fumbled over the ground separating her from her father. "Stop!"

Crockett was at her side in an instant, his warm hand gripping her elbow, supporting her, strengthening her, as his steady gait propelled her securely across the remaining distance. Jackson fell into step behind them.

"What are you doing?" Joanna wrenched her arm away from Crockett's hold when they reached the men and threw herself at the marshal. She shoved against his shoulder, hard, forcing him to stumble backward a step. "You can't arrest him. Jackson's shooting was an accident."

Marshal Coleson stoically regained his footing and regarded her with a cool gaze. "I'm not arresting him for the shooting."

"Then why are you treating him like a prisoner? He hasn't done anything!"

"On the contrary, ma'am, he's confessed to multiple counts of robbery. Coaches, trains, even admitted to kidnapping the parson, here."

"Which I still have no intention of pressing charges for," Crockett said from behind her. But his generosity didn't matter, not really. Not if her father had admitted to the rest.

"Daddy?" She searched his face for answers, but his oddly composed features revealed nothing.

Why would he confess? Why now, after all these years? Was it greedy of her to want to keep both the men she loved? Must she sacrifice her father now that Crockett was safe?

Her father lifted his bound arms and looped them over her head. She flung her arms about his waist and clung to him with desperate strength, closing her eyes to block out the truth of what was happening. In her mind, she was a little girl again running to her father for comfort. And when his lips brushed her forehead in the same manner they used to press against a scraped elbow or a hen-pecked hand, her tears fell.

His arms tightened about her, and his husky voice echoed softly in the night. "It's time, Jo. Time to stop hiding from the past."

She shook her head adamantly against his chest, squeezing her eyes shut so firmly that her cheeks nearly met her brows.

"Come now, Jo. It's the right thing to do. Deep in your heart you know that. Doesn't the Good Book say we need to confess our sins to receive God's forgiveness?"

"First John 1:9," Crockett murmured softly.

"See," her daddy said, a near laugh in his voice, "the parson knows what I'm talking about." He lifted his arms back over her head and gently eased himself from her hold.

Determined to be strong for him, she didn't fight. She stepped back and dried her cheeks with the back of her hand. When the knuckles of his bound hands chucked her softly under her chin, she bit her lip to keep it from trembling and raised her gaze.

"Don't you see, darlin'? If I'm gonna be joinin' up with the Lord, I can't keep hangin' on to the secrets of my past. I have to own up to what I did and face the consequences. He ain't the kind to be satisfied with me handin' over half the loot. He wants the whole thing."

Shivers coursed over her skin at the same time a floodgate of warmth opened in her heart to surge through every vein. This was the moment—the moment for which she and her mother had prayed year after year.

Tears rose to blur her vision, but she blinked them away. She didn't want him to remember her tears; she wanted him to remember her joy. Joanna beamed a smile at him, a smile that wobbled a bit, but one that matched the feelings of her heart.

"I'm proud of you, Daddy. Prouder than I've ever been in my entire life."

"Yeah . . . well . . ." He coughed and turned away, but not before she noticed how his eyes gleamed suspiciously bright in the moonlight. He coughed again, then focused on a point above her head. "You'll see her home, Archer?"

"I will." Crockett placed his hands on her shoulders, his thumbs making comforting circles on her back. And while his confirmation was what any gentleman would offer, the solemnity of his voice carried a weight that extended well beyond escort duty.

Her father nodded once, then turned and reached for Gamble's saddle horn with his bound hands. "No sense dragging this thing out, Coleson," he said gruffly as he mounted in a less than graceful manner. "Let's get the boy home so we can be on our way at first light."

The marshal gathered Gamble's reins and climbed aboard his own mount. "Come on, Jackson. You can ride with me." Coleson removed his boot from the stirrup and reached a hand down to help the boy mount behind him.

Jackson shot a questioning glance at Crockett, then at his nod, scrambled up behind the marshal.

As the threesome disappeared into the night, Joanna stood frozen, too numb and exhausted to do more than stare after them. Her soul rejoiced at her father's spiritual surrender, but her heart agonized over the price he might pay. Crockett wrapped his arms about her shoulders and pulled her back against his chest. His heat soaked through her chilled skin as he held her close. Then he leaned his face down, pressing his cheek against hers, and whispered words that revived her weary hope.

"It's not over yet, Jo. It's not over."

42

The following afternoon, Joanna marched out of Miss Bessie's boardinghouse, ready to do battle with Marshal Coleson. Crockett had driven her to Deanville first thing that morning, settled her at the boardinghouse, and then rode on to Caldwell in search of a lawyer. Jasper, Frank, and Carl had chipped in from their savings to cover the attorney's fee, but they chose to stay behind and tend the ranch. That and keep themselves out of the marshal's line of fire.

She didn't blame them. In fact, she was glad they were staying away. Her heart was battered enough already. It couldn't take much more.

Thankfully, she had reinforcements marching alongside her. Miss Bessie, looking stern as ever in her tight bun and pursed mouth, matched Joanna's stride. Both women's arms overflowed with items geared to a man's comfort. Blankets, reading material, food. Miss Bessie had even scrounged up a deck of playing cards that had been left behind by one of her boarders. Knowing her father didn't sleep well if he didn't have her mother's paintings around him, Joanna had brought two of his favorites from home, along with her mother's Bible.

No way would she let him rot in a stark jail cell, surrounded by nothing warmer than stone and iron. When she ran into the marshal coming out of the bank that morning, he'd approved her bringing her father a few personal items. Well, her definition of *few* might be a bit liberal, but she aimed to see that Coleson stood by his word, even if she had to bully him to do it.

As she stepped onto the boardwalk that ran in front of the jailhouse, one of the paintings under her arm began to slip. Without a free hand to adjust its position, all she could do was clench her elbow to her side and bend her posture so her thigh could slow its downward progress. Fortunately, the door to the jail stood ajar, and Joanna managed to nudge it open with her foot. Hurrying to reach a raised surface before she completely lost her grip on her mother's *Sunrise on the Brazos*, she surged forward and dropped her load onto the first table she came to. A table that happened to be the marshal's desk.

One thing she could say for the marshal—he had good reflexes. The man jumped to his feet and in the same motion snatched his coffee cup and a stack of wanted posters out of the avalanche's path before the *Brazos* could inflict any damage.

He raised a supercilious brow. "Are you thinking to bribe me, Miss Robbins?" His dry tone reeked with sarcasm. "I'm afraid I'm not much of an art collector."

"Don't be ridiculous, Marshal." Joanna jutted out a hip to keep the *Brazos* from sliding off the edge of his desk and quickly stacked *The Lazy R Pines* on top of it, freeing her hands to settle her special surprise on the floor against the front of the desk. "These things are for my father. I only brought a few," she said with a smile. "Just like you instructed."

Bessie came in behind Joanna, looked directly at Marshal Coleson, and deliberately dropped her market basket atop the handful of telegrams sitting on the one section of his desk that hadn't been overrun by artwork.

"Land sakes, woman! You're in on this, too?" The lawman growled, looked around for a place to set his coffee, settled on the back of the small cast-iron stove behind him, and growled again. "Listen, ladies. This here ain't no pleasure palace. It's a jail. It's not supposed to be cozy. It's supposed to be hard. Cold. So downright disagreeable, in fact, that once folks visit, they decide to change their ways so's they don't have to come back."

Joanna crossed her arms over her chest and raised her chin, not about to give in. "But my father doesn't have to be convinced. He changed his ways sixteen years ago. Therefore no harm will come from a few blankets and knickknacks."

"Knickknacks?" A rather sour chuckle rattled in his throat. "Lady, your knickknacks are about to swallow my desk."

"You don't plan to starve your prisoner—do you, Brett?" Miss Bessie flung back the towel covering her basket to reveal the feast waiting within. "Fresh bread, jam, cheese, apples. Just some snacks to sustain him between those paltry meals Mrs. Elliott brings." The marshal leaned close to inspect the hamper and inhaled deeply.

"Those your strawberry preserves, Bess?"

"Yep. I thought you might enjoy sampling the wares, too." She pushed the basket more directly under his nose. "If you dig deep enough in there, you might even find a thick square of my lemon pound cake."

The man's head jerked up, and Joanna swore she could hear him salivating. "You *are* trying to bribe me." He slashed a frown at Bessie, but his gaze twitched back to the hamper, giving him away.

"It's not a bribe. It's a reward for doin' a good deed." Bessie reached across the desk, and for a moment, Joanna thought she was going to touch the marshal's hand. But then her fingers detoured to the towel and drew it back over the food. "Let her hang her pictures, Brett. It ain't gonna hurt nothing."

"Seems a waste of time to me," Coleson grumbled, but he picked up the first painting and started scrutinizing the frame and the back, as if checking for contraband. "The circuit judge is gonna be here next week. Hearing's set for Tuesday."

Tuesday. A moan rose in Joanna's throat. Six more days of wondering what would happen. Six more days of separation from her father. Joanna's spine started to slump along with her spirits, but she forced them both straight. Six more days to pray for a favorable outcome.

"What's this?" Coleson dug a hammer out of the food basket and waved it under Joanna's nose. "Trying to sneak weapons in to your father?"

Bessie harrumphed in disgust. "Don't be an idiot. That's to hang the pictures. There's a handful of nails down there, too. We just didn't have enough hands to carry it all. Had to put it in the bottom of the hamper to keep it from smashing the bread."

Coleson turned to face Bessie and raised a doubtful brow. "You expect me to just let you waltz into that cell with a weapon that Silas Robbins can use against me?"

"No." Bessie aimed a look at the lawman that seemed to question the man's intelligence. "What I expect is that you will take charge like you always do and go in there and hang the pictures yourself. Really, Brett. It's what a gentleman would do."

"For pity's sake," the man grouched. "Give me them nails. You can hand me the blasted paintings through the bars." He stomped off toward the back of the jailhouse, muttering under his breath about fool women and their crazy schemes.

Bessie smirked at Joanna, then picked up the blankets, playing cards, and Bible, leaving the food hamper on the marshal's desk. She shrugged off Joanna's questioning glance. "I really made it more for him than your father. To soften him up, you know. He loves my cooking."

Joanna hid a grin as she collected the paintings. If she didn't know better, she would swear Miss Bessie had a soft spot for the town marshal beneath that prickly exterior. And judging by the man's reactions, he was probably fond of more than her food.

By the time the women made it back to the trio of cells at the rear of the building, the marshal had already restrained Joanna's father by placing his arms through the last cell's bars and cinching a leather strap around his wrists. Her father leaned submissively against the bars while Coleson fit a key into the door's lock.

Joanna set the paintings against the wall and rushed up to her father, covering his hands with her own. "Are you all right, Daddy?"

He smiled at her and nodded. "I'm fine, darlin'. You don't need to be fretting about me."

"Crockett's on his way to Caldwell to hire a lawyer. We're going to fight this. It's not over."

Her father's gaze met hers through the bars with a level of peace that stunned her. "God's in control, Jo. Whatever happens, he'll take care of me." He raised his bound hands along the bars until his fingers were able to capture a piece of her hair that dangled by her temple. "He'll take care of you, too. If I didn't believe that, I wouldn't be here now."

Her eyes grew moist. "I know," she said, her voice trembling slightly. "I trust him, Daddy. I do." After so many years of hoping and praying for her father to express such faith, it nearly undid her control to hear him do so. But a weepy woman would serve no good purpose. So she blinked away the unwanted liquid from her eyes and cocked her chin enough to shoot him a grin. "I brought you a few things."

Marshal Coleson snorted. "A *few*? The woman's trying to turn my jail into a lady's parlor."

"Oh?" Her father quizzed her with a look.

Joanna shrugged, then turned and clasped a frame in each hand. "I know how you like having Mama's paintings around, so when I left the house this morning, I brought a couple with me."

His eyes lit with surprised delight. "The *Brazos*?"

Joanna smiled as she held up the painting for her father to see. "Of course." She handed it through the bars to the marshal, who had come up alongside them. Her father's gaze followed its trail, caressing the familiar scene with hungry eyes.

"I brought our pines, too." She held out the last painting her mother had completed before her death, the one she'd claimed was her favorite because it was bathed in the love of home.

He stretched a reverent fingertip toward the canvas. "Ah, Martha." The words were whisper-soft. Joanna bowed her head, her heart squeezing.

After a pair of thumps from the hammer, the marshal returned to collect the second painting. The first hung rather crooked on the wall above the cot that served as a bed, but it was up. Joanna nodded her thanks to the grumbling lawman and handed him the next one.

Her stomach lurched as she reached for the final item stashed by the wall to her left. "I brought one of mine, too. A new one." Heat rushed to her cheeks, and she found it hard to look her father in the face. Her hands shook as she lifted the recently framed piece before her.

"One of yours?" Curiosity warmed his voice. "That's wonderful, Jo. I haven't seen a new work from you since . . . well . . . in a long time."

Not since her mother's death.

Joanna bit her lip and slid the portrait free of the pillowcase she'd wrapped it in. Holding her breath, she let the white cotton fall to the ground and turned the painting around to let her father see it. "I had planned to give it to you for your birthday, but . . ." She lifted her head, and the rest of the sentence turned to dust in her mouth as she saw what could only be described as awe wash over her father's face.

He offered no compliments. No flowery praise. Not even a smile. He just stared at the likeness of his wife as if nothing else existed. His hands opened, and Joanna set the bottom edge of the frame across his wide palms. His lips silently formed her mother's name at the same time that a tear rolled down his weathered cheek.

Joanna glanced away, the moment too intimate for even her to invade. It was only then that she noticed the complete stillness surrounding her. Bessie stood by the cell door, eyes wide in disbelief and wonder. Even the marshal looked nonplussed.

"I'll just . . . uh . . . place a nail and let you hang that one when you're ready." Coleson backed away and quickly pounded a nail into place near the head of the cot.

The two sharp taps from the hammer seemed to break Silas from his trance. He blinked and finally lifted his head.

"You brought her back to life, Jo," he rasped. "Thank you."

"She'd be so proud of you, Daddy." Joanna scooted close and wrapped her hands under his as he held the frame.

The cell door rattled closed, shaking the bars. Joanna stepped back, taking the painting with her when the marshal approached. As soon as Coleson unfastened her father's bonds, however, she passed the painting through the bars.

"I put the blanket, cards, and Bible on the cot, Robbins."

Her father hugged the painting to his chest but focused his attention on his daughter. "Martha's Bible?"

Joanna nodded. "You've been reading it so faithfully lately, I thought you'd like to have it. I was hoping you'd find strength and comfort in its pages."

"I'm sure I will." He set the painting down, leaning it against the bars, and held a hand out to her. "Come here, Jo."

She went immediately, stretching her arms through the bars to hold as much of him as she could.

"I love you, darlin'," he said, the words burning a hole directly to the center of her heart.

"I love you, too, Daddy, and I'll be praying for you every day."

He patted her shoulder in that slightly awkward way of his that always made her smile. "You do that, girl, but remember . . . if God don't give you the answer you're wantin', don't be holdin' it against him. He can still be trusted, even when he says no."

Joanna had to work hard to swallow the melon-sized lump in her throat. Her father had truly made his peace with God. She locked her gaze with his and lifted her chin. "I'll remember."

43

All of Deanville turned out for the hearing—the nosy tele-graph clerk, the barber, even the minister who used to preach from the pulpit Crockett now occupied. Crockett recognized several faces from his own congregation, as well.

Joanna hadn't wanted to leave her father in the days leading up to the court date, so after Crockett returned to town with the attorney, he'd left her in Miss Bessie's care and returned home, not only to conduct worship services, but also to organize a special prayer meeting Sunday evening. He had been humbled by the number of families that had turned out. And when he put out the word to recruit character witnesses willing to testify on Silas's behalf, several volunteered and were in the courtroom now, waiting.

Jackson had begged to be included on the witness list, but Mr. Gillman, the attorney, had been afraid the marshal would bring up the shooting incident if Jackson took the stand, and that wouldn't do Silas any favors.

The door to the judge's chambers cracked open, and Joanna squeezed Crockett's hand. He stroked the pad of his thumb over her knuckles and shifted closer to her on the wooden gallery pew, his own nerves on edge.

The judge, a surprisingly short, slender man with a balding pate, strode into the courtroom. He seemed to grow in stature, however, as he ascended to the bench, and when he pounded his gavel, all chatter died. With no more than a flick of the wrist, the man had taken command of the room.

Crockett and Joanna rose to their feet along with the rest of the crowd, but the judge quickly waved them all back down. Gillman had assured him that Judge Wicker was a fair man who didn't stand on ceremony, and it appeared that at least the latter half of that assessment was true. Crockett prayed the first half proved accurate, as well.

"Silas Robbins." The judge's voice echoed through the crowded room with an impressive boom. Mr. Gillman stood and urged Silas to do the same. The judge shuffled some papers around on his desk as he continued. "You are charged with an ambiguous number of robberies." He looked up and pierced Coleson with a glare of displeasure. "Apparently the good marshal, here, was unclear as to how many crimes to actually charge you with."

"That's my fault, Your Honor," Silas said, ignoring the lawyer at his side who was muttering furiously at him to be quiet. "When I made my confession, I couldn't recall the exact number of stagecoaches. Probably around twenty or so. I only robbed three trains, though. Four if you count the time I abducted the parson." He jabbed his finger over his shoulder.

Crockett raised his hand and waved at the judge.

"What are you doing?" Joanna hissed.

Crockett bent toward her and whispered out of the side of his mouth. "Trying to show there are no hard feelings over that incident."

The judge raised a brow at Crockett and turned back to Coleson. "I don't see kidnapping listed among the crimes."

"That's because the parson refuses to press charges." The marshal folded his arms across his chest, and Crockett had no doubt the lawman's glare would've scorched him if he had actually glanced in his direction. "'Course, I hear he's marryin' up with the defendant's daughter, so that might have something to do with it."

"The parson's matrimonial prospects are not the concern of this court, Marshal. I'll thank you to keep your suppositions to yourself so that we may progress in an orderly manner. Do I make myself clear?"

Coleson scuffed the sole of his left boot against the oak floorboards. "Yes, sir."

The judge redirected his attention to Silas. "Now, Robbins, since you have been so forthcoming about the events for which you are charged, and since I have a statement from Mr. Coleson indicating that you have confessed to the crimes in question, may I assume that you are entering a guilty plea?"

Silas straightened his posture and lifted his chin in a way that reminded Crockett of Joanna when she was determined to see something through. "Yes, Your Honor."

Joanna whimpered softly, and Crockett wrapped his arm around her, wishing he could do more to protect her heart from this emotional pummeling.

"An honest criminal," Judge Wicker remarked. "That's a rarity in my line of work. Refreshing." He made a note on one of the papers in front of him, then gestured to Mr. Gillman. "Before I pronounce sentence, do you have any witnesses who wish to offer testimony on Mr. Robbins's behalf?"

"Yes, Your Honor," the lawyer replied.

"Very well. Call your first witness."

"I call Silas Robbins."

After giving his oath to tell the truth, Silas took the stand. Mr. Gillman strode up to Silas, then turned slightly to include the audience as well as the judge in his questioning. "Mr. Robbins. How many years have passed since the last time you stole something? A material possession of any value."

Silas cleared his throat. "Sixteen years."

The lawyer paced before the judge's bench, hands behind his back. "And after sixteen years of lawful living, what prodded you to suddenly confess these past wrongs?"

"Got tired of carryin' the past around with me while dodgin' God and my conscience. Finally stopped dodging and realized it was time to come clean. I couldn't be God's man otherwise."

Mr. Gillman smiled. "I see. So not only have you been a law-abiding citizen for the past sixteen years, but you have also recently become a man of religious conviction. Admirable, indeed. No further questions."

"You may be excused, Mr. Robbins." Judge Wicker directed Silas back to his seat. "Call your next witness."

Gillman turned to face the gallery. "I call Mrs. Idabelle Grimley."

A shuffle echoed behind Crockett as Mrs. Grimley made her way forward, clutching her handbag nervously before her. Her gaze found his as she passed his row, and Crockett nodded encouragement to her.

At Mr. Gillman's prompting, she told the court about the time Silas had shown up on her family's doorstep with two of his men in tow offering to cut hay after her husband had been laid up with a broken leg. Mr. Robbins hadn't accepted a thing in payment beyond the cherry pie she forced him to take home in thanks.

Two other church members took the stand following Mrs. Grimley, each painting a picture of Silas as a hardworking rancher who kept mostly to himself but who could always be counted on to help his neighbor in time of crisis. When the attorney turned toward the crowd to call the fourth witness, however, Judge Wicker interrupted him.

"You've made your point, Gillman. Robbins has been a model citizen and a decent neighbor to these folks." He waved his hand impatiently, as if trying to erase names from an invisible blackboard. "I think we can dispense with the rest of the witnesses if they all have a similar testimony."

"Yes, Your Honor." Gillman took his seat.

Judge Wicker turned to Coleson. "You have any refuting witnesses?"

The marshal slowly gained his feet. "Uh . . . no, Your Honor. But the man's confessed," he hurried to add, "so that should tell you all you need to know."

The judge frowned. "Did you not wire area lawmen to see if there were witnesses willing to testify regarding Mr. Robbins's crimes?"

"I did. But of the two men who came forward, neither could identify him. Robbins always wore a bandana over his face, you see. And with all the years that've passed . . . well . . . the witnesses weren't willing to swear on a Bible that he was the man who'd robbed them."

Judge Wicker glared his displeasure at the marshal until the man finally took his seat. "This is highly irregular," the judge grumbled. "A confession of decades-old crimes from a criminal with no accusers." He set aside his papers and let out a heavy sigh.

Joanna tensed. Crockett rubbed her arm, his own chest growing tight.

"Mr. Robbins," the judge intoned, his scowl locking on Silas as Joanna's father pushed his chair back and rose to accept his sentence. "You present me an unusual dilemma. You have pled guilty to the charge of robbery. Therefore, I must assign a sentence appropriate to the crimes for which you have confessed. Usually a minimum of five years."

"No," Joanna whispered, her quiet anguish a shout in Crockett's ear.

"However," the judge continued, "I find myself asking what, exactly, that five years in prison would be expected to accomplish.

"Incarceration serves a twofold purpose. First, it is a punishment for crimes committed against society and a deterrent against future illicit behavior. But second, and I believe most crucial, incarceration provides an opportunity for reformation of the criminal character. That is why we have libraries and chaplains in our prisons, why we teach our inmates a marketable trade. We want them to reenter society changed and prepared to contribute in a positive manner."

Judge Wicker paused for breath, then pointed a stubby finger directly at Silas.

"You, sir," he declared, a note of accusation ringing in his voice, "have already reformed."

44

Joanna blinked. Had she heard correctly? Had the judge just accused her father of being *too* rehabilitated? She shared a brief glance with Crockett, but he appeared equally perplexed. He rubbed her arm again, though, and the simple touch buoyed her. She didn't know how she would have survived this day without him by her side, always ready with a smile or a gentle reassuring touch.

Her father stood so straight and tall, his shoulders squared as he listened to the judge's pronouncement. He'd stood the same way at her mother's funeral, as if braced for a blow he couldn't defend against.

"Since you have already renounced your criminal ways and have been an exemplary citizen for the past sixteen years, I am reluctant to enforce prison time."

Joanna's heart hiccuped in her chest. She grabbed Crockett's knee. *Please, Lord. Please.*

"However," the judge continued, his expression grave, "there is the element of punishment that must be addressed. In such cases, I would normally insist that you make restitution to those you have wronged. Yet it seems we have no victims on which to confer such compensation. Hence my dilemma. I cannot let a guilty man go free with no consequences for his actions. Nor will my conscience allow me to sentence to prison a man who has already proven himself reformed.

"That leaves me with only one recourse. Therefore, it is the ruling of this court that you, Silas Robbins, will make restitution to the community at large in lieu of individual victims. Instead of time served in prison, your five years will be probated on the condition that during each of those five years, ten percent of all income, whether personal or the product of the Lazy R ranch, be donated to local charitable or civic organizations approved by the court. The court will appoint a business manager to oversee your finances during this period and to keep an accounting of all earnings and expenditures. Do you agree to abide by these conditions?"

"Yes, sir." Her father gave a shaky nod. "I do."

"Then the ruling stands. This court is adjourned." Judge Wicker pounded his gavel, rose from the bench, and strode to his chambers.

Applause reverberated through the room along with a handful of hearty cheers, but it was nothing more than a buzz in Joanna's ears. All of her attention focused on her father and her need to get to him. Now.

She tried to squeeze past Jackson and Miss Bessie to get to the aisle, but they were too busy celebrating—Jackson with loud hollers and Bessie with timid claps as she backed up to avoid being impaled with a flying elbow or jerking knee. Crockett must have sensed Joanna's growing desperation, for when she turned his direction to look for an escape route, he seized her about the waist and hoisted her over the barrier separating the court from the gallery. With a wink, he shooed her toward her father.

Loving him for knowing her so well, she blew him a kiss,

then pivoted and threw herself into her father's arms, not caring that he was occupied with a handshake from Mr. Gillman at the time.

"Oh, Daddy! You're free." Free from the past. Free from prison. Free to be the man God always intended him to be.

His arms tightened around her, and he dropped a kiss on her head. "That I am, darlin'. That I am."

Joanna pulled slightly away, her gaze drinking in his beloved face. He smiled, and the light in his eyes shone brighter than she'd ever seen it. A laugh of pure joy bubbled out of her, and her father's rich chuckle joined it on its journey to the rafters.

"Hey, Parson!" Her father loosened his hold on her in order to include Crockett in their circle. "I need you to do me a favor."

"What's that, Si?"

This time her father was the one to wink. "Find me some water."

Joanna was slow to understand, but when the Deanville preacher stepped up and pounded her daddy on the back, saying he knew just the place to do the deed, comprehension dawned. Joanna's stomach swirled in jittery delight as her former minister led the way down the aisle, his pulpit voice ringing out in song.

> "Shall we gather at the river,
> Where bright angel feet have trod,
> With its crystal tide forever
> Flowing by the throne of God?"

The man gestured to the crowd to follow them, and soon an entire throng was singing and laughing on their way down to the town creek. Joanna grinned through the tears pooling in her eyes and added her trembling voice to the mix as she allowed herself to be herded along with the rest.

"Yes, we'll gather at the river,
The beautiful, the beautiful river,
Gather with the saints at the river,
That flows by the throne of God."

The longer she sang, the stronger her voice became. Crockett grabbed her hand, his deep baritone blending with her alto as they escorted her father to a tree-shaded area out behind the schoolhouse.

The Deanville preacher stepped aside once they arrived at the swimming hole, giving the three of them some privacy as he led the congregants in another hymn.

"What can wash away my sin?
Nothing but the blood of Jesus.
What can make me whole again?
Nothing but the blood of Jesus . . ."

The singing continued, but Joanna's voice faltered. The reality of the moment pierced too deeply.

"Archer?" Her father shrugged out of his suit coat, and then paused and regarded Crockett with an intense gaze. "Son, would you do the honors?"

"Nothing would make me happier, sir." Crockett clapped him on the shoulder, then quickly divested himself of boots, coat, and tie and waded into the water.

Joanna collected the discarded clothing and held it tight to her breast, as if doing so would enhance her connection to the two men she loved more than life.

Can you see this, Mama? Your prayers are being answered.

The men ventured away from the bank until they were waist-deep in the creek. The crowd hushed. Crockett asked her father for his confession, and when her daddy claimed Jesus as his

Lord, Joanna couldn't hold the tears back any longer. Tiny sobs of long-awaited joy shook her shoulders as Crockett buried her daddy in the water and brought him back up a new man in Christ.

And as the crowd shouted their amens and burst into a rousing rendition of "Let Every Heart Rejoice and Sing," Joanna could have sworn she heard her mother's clear soprano joining in the praise.

Epilogue

Crockett stood before his congregation three months after that triumphant day, a pile of ravaged nerves. Knots twisted his stomach and tiny pinpricks needled his neck as he gazed over the heads of the crowd, a condition that hadn't beset him since his first day in the pulpit. But then, he wasn't in the pulpit today. His mentor, Amos Ralston, had that distinction. After all, a man couldn't perform his own wedding ceremony.

Jackson waved at him from the back of the sanctuary, sporting his new duds. Silas had offered the kid an official position at the Lazy R along with a set of clothes and an assigned horse to ride while on duty, and Jackson had been strutting around the ranch ever since, his pride nearly busting the buttons off his store-bought shirt. He still showed up early at the church every Sunday to ring the bell, and that was where he stood now—manning the pull rope in order to set the church bell to ringing the instant Brother Ralston pronounced Crockett and Joanna husband and wife.

Husband and wife. Crockett swallowed hard.

"If you tug on your collar one more time, Crock, the thing's gonna pop clean off."

Crockett glared at his big brother. "You know, Trav," he muttered out of the side of his mouth, "Jackson volunteered to stand up with me. It's not too late to switch you out."

"Yes it is." Travis chuckled softly and nodded toward the back of the church. "Your bride's coming."

Crockett's pulse leapt at the telltale squeak of hinges. The gap in the door widened. Silas, wearing the new suit coat Joanna had bought him for the trial all those months ago, stepped through the entrance and held his arm out to his daughter somewhere behind him.

Straining to see past his soon-to-be father-in-law, Crockett stretched his neck only to have his breath catch in his throat.

Joanna glided through the doorway, resplendent in a dark green gown dripping in ivory lace. Her glorious red curls hung loose past her shoulders with a halo of golden wildflowers and streams of ivory ribbon as adornment. Her chin dipped in demure shyness, she was halfway down the aisle before she raised her lashes and met his gaze.

When she did, Crockett felt the impact clear through his chest. Soon this beautiful woman would be *his*. His helpmeet, his partner, his wife. The love glowing in her blue-gray eyes banished his nerves, and his heart swelled with pride.

His attention never leaving her face, he stepped forward and accepted her hand from Silas. Her gloved fingers curved around his and his pulse thrummed. Her pixie face, delicate within the mass of those burnished curls, blushed at the intensity of his stare. Reeling in his desire, he winked at her to break the tension, then grinned like an idiot when she smiled at him.

As Crockett turned to face the minister, he caught Travis rolling his eyes at his smitten behavior. But then a gurgling noise from the front row transformed his brother's mocking expression into one of indulgent adoration as his six-week-old son, Joseph, flailed his arms in happy, jerky motions from where he lay cradled in Meredith's lap.

Yep, the Archer men were soft as cornmeal mush when it came to their women. Apparently their children, too. Even Jim, the most stoic of the bunch, hinted at a smile when his Cassie snuggled close as the minister began addressing the congregation. Maybe Neill would be different when his turn came around, but as Crockett hugged Joanna's arm into his side, he sure hoped not.

Loving a woman might soften a man's heart, but receiving her love in return made him infinitely stronger than he could ever have been alone.

Two-time RITA finalist and winner of the coveted HOLT Medallion and ACFW Carol Award, CBA bestselling author **Karen Witemeyer** writes historical romance because she believes the world needs more happily-ever-afters. She is an avid cross-stitcher and shower singer, and she bakes a mean apple cobbler. Karen makes her home in Abilene, Texas, with her husband and three children. Learn more about Karen and her books at www.karenwitemeyer.com.

If you enjoyed *Stealing the Preacher*, you may also like...

BETHANY HOUSE

More Laughter and Romance from Karen Witemeyer

To learn more about Karen and her books,
visit karenwitemeyer.com.

She thinks he's arrogant. He thinks she's vain. Yet they are both completely wrong...and maybe completely right for each other.

A Tailor-Made Bride

Eden Spencer prefers books over suitors. But when a tarnished Texas hero captures her heart, will she deny her feelings or create her own love story?

To Win Her Heart